PENGUIN BOOKS

# THE INQUIRING EYE

One of the outstanding political journalists of his generation, David Watt was born in Edinburgh in 1932 and educated at Marlborough and Hertford College, Oxford. He began his career as a journalist writing drama criticism for the *Spectator*. After working for several other papers he returned to the *Spectator* as political correspondent. In 1964 he joined the *Financial Times* as its Washington correspondent and rapidly became one of the most influential political commentators in the British press. In 1968 he returned to London to become the paper's political correspondent, a post he held for ten years. In its tribute to him the *Financial Times* wrote of his 'invaluable contribution to this newspaper's coverage of domestic and international politics' and described his writing as 'sharp, perceptive, witty but always fair'. During 1978 to 1983 David Watt was the director of the Royal Institute of International Affairs. He was joint editor of the *Political Quarterly* from 1979 for six years and also contributed a weekly column to *The Times*. At the time of his death, in 1987, he had just completed the preparatory work for a major book on American foreign policy since the Second World War. He was a Fellow of All Souls from 1981 to 1983.

Charles Wilson, the editor of *The Times*, described David Watt as 'one of the leading journalists of his generation . . . a man of strong personal courage, which he showed both in his varied professional life and in his long personal battle against the physical effects of polio'. Rudolf Klein wrote in the *Political Quarterly*, 'David Watt was a kind and courteous man with a nice, tart sense of humour: as generous and humane in his personal as in his political sympathies.'

Ferdinand Mount, political columnist of the *Daily Telegraph*, was formerly head of the Prime Minister's Policy Unit. His most recent books are *The Subversive Family* and *The Selkirk Strip*.

---

**The Inquiring Eye** is published to coincide with the establishment of the David Watt Memorial Prize. This prize will be awarded for outstanding contributions towards the clarification of international and political issues and the promotion of greater understanding of such issues.

**The David Watt Memorial Prize** is being introduced, organized and administered by Rio Tinto Zinc Limited. For further information, please contact RTZ Ltd, 6 St James's Square, London SW1Y 4LD.

# The Inquiring Eye

## The Writings of David Watt

**Edited by**
**FERDINAND MOUNT**
*With a Foreword by the*
*Rt Hon. DAVID OWEN, MP*

PENGUIN BOOKS

PENGUIN BOOKS

Published by the Penguin Group
27 Wrights Lane, London W8 5TZ, England
Viking Penguin Inc., 40 West 23rd Street, New York, New York 10010, USA
Penguin Books Australia Ltd, Ringwood, Victoria, Australia
Penguin Books Canada Ltd, 2801 John Street, Markham, Ontario, Canada L3R 1B4
Penguin Books (NZ) Ltd, 182–190 Wairau Road, Auckland 10, New Zealand

Penguin Books Ltd, Registered Offices: Harmondsworth, Middlesex, England

First published 1988

Made and printed in Great Britain by
Richard Clay Ltd, Bungay, Suffolk
Filmset in 11/13 Monophoto Times

No man hath walked along our roads with step
So active, so inquiring eye, or tongue
So varied in discourse.

*Walter Savage Landor, 'To Robert Browning'*

# Contents

## III   The British Scene

# IV  Great Contemporaries and Others

# V  The Commentator At Large

# Foreword

For me, David Watt was not just a very close friend but also a dispassionate critic. It is so hard to find a single word to describe him. But courage shines through his life like a golden thread. At Marlborough he was a spectacularly good athlete, a formidable wing three-quarter. For those of us who knew him only after his polio, it is hard to realize what a shattering blow it must have been to have found himself, at Oxford, totally paralysed in an iron lung, able only to move his head and hanging on to life itself. Always cheerful, he even then never lost his capacity to joke. He described his experience in an iron lung in the *Spectator* in 1955:

> It is not an easy machine for the beginner. He breathes whether he likes it or not, and it is some time before he likes it at all. If he works against the rhythm of the thing, he splutters and gasps, and the bellows creak on without paying him the slightest attention. He cannot return the compliment because it is as if an asthmatic dormitory was tossing on its rusty springs all around him; there is an ominous click and a deep grunt, followed by a noise like the pulverizing of many sardine tins, a pause, and then the whole machine gathers itself together for a final long drawn wheeze . . . He longs for his lungs as much as a tramp might long to get into the police cell out of the rain, and for the same reason: ease and security are worth paying for in self-respect. For it is a battle against his own fears and laziness that he is fighting as much as against his physical weakness. Breath comes to him only in small, hard lumps that have to be shaken down like pills; but he cannot help feeling that he would take them without a murmur if they were sugar, if he were not demoralized, if he were the kind of person he had always wanted to be. Pride demands that he should spend a little longer each day breathing his own air; everything else demands that he think of plausible reasons why he should not.

There is no doubt that that experience made David an exceptional person. No longer able to play games or the piano, his whole lifestyle changed. From it came the self-discipline, the resolution, that forged a personality of rare integrity and of fastidious intellectual honesty. I am told that it was from his father that he derived his superb sense of humour. David's humour was mischievous as much as caustic, and he was a delicious gossip.

Challenges presented themselves to him to be overcome. Even if we were walking together and the cold wind affected his breathing, he would refuse all suggestions that we should go back home, insisting that, having embarked on a walk, we should finish the circuit. Often in pain, he never complained.

It was for self-respect that he insisted on returning to India after he had had to come home because of trouble with his breathing. It was as if he had to demonstrate to himself, again and again, that he was capable of overcoming every physical obstacle to living a normal life.

It was, however, his razor-sharp mind which captivated so many of us and his capacity to shift from the serious to the frivolous and back again, whether we were *en famille* or by ourselves, talking late at night around a log fire.

He loved the United States and knew it well from his time in Washington. But he was never seduced by America. In a book review in the *Observer* on *The Protestant Establishment* he wrote:

> Anyone who has had his antecedents sniffed over by an old-fashioned Ivy Leaguer, or been to a point-to-point in Virginia, or lunched with conformist young executives at a big corporation, or tried to take a Jewish girl to a private dance, or seen a swarthy complexioned stranger being ignored in a country club, knows that the sheer ruthlessness of American upper-class snobbery can sometimes make the English variety look positively Franciscan in its charity.

Playing chess with David was itself a formidable undertaking, demanding total concentration; but read his description of the 1972 World Chess Championship in the *Financial Times*, starting with Fischer:

> To watch him in action is to sense the torture and the tension at work in him. He shuffles like a bear on to the stage, blinking at the lights and the public. He fingers the chessmen on the table as if to establish some mystic connection with them. He twines himself torturously around the limbs of his special swing chair. His hands knead his temples feverishly and his body alternates between galvanic tension and sullen lassitude.

No one else could have written that.

In his final article for the *Financial Times*, in a column which politicians of every hue had grown accustomed to read first on a Friday, David wrote:

> I have picked this aspect (the problem of coming to terms with a mass electorate) rather than any others in my farewell to this page because it has haunted me personally for the whole period I have been writing. By background and temperament I share all the values and fears of J. S. Mill. But journalism imposes other values of its own – a belief in public discussion, a distrust of closed societies, and a belief that ordinary people can be persuaded to act rationally and farsightedly if things are adequately explained ... The distribution of power and wealth and amenity is too complex and too sensitive to be encompassed either by paternalism or by a return to *laissez-faire*. The only alternatives are education, persuasion, debate, trust.

The reason why David was such an effective writer about politics is that he carefully analysed the politician's role, never better than in a lecture which he gave in the 1970s:

> What, in the end, is the whole political exercise about in a democracy? It is, surely, the acquisition of legitimate power based on support and its exercise in a way that involves the maximum of consent and the minimum of compulsion. Now, the skill of a politician – and it is ... one which is equally applicable in the complicated relations of the workplace and the happy home – is to spot where potential support lies, to grab it and to hang tight on to it.
>
> This is not, in some ways, a skill that reflects the best in human nature. It requires in the politician not only a love of power itself – suggesting more than a touch of vanity and self-importance, to say nothing of other, baser instincts – but it also implies a certain feminine power of sympathetic flexibility, an ability to sense a change of mood in one's interlocutors and to adjust rapidly and ruthlessly to it before support melts away.
>
> It is this quality, of course, which is the origin of Sainte-Beuve's charge of charlatanism and the cause of so much fashionable criticism of the dishonesty of politicians today. Nor can it be denied that the critics can find plenty of ammunition in the pages of recent history to support the attack on political quackery and naked self-interest. What is wrong is to proceed to the general indictment of the race of politicians on this charge. A politician can honourably prevaricate and shift his ground; and indeed if an open political system is working properly it is difficult to see how these tactics can be dispensed with.

David was often at his most perceptive on the Anglo-American relationship, a fact recognized in an obituary article entitled 'Uncle Sam, John Bull, and David Watt' by Elspeth Rostow from Austin, Texas. She drew attention to the book *The Special Relationship: Anglo-American Relationships 1945–83* \* and David's luminous essay, characteristic of the man. He wrote about this country's role as being

> to act emphatically as the European power it has actually become but to bring to European capitals the important elements of pragmatism, balance and global perspective which are her distinguishing character-istics . . . To demonstrate that the British have developed since 1940 the important ability to understand the American mind better than any of their European partners. They are able to say . . . that trans-Atlantic conflicts of interest are manageable, even among unequal partners, provided there is a minimum of shared objective and provided both sides are prepared to devote real energy to cultivating the habits of close and civilized intercourse.

He couldn't have written this without his period at Chatham House, nor would he have held out against the fashion in arguing for dialogue in South Africa and advising R T Z, if he was not a rooted inter-nationalist. Yet Peter Hennessy once described what he called 'one of those off-the-record occasions at Ditchley Park, where the mighty of the Western World celebrate in private' and how David 'sang a song of old England' (to borrow a phrase of Stanley Baldwin's), enumerating most things his country might lose if his admitted desire of an in-tegrated Europe came about; he talked of 'Cox's Orange Pippins giving way to Golden Delicious apples and the disappearance of narrow lanes, hedgerows and draughty houses'. The fact is that David was a romantic.

In one of his last pieces for *The Times*, entitled 'Old-fashioned and proud of it', he wryly observed in his defence:

> I am instructed by my children in 'teenspeak' and the finer points of the charts. Am I not the possessor of a computer which I have learnt how to manipulate for all sorts of professional purposes? Can I not summon up a vast library of facts on my desk at the touch of a button?

He went on to say:

14

\* See pp. 85–99.

The important question is not so much which 'old-fashioned' (i.e. un-fashionable) opinions and attitudes should be thrown out as which ones still deserve to be rescued . . .

He chose to elaborate in that article on the three guiding principles of his youth: pragmatism, responsibility and internationalism. They summed up the man. He wrote, 'Anyone who unrepentantly proclaims their validity in 1987 will still have the present and the future, as well as the past, on his side.'

We who love him will always miss him.

*David Owen*

# Introduction

'We are living through a period where almost anything can happen, and the main qualifications for successful punditry are wholesale effrontery, a short memory and an ability to spell the word "Armageddon".' Even in the swamplands of the mid-1970s, David Watt's political commentaries never lost their sense of proportion – or their charm. We used to look forward to Friday's *Financial Times* and, later on, to Friday's *Times* for a mixture which, I think, was then, and still remains, unparalleled: of seriousness and good humour, of charity and wit, and of wisdom without solemnity.

David Watt was master of the conversational tone, being able to lead the reader gently on through a complicated argument or a series of hypotheses and scenarios without any feeling either of arduousness or of oversimplification. The best of his pieces are like a walk on level downland turf, with leisurely halts allowed for admiring the scenery (or for a pull at the hip flask). Those who think of political commentators as by nature overbearing and tendentious may be surprised and pleased to discover one who is neither. Watt is a tremendously *unforcing* writer. He leaves you in no doubt as to what he thinks ought to happen or, often a sadly different matter, what is likely to happen. But he also leaves you with plenty of room to make up your own mind.

Now and then, he allows himself a waspish wisecrack or put-down, Harold Wilson being a frequent victim: one of his speeches on the European Community was described as 'of the modern gents' rainwear variety – cheap, lightweight and infinitely reversible'. Wilson's notorious ability to recall his own past speeches in order to justify his present position prompted Watt to remark that 'if he had actually been in St

17

Paul's sandals on the road to Damascus, I have no doubt he would have pointed afterwards to a passage in the speech in Beersheba of March 17, AD 33, in which he had mentioned the possibility that Christianity might, under certain circumstances, have something to be said for it.' But he was fair to Wilson too, as to all the politicians he wrote about. Richard Crossman, quoting in his diaries from Watt's description of Wilson's speech at the 1967 Labour Party conference, remarked: 'Harold won't like that kind of discriminating praise, but it's worth a great deal more than the uproarious backslapping which the popular press has given him.'

For all his own enthusiasm for the Community, Watt was certainly not starry-eyed about the dismal scene it sometimes presented: 'Chancellor Schmidt bored and restless, President Mitterrand glowering, Mrs Thatcher in her "Keep-Death-off-the-Roads weeds", and the wretched and ineffectual M. Gaston Thorn, President of the European Community, scolding them for their lack of "Community spirit".' Again, he often wrote warmly of Ted Heath, picking up sympathetic vibrations from Heath's unmistakable honesty of purpose, but no one could have summed up more mercilessly the débâcle of the second 1974 election campaign, in which the Tory leader, according to Watt, 'has been going around this last week with a smile of brave, uplifting sorrow like Dean Farrar or some similar Victorian worthy confronted with fresh and irrefutable evidence of Man's bent towards sin'.

Yet these talents to amuse, obvious from the moment he began to write for the *Spectator* in the mid-1950s, were not allowed to luxuriate unchecked. They were put to proper service. What made David Watt so unusual and so formidable among British political journalists was his unswerving and sometimes unnerving integrity. In another age he might have been a Protestant divine of the best sort: good-humoured, witty, generous, but with an intense moral seriousness, except that there was no 'but' about it in such an open character, someone so much of a piece. He was clergy-boned, indeed the son of a clergyman. Without being in the least portentous, he could make politicians, especially of the Harold Wilson variety, all too conscious that they were 'falling below the level of events'.

His attitude towards politics and politicians was simultaneously playful and respectful. He saw their task as a tricky and gruelling one: 'This role of judging the erratic current of public opinion and turning its force to the purposeful resolution of conflicts in society, with consent – that is, ultimately, what politicians are for.' And when they failed to bring off these delicate feats, the consequences were liable to run right through society, breeding mutual recrimination and misplaced blame on a disastrous scale. He had no doubts, for example, as to where the blame for the appalling events of 1974–5 should rightly be placed: 'What has happened is that British politicians, and perhaps the whole British middle class, has lost its nerve, and until it recovers it, the prospects are bleak. It is not that Britain is ungovernable; it is that the governors refuse to govern.'

All the same, he charted the foibles of politicians with an indulgent eye, understanding the professional deformations to which they were peculiarly prone. On their tendency to embroil themselves in pointless and damaging squabbles, Watt pointed out that 'politicians, like dental patients and women after childbirth, are protected by a kind of natural defensive amnesia from remembering just how ghastly the last occasion was'.

But he had high expectation of them, none the less. He was not ashamed to admit to a belief in political élites; a country was better governed by men and women who were brought up to be practical, responsible and internationally minded; narrowness of any kind – whether nationalist or ideological – would in the end turn out to be costly and counter-productive. Naturally, it was important to be clear-eyed and undeceived about the realities of co-operation between allies. The Anglo-American 'special relationship' had never been quite so special as it was cracked up to be; the Common Market was constantly disappointing its supporters' hopes. All the same, it was this framework of alliances which constituted our best interests. Watt's five years as Director of the Royal Institute of International Affairs may not have been the easiest part of his life: he was probably not an administrator by temperament. But he served Chatham House with dedication and distinction, and it undoubtedly stood for many of the things he most passionately believed in.

'Passionately' is, I am sure, the right word. In one of his most delightful columns for *The Times*, he reflected on the accusation that he was always 'detached' in his attitudes, and he recalled Tony Crosland towering above him and shouting: 'You'll never influence anyone unless you join up.' But he asserted stoutly:

> in spite of the fashion for 'commitment', the uncommitted voice has its own right to be heard . . . detachment is the state of mind of the majority of the British public towards politics. Politicians want loyalty, but the ordinary reader may occasionally want to hear from someone more like himself.

Indeed, a kind of uncharacteristic ferocity broke out whenever he defended this sort of position:

> In spite of all the contemptuous labels that have been hung round its neck in the past few years – 'opportunism', 'cynicism', 'superficiality', 'lack of conviction', 'wetness' and so forth – this commonsensical frame of mind, which naturally tends to centrism, has preserved us from extremism and folly in the past, and the lack of it has been the most dangerous deficiency of the present government ... we often seem to me to be even crazier in our weakness than the Americans are in their strength to exchange 'old-fashioned' outward-lookingness for self-deceiving nationalism and catchpenny isolation.

Being 'detached' or 'old-fashioned' certainly did not entail being luke-warm.

His own personal political beliefs were clearly set out in what he wrote, but were modestly placed on a side-stand and not allowed to dominate the centre-stage as the *pièce de résistance*. He belonged to what I suppose might be called the liberal hard centre, in the rough jargon of political geography, and although he had friends all over the place on both sides of the Atlantic, they were concentrated in that amiable region. He was robust on defence, an unabashed believer in NATO, the Atlantic Alliance and the European Community, libertarian on social issues, in favour of the welfare state but not blind to its weaknesses, and rather more hesitantly in favour of some government intervention in the free market but sceptical about public ownership. In his twenties he, like most of his friends, was a critical supporter of the Labour Party; they were virtually all among the early enthusiasts for the formation of the SDP. Watt shared their distaste for what he called 'the masochist triumphalism of Mrs Thatcher'. Yet he felt, perhaps more acutely than many of them did, that throughout his career 'the most significant thing I have been reporting, though I have not always realized it, is the decay of a political culture and the demoralization of a political class.' This sense of national decline – and of the painfulness of the remedies required to reverse it – brought him even closer to his long-standing friend, David Owen.

Another old friend and sparring partner, Tony Howard, writes that Watt had tended to move to the right in recent years. I'm not so sure. He simply saw no reason to shift with the crowd. If there had once been a moral and prudential case for continuing to invest in South Africa (the theme of the last article I read of his), as previous Labour governments had thought, then so there was still. The Labour Party left him, rather than the other way round.

This strength of character has been attributed to the polio which crippled him as a young man, and which continued to make the most ordinary activities exhausting. When he was a neighbour of ours in the 1970s, we used to see him grey with fatigue after backing the car into the garage he had insisted on building in his basement. He could still play a better game of golf with one good arm than many with two, and I shall miss the wry-necked, bespectacled figure chuckling and gossiping his way along the fairways.

His severe physical handicap was an indirect contributory cause of the accident which caused his death. Some years after becoming a fellow of All Souls, the college had rented him an old farmhouse at the foot of the Chilterns where he could work during the week (and preside over ruthless games of family football at the weekends). Fierce storms on 27 March 1987 had brought down the power cable and blocked the driveway. He needed to get back to London for a session on his respirator. Being assured that the power was off, he picked up the cable and was killed instantly. He was 55.

David Watt was educated at Marlborough and Hertford College, Oxford. He was on the *Spectator* as dramatic critic 1956–7 and as political correspondent 1962–3. He served as diplomatic correspondent on the *Scotsman* 1958–60 and as Common Market correspondent on the *Daily Herald* 1960–1, before joining the *Financial Times* as Washington correspondent from 1964 to 1967 and as Political Editor from 1968 to 1977. He was then at Chatham House from 1978 to 1983, and started his weekly columns in *The Times* in 1981. He was also a fellow of All Souls from 1981 to 1983, having been a Visiting Fellow there ten years earlier. He was joint editor of the *Political Quarterly* 1979–85 and, among other public service, a member of the Board of Visitors at Wandsworth Prison and of the Fisher Committee on Self-Regulation at Lloyd's. At the time of his death, he had just finished the preparatory work for his large-scale book on American foreign policy since the war. Nobody could have been better fitted than he to deal with this highly complex and contentious subject, and it is hoped that the work can be brought to a satisfactory – and publishable – conclusion.

In putting together this selection of his work, I have tried both to emphasize those subjects which most interested him and brought the best out of him and also to be true to the breadth of his range. I am painfully conscious of the danger of falling between two stools – to use the sort of stale metaphor which would have provoked a genial snort from him – but I hope that admirers of David Watt's work will find some at least of their favourites here.

On the whole, I have grouped pieces round themes, but there were times, as when he was in America, where it seemed more appropriate to put them roughly in date order. The pieces are reprinted as they first appeared, except where I have removed the odd reference which might irritate or confuse the reader – for instance, mentions of other contributions to a collection of essays or the date of some impending minor political happening, such as a ministerial visit to Washington. David Watt's work is so clear and he is so considerate to the reader that, even at this distance in time, none of the pieces seemed to need much in the way of footnotes. I have changed many of the titles which the articles were given when first printed, for reasons of clarity or euphony or both. My aim has been to chart, as faithfully as possible, the working life of a political journalist over thirty years.

My thanks go to the Royal Institute of International Affairs for permission to reproduce the lecture marking the bicentenary of the Foreign Office. I would also like to thank the publishers who have let me reprint contributions to the following volumes: *The Special Relationship*, edited by W. R. Louis and Hedley Bull, OUP, 1986; *The Troubled Alliance*, edited by Lawrence Freedman, Heinemann, 1983.

*Ferdinand Mount*

# Acknowledgements

For permission to reproduce copyright material, grateful acknowledgement is made to the following: the *Financial Times*, the *New Statesman*, the *Observer* and the *Spectator*.

# Summits
# and Foothills

# I

# The Bear, the Squirrel and the Ticket-collector

## British Diplomacy in the 1980s: from Power to Influence ▮▮▮▮▮▮▮▮▮▮▮▮

A few weeks ago, I am told, the chief Soviet delegate to the Geneva negotiations on the control of nuclear forces, Mr Yuri Kvitsinksy, drew aside a member of the American team and recounted the following fable. A bear was once sitting in a railway carriage when the train stopped at a small wayside station. The compartment door opened and a squirrel scampered in and sat down on the opposite seat. The train moved off, and the travellers remained silent for a while. Eventually, however, the bear, irritated by the squirrel's inability to sit still, inquired, 'Is anything the matter? You seem remarkably nervous.'

'As it happens, I am,' replied the squirrel. 'I have no ticket and no money, and I am afraid the ticket collector is going to come along and throw me off the train.'

'Don't you worry, my little man,' said the bear. 'The inspector may never come – and if he does, I will look after you.'

Unfortunately, no sooner had he spoken than a voice was heard in the corridor crying, 'Tickets, please.' The bear, as good as his word, with one hand picked up the squirrel and held him out of the window, and with the other prepared to offer his ticket for inspection. The guard punched the ticket and thanked the bear. 'But what have you got in your other hand?' he asked.

'Nothing,' said the bear – and when he drew in his paw it was empty.

27

This pregnant and not entirely heartening parable opens up an almost endless vista of inquiries. Who is supposed to be the bear? Who is the squirrel? Who, for that matter, is that faintly sinister *deus ex machina* the ticket collector? And why was the story told by that narrator to that particular audience? Is it a subtle invitation to the Americans to sell out the Europeans in the negotiations? Is it an even more delicate – and improbable – hint that the Russians might, if challenged in the right way, ditch some of their own protégés? Or is it just the kind of story that gets told in the bar of the superpower club-house? Everyone will draw his own conclusion, and his own lesson. From the point of view of squirrels (and I assume that by comparison with the bears and railway guards of the international system, Britain is strictly in the squirrel league these days) I should say that two morals are to be extracted.

The first is that would-be free-riders do not always reach their destination. The second is that protection is a rather flexible concept. Now I don't imagine that these are quite the conclusions Mr Kvitsinksy intended, but none the less I would ask you to keep them in mind during our discussion this evening. Their relevance to the problems of adapting British foreign policy to the circumstances of the next decade will, I hope, become apparent as we go along.

First of all, though, it may be asked why any serious adaptation of our foreign policy is required. The objectives of British diplomacy have already been recast in the most radical fashion twice since the war. In 1947, as Professor Michael Howard described in his lecture here two weeks ago, Atlee and Bevin took (in the withdrawal from India and the withdrawal from Greece) the decisive first steps towards transforming our aims from those of a superpower to those of a member, albeit an important one, of an alliance led by the United States. In the 1960s another shift changed our orientation from that of a global power to that, essentially, of a European one – a member of the European Community. We have still not fully digested the second of these moves and occasionally, it seems, not even the first. Surely another series of changes is not yet required. The answer to this is that the pace of change in world affairs has itself changed, and two decades – the period since Mr Harold Macmillan began to beat on the door of the European Communities – is now a very long time indeed, and the world has changed, almost out of recognition.

– The two superpowers have vastly increased their military capacities and the United States has, in the process, lost its commanding superiority over the Soviet Union. The two are now deadlocked by a position of more or less equal nuclear arsenals and their fear of confrontation with each other.

– At the other end of the spectrum of power, recent experience – from Vietnam to Afghanistan – has shown that terrorist and guerrilla techniques make large-scale conventional conquest of another state exceedingly (and usually prohibitively) difficult and expensive.

– This relative ineffectiveness of conventional military power has finally destroyed colonialism and has left nationalism (parcelled into a large number of new states) in virtually unrestricted control of large parts of the world and its raw material and energy sources.

– Economic power has also been broken up into small pieces, some of them, like the multinationals, outside the normal boundaries of the state system altogether; and attempts to put the bits together again in the shape of groupings like the European Communities or OPEC, have been only fitfully successful.

– Communications of all sorts have been eased and speeded up to an extraordinary extent by the growth of jet travel and by the invention of the satellite – and in the field of information technology we are already well over the threshold of a revolution as earth-shaking as the invention of printing.

A number of very different conclusions can be – and are – drawn from these developments, and I shall discuss some of them in detail in a moment or two. But three general deductions can be made instantly and without any controversy at all. First, the world has become vastly less stable in the last twenty years, both politically and economically – and Britain's normally quite high exposure to unpredictable and calamitous shocks has actually been greatly increased. Secondly, since neither of the superpowers is able to control this turbulence, it is only prudent that medium-rank powers like our own should at least review their own means of coping with these challenges. Thirdly, if we are looking at alternative policies that might take us through this extremely dangerous period, the major criteria for judging them must be whether they are actually relevant to reducing our vulnerability and whether they are likely to get round the problem of our lack of power. In other words, can they be made to stick or, if they are likely to upset others, can we get away with them?

It seems to me that there are in fact three broad strategies at our disposal, each of which has at least some plausibility and each of which has its own strong adherents and critics. Let us start with what is in some ways the most fashionable of them – a modern version of the Little England position of the mid-nineteenth century. I shall spend a little time on this because it is the most radical and therefore sheds the most contrasting light on the other two possibilities.

The argument goes like this. If the superpowers are in deadlock, the chances of the Russians risking confrontation with the United States by invading Western Europe are remote, and even if they did anything so foolish, they would find they had bitten off far more than they could chew. The present troubles in their own East European empire are a pale shadow of the headaches they would get in a Western one. Similarly, if it is impossible for the West in its turn to make any serious impact on the Third World by military means, why waste resources in preparing to do so? On both counts we can and should reduce our defence expenditure by quite large amounts. And if the Americans claim that we are not paying our way, it does not matter too much. They are bound to defend our vital interests – in so far as military defence is possible and relevant – in order to defend their own.

Or take our relationship with the European Community. The conventional pro-Market case in the last twenty years has boiled down to the proposition that the combined power of the main Continental countries is likely to be such that we cannot afford to be left out. But it apparently turns out that we are living in a world in which the Community does not have the political clout to protect itself from the rapacity or instability of countries in the Third World (particularly OPEC) or the economic strength to avert the consequences of economic mismanagement in the United States. What is the point of paying the costs of membership, which are financially onerous and restrain our economic and political freedom of manoeuvre, when we should fare much better as economic opportunists and freebooters, buying food and raw materials in the cheapest markets, protecting our industries, as the Japanese have done, with a series of high-handed expedients, and being clever enough to present our flexion of the rules as the result of unfortunate cultural accidents for which we can hardly be blamed?

Most of this is not complete isolationism in the American sense, any more than the little-Englandism of Cobden and Bright was. Our perennial tendency to insularity hardly needs underlining. Cromwell was right when he said to Parliament in one of his last speeches, 'You have accounted yourselves happy in being environed with a great ditch from all the world beside.' But nobody, except perhaps on the lunatic fringes of Left and Right, supposes that a country of our size and industrial balance can entirely cut itself off from the outside world, sufficient to itself. Even our relative affluence, for the time being, in energy supplies does not provide immunity from outside disruption. The position I am discussing here is much more like that of our old friend the squirrel free-rider. The notion is that it is possible to get the benefits of a relatively stable international system and of an alliance without having to contribute much – or perhaps anything – to it. We could put up tariff, and non-tariff barriers, and impose exchange controls to protect our industries, while others continue to bear the cost of obeying the rules. We can, to a considerable extent, opt out of the defence of northern Europe, because others will continue to defend it without us. And there is no need to bother too much about our relations with the Third World, since there is nothing we can do to control it in any case.

In saying, as I do, that the first great question of British foreign policy in the 1980s is whether or not we should adopt this rather anti-social stance, I expect to encounter some resistance from an audience celebrating the bicentenary of the Foreign Office in a house which has not infrequently been regarded as the headquarters of the British foreign policy Establishment – some of whom may possibly be here tonight. I shall no doubt hear that such a strategy is so obviously absurd in an age of interdependence that it is not worth discussing at all. Simultaneously, and contradictorily, I shall probably be told that I should not give aid and comfort to dangerous opponents by taking their ideas too seriously.

There is something in these objections, but not, I think, enough. In the first place, the notion is not as daft as all that. There have been, and are, some very notable and successful practitioners of it, even in recent times. The French, for instance, with their ferocious sense of national identity and national superiority, are past masters at amassing advantages while at the same time refusing to restrict their freedom of manoeuvre. General de Gaulle's strategy depended ultimately upon the American deterrent and on the existence of NATO, but he professed to ignore the first for French purposes and withdrew his practical co-operation from the second. The neutrals – like the Swiss and the Swedes – have refused to contribute to arrangements which, had they done so, might have prevented the wars from which they later self-righteously claimed exemption. But since they actually escaped the consequences themselves, their policy cannot be said to have been a failure. Even some full members of NATO, notably the Canadians and the Italians, pay far less than their per capita fair share without raising too many eyebrows. Nor is security the only question involved. Economic arrangements are equally open to this kind of manipulation.

The Japanese, for example, have flourished greatly since the last war through their own efficiency and hard work, but also as the result of evading the implicit rule of the international economic system, which ordains that their markets ought to be as open to foreign competitiors and investors as others are to theirs.

But even more important than the plausibility of the free-rider philosophy in our present situation is the fact that derives from its plausibility – namely that it is reflected in a wider range of opinion in this country than at probably any time in the two hundred years since the Foreign Office was founded. This may sound too dramatic; and it is perfectly true that in its pure form it is adopted only by the left wing of the Labour Party. But the psychological roots of it – the idea that Britain has been too responsible for too long, and that we must now pay the highest attention to our own immediate interests for a change – are spread very wide indeed, and vigorous offshoots of the policy consequently appear in some significant places. They have sprouted in many parts of the bureaucracy, particularly in the Treasury; they have overrun one of the main political parties of the state completely. They are tended to splendid and luxuriant growth by the Institute of Applied Economics in Cambridge. They crawl over the pages of every popular newspaper. And they have even shown a tentative tendril or two in Number Ten Downing Street. This growth cannot, whatever one thinks of it, be ignored or brushed aside.

That is not to say, however, that it cannot be defeated by argument, or found wanting when put up against the criteria we have just laid down. First of all, is it relevant to limiting Britain's vulnerability in the world? The reply is that if it worked, it might be. If protectionism is all that Mr Wynne Godley cracks it up to be; if world food prices do not rise drastically; if the Russians do not actually invade Western Europe or take over the Persian oilfields before the Americans get there; in short, if the train stays on the rails and proceeds in an orderly fashion to its destination to peace and prosperity, then boarding it, even without a ticket, does at least have some point.

But there is still the question of whether we shall be challenged for payment. How much can we get away with? In the trade field, Mr Tony Benn's economic advisers believe we could get away with higher tariff barriers provided they were raised all round and did not add new discrimination as between one trading partner and another. But this ignores the political context. We could not introduce a major protectionist package of our own without, in effect, being thrown out of the European Community, and while this is not necessarily a drawback in the eyes of the Left, there is not much doubt that our European partners would be in a sufficiently vindictive frame of mind to exact a severe penalty. It is not enough to say 'the Japanese have got away with it'. The trouble is that they got there first by a good twenty years, and have spoiled the market for all other freebooters. And even they are now finding that they are obliged to liberalize their arrangements in response to pressure from the United States and Europe. More significantly still, they have begun to engage in an active diplomacy in order to secure their sources of supply in the Pacific region, in South-east Asia and the Middle East. If they, with all the strength that they have built up, are yielding to the pressure of these forces, we could hardly hope to do otherwise.

Where security is concerned, I believe that we could, strictly speaking, get away with much more than we do. If, for instance, Britain were, as Labour suggests, to reduce her per capita expenditure on defence to the average of the rest of the Alliance, or even if she were to withdraw her twenty thousand troops from the Rhine army, or abandon the NATO role in the North Atlantic, the effect would not be to cause the United States to start withdrawing troops of her own. We are much too easily impressed by American senators and Congressmen who appear in London and tell us that unless we 'shape up', their colleagues (never, by the way, themselves) will start reducing American military commitments, in the most irrational and irresponsible defiance of American interests and at a time when the Russian menace is supposed to be more dangerous than ever before.

On the other hand, we do have to consider the wider political effects of our own actions, and on this basis the free-rider role looks rather less attractive. The real danger about refusing to pay the normal fare is that, like the wretched squirrel, you have no right to prevent your powerful friends acting on the spur of the moment in ways that may be detrimental to your health. What we have to consider is whether it is in the British interest that American presidents, spurred on by American public opinion, should feel that they are alone in the world and are therefore tempted to act and react and over-react around the world – in the Gulf, in Latin America, in Africa, or even in Europe – as their lonely fears dictate, and without reference to the opinions and needs of anyone else. For the most part, no doubt, nothing untoward would happen, and in this sense we can 'get away' with a certain amount; but there are limits beyond which the risks of misadventure start to mount quite rapidly.

To sum up this part of the argument, I should say that if we try to

33

make ourselves less vulnerable, either by ignoring our friends and trying to conduct a solitary and inward-looking foreign policy, or by quarrelling with them and trying to get them to support us on the cheap, we are likely to land in serious difficulties. It is, to put it at its best, a very high-risk strategy, and at its worst it is a recipe for complete helplessness. The world owes us nothing, and we shall get reliable support only in so far as we can collaborate, with others on the basis of rough equality of effort.

Does this conclusion, then, endorse the second of our strategies – that is, the foreign policy that has broadly been adopted for the past ten years or so? With the present Foreign Secretary in the audience, as well as the immediate past Prime Minister, it would certainly be polite, and possibly prudent, to say that it does. And up to a point, I do. Recent British foreign policy has put heavy emphasis on co-operation and consultation; it has been in favour (for the most part) of free trade and the free movement of capital; it has made a greater effort to contribute to the common defence than any of its allies, with the exception of the United States, and it has paid a high – most would say too high – subscription to the European Common Market. We have shown periodic traces of extreme insularity and bloody-mindedness, of course, as we always have, but on the whole we have displayed most of the solid virtues that the free-rider position derides.

The question is whether we have not become too solid and therefore too inflexible for the new circumstances I have been describing. The way in which our policy has developed since 1950 has, in fact, brought us to an awkward dilemma. For twenty years after Bevin, we put our money firmly on the American alliance. Churchill's grandiose rationalization of our position in terms of the three overlapping circles of the Atlantic relationship, Europe, and the Commonwealth, was basically backward-looking and rapidly gave way to Macmillan's Jamesian picture – a characteristic Highland mixture of melancholy romanticism and brazen self-interest – of Britain holding out civilized hands to the brash Americans and leading them to their global inheritance as the Greeks did the Romans. The attempt to join the Common Market, which, as I have already said, looked like another change, was less of one than it appeared to be. It certainly marked our decisive transition from being a global power to being a regional one, and reduced the Commonwealth circle to a poor ghost. But Europe was

**34**

seen by the British government at that stage first and foremost as an adjunct to the mid-Atlantic alliance rather than as an alternative to it.

Subsequent Labour governments – and indeed all, with the brief exception of Mr Heath's – have until very recently taken pretty much the same view, which is that there is nothing incompatible between the idea of Europe and the idea of an Atlantic Community. There is no choice involved, and indeed in so far as Britain has a 'role' (in the sense that Dean Acheson lamented that we had not) it is to rescue our European partners from their delusion that a serious tension exists.

Subsequent experience has shown that the Europeans were right. It has never been easy to square this circle, as has been proved over the years by frequent accusations from the United States that the British are as unreliable as the rest of Europe, and from the Europeans that we are an American Trojan horse. But we have stuck grimly to it, constantly attempting to finesse our position so as to give the least offence to both sides. The question is, how much longer can this feat be performed, and whether the events and forces we have been considering are going to make it impossible.

If we apply to it the two criteria to which we subjected our first strategy, it is doubtful whether it passes either test. If one asks, can we 'get away with it', the answer is that that is getting pretty difficult, and may well get worse. The rifts of interest and perception between the two sides of the Atlantic have now become so wide that in a lot of cases a choice simply has to be made. There is no time this evening to discuss the rights and wrongs of these divergences. But on the general question of how to deal with the Soviet Union world-wide, as well as a number of particular disputes – let us say, energy policy, or the wisdom of setting up bases in the Middle East, or the significance of the Palestinian issue, or the efficacy and appropriateness of economic sanctions against Poland – the political credibility of Britain as a major partner in Europe already depends upon her distancing herself at least some way from the American administration, even if we did not, for geographical and other reasons, in fact see our interests as lying on the European side of the argument. Yet that is what the Americans regarded as a matter of betrayal. In their present embattled mood, the slogan is 'he who is not with us is against us', and he who is against us is a duplicitous – well, a less than frank fellow. This hardening of attitudes makes the policy of the 1970s much harder to sustain; but the other criterion – 'would it serve its purpose?' – is equally damaging to the idea of Britain poised gracefully between the two sides of the Atlantic. In the world of the 1980s and 1990s, Britain is confronted with a vast variety of problems for which neither the

35

present American alliance nor the present European Community is necessarily the most appropriate answer.

A British government that wants to protect its important economic interests in, say, Nigeria or Malaysia, or promote them with China or the OPEC countries, cannot hope to do so in one dimension only. Our own unaided leverage is at present small, even in the old Commonwealth countries – though it might perhaps be greater with a bit more cultivation. The European Community is still not functioning very satisfactorily as a political entity, and its attitude to the Third World is likely to remain spasmodic and hard to co-ordinate for as far ahead as one can see. The Germans have severe inhibitions about getting involved except on a strictly commercial basis; the French have their own fish to fry, as usual. For the rest – sometimes you see them, sometimes you don't.

As for the Americans, they may announce that they will look after us. But, like the bear in Mr Kvitsinksy's story, their protection can be a mixed blessing. For one thing, their status and accumulated reputation in the Third World as a reactionary element in world politics makes their purely persuasive powers remarkably difficult to deploy, especially in public. The instinctive reaction of national pride to American arguments is 'superpower bullying'. More forceful American inducements, such as threats to cut off aid or to reduce arms sales or even to use force – that is, *real* superpower bullying – are apt to backfire, either because there is another, rival superpower available to be played off against the United States or because the country concerned has observed the phenomenon we discussed at the beginning – namely the difficulty, under modern conditions, of actually applying power. Being associated with these difficulties as a close ally is not yet prohibitively quixotic, and there may well be moments in the future when we shall be very glad of the American Marines. But in the normal conduct of our relationships with any parts of the world, the maintenance of a certain distance from the United States is often prudent.

Whether this argument for greater flexibility really deserves the title 'a brand-new strategy' – the third in our triad of possibilities – I am not sure. Some people here present would probably maintain that these conclusions have long since been drawn by the Foreign and Commonwealth Office, and are indeed old hat. On the other hand there is a different school of thought that would argue that it is new and rather disgraceful to be talking about distancing oneself systematically from one's greatest ally, or refusing to play the global game entirely by

European Community rules. I would merely claim that it is a modification of past norms and that we should be conscious of making it.

Certainly it would be to the advantage of the Alliance as a whole as well as to British interests if it were generally recognized in America as well as in Europe that the logic of the present situation points in the direction of a complicated 'variable-geometry' system instead of the grand and solid designs of yesteryear. Without question we need the American relationship for our immediate safety, as well as for all the psychological reasons on both sides of the Atlantic that I have mentioned. Even without the cultural and historical ties that bind us together, we would continue to regard the United States, ultimately, as 'our' superpower. There can be no question of neutralism. But there is no reason why the European Community should not begin to think more about its own defence arrangements; or why it should not adopt views and make relationships outside Europe which the United States may find misguided or distasteful, but from which the West may actually benefit because its medium-sized members are able to operate in ways in which the United States itself is not. As I have said, I do not believe that this agreement occasionally to disagree need bring down a terrible and irrational vengeance from American public opinion. But some new framework in which to discuss these questions is desirable. Last year I and some colleagues in other institutes in Europe and America published a plan for making consultation on extra-European matters more effective, as well as more acceptable to the United States, by means of a kind of Directorate including the Europeans, the United States, and Japan; and it is interesting to see that President Mitterrand has revived the Gaullist idea of an intra-European one. But the American and European arrows are not the only ones in the quiver. If we wish to influence the Third World, for instance, we probably need to try to make other institutions more effective and instrumental to our purposes – the OECD, the Commonwealth, and even the UN itself. And finally, if we fail on all these levels – as we may, given the unpredictability of the American administration, the internal difficulties of an enlarged Community, or the simple chaos of the Third World – we must be prepared to maximize British interests by the application of our own judgement, our own skills and our own national influence, however limited in comparison with the past. Having rightly insisted on turning our back on Little England, the next most important and difficult psychological task is to prevent ourselves becoming Little Europeans or Little Atlanticists.

So far, I am conscious that I am to some extent guilty of offences under the Trade Descriptions Act. I advertised a lecture about British diplomacy in the 1980s, and I have been talking mainly about foreign policy – which, as Frederick the Great remarked, bears the same relation to diplomacy as music does to an orchestra. I do not actually think I was wrong to concentrate on the wider theme, but I now turn briefly from the score to the manner of its execution.

When I was making a radio programme for the BBC World Service the other day, also in celebration of the bicentenary, we asked Sir Michael Palliser, the Permanent Under-Secretary of the Foreign and Commonwealth Office, and also a young member of the Diplomatic Service still in his twenties, the same question: 'What changes do you expect to see in the Foreign Office within the next generation?' They both answered in the same way – that the only major change would be in communications, which would allow a certain amount of gadgetry to perform tasks at present requiring much expensively produced paperwork.

In a sense – perhaps the most important sense – I am sure that this is right. The functions of diplomatists are not going to alter fundamentally in the next thirty, any more than they have in the past four hundred, years. To report, to represent, to negotiate, to advise, and, ideally, to do all these things in the spirit of Satow's elegant definition of diplomacy: 'the application of intelligence and tact to the conduct of relations between governments'.

All the same, I am not sure that this diplomatic reply quite did justice to some of the practical consequences of the changes in the international environment that we have been discussing.

For instance, take the vast increase in the number of states under the impulsion of nationalism. This looks like a relatively simple problem. You expand your diplomatic service so as to set up embassies in the countries of the most important newcomers, and for the lesser ones, double up with neighbouring statelets or find other expedients like mini-missions to reduce costs. All this we have done. But the repercussions are not by any means over. One fine morning, our mini-mission in Terra Nova reports that oil has been found in vast quantities beneath the inhospitable surface of the territory; that civil war has broken out; that a large party of Czech advisers has suddenly appeared to help put down the rebellion; and that General Bonaparte McCutcheon, the Head of State, has indicated that any British representative in his capital short of a full Ambassador is not consonant with Terra Novan dignity and will not in future be received by him or his ministers. In other words, the pressure is on, because the volatility and the importance of the Third World is likely to go on increasing. At the same time, the complexity of international relationships is also increasing at an exponential rate. The new countries are attempting to combine in order to combat their weaknesses, and the old countries are doing likewise to defend their interests; but the nature of nationalism ordains that not much delegation of authority to supranational bodies takes place, and therefore a vast number of multilateral organizations and negotiating forums has appeared on the scene, haggling and politicking over every aspect of international affairs. Dr Henry Kissinger's famous 'web of international relations' in which he hoped to enmesh the Soviet Union turns out to be a gigantic cat's cradle in which we are ourselves entangled.

A Foreign Service capable of ensuring our survival in the midst of this kind of menagerie needs first of all to be large – at a time when the Treasury is looking constantly for cuts. It needs to be young – since a career structure which insists that the many important responsibilities just mentioned only go to senior officials is hopelessly wasteful of the lower ranks. It needs to be extremely versatile – and particularly well versed in economics, which is now the most common currency of international exchange.

No doubt this can be achieved with a little more effort, and the last point naturally raises the delicate question – what is and is not foreign policy? Interdependence of states and their economies has certainly blurred the old distinctions. Vast numbers of subjects that have been regarded in the past as domestic are now seen as international – and vice versa. Telecommunications policy, energy policy, agricultural policy, investment policy, exchange-rate policy – all these concerns of the sovereign state are now up for international grabs. All have highly emotional and political content, but all are very technical and require handling as much by domestic ministries as by Foreign Offices, and by experts in the subject matter as much as by diplomatic generalists.

What follows? First, that there will have to be much more flexibility in the interchange between the Foreign and Home Civil Service (whether or not one eventually goes as far as the Berrill Report and amalgamates the two). Secondly, there will have to be a much more elaborate form of inter-departmental liaison than now exists to co-ordinate our foreign policy interests. The Cabinet and its sub-committees work reasonably well where traditional functional issues like defence interact with foreign relations; less well on geographical areas, such as the European Community, where large numbers of departments are concerned; and often not at all where the ministries are as ill-assorted as, say, the Foreign and Commonwealth Office, the Department of Education and Science, and the Department of Health and Social Security, handling various aspects of the overseas students question.

As far as I can foretell, all this will tend, over a period, to enhance the power of the Prime Minister at the expense of the Foreign Secretary, of the Civil Service at the expense of ministers, and of the Cabinet Office at the expense of departments – but perhaps that is peering too far into future controversy for a celebratory occasion like this. As any fairground palmist will tell you, there are moments when it is a mistake to see – or at least reveal – too much.

What I hope I have been able to convey is my own sense, as I look at the world in the 1980s and towards the world of the 1990s, that an active foreign policy and diplomacy is essential for this country.

Our vulnerability to all sorts of pressures and disasters is very great, and the only sensible defence in a chaotic and protectionist environment is to mobilize other people's self-interest on as many different levels, multilateral and bilateral, as possible. To put it crudely, we shall get at least some of what we want from those with whom we collaborate and whom we help, from those we can convince that they will make money with us and out of us, and from those who can be brought to believe that we are the sort of people it is a pleasure and privilege to do business with.

In mobilizing our assets to this end, a certain amount of risk and expense is inevitably involved, including a serious defence effort, a subscription to the European Community that may be too high, an overseas aid programme, and a willingness to support unquantifiable assets like the British Council, the Overseas Service of the BBC, and (dare one say it?) Chatham House. It is hopeless to try to fortify ourselves in the bunker. And even more dangerous to expect others to look after us for nothing. As Mr Kvitsinksy would agree, the track behind us is littered with the corpses of small furry animals who have tried it. St Thomas à Kempis said, 'it is safer to remain in subjection than to govern'. But it is still safer to rise than to fall.

*Lecture to mark the bicentenary of the office of Foreign Secretary, Chatham House, 18 March 1982.*

# The Pros and Cons of Summitry

Nothing could be more fatal than the habit (the at present fatal and pernicious habit) of personal contact between the statesmen of the world. It is argued, in defence of this pastime that the foreign secretaries of the nations 'get to know each other'. This is an extremely dangerous cognizance. Personal contact breeds, inevitably, personal acquaintance and that, in its turn, leads in many cases to friendliness: there is nothing more damaging to precision in international relations than friendliness between contracting parties. This is no mere paradox. Diplomacy is the art of negotiating *documents* in a ratifiable and therefore dependable form. It is by no means the art of conversation. The affability inseparable from any conversation between ministers produces allusiveness, compromises and high intentions.

The author of this passage, Sir Harold Nicolson, wrote it in an agony of disillusionment after the Versailles Conference where President Woodrow Wilson's personal diplomacy had proved such a disaster. But it is worth reviving the quotation as the world prepares for the Downing Street economic summit in two weeks' time, because it encapsulates an ancient[1] and respectable strand of thought which has certainly not disappeared from the minds of members of the professional diplomatic community, and probably deserves more consideration than present fashion allows it.

It would not be difficult to make a case along these lines against the Downing Street meeting. The colloquy will take seven heads of government away from their desks and their domestic political responsibilities at a critical time and catapult them into unfamiliar surroundings liable

[1] The fifteenth-century diplomatist Philippe de Comines, wrote, 'Two great princes who want to establish good relations should never meet each other face to face.'

41

to warp their judgements. It will not be possible in the time available to discuss the matters in hand in any but the most general terms and yet they are matters – international monetary reform, nuclear energy, arms control and the commodity markets – where everything turns on the details.

Moralizing rhetoric and brute force of personality rather than the accommodation of conflicting interests will be the order of the day. Public expectations will be aroused which cannot, in the nature of things, be met and which will have to be frantically damped down by the publication of an anodyne communiqué 99 per cent of which has already been composed and agreed between high officials in Washington this week. The whole exercise, it can be argued, is therefore likely to be profitless at best; and at worst dangerously deceptive.

A quick look at the previous two meetings in this series – the Rambouillet summit of November 1975 and the Puerto Rico summit of last June – does not necessarily invalidate this critique. In retrospect, one can see that neither meeting did any positive harm, but in spite of all the ballyhoo at the time, neither achieved anything very solid either – or at any rate anything that could not have been achieved more easily by the normal means. Rambouillet endorsed the sale of gold by the IMF, for instance, but this had been settled by the technicians already and its full announcement might have been made earlier if it had not been thought necessary to reserve something for the summit to 'agree' about. Puerto Rico enabled President Ford and Dr Kissinger to have a final international fling in front of the American electors but produced nothing at all.

Similarly, the Downing Street meeting will presumably endorse a new IMF agreement on exchange rate policies. It will likewise be attended by much cordial razzmatazz from which Mr Callaghan, as the courtly host, and Mr Carter, as the gracious chief guest, will expect to derive some political advantage. (Let us not forget the President's half-serious remark during the election campaign: 'Whenever I run into problems with the Congress, I'm going to have to go abroad.')

But can we expect anything from the encounter other than a lot of private misunderstandings and public clichés? It is all very well to say, in the words of the Rambouillet communiqué, 'We are confident that our present economic policies are compatible and complementary and that recovery is under way,' or 'a co-operative relationship and improved understanding between the developing nations and the industrial world is fundamental to each,' but, as the subsequent eighteen months have shown, it is quite another thing to turn this unexceptionable consensus into practical progress. And in any case, do we need this kind of meeting to bring forth these bland mice?

The answer to this question is really the modern answer to the Harold Nicolson thesis about diplomacy. And it is 'yes'. We probably do need this kind of meeting precisely for the purpose of propagating, in the first place, a number of virtuous clichés and, if possible, a number of home truths of a less obvious kind. Nicolson, writing in the 1920s, did not make sufficient allowance for what has become a more and more critical factor in the conduct of foreign relations – namely, the existence in all the western countries of a powerful public opinion sufficiently sophisticated to perceive a connection between international events and its own well-being.

The discreet, upper-class diplomatists of nineteenth-century Europe, padding about the Chanceries and exchanging confidences in beautifully modulated French accents, did not, of course, have everything their own way. Opposition of a narrow but menacing kind could be aroused where manufacturing and commercial interests were threatened and occasionally on a wider scale the passions of the mob could be inflamed by some issue of national honour or prestige. But on the whole for more than half a century after Waterloo the politicians and professional diplomats of the day were able to behave as if foreign policy was a matter which they could handle in the light of their own judgement and a manageable range of domestic pressures.

All that has now been swept away, and indeed had already crumbled almost to nothing by 1919. Woodrow Wilson's 'democratic' approach to diplomacy was not an aberration, as Nicolson may have supposed, or even a mistake. It was a necessity for him. It is arguable that if he had stayed at home a bit more, he might have had a better chance of stemming the tide of isolationism in the Congress but he evidently believed that he could dramatize to the American people by his own presence in Paris their stake in the shape of the post-war world. The gamble did not come off for a variety of complicated reasons; but so long as American public opinion was worth influencing (and it was) it is hard to believe that he was wrong to come to Paris at all.

Wilson's problem was bad enough sixty years ago to defeat him. For an American president, it is far worse today and it has invaded the preserve of every political leader in the old world as well. A summit meeting is a useful, perhaps even an essential, tool in the hands of a competent politician for dealing with it.

The seven men who gather at Downing Street on 7 May are already well aware of the problems that confront them – inflation, unemployment, the energy crisis, nuclear proliferation, the growing military and ideological pretensions of Soviet Russia, the increasing and unpredictable power of primary commodity producers. They are also well aware of each other's arguments, political difficulties and, if it comes to that, personalities. Nothing much therefore that any of them can say in private is going to come as a surprise or an enlightenment. Yet everything they agree publicly, however banal, and everything that they do and the very fact that they are meeting at all gives them a chance individually and collectively to convey something dramatically to their own domestic opinion.

The most important message is in fact the tritest. It is the message that all seven are agreed on what they would like to avoid – on the wickedness, if you like, of sin. This is the point of those endless communiqués and declarations. Just as a religious litany proceeds from the psychological assumption that if you say over and over again in public that you disapprove of this or that course of action, you are less likely to perform it in the future: so the summit meetings proceed on the assumption that if the leaders of the western developed world stand up and chant in unison, 'we believe in open, democratic society, dedicated to individual liberty and social advancement; in interdependence and constructive dialogue; in steady economic growth; and in free trade for ever and ever, Amen,' it will have some effect on their propensity to virtue thereafter. It will also commit their public opinion at home to virtue as well, and because the commitment was made in a palatable ritual form it will not raise immediate political reactions.

This sounds a childish exercise, perhaps, but it seems probable that incantations of this kind have had a real effect in enabling politicians to contain the domestic pressures for protectionism in all the western countries during the recession so far. There is the more general point, moreover, that when people see on their television screens the leader of their own country hobnobbing amicably with others, in what is evidently very high-powered dialogue, they conclude that there is some offsetting advantage for any national sacrifices they may have to make in order that virtue may flourish.

The question, of course, is whether any of the leaders will go further than the rather passive exploitation of the opportunity implied here and have the courage to use the dramatic occasion for a more direct confrontation of public opinion with the real issues. How many can we expect to tell the world from this platform about what must be done to limit the growth of expectations in the West, if the political and economic problems arising from the present distribution of global resources are not to engulf us all? Mr Carter is trying in a way to do something of the kind and he will obviously use the summit to heighten the effect of his appeal. So far, the Europeans and the Japanese show little sign of seizing the same opportunity to spell out, in genuinely clear terms, the implications of our predicament. The truth is that there is nothing wrong with communication between states or their leaders at present. The gap today comes between the rulers and the governed who have the power to frustrate the best-devised agreements of princes.

*Financial Times*, 29 April 1977

# Why We Need to Keep the Bomb

**W**ould the world be a better and safer place without nuclear weapons? The Easter marchers obviously think so and it seems that President Reagan does, as well. In his 'Star Wars' television address on 23 March, he did not, it is true, go quite to the lengths of trying to abolish the bomb overnight, but he did hold out the prospect of making nuclear weapons 'impotent and obsolete' by the expedient of inventing an impregnable defence against them and thus 'paving the way for arms control measures to eliminate the weapons themselves'.

On the face of it, the US government is now officially committed, therefore, to sharing at least one axiom with the peace movement: the fewer nuclear bombs there are lying around, the less likely they are to be used; the most desirable state of affairs is one in which there are no nuclear weapons at all.

It is hard to argue with such a proposition these days without being instantly denounced as a warmonger and fascist beast; but still, I must say that in the form I have just stated it (which is the form in which it is usually heard) the idea is sentimental, simplistic and dangerous.

'Why?' you may ask. 'After all, you are always writing that nuclear weapons are extremely expensive and terribly destructive and both the US and the Soviet Union have far more of them than is necessary. You obviously agree that we should negotiate arms control agreements in order to save resources, and to limit disaster if war actually breaks out, and to unwind the dangerous psychological tensions and illusions that a competitive arms race creates. What is wrong, then, with looking forward hopefully to a day when these negotiations have been so successful that nuclear weapons have been abolished – or, to put it in Mr Reagan's way, to a day when the definitive answer has been found to them?'

God knows there is no great mystery about the answer after forty years of argument on this subject, but its elements are worth repeating in the present hectic atmosphere. First of all, nuclear weapons, though unimaginably terrible, are still weapons; that is, they have been called into existence because men wish to advance their interests and to defend themselves and will always seek the most effective way of doing these things, including the use of force.

If, by some magic wand, we could 'disinvent' nuclear weapons, we should not be able to prevent great powers attempting to further or defend their interests, either through the development of even more terrible weapons or perhaps by threats of so-called conventional war (which is now likely to be so much more destructive than the Second World War that it scarcely deserves the title 'conventional').

What will restrain the actual use of force in these circumstances? 'A new world-order', perhaps? Yes, a juster world and new international institutions with greater powers might help; but can one realistically see the Soviet and American governments allowing their freedom to be circumscribed by paper treaties or international bodies in a really serious conflict of interests?

What about moral restraint, then? Again, yes – but only up to a point. Morality has certainly been an important element in preventing the US from using atomic weapons when they could have done so with impunity in the late 1940s and 1950s. Even later – in Vietnam, when other considerations of prudence entered in – the ethical factor prevented the nuclear bombing of Hanoi and indeed ultimately caused the collapse of the US position.

The trouble is that we cannot be certain that the Russians would display similar squeamishness if there were no Western nuclear weapons, or if they managed to solve the problem of shooting down American rockets with certainty before the Americans solved the problem of shooting down Soviet ones. In conventional situations when there has been no external constraint, such as Afghanistan or Eastern Europe, Soviet behaviour has been brutal.

This does not leave much to rely on except some form of deterrence. Four thousand years of experience show that the possession of a large conventional army, though certainly a help, is not always protection against aggressive powers, because the risks associated with losing a conventional war often seem less, at the outset, than the prospective gains of winning it. The vital question is whether nuclear deterrence is likely to do any better.

On this point, all we can say is that it has done remarkably well so far. There has been no nuclear war since 1945 and what is more this success has spilled over into the conventional field. The superpowers have been so afraid of the possibility that conventional confrontation would escalate to the nuclear level that they have so far shied away from situations that entail Russian and American troops fighting each other on the ground. The chances of this period of relative peace to have lasted so long if nuclear weapons had not been invented are slim.

Of course, there is a counter-objection at this point and it is that the consequences of a failure of nuclear deterrence are so frightful that they outweigh the increased chances of nuclear or even conventional peace. An honest proponent of this line might say: 'I would rather accept a high risk of another world war than an even infinitesimal risk of a nuclear holocaust.' This is a matter of taste, and all I can say is that I don't agree.

Nor is it easy to see why the sheer numbers of nuclear weapons in the armoury of each side makes any difference to this part of the argument. A balanced reduction of numbers is a good thing for all sorts of reasons but it doesn't make the weapons any less likely to be used – until, that is, there are no nuclear weapons at all.

If this is right, President Reagan's vision of an infallible anti-ballistic missile system is an appalling one. It separates the United States from her allies, of course, because it raises the possibility of a war in Europe from which the Americans could stand aloof. More generally, though, the perfect A B M would be extremely de-stabilizing. If one superpower possessed it and the other did not (a situation which in any case could not last more than a year or two) then one superpower would have the whip hand – which is all right if it's us, not so good if it's them. On the other hand, if both superpowers lost the capacity to destroy each other we are back to the 1930s and an era in which regional conflict forever threatens to escalate into conventional war on global levels – which may seem 'tolerable' because political leaders compare it in their minds with a nuclear Armageddon.

Very few things in this world are wholly bad, and fear is not one of them. In forty years fear of nuclear weapons has done more to undermine war as an instrument of policy than anything else in the history of mankind. Remove that fear and we are back to where we started.

*The author is director of the Royal Institute of International Affairs, Chatham House. He writes here in a personal capacity.*

*The Times*, 8 April 1983

# Where Truman Went Wrong

The passion for anniversaries has already conjured up so many dubious spirits this spring that I hesitate to raise another. Nevertheless my particular ghost deserves, I think, his walk on the battlements.

Thirty-five years ago this week, on 25 April 1950, the US National Security Council approved a top-secret document known as NSC 68. Prepared by order of President Truman, it set out to 're-examine American objectives in peace and war' in the light of the explosion of the first Soviet atomic bomb in 1949. It chartered, in fact, the course of US foreign policy, and indeed much of world history, up to the present and must be considered one of the two or three most important state papers this century.

It is hard to convey in a few paragraphs the flavour and significance of an argument sixty pages long, but its essential point is to say that NSC 68 accepted, for the first time, the burden of imposing an American order on the whole of world affairs. At any time between 1946 and 1949 there would have been general assent in Washington to some of its main propositions – Moscow's implacable enmity and aggressive intention towards free institutions in general and the US in particular: the impossibility of a return to pre-war isolation; the vital need, in the interests of American security, to prevent Western Europe, and possibly the Middle East, from falling under Soviet domination.

That, after all, had been the rationale for the Marshall Plan in 1947 and the foundation of NATO in 1949. What was not asserted until NSC 68 was that the whole globe was strategically a single battlefield and that any fresh increase of Soviet influence in any part of it was a threat to America's own ability to flourish in freedom. The logic by which this far-reaching conclusion was arrived at was by no means simple. It was probably as much an emotional as a logical process. But the main elements were:

– A growing belief that the Soviet leaders really were bent on 'world domination'; and that they were guided by 'the simple consideration of weakening the world power position of the US'. In this situation a 'spheres-of-influence settlement' was unreal.

– A perception that Soviet military strength, now boosted with atomic weapons, gave the Russians the capacity to confront the US with an impossible dilemma – that of either 'reacting totally to a limited extension of Soviet control or of not reacting at all'. This would lead to 'gradual withdrawal under the direct or indirect pressure of the Soviet Union, until we discover one day that we have sacrificed positions of vital interest'.

– A new fear about the effects of an *appearance* of American weakness. 'The risk of having to capitulate or precipitate a global war is bad enough, but it is multiplied by the weakness it imparts to our position in the cold war. Instead of appearing strong and resolute we are continually at the verge of appearing and being alternately irresolute and desperate.' The danger was that allies and potential allies would, as a result, 'drift into a course of neutrality eventually leading to Soviet domination'.

What, then, was to be done? One possibility specifically raised in NSC 68, but firmly rejected, was of a pre-emptive military strike against the Soviet Union before it could match US nuclear superiority. This was dismissed partly on the creditable ground that the idea of 'preventive war' is 'generally unacceptable to Americans' and partly because of an estimate that an American atomic attack alone 'would not force or induce the Kremlin to capitulate'. The only alternative was to ensure, by means of a rapid and sustained build-up of strength, that Western superiority was continued – for, as the paper roundly asserted, 'without superior aggregate military strength, in being and readily mobilizable, a policy of "containment" – which is in effect a policy of calculated and gradual coercion – is no more than a policy of bluff'.

For the authors of NSC 68 the crucial question was whether the US public would stand for such a policy. For themselves, they were not too troubled by doubts: 'The integrity of our system will not be jeopardized by any measures, covert or overt, violent or non-violent, which serve the purpose of frustrating the Kremlin design.' But they acknowledged that in a free society the resort to force 'must commend itself to the overwhelming majority as an inescapable exception to the basic idea of freedom'.

This entailed a willingness to negotiate (not, for the foreseeable future, 'as a separate course of action but rather as a means of gaining support for a programme of strength, of recording . . . progress in the cold war'). It also meant a dramatic presentation of the issues to the American public.

An ironic feeling of uncanny continuity is the main sensation one gets from re-reading NSC 68. Quite apart from the fact that its main author was none other than the veteran Paul Nitze, now the Reagan administration's (moderate) adviser on arms control but then head of the State Department's policy-planning staff, it states the East–West policies of President Reagan's first term in a form, rhetorical as well as substantial, that the most vociferous Republican 'hawk' would find acceptable. And since, in the context of 1950, with Stalin at the height of his power, such policies have rightly entered the Western historic consciousness as right and even heroic, the inevitable question arises: why (except to the ardent New Right) do they strike a jarring note today?

A brief answer would be that NSC 68, for all its bravura, was flawed even in 1950, and that because no subsequent American administration has entirely freed itself from its assumptions, these flaws have become more and more serious. First, it defined Western interests almost entirely in terms of Soviet policy and not in terms of their comparative real importance to the US, thus, in effect putting the initiative for American policy into Moscow's hands. Secondly, its implications could be sold domestically only by scaring the American people. And finally, it offered no coherent strategy for negotiation or coexistence with the Soviet Union to whom a complete Western victory was hardly likely to appeal.

The first course led ultimately to Vietnam; the second to McCarthyism and the wild fluctuations of the 1960s; and the third to the very frustration among Western allies that NSC 68 feared most. In thirty-five years we ought to have learnt something from all this. Sometimes I even think we have.

*The Times, 26 April 1985*

# Goodbye to Brussels

Historians, I am sure, will regard the Brussels negotiations as a mere fragment in the prolonged story of how Britain rejoined Europe, and the politicians cannot really be blamed for anticipating them, whatever their motives. But, for me, Brussels – that dingy, rainy, money-grubbing caravanserai – has already become a distinct chapter of my life, closed ten days ago and now almost dreamlike in its completeness and isolation. The fat bankers' wives, stuffing themselves with cream cakes amid the gilded imperial fantasies of the Metropole Hotel; the white-faced 'hostesses' beckoning above their knitting from behind the nylon net curtains in the Boulevard Jacquemin; even the journalists of several dozen nations clustering in a daze of rumour and discomfort in the sick-coloured marble foyer of the new Belgian Foreign Ministry – they all belong to a world which I doubt if I could enter again, however often I go back to Belgium and even if the negotiations were to start again in two years' time.

Try to reduce this strange, chaotic interlude to order in one's mind at this distance of time is a useful private exercise, but a public impertinence. I offer here no more than some gropings towards the answer to a single traumatic question – was it worth while? Has the cream of Whitehall (not to mention the skimmed milk of Fleet Street) wasted sixteen valuable months which should have been spent in raising Britain by her own shoelaces?

The first thing to be established, with all the brilliant penetration of hindsight, is whether General de Gaulle ever had the slightest intention of allowing Britain to join the E E C. If it could be proved, perhaps the most damaging accusation against the British Cabinet would be that they failed to read the plain evidence of their senses, and led us on an obstacle race which ended at the edge of a cliff. One member of the British delegation admitted to me the other day: 'If we had known then what we know now about de Gaulle, we should probably never have started negotiations.' But how could they have known? Had de Gaulle in fact made up his mind early in the negotiations? And even if he had done so, was there any way short of astrology in which the government could have divined earlier that he had turned down his thumb.

It is true that on the evidence of the Memoirs the presence of Britain in the Common Market was bound to be thoroughly inconvenient to him, since it would probably prevent France from becoming the strongest power in Europe. It was equally inconvenient to admit a new member who might, in order to please the Americans, dispute the necessity of building up a third-force Europe. But if he was determined to exclude us for these reasons, why did he not challenge us from the beginning? He was obviously disconcerted at the British government's application and Mr Heath's bland acceptance of the outlines of the Rome Treaty in October 1961. But the political arguments were as good then as they are now and the risks of breaking up the Community by imposing a veto no greater. The British government not unnaturally drew the tentative conclusion that the General was sceptical, unenthusiastic and prepared to squeeze us until the pips squeaked, but in the last resort resigned to our entry if his partners insisted upon it.

Such was certainly the genuine view of French diplomats at the time, and such was the basis on which French tactics for almost the entire course of the negotiations were founded. French economic interests, particularly agricultural ones, are protected by the Rome Treaty for the very good reason that during the 1957–58 negotiations the French refused to sign until they were. A strict stand on the Rome Treaty, therefore, had the triple advantages of maintaining French interests, making things difficult for the British and forcing the European Commission as guardians of the Treaty to side with France. The possibilities of the position were brilliantly exploited by Couve de Murville, the French Foreign Minister, and his chief official and golfing partner Olivier Wormser. With undertakers' affability they would rub their hands over an abstruse article in the Treaty or the agricultural regulations as if it were a stymie; they would point out '*équivoques*' and '*malentendus*' to the British position with the sad satisfaction of one finding his opponent's ball in a bad lie; they would cede gracefully on minor points like easy putts and watch with polite irony while

Britain tried to sink difficult ones. Whenever Britain made a concession, the French minions would appear magically among the anxious journalists and point out how easy everything was when Britain adopted the Treaty. In short, standard French diplomacy – and fair game up to a point.

Suddenly, on 14 January, this long and satisfying professional match was brought to an abrupt end by the General, who made it quite clear that the Rome Treaty was not in the rules. The French delegation was frankly astounded, then furious, and finally acutely embarrassed. They had been made to look foolish. They could hardly blame themselves, but one of them went as far as to suggest to me that Couve himself should have resigned.

If the French delegation were thus hoodwinked and finally betrayed, one can scarcely blame the British delegation for being similarly taken unawares. There still remains, however, the question of Mr Macmillan's two personal encounters with the General. Surely some sense of how the great mind was working must have filtered through to the Prime Minister. Here, I fear we are up against an unhappy fact of nature – that Mr Macmillan and the General are and always have been incapable of understanding one another. If this is not proved by the present rumpus over Rambouillet, it was obvious after the Prime Minister's visit to Champs last June. The French Ministry of Information telephoned the British correspondents in Paris to inform them that Mr Macmillan had abjured the Atlantic Alliance; the Quai d'Orsay, enraged, rang them up to say that he had done nothing of the kind; while the wretched British Embassy, which had apparently heard almost nothing of the Olympian dialogue, could do little but confirm that it had all been frank and friendly. The '*esprit de Champs*' upon which so many hopes were built might, in short, have meant everything or nothing at all.

Looking back on it, I have a feeling that a very far-sighted character might have read the signs even at Champs. Last time I saw the General was that sunny afternoon, stepping recklessly out of his car to be mobbed by the villagers and the Sunday sightseers, his surprisingly fat head towering pallidly over the sunburnt crowds. His astonishing serenity and his effortless magnetism foreshadowed the sweeping successes of the referendum and the election. The election, I believe, and the gradual establishing of a psychological ascendancy over Dr Adenauer in the exchange of visits in the summer were probably the deciding factors in the General's mind. The first marked the end of the first phase of the Grand Design – the establishment of a secure home base;

the second marked the recovery from the setback in the spring when Italy and Benelux refused to proceed with political union in Europe without Britain – with a Franco-German treaty in prospect, de Gaulle felt he could afford to disregard the Italian–Benelux axis. The insecurity of the British government after the autumn by-elections, the ascendancy of Mr Gaitskell's anti-Market line and, finally, the Nassau agreement clinched the argument.

Only a government endowed with second sight could have seen for sure that this was the way things would go, and even if the analysis is correct, Britain was therefore perfectly justified in opening the negotiations. There is still, however, the question whether, having begun to negotiate, the right tactics were used. The problem as presented to the British delegation was to implement Mr Macmillan's characteristic policy of doing good by such slow degrees that the electorate cannot detect it. A vast change was to be wrought in British public opinion and in Parliament in favour of the Market while an orderly retreat in Brussels was presented to them in the heavy disguise of an orderly advance. It was a task calling for immense diplomatic agility and a political sleight-of-hand to prevent one half of this operation from getting out of step and tripping up the other. How, for instance, was the government to convince the House of Commons that these were 'exploratory' talks which would leave everything open for a big decision later on and at the same time to convince the Six that we were whole-hearted Europeans? How to arouse enthusiasm for the Market and bring the Tory Party into line without convincing the Six that we would come in at any price? How to reassure the Commonwealth, EFTA and the British farmer that we would fight to the death for them, without losing all momentum in Brussels?

The answer to the Brussels half of these questions lay mainly in the person of the Lord Privy Seal. It has been absorbing and at the same time a little frightening to watch Mr Heath at work these last sixteen months. For Mr Heath is, frankly, a new type of British politician – the whizz-kid. He would be at home in President Kennedy's Brains Trust – even, I dare say, in President Kennedy's rocking-chair itself. He is probably less quick-witted than the White House boys, but he is certainly less of an intellectual snob. What he shares with the new Americans is a passionate empiricism and a deep-seated belief in efficiency as the ultimate political good. It is these which have given him his immense staying-power during the negotiations. He really believes in Europe not, as he may whimsically tell you, because he hitch-hiked there before the war, but because he believes it is the shortest cut to making Britain efficient and hence happy. His beliefs have also given him, like his American counterparts, a penchant for the hard technical details of his business and for the solution of problems by an endless discussion of them by clever colleagues – a kind of 'total recall' technique requiring exhausting hours of thought, especially from the colleagues. He is too reserved to be loved, but tenacious enough to be sincerely admired and able enough to be respected by his officials and his opponents. Until, through no fault of his, the Tory Party Conference in October followed its leaders with a blind excess of enthusiasm, leaving him with no negotiating position to speak of, it was impossible to imagine a man better equipped for waging a patient, expert and subtle war than Edward Heath; nor could he and his delegation have done it better given their presuppositions.

If there was a fault it lay in the presuppositions themselves, and these were primarily the responsibility of Mr Macmillan. If the British delegation often behaved as if this were an ordinary tariff negotiation between equal partners in which there was all the time in the world (apart from the limit imposed by the British general election) for horse-trading and didactic attrition, it was because they were picked and equipped and instructed to do so. It was the government which failed to read the General's mind and draw the correct conclusion. I have argued that nothing less than astrology could have done this with accuracy, but I still believe that even taking the most favourable possible estimate of the General's intention there was an obvious need for haste, before he changed his mind and before some new calamitous factor arose.

To have gone faster would have certainly involved political risks at home, which was presumably the main reason that strategy was decided as it was. It cannot be seriously maintained, as some optimists have done, that Britain could have 'signed the Treaty and negotiated afterwards'. Even the eloquence of a Churchill (which, heaven knows, is not that of Mr Macmillan) could not have persuaded the House of Commons to swallow the disappearance of Commonwealth preference as quickly as that. But there was no reason why the task of educating the public should have proceeded at such a funereal pace. It was not until after the Commonwealth Prime Ministers' Conference that the government's propaganda campaign was 'unleashed', so presumably it was calculated that an earlier drive would have given unnecessary ammunition to Sir Derek Walker-Smith and his friends. Still, it was a gamble which should have been taken. Another vital six weeks or two months might have been saved by moving far more quickly from the fact-finding phase last spring to the actual business of negotiation. Above all, I believe that quicker progress could and should have been made over British agriculture. If the government had been prepared to accept a deal for the British farmer as tentative and unsatisfactory to some interested parties as that which it was apparently willing to accept for the Commonwealth, much time and temper would have been saved. A political decision was evidently taken that this was one thing the Tory Party would not swallow and, having been taken, it was backed by a particularly stubborn team from the Ministry of Agriculture. Nevertheless, a senior minister told me not long ago that he believed that in the last resort the government could probably induce the party to swallow the latest proposals to the Six on agriculture. In view of what happened, this should surely have been tried.

These arguments can now be left to the historians and to members of the British Cabinet, who will no doubt dream them over after every heavy dinner for the rest of their days. What matters from the practical point of view is this. The negotiations proved that entry to Europe is perfectly feasible for Britain – given a minimum of political good will on the Continent. The past eighteen months have done very little to weaken the general arguments in favour of entry. If one looks back over the great bleak battlefield of words it is remarkable how few casualties the original Marketeers have suffered. The endless argument over the strict economic advantages and disadvantages to Britain of entry has admittedly been fought to a draw. The government overestimated the economic benefits at the outset of the proceedings perhaps because one of the main impulses in favour of entry came originally from one school of thought within the Treasury. But the psychological arguments still look in good shape, in spite of the scorn that has been poured on the 'pseudo-idealism of the younger generation'. It may be that there was something escapist and gimmicky about the government's clutch at Europe – Mr Macmillan seldom allows himself the luxury of romanticism without satisfying himself that it has political possibilities. But since nothing, not even a Labour government, seemed likely to jolt the country out of a bankrupt complacency, the only initiative in sight was well worth attempting.

Events have been slightly kinder to those critics who maintain that the Community was an inward-looking protectionist group. Nobody who has listened in the last year to the Dutch and Germans talking about aid to under-developed countries, or the French talking about food imports to Europe, is likely to maintain that if left to themselves any of these countries would have particularly wide horizons. And no one who has sat through a day or two of airless tedium in the Strasbourg parliaments will deny that there is a strong streak of anti-Americanism latent in the European movement. And yet the whole of this argument depended on the belief that if Britain joined she would be engulfed in a system which her presence could do nothing to change. This, in retrospect, was the crux of the difference between the pro- and anti-Marketeers. Mr Gaitskell and the majority of the Labour Party (to the exasperation of continental socialists) believed that Big Business would see to it that the roles of the Community were worked against planning, social welfare and low tariffs. The Right was equally convinced that the Commonwealth, the American alliance and the Queen would go under to a mob of faceless bureaucrats and foreigners. But the negotiations have justified those who believed that a community that included Britain would be very different from what it is now. Politically it has been proved that de Gaulle's anti-American third-force notions could not have survived our entry, and will hardly survive now. The Right can derive at least this much satisfaction, too, from de Gaulle's action – that it demonstrates how a major power can exercise a negative force within the Community. Socially it was shown a hundred times that while we were unlikely to export socialist planning where it did not already exist on the Continent, the British Welfare State was not in jeopardy. Economically, the negotiations were tending to a result which would have given us, as members of the Community, just enough moral and political leverage to see that in future the rest of the world was not shut out.

Above all, the negotiations have educated public opinion to the great issues of the time as nothing else could have done. In Europe the ultimate choice between a loosely knit political group under de Gaulle and a more unified but outward-turning system has had to be faced. The Five who began the negotiations supporting British entry as a counterweight to de Gaulle have ended by supporting it for wider reasons as well, among which is a better understanding of the Commonwealth.

In Britain the education has been even more radical. Anyone whose profession has been to swell the volume of words which have been written during the controversy will confirm that he has had to become, if only superficially, conversant with the problems of the Atlantic Alliance, GATT, world commodity markets, East–West relations and economic planning – not to mention social security benefits, East India kips, the *Mezzogiorno* and the number of grains that a chicken eats in order to put on a kilogram of weight. If (as I admit I have sometimes doubted) even a small proportion of these words has been read, the effects must have been profound.

Already some deep-seated illusions have been dispelled. The idea is dead that the Commonwealth can provide an economic alternative to Europe, far less a harbour for visions of imperial grandeur. The present food subsidy system in Britain is doomed. The independent deterrent is moribund. The notion that Britain somehow belongs to Europe has gained ground – partly perhaps for the admirable negative reason that anything opposed by General de Gaulle and Dr Adenauer must have something in it, but more, I believe, from a general realization that far from losing an identity in Europe, Britain might find one. 'Blistered in Brussels, patched and peeled in London,' the European ideal still survives to fight another day.

*Spectator*, *8 February 1963*

# My Vote Is Still 'Yes'

I believe we should go into the Common Market because I do not think that Britain (or for that matter any but a super power) can any longer realize alone her full potential either as an industrial nation, a leader of world opinion, a source of assistance for the underdeveloped world, or a stabilizing democratic influence in the Western alliance . . . I am not alone in thinking this. My friends, my generation, if you like – I am thirty – grew up in the war and the post-war years. This period has rubbed our noses in two harsh facts: Britain's loss of power and the sad impossibility of building Jerusalem in the midst of nuclear, nationalist anarchy. Any socialist with a spark of imagination must see the Common Market as Labour's dreamed-of chance to spread its ideals and practical wisdom outside the narrow confines of Britain.

I must apologize for this quotation – not its content, with which I heartily agree, but its authorship. I wrote it myself thirteen years ago in an article in the *Daily Herald* (of which I was then Common Market Correspondent) in answer to one by Mrs Barbara Castle. I turned up her diatribe and my own the other day in order to try to pin down what it was that I felt had changed about the argument since those far-off days when Mr Harold Macmillan was in Downing Street, Mr Hugh Gaitskell was leading the anti-Market crusade and the Watt waistline was several inches smaller. The yellowing cuttings, like all such ephemera, give off their own special smell of sadness and decay, but there is an additional lugubrious quality about a walk down this particular Memory Lane that I find both depressing and in-structive.

For one thing, both 'pros' and 'antis' made certain automatic as-sumptions about Britain's power and influence in the world. Mrs

61

Castle's pitch – to which almost the whole of her article was devoted – was the question of the Commonwealth. She really believed that the Commonwealth was a viable alternative and she was, to do her justice, prepared to make sacrifices in order to see that it remained one. I remember her pounding her fist at me over a Brussels restaurant table, and shouting, with some justice, that I had no right to talk about the Commonwealth until I had had to defend the import of cheap Commonwealth textiles, as she had, on a street corner in her Blackburn constituency.

These perspectives have almost completely disappeared. I heard Mr Harold Wilson tell a Yorkshire audience last Tuesday that 'the Commonwealth is an important issue in this campaign', but there was no flicker of response from his Labour listeners for what was patently little more than a pious platitude. Even the Prime Minister was obviously far more excited by the new cliché about his discussions with 'tough' Common Market heads of government, than with the old cliché about Britain's leadership of a world-wide multi-racial grouping.

But this is only one aspect of a fundamental change affecting both sides of the argument – and one which is as glaring from a glance at my 1962 article as from Mrs Castle's. My tell-tale phrases – 'a leader of world opinion', and 'a stabilizing democratic influence in the Western world' imply a degree of power and still more of self-confidence in Britain that scarcely figure at all in the present campaign. Mr Edward Heath, whom I followed in Lancashire earlier this week, talks in terms of 'extending Britain's influence in the world' and even of the 'controlling interest' (a most revealing phrase) which membership of the Community would confer on us.

This, of course, is the essence of the Churchillian conception of European integration (vintage 1948) and the Macmillan conception (vintage 1961). Britain faced the loss of an empire, and could not rely indefinitely on her special relationship with America as a substitute; very well, she would assume the leadership of another grouping. But, here again, this has become a highly eccentric proposition. The normal assumption on the pro-Market side is that Britain can play some part (no more) in the construction of a new Europe, and on the anti-Market side that in staying in we shall be entirely swamped.

The most striking – indeed terrifying – aspect of the whole referendum campaign is apparent here. The heart of the argument is no longer the question of whether Britain can 'best realize her full potential' in the EEC or as head of a multi-racial Commonwealth. It is not even a question of whether certain trading or political arrangements suit us better or worse. The fundamental argument now turns on whether we are more likely to survive at all within the Common Market or without.

The anti-Marketeers – and it is by far their most effective argument – say that we are in such a bad state that we must face a long period of convalescence in a kind of economic sanatorium. The cold shower of Common Market competition will kill us off. The pro-Marketeers reply that there is no such thing as a real sanatorium these days; and that any attempt to build one would be frustrated by the withdrawal of Arab finance and the retaliation of American and Continental demolition gangs. An alternative, and to some extent contradictory set of arguments is represented by the anti-Market belief that we shall never summon the resolution to put our own house in order unless we are obliged to do it on our own; and the pro-Market retort that we need the assistance which membership of the EEC will provide.

In either case it is common ground between the two sides that the EEC is either a lifeline or it is a competitive jungle in which we shall be lucky to survive. The idea that it is an organization which is going to be, to a large extent, what we consciously help to make it is not a notion that is being promoted.

This fact naturally introduces the other glaring difference between the discussion of 1962 and the argument today. There is, so far as I have been able to detect, terribly little positive enthusiasm in this country at present either for staying in Europe or for coming out. The arguments are negative ones. The price of food will go up (no it won't); unemployment will rise (rubbish); the Commission will usurp the role of Parliament (ridiculous!). Idealism of any kind does not enter into the equation and there is neither zest nor vision in most of what is being said on platforms up and down the country.

Why this should be so is really the central puzzle of the campaign. It is not as if emotional arguments were lacking even on the anti-Market side. Admittedly the Commonwealth and EFTA do not look frightfully inspiring alternatives to the EEC. But something could surely be done on Land of Hope and Glory lines to paint a picture of a country whose distinctive features were so valuable and unique that almost any sacrifice was worthwhile to preserve them. This is a note which many Conservatives used to strike thirteen years ago but hardly any are striking today.

More distressing still is the failure of the pro-Marketeers to preach a positive creed. One can understand the reasons, of course. Practical politicians naturally tend to take their tune from what they conceive to be the public mood, and the present British mood is one of fear. Tactically speaking, therefore, there is a good deal to be said for cashing in on this phenomenon and demanding support for the status quo – which is now British membership, whereas before it was British non-membership. The kind of thing I was writing in 1962 about European federalism and the prospect of direct elections to a European parliament are entirely out of tune with the majority of British opinion at present (though not with mine), and one can hardly blame pro-Market speakers for not venturing on to this treacherous ground.

It also has to be admitted that a lot of the idealism has drained out of the Community on the Continent. The French veto and the prolonged haggle over the British question, to say nothing of bureaucratic arthritis, and perhaps even the enlargement of the Market, have had the effect, for the present, of reducing the whole enterprise to something not much more than the minimalist conception allowed by General de Gaulle himself. Public opinion in France and Germany apparently tends to regard the EEC as a humdrum fact of life – moderately useful, moderately boring.

And yet it is a far cry from this pragmatic acceptance, unenterprising though it is, to the present tendency of most British politicians to sell the Common Market almost exclusively on the general basis that 'out of the Community our future would be grim'. Personally I believe that this is true. But it is not the whole story and there are serious dangers from concentrating upon it to the exclusion of any long-term idea of the Community's potentialities. For one thing, fear is an uncertain and double-edged weapon. For another, there are classes of people, particularly the young, for whom some kind of vision is by far the most convincing framework of argument. I saw Mr Heath having a fairly rough ride at Lancaster University the other day on the question of whether he would or would not accept the verdict of a referendum. But a notoriously left-wing audience of students listened to him in silence and with respect while he expounded his views on the EEC, precisely because, I suspect, he is one of the few politicians who is still talking with the idealism of the 1950s and early 1960s.

The other point is that we have to live in the Community even after the referendum is over, and while to my mind it is better that Britain should stay in in a mood of sullen fear than that she should not stay in at all, the outlook for the Community, as well as for Britain's role in it, will be pretty miserable for a long time to come. I am prepared to believe (which is one reason I favour staying in) that our self-confidence is more likely to be restored and our political life lifted out of its present gloom if we are inside rather than out. But the Community's ability to help us to help ourselves will be powerfully influenced by our frame of mind at the moment when the die is cast.

Some of the reasons I offered in 1962 for joining the Market are no doubt a bit hollow at present ('a stabilizing democratic influence in the Western alliance'). But they are still the main reasons why I shall vote 'Yes' next Thursday. And to these I would even add, unashamed, the grandiloquent sentiment of my younger self: 'To share, to co-operate, to pull down barriers and build a new structure from the shreds of a thousand years of war – that is a tremendous and inspiring aim worthy of any idealist.'

*Financial Times*, *30 May 1975*

# The Realities of Yalta

The fortieth anniversary this week of the Yalta conference which settled the post-war fate of Europe was bound, I suppose, to be a field day for ideologists. In the United States, and to an only slightly lesser extent in Britain, the steamroller of right-wing fashion is busily effacing as many as possible of the political and intellectual landmarks erected in the unprincipled collectivist years of 'consensus' and 'betrayal' and laying down a smooth surface on which gleaming vehicles such as untrammelled enterprise and uncompromising anti-communism can be parked with pride.

In this vast revisionist activity the post-war settlement is central, and Yalta is the key element. Suitably interpreted, it provides a simple explanation, replete with scapegoats, of the deplorable but inescapable fact that the Russians took over Eastern Europe; it alleviates the frustration which arises because even the New Right still cannot see quite how to get them out; it stokes up the fires of righteous indignation; and it provides an 'awful warning' for negotiations with the Russians in future.

The 'suitable interpretation' in question comes in two main parts. First, it is said that Roosevelt and Churchill behaved with almost criminal weakness and gullibility towards Stalin who, in the words of Zbigniew Brezinski, had been conducting 'a carefully calibrated diplomacy designed to obtain Anglo-American acquiescence to a preponderant Soviet role in all of Europe'.

The second, and more important, claim is that if the two Western allies had in fact been prepared to get tough with Stalin over Poland (the critical issue to which seventeen hours of dispute were devoted at Yalta) he would have backed away and allowed the East European countries to develop democratically.

There is no space here to discuss these propositions in detail. Some things, however, stick out a mile. One is that whatever may be thought, or proved, about Roosevelt's fatuous belief in his own ability to 'handle' Stalin in 1944 and 1945, Churchill had very few, if any, illusions about what sort of a man, or power, he was dealing with. The whole record shows that most of Churchill's actions in this context were based, as so many Western actions have rightly and necessarily been based since, on a conscious and tortured effort to make the best of what he knew was a bad job, and rescue what he could from the jaws of circumstance.

Another important point is that even if Roosevelt had not been so deluded, that would not have made much difference to the outcome, which was determined mainly by the underlying facts of the situation. These were (a) that thanks to the difficult (and, militarily speaking, probably correct) decision not to invade France in 1943, the Red Army reached Eastern Europe before the American and British forces; (b) that the Americans were convinced they would need Russian help to beat Japan; and (c) that neither British nor American public opinion would have understood or countenanced a military 'show-down' with Stalin in 1945.

These facts do not excuse some errors of self-deception and gratuitous appeasement made by the American and British leaders – particularly the handing over to the Russians of prisoners whose fate they knew was thereby sealed. But it is fruitless as well as unhistorical to go backwards and demand that Roosevelt and Churchill should have adopted (with Germany and Japan still undefeated) a set of broad strategic priorities, with the containment of Soviet Russia at the top, which would have made sense to them only if they had been able to foresee the history of the next thirty years in full, and which, even then, they might not have been able to pursue in the face of domestic political and military opposition.

They did, by and large, what was possible, and no survivor of these days need feel any sense of guilty responsibility for the general outcome, even though he may reproach himself in detail. As for politicians of succeeding generations, it is their business to work with the material, however unpleasant, that is at hand and not to agonize about why things are as they are.

That, today, is the important point. It is remarkable how often, in modern political controversy, appeals to historical experience or analogy are intended to use past injustices to arouse and exploit present feelings of guilt. The Zionists have made it their stock-in-trade for years; the Third World does it constantly (to a chorus of derision from the New Right). In the 1960s it was a favourite thesis of left-wing revisionist historians that the Cold War had been an invention of President Truman. We were implausibly invited to believe that the Russians took over Eastern Europe because the West brushed aside the hand of friendship Stalin had offered us and embarked on an anti-Soviet crusade – the implication usually being that we should atone for this behaviour by letting Khrushchev or Brezhnev get away with something.

Now that the revisionists on the other side are up to similar tricks, though with the opposite purpose, we should be equally on our guard against submitting to moral blackmail. A sense of guilt, even if it is valid (which in this case it is not), is a rotten guide in power politics and generally leads to someone innocent getting it in the neck. By all means let us draw from Yalta the obvious conclusion that the Russians are often duplicitous and invariably dangerous; but let us not be bounced by bad history into trying to ignore the bitter realities about the division of Europe.

These are, first, that the only possible condition for reuniting Europe is one that we are no more prepared than the Russians to accept (namely a more or less reunited Germany that belongs to neither bloc); and secondly that there is virtually nothing that anyone outside the communist bloc can safely do to ameliorate conditions within it except to encourage a climate of *détente* which inevitably appears to legitimize the present situation. It is, as George Kennan says in his memoirs, 'a bad show', but we will not make it better by conjuring Crimean ghosts.

*The Times*, 8 February 1985

# The Democrat's Dilemma

**F**oreign politics demand scarcely any of those qualities which a democracy possesses; and they require on the contrary a perfect use of almost all those faculties in which it is deficient ... A democracy is unable to regulate the details of an important undertaking, to persevere in a design, and to work out its execution in the presence of serious obstacles. It cannot combine its measures with secrecy, and it will not await their consequences with patience. These are qualities which more especially belong to an individual or to an aristocracy; and they are precisely the means by which an individual people attains to a dominant position.

Alexis de Tocqueville, who wrote those words 140 years ago, was applying his analysis to the America of President Jackson, but he would no doubt have felt it equally applicable to the America of President Gerald Ford or the Britain of Prime Minister Harold Wilson.

Dr Henry Kissinger was in London last week and apparently spent much of his time bewailing the recent interference of the US Congress with his grand designs. His hosts in the British government are said to have expressed sympathy and alarm at the effects of this unpardonable assertion of democratic rights, blithely unaware of any irony in the fact that they were at the same moment carrying popular participation in foreign policy-making to its ultimate limit in the form of a referendum on the EEC. This strange juxtaposition prompts one to ask a new version of the old question. Can democracies conduct a satisfactory foreign policy under modern conditions – granted (a) that the world has become an unprecedentedly complex place and (b) that 'democracy' is now interpreted in an increasingly participatory sense?

Naturally this is not a question which politicians ask out loud. They might find themselves obliged, in honesty, to answer 'no' – and that would never do. It was almost ludicrous to read the Commons debate on the referendum without finding a single opponent of the principle coming out bluntly with the sentiments that most such opponents really hold – to wit, that the voters are too ill-informed to be trusted with the issue, and either too stupid or too lazy to remedy the defect. Similarly Dr Kissinger was not really prepared to echo de Tocqueville, although he must surely believe that, so far as foreign policy is concerned, the arrangements envisaged under the American Constitution are almost bound to negate the interests of the country. Everyone is obliged to pay lip-service to the competence of the People and their representatives even when his instincts and arguments are against it.

What, then, are the realities? Let us take each case in turn. Dr Kissinger's predicament arises from the sudden revolt of the new Congress, which is refusing to grant the President's request for funds for the supply of ammunition to the Cambodian government, and also insisting that aid to Turkey shall be withdrawn in retribution for the Turkish actions in Cyprus. More generally, there are signs that Dr Kissinger's policies, *vis-à-vis* the Russian *détente*, the Middle East and, to some extent, energy are under challenge from Capitol Hill. Anyone who has studied his style and his arguments over the years will have a fair idea of what Dr Kissinger's attitude to this trend must be.

As Mr Anthony Hartley points out in an excellent Adelphi Paper[1] published recently, the essence of Dr Kissinger's diplomatic philosophy is an extreme flexibility both in strategy and tactics and a complete absence of the moralistic approach usually adopted by American statesmen. In the service of this diplomatic style President Nixon and Dr Kissinger also introduced two functional innovations – centralization and secrecy. The normal post-war form of American foreign policy had had a broad, cumbersome ideological outline within whose framework individual policy decisions were reached after endless bureaucratic in-fighting and much tedious negotiation with potentates and interest groups in the Congress, all parties in the discussion leaking constantly to the Press. The Nixon-Kissinger foreign policy has been very different – an extremely

[1] 'American Foreign Policy in the Nixon Era', International Institute for Strategic Studies.

limited statement of external commitment (the Nixon doctrine) within which a tightly knit group of men operated according to its own conception of American interest at any given moment and as opportunities presented themselves – all this without more than the absolute minimum of reference to the State Department, the Congress, or the Press.

That all this was quite deliberate can be easily deduced from Dr Kissinger's writings before President Nixon brought him to the White House. His critique of American foreign policy between 1945 and 1968 (to say nothing of his excursions into nineteenth-century history) shows a clear dissatisfaction with the traditional open style of American diplomacy and its notable rigidities. Today, moreover, one suspects that Dr Kissinger would maintain he had been abundantly justified, not only by detailed results in the field of *détente*, in China and in the Middle East, but by the evolution of world politics themselves. With the emergence of a multi-polar world in which the US no longer had the vast preponderance of strength she possessed in the twenty post-war years, American influence and security could only be maintained by a far more alert, manipulative and, if you like, cynical diplomacy. Since the Congress, the State Department, and the American public were quite incapable of endorsing, far less playing, this kind of subtle power-politics game, there was literally no choice but to cut them out.

The case is an intensely interesting one and not, if one is honest, entirely simple to meet. The easy answer is to say that the Congress is suffering as much from hurt pride as anything else, and that much of Dr Kissinger's trouble could have been avoided if he and President Nixon had taken the precaution to butter up the Congress in the traditional fashion. According to this analysis the revolt in Cambodia may have taken place as a result of analogies with the Vietnam War which are ineradicable (and perhaps rightly so); but the Congress would have been perfectly open to persuasion on Turkey if the administration had gone about it properly and even on the wider issues a serious educative effort would have borne fruit.

And yet the fact remains that members of Congress are limited in their ability to respond to the blandishments of the White House by the mood of public opinion and if public opinion in the US is weary, disillusioned and sceptical of America's global role, the Congress will reflect it. An apologist for Dr Kissinger would presumably put it like this: 'Very well, I can see that we could have handled Congress better and it's possible (at any rate up until Watergate) that President Nixon might have appealed over the heads of Congress to the American people, but what could he have said that would have had the desired effect? A democratic country of the size and diversity of America can only be mobilized on the basis of some great moral certainty – a crusade against the forces of evil. The world is not like that any more and it would be both dangerous and dishonest to say that it was. Teaching 200 million people about the balance of power is like teaching an elephant to walk on a tightrope.'

A similar objection, of course, arises when one turns from the American situation to the British. It simply is not possible, with the best democratic will in the world, to suppose that more than a small proportion of those who will vote in the EEC referendum have more than a very hazy picture of what the Common Market is or what membership of it entails in all its complexity. Ah, comes the reply, but that does not mean that the voters are incapable of taking a common-sense view on the matter and taking a rational decision. The trouble about this kind of retort is that it fails to recognize how much conscious will is required to disentangle facts from threads of memory and emotion, and how seldom people are used to making the effort.

The outcome of the referendum is going to turn very much on the emotive power of words like 'sovereignty', 'the British way of life', 'outward-looking', 'influence' and the like. To say, as many people do, that the British people are entitled to their emotions is all very well, so far as it goes, but it is no more than saying that the British people have the right to make their own mistakes. That may be true too, but it concedes the basic proposition of de Tocqueville about the difficulty of combining democracy and a rational foreign policy.

This is a dilemma from which there is no escape except by compromise. Some kind of trained and effortful rationality has got to be interposed to mediate between public emotion and state policy. That means the public accepting some degree of diminution of its sovereign power in the interest, hopefully, of better government. (It also entails, incidentally, politicians accepting responsibility and not pushing the decision back to the people when they find it difficult.)

At the other end of the scale it entails Dr Kissinger and his fellow-élitists accepting some degree of boredom, inefficiency and messy emotion in the conduct of foreign policy as a result of trying, and inevitably failing in fact, to persuade the representatives of popular opinion. Emotion, which finds no response from reason, generally has its revenge in the end; and it is even possible that a US at peace with itself and its own conscience, will be not much less effective than one which its rulers are trying to lead about the world blindfold.

*Financial Times, 14 March 1975*

# The Arts of Politics

Abusing politicians has been a favourite pastime ever since that moment, in the dawn of civilization, when some caveman or other successfully employed qualities of mind and speech to grasp power from another endowed with mere physical strength. But out of the many thousands of insults hurled at the victors I would like to start by selecting one from Sainte-Beuve: partly because it is an appropriate reminder of the very distinguished scholar of French literature – and of Sainte-Beuve himself – after whom this lecture is named, and partly because it is so contemporary in tone.

'*Charlatanisme,*' said Sainte-Beuve, '*il en faut, je crois, dans la politique, dans l'arte de gouvener les hommes ... mais dans l'orde de la pensée, dans l'arte, c'est la gloire et l'éternel honneur que le charlatanisme ne pénètre pas.*'

There, it seems to me, is the voice of the intellectual not just in Louis Napoleon's France but in Harold Wilson's Britain. The politician is a plausible quack, peddling gilded pills on the street corner, chiefly for his own advantage. Perhaps he and his deceptions are a necessary part of the scene: but two things about that scene are supposed to be incontrovertible. First, it is sordid; and second it is sheer self-deception to suppose that another sort of 'honest' politics is possible.

The politicians you think were honest, like John F. Kennedy, turn out to have made dirty deals and ordered secret assassinations just like the rest; or else when they really try to be honest, like Hugh Gaitskell or (to stretch the point a bit) like Edward Heath, it turns out they cannot command enough support to be effective.

This prevailing cynicism is usually imputed by those cynics who

74

bother to analyse their own feelings to our having lived through a period of British politics in which there has been a great deal of political promising and conspicuously little political fulfilment, especially on the central issue of economic affairs. Half the critics want to reduce the promising and the other half to improve the performance. The first group argues that democratic politics is meeting the fate predicted for it by de Tocqueville and other nineteenth-century conservatives. A force has been created by universal suffrage which no politician can withstand and it has been exerted in favour of demands which no politician can meet out of existing resources. So what does the politician do? He promises delivery and then resorts to the bank or the monetary printing press to bail him out.

The other school of thought believes that there is nothing unreasonable in the popular demand for steadily rising living standards, and that this demand could be met without resort to draconian financial orthodoxy if it weren't for the party politics which leads politicians to dissipate their energies and the country's resources on absurd and irrelevant dogma.

I may as well declare at once that I don't subscribe to either of these visions of our present troubles and in the rest of this lecture I will try and explain why I prefer to see the problem in terms of political skill – the conditions which cause it to grow in politicians and the conditions which allow them to exercise it.

There are two possible approaches to the question – one functional, the other psychological. We can define the roles of a modern democratic politician and ask what skills might be needed to make them better filled. Alternatively we can attempt to discover the essence of the attitudes of the successful politician – whether college politics, or office politics, or international politics, or sexual politics – and then see whether our real politicians are possessed of it.

First, then, the democratic politician is a representative in the narrow sense of a man or woman sent to Parliament to protect as far as possible the interests of constituents. This seems to me a function that British MPs now fulfil pretty well – in some ways better than their predecessors. They are, of course, at the mercy of economic forces and, unlike their American counterparts, they are in no position to bargain from strength in the allocation of federal funds to prevent hardship from the incidence of general unemployment or even, unless the case becomes notorious, from the closure of particular firms. On the other hand where the individual concerns of his constituents are at stake he still has considerable pull and uses it.

It is arguable that his ability to get grievances redressed in individual cases is imperilled by the sheer weight of the work and the ponderousness of the bureaucracy; but my impression is that a remarkable amount of social casework is effectively performed by MPs in the interstices of the Welfare State; and the opinion polls show that the public is both aware of this and grateful for it. The price that has to be paid, of course, is in sheer time. MPs spend an enormous amount of energy holding surgeries, meeting groups of constituents or showing them round the Palace of Westminster, writing to ministers and answering constituency correspondence; and the first question arises – is it time well-spent? To the extent that it is partly public relations, is it necessary? And to the extent that it is social work, should not others, better trained, be doing it?

Let's leave this for a moment and turn to the second aspect of a politician's representative function – his ability to act as a channel of communication between some interest groups and his government. A certain number of MPs are retained for a fee to look after parliamentary relations of, say, the Police Federation or the Bookmakers Association. Others find themselves involved in speaking up for consumer groups perhaps or motorists simply because of their own tastes. Others still, let us say an MP for a farming division, are obliged to attach themselves to some large interest in which their constituents are involved. But in all these cases the principle is the same. It is part of the politician's job to see that the views of interest groups are made known to the government, to other MPs and to some extent to the public; and it is equally his job to see that the views of the government (and if necessary the public) are transmitted back to his friends with the limits of the 'politically possible' marked clearly upon them. This mediating role can be filled to some extent by ordinary jack-of-all-trades MPs but the operation only takes on three-dimensional life if the main interest groups of the society are directly and forcefully reflected in the composition of Parliament.

In the past this has frequently been the case. In the mid-nineteenth century for instance there were actually present at Westminster, either in Lords or Commons, important members of the landed interest, the manufacturing interest, the railway interest, the West India interest, the East India interest, the Church and so forth; and it was therefore possible to hammer out a genuine consensus (with the government holding the ring) by the classic process of representative bargaining. Today this is simply not feasible. The decline in power of the Lords has something to do with it but there is also the fact that the Commons itself is in this sense less 'representative' in important respects than it once was. The bulk of MPs – and therefore Cabinet Ministers – are drawn from a decidedly narrow circle of professions and trades. There are certainly more working-class members than sixty years ago – though fewer than thirty years ago – and fewer landowners and soldiers. But women are grossly under-represented; so are the under-thirties voters. There is a disproportionate quantity of teachers, lawyers and PR men, and an under-representation of industrial managers, engineers, craftsmen, shopkeepers and sales representatives. The unions are at present well (some would say too well) represented by the Labour Party itself, but it has not always been so and may not be again. Meanwhile they must be content to have their case put mainly by elderly second-raters whose pocket boroughs are the reward for long service and uncomplaining loyalty.

This parliamentary penchant for professions which are in some sense parasitic rather than those which might be called first-order activities is understandable in a way because politics is itself not a first-order activity and itself attracts manipulators. But it has the unfortunate effect of making it seem even more pointless for the interests to conduct their relations with government through the democratic forum of Parliament. To them Parliament has become something of a side-show. It is much more promising to make a direct approach to the bureaucracy in Whitehall.

Let us now turn very briefly to the politician in his third role – as legislator and overseer of government activity – the most time-consuming function of the back-bench Parliamentarian. By common consent this is a task that it is increasingly difficult for any British politician to tackle satisfactorily under present arrangements. Far too many Bills come before Parliament for any but a few to be discussed properly, and the range of government activities is now so wide that without vastly more professional assistance than it now possesses, Parliament's oversight can only be patchy and superficial. On the other hand it is also generally agreed that if any reforming Cabinet really wanted to do so, there is no reason why it should not remedy some of these defects. A shorter legislative programme and a system of specialist committees designed both to take some of the legislative burden from the House of Commons as a whole and also superintend the operation of the laws after they are enacted, would achieve wonders, particularly if it were combined with a reformation of MPs' pay, working conditions and research facilities.

Why this obvious course has never been taken is a long story, but so long as a strong British Executive continues to insist that the legislature shall be subservient rather than independently effective, it is hard to see how any group of legislators, however distinguished, could transcend the difficulties.

So far we have considered the British politician as representative, as mediator and as legislator. But what about his most visible role as policy-maker and administrator? It is on this that the reputation of politicians as a class really depends. There has never been a period in British history when the House of Commons has not been liberally sprinkled with incompetents, lunatics and crooks – and that is as true today as it has ever been. But the great British public, in its wisdom and mercy, puts up with this on the 'it-takes-all-sorts' principle *provided* that the system throws up people at the top who are capable of making credible political leaders and of running the country with tolerable efficiency. The main trouble at the moment is therefore the manifest fact that for the last ten years political leaders have not been delivering the goods – defined as prosperity and stability – and it is natural to ask whether it is the system that is at fault.

Certain it is that the *cursus honorum* of British public life does not strike one as ideally designed for the production of platonic 'Guardians'. The political heads of the great departments of state all reach and retain high offices by an astonishingly haphazard process. Leaving aside the procedures whereby MPs are selected in the first place, their feet are usually planted on the first rung of the ladder not by overpowering ability but by tame obedience to the Whips or by the chance that their regional and political 'profile' happens to fit the Prime Ministerial needs of the moment. In any case it may be anything up to ten years before a new MP's chance comes – and if his party happens to be out of favour with the electorate as Labour was, for instance, between 1951 and 1964, then the wait may be twice as long.

But even when the politician is on his way, his education as an administrator is very patchy. As an under-secretary he will inevitably do a lot of the departmental chores – answering letters, opening buildings, meeting unimportant delegations – but unless his political superior consciously sets out to 'train' him (and most do not) these menial tasks will never involve him in the central policy-making of the department. He will usually earn his promotion by being agreeable, by speaking competently on minor motions in the House of Commons, or by cultivating an independent political base in his party through articles and speeches. If anyone wants to understand the bewilderment and unimportance of a new senior minister let him read the first volume of

Richard Crossman's diary with care. Crossman was admittedly a slightly special case in that he was a senior politician who had never for a variety of reasons held office at all until he was nearly sixty, but in essentials his situation was the same as most incoming ministers. He didn't know his subject. He didn't know his way round Whitehall. He was for a considerable time at the mercy of his senior civil servants who promptly cut him off from the outside world. And he was moved to another post in the government not long after his learning period was complete.

There is no time here to go into the labyrinthine argument about the organization of central government but it is worth noting once again the essentials of the problem. The fact that the Executive is drawn from the legislature in Britain means that the aspiring politician faces a long waiting period on the back benches and in junior office where little expertise is gained that is relevant to the administrative tasks of government and where, on the contrary, ennui and frustration take a heavy toll. When he finally reaches the sunny uplands of Cabinet work, he is awed both by his eminence and by his ignorance, and either fails to grasp the subject or becomes so engrossed in it that he cannot see the wood for the trees.

This rather melancholy survey is not by any means complete, but even in its truncated form it does suggest at least one basic difficulty about improving British politicians. Our rather peculiar constitutional arrangements mean that we expect our politicians to play too many parts – simultaneously and consecutively. The young back-bencher is supposed to be at one and the same time in his constituency doing welfare work and at Westminster mastering the details of legislation. He is supposed to be a dedicated member of some non-political trade bringing its expertise and interest to the common debate; but he is also supposed to be a professional politician engaged in the full-time occupation of protecting the public against the depradations of the State. He is supposed to be lobby fodder, welfare worker, mediator, and legislator for years and years – but then, suddenly, this conglomerate caterpillar is supposed to turn effortlessly into a ministerial butterfly with smoothly functioning wings and sensitive political antennae. It can't be done unless we do one of three things.

We could, in theory, change the Constitution radically and institute a separation of powers. We shan't. We could abandon one, or indeed all, of the functions I have described – let M Ps be chosen from a party list and cease to represent constituencies, let government deal directly with the interests without the assistance of Parliament – come to that, let the Civil Service rule the country. Some people advocate the first surrender and others would say that the other two have already been made. But personally I prefer a third quite different solution. I should like to make the existing system, or at any rate something very like it, work – by making far better use of the resources which lie buried in it.

What *kind* of resources is best explained by abandoning functional analysis at this point and adopting the alternative psychological approach to the politician's role. What, in the end, is the whole political exercise about in a democracy? It is, surely, *the acquisition of legitimate power based on support and its exercise in a way that involves the maximum of consent and the minimum of compulsion.* Now, the skill of a politician – and it is, as I said earlier, one which is equally applicable in the complicated relationships of the workplace and the happy home – is to spot where potential support lies, to grab it and hang tight on to it.

This is not, in some ways, a skill that reflects the best in human nature. It requires in the politician not only a love of power itself – suggesting more than a touch of vanity and self-importance to say nothing of other baser instincts – but it also implies a certain feminine power of sympathetic flexibility, an ability to sense a change of mood in one's interlocutors and to adjust rapidly and ruthlessly to it before support melts away.

It is this quality, of course, which is the origin of Sainte-Beuve's charge of charlatanism and the cause of so much fashionable criticism of the dishonesty of politicians today. Nor can it be denied that the critics can find plenty of ammunition in the pages of recent history to support the attack on political quackery and naked self-interest. What is wrong is to proceed to the general indictment of the race of politicians on this charge. A politician can honourably prevaricate and shift his ground; and indeed if an open political system is working properly it is difficult to see how these tactics can be dispensed with. There are three basic operations involved. The first is the discovery of people's needs; the second is the business of persuading them that yours is the appropriate way of meeting those needs; the third is the simultaneous process of persuasion and discovery by which you as a politician and they as citizens react to the assessment of what you are in the process of doing or have already done.

None of this can be accomplished without a continuous flow of communication between politician and public and between public and politician. It was Burke's dictum that 'it is the business of the speculative philosopher to mark the proper ends of government. It is the business of the politician, who is the philosopher in action to find out the proper means to those ends and to employ them with effect.' In these democratic times, the theory has been modified. It is now the electors and not the philosophers who mark the proper ends and while it is still the politician's business to find out the means, he will not 'employ them to effect' or even survive unless he is listening and constantly persuading and manoeuvring in order to persuade.

If we reverted to aristocratic rule or to tyranny this might not be necessary. But assuming that we want democracy to survive, the proper criticism of modern politicians is not that they 'politick' too much but that they do not do it enough, or at least not effectively enough. You may well expect this diagnosis to be a prelude to an impassioned plea for a greater degree of participation, devolution and the like in our lives; or (if you are particularly cynical and have taken note of my trade as a journalist) you may anticipate a pitch for open government and the repeal of the Official Secrets Act. If I were a television man, I would probably spend the rest of my time urging the televising of Parliament. As it happens, I am in favour of all these things, but the point I wish to make here is a rather more general one.

It is that politics in this country has become quarantined from the society. Our politicians are no less talented, sensible, honest or well educated than those of other countries or of other times. The trouble is that what they do is regarded by the rest of their fellow countrymen as a task apart. 'They' are doing something to 'us', rather than 'we' doing something to ourselves.

In the nineteenth century, politics was broadly coterminous with the culture. The values of the middle and upper class, whose business politics admittedly had its limitations, were accepted by society as a whole and it was able to conduct the nation's affairs on the basis of shared assumptions. The institutions of British politics – the club-like atmosphere of the House of Commons, constitutional conventions governing ministerial responsibility, the organization and recruitment of the higher Civil Service – are all based upon the proposition that our affairs are still run in this way. But, alas, this is not so. Society no longer accepts the assumptions of the middle classes and it follows that the institutions have got to be opened up so that political communication on a wider scale can be set in motion. Television, as I have said, may have a part to play, and politicians are only just beginning to learn how to use it effectively. But the most important thing for the future is that the politicians and the public should be able to touch each other and influence each other and learn from each other and work with each other at a far greater number of points.

This means, ideally, breaking down the distinction between what is a 'political' question and what is not (an attempt which is regarded as highly dangerous when indulged in by trade unions, but which cannot, in this kind of society, be avoided in the long run). It also involves breaking down the barriers around what is supposed to be the 'political life'. Not everyone has, or wishes to acquire the highest political skill. But it ought to be easier than it is for people to flit in and out of politics, widely defined, as they do in America, not merely at local level but also at national level. Since there are only 635 members of Parliament it might seem that the scope here was limited. But it is not as limited as it looks. A system which paid MPs enough money to employ a couple of research assistants, which vastly extended the staff of parliamentary committees and which instituted ministerial *cabinets* on the Continental level would immediately extend the range of the political process by an amount out of all proportion to the numbers involved. Intelligent young people would have a chance, for a change, to see politics at first hand as a channel for practical idealism. Academics could take more frequent excursions into the world they aspire to analyse. The ears and eyes of politicians would be multiplied and their ability to combine their present impossible variety of roles enhanced. The answer to many of the problems posed in the first half of this lecture as well as those posed in the second is to be found here.

But what, you may ask, is going to split the old shell open? Television and the Press can do only so much, and the politicians themselves are bemused by the horizons of work and custom which have closed in on them. The real impetus has got to come from the voters themselves – from comfortable people who complain that politicians are an inferior lot, but never sully their own hands with politics; that democracy is doomed, but do nothing about revivifying it; that the party system is corrupt, but are not prepared to take part in the foundation of a new one; that their sectional interest is unfairly treated, but only use back-stairs methods to try and remedy matters. It is an old truism that we get the politicians we deserve, and the reason is that politics, like the tango, takes two partners. Or to put it another way, it is only when we recognize that politics is too important to leave to the politicians, that we will acquire politicians to whom, at a pinch, we could safely leave it.

*Sainte-Beuve Lecture given in 1976*

# II

# Anglo-
# Americana

# The Beneficent Myth

The first thing that must strike anyone who thinks objectively about the Anglo-American relationship is the contrast between its coolness for most of its duration and its warmth in modern times. Only for a mere forty-five years in total, corresponding to much less than a quarter of the life of the American Republic, has it amounted to what might be called an 'alliance'.

It is not altogether easy to rescue this fact from beneath the mountain of rhetoric that now enshrines it. Every British Prime Minister from Churchill onwards has made it his business to suggest that 'our joint aims', 'our common heritage', and other emblems of 'the unity of the English-speaking peoples' has the patina of great antiquity. Equally, from the moment the United States entered the last World War, leading American politicians began to pay their own lip-service to the notion that there is a natural and immemorial affinity between the two countries; and though one hears less of this from the American side of the Atlantic than twenty years ago, it still reappears today from that quarter as an occasional basis of flattery or reproach.

This has been a powerful and often beneficent myth, and it was no doubt emotionally valid for Churchill himself, and later Macmillan, with their American family connections. But it does not bear critical inspection. At the popular level, a shared language and a joint adherence to the common law did not make our nineteenth-century forebears feel any very close affinity. The average Englishman, right up to World War Two, regarded the Americans as surpassingly strange and largely irrelevant (though the cinema and popular music had perhaps begun to soften this view among the young in the 1930s). The general American image of the British for 150 years was of a nation of more or less menacing snobs, and almost every successive wave of immigration into the United States from the Irish famine onwards added to the sum of Americans who either had a positive animus against Britain or at least had no particular cultural bias in her favour.

At the level of state relations, it is true that for most of the nineteenth century, and certainly after the settlement of the *Alabama* claims in 1872, there was no great reason for hostility between Britain and the United States. But neither was there any pressing need for them to come to grips with each other at all. It suited the British (with only occasional qualms) to leave the Caribbean and most of the Pacific to a relatively harmless power, thus freeing themselves to concentrate on the higher priorities of their imperial lifelines and the balance of power in Europe. It was equally convenient to the United States to leave the British Navy in protective control of the Atlantic. There was a certain objective congruence of interest here which survived the German attempt in 1897 to disrupt it; but there was no explicit understanding.

America's late entry into the First World War created a genuine alliance for the first time, but it was an odd kind of partnership, intense while it lasted but also curiously remote. The Americans were determined to maintain their freedom of manoeuvre at all costs. President Wilson, in order to avoid accusations of foreign entanglement, invariably insisted that the United States was not an ally of the Allies but an 'associate' and kept American representation in the Supreme War Council to a discreet minimum. The Allies themselves, at the political as well as the military level, were inclined to patronize the American contribution and, considering that until the summer of 1918 there were no more than the equivalent to nine American divisions on the Western front out of more than 170, they had some justification. The turning-point came when, in the desperate situation of June 1918, the Allied Prime Ministers were obliged to make their famous appeal to Wilson: 'There is great danger of the war being lost unless the numerical inferiority of the Allies can be remedied as rapidly as possible by the advent of American troops.'

Whatever may be argued about the subsequent contribution to victory of the additional 300,000 American soldiers shipped over in answer to this call, Wilson was afterwards in a position of moral equivalence and even superiority to the Europeans. This greatly increased his influence at the peace conference. It also made an indelible impression on British foreign policy, which has never entirely ceased from that moment to see the American connection as being, on balance, a potential aid to the furtherance of British interests rather than as being neutral or a positive hindrance.

Even so, the joint experience of World War One still did not succeed in bringing about a deepening of the Anglo-American relationship in the inter-war years. This failure was largely due to the American withdrawal into isolation which frustrated a number of tentative British attempts to draw the United States into multilateral political and economic enterprises. But it also owed something to the British reversion to pre-war imperial preoccupations, which were now tinged with a new element of rivalry and fear of American power on the economic and strategic (particularly naval) planes. Anglo-American relations at the outbreak of World War Two were about as distant as it is possible to imagine between 'friendly' powers and, of course, infinitely less warm than British relations with the French.

It is worth labouring this contrast between the situation prior to the fall of France and the situation after it (the important change in American, as well as British, attitudes dates from that event rather than from Pearl Harbor), for it makes the essential point to which the essays in this book bear witness – namely that the underlying basis of the Anglo-American relationship has always been interest and not, in the first place, emotion. Sentiment has indeed flourished in the soil that interest has watered, and has itself borne fruit, but it cannot be relied on to remain a vigorous and fertile plant for more than a limited period when interest on one side or the other is withdrawn.

In its broad outlines, the historical framework of the last forty-five years illustrates this proposition. The United States was confronted in 1940, as in 1916, with the prospect that its interests, which had become global, would be seriously threatened if the balance in Europe were destroyed and the continent dominated by a single power. The destruction of France not only made this a very possible outcome, and would almost certainly have forced America into the war eventually, irrespective of the Japanese attack. It also made the alliance with Britain obligatory; no other serious resistance to Germany was available. Once this enterprise had been brought to a successful conclusion the United States showed every sign of reverting to its old unilateralism, if not actual isolationism, and to the pursuit of its latent rivalry with Britain and the British Empire. Roosevelt played with the idea of American non-alignment between Britain on the one hand, colonialist and slave to immoral practices such as the balance of power, and on the other a paranoid, obstreperous, but ultimately manageable Soviet Union. This course was ruled out by another crisis in Europe. The continent was again threatened by a single power whose global pretensions were evidently turning out to be even more menacing than Germany's had been. Once more, with France, Germany, and Italy prostrate, an intimate alliance with Britain was the only possible expedient. As Professor Ullman remarks, 'without the spectre of Soviet expansionism seemingly ever present ... the Anglo-American relationship might have taken quite a different course'. But the intimacy and cordiality of the relationship was conditional on Britain's remaining the single most effective adjutant in the task of containing the Soviet Union and its allies. This condition applied for ten years after the war but was gradually dissolved as British power diminished and other allies, above all Germany, were revived.

At the point we have now reached, Britain is still an important ally of the United States. She remains, moreover, a *more* important ally than her size and economic strength would justify, for her situation has some unique features. Possession of nuclear weapons, membership of the Security Council, access to political and military intelligence, political stability, and willingness (at any rate hitherto) to devote an unusually high proportion of GNP to military purposes – all these are valuable to the United States. British membership of the European Community is an asset of even greater importance, but it is an ambiguous one. On the one hand, so long as Britain maintains her Atlantic outlook, it helps to keep the Europeans from neutralist and protectionist excesses. On the other hand there is a dual risk: first, that Britain will be seduced into European heresies herself and, second, that a Britain that appears to be too close to the United States will be regarded by her Community partners as a 'bad European' and will therefore lose her utility. This situation ensures that British views are taken into account in certain specific areas of policy. But they are no longer strong enough to ensure either (*a*) a purely British veto over any single American policy (except where, as in the case of bases in Britain, British sovereignty is directly involved) or (*b*) a purely British ability to influence the general direction of American foreign policy.

The question of where, along this path, the 'Special Relationship' can be said to have ended is to some extent a semantic one. My own definition, which would require the degree of British influence that I have just defined, implies that the 'special relationship' in the broad sense ceased to exist in the early 1960s and perhaps even earlier. On the other hand it is clear from a number of the essays which follow that in some specific areas of policy (particularly in certain military and intelligence matters) a close functional connection has lasted up to the present.

The question of how far sentiment has affected the logical train of events is one of the central themes of this book. In the first place, as David Reynolds explains, once confidence had been established it smoothed the working of the wartime alliance. It is debatable to what extent Roosevelt and Churchill ever really liked or even fully understood each other; certainly, neither was always entirely frank with the other. But it is obvious that they established an unusual degree of personal communication and a reasonable degree of mutual trust. At lower levels, military and official, habits of easy intercourse also took root and many permanent friendships were formed. This kind of sentiment survived the war, and continued in the first ten years of peace. The sense of overall common purpose and mutual need which the Truman and Eisenhower administrations shared with their British counterparts made it possible, until the end of the 1950s at any rate, for politicians and officials in Britain and the United States to converse with an openness and regularity that was exclusive and on a different level from the normal cordiality of allies. This resulted in an instinctive understanding of the political and emotional patterns and constraints of the other side and greatly increased speed and ease of operation in any joint enterprise. As for the mystique created by Churchill, it has and was deliberately intended to have the effect of providing a climate of public opinion in which it was easier for both governments, if they so wished, to override special interests and nationalist objections to mid-Atlantic compromise. This has become a more and more fragile instrument, particularly in the United States where special interests are institutionalized, but it has played some part even as recently as the Falklands crisis.

Common sense, as well as the testimony of innumerable participants, confirms the operational importance of these links. But how far did they ever cause the American government to decide to act in a way which the logic outlined earlier would not have dictated anyhow? There certainly were plenty of instances, even at the height of the 'special relationship', in which they failed to prevent American administrations following a very cold-blooded course. Professors Perkins, Gardner, Watt, Gowing, and Louis, as well as Sir Harold Beeley, elaborate some of the most notable examples of the first post-war phase: the abrupt ending of Lend-Lease, the insistence on sterling convertibility, the refusal to share nuclear technology, the exclusion of Britain from the ANZUS Pact, the failure to join the Baghdad Pact, and, most traumatically of all, the stop on the Suez operation. To what extent these unpleasantnesses were due to a simple, overriding consciousness of American national interest and how much to the strong residue of anti-colonial moralism analysed by Professors Beloff and Louis is arguable. What is certain is that in each case pro-British sentiment was relatively easily overcome even in the heyday of the 'special relationship'. Moreover, cases of the opposite kind are, almost by definition, unsubstantiated. One can speculate, for instance, that Harold Macmillan's emotional appeal to President Kennedy at Nassau in 1962 powerfully affected the decision to provide Britain with Polaris as a replacement for Skybolt. But the arguments from national interest (which included, on the negative side, the danger of being seen to let down a major ally) were finely balanced; and one cannot be absolutely sure that Kennedy would have replied any differently to a cooler approach from a Prime Minister who had not taken pains to cultivate a personal relationship with him. Similarly, in the case of the Falklands it is tempting to guess that the Latin American faction within the State Department might have defeated the Atlanticists if the European protagonist had been France instead of Britain; but this is not at all certain. There were plenty of good arguments for opposing General Galtieri and backing a major member of NATO and these arguments might well have prevailed even without the pro-British emotions of the Secretary of State and the Secretary of Defense.

It appears from these examples that these major incidents are not very helpful for isolating and assessing the importance of emotion. So many factors were at work that individual motives cannot be satisfactorily separated out. The same applies, for slightly different reasons, to the World War Two period, when the parity of power between the two partners made the element of feeling, in a sense, less important. The obvious fact that in many areas the United States simply could not act successfully without British acquiescence and co-operation meant that the emotional and ideological links seldom, if ever, had to bear the whole weight of the relationship. For these reasons it seems better to take the years after 1946 as the test, and to take them as a whole. On this basis it appears that what I have rather loosely called sentiment did have one substantial though not easily definable effect.

The simplest way to describe this is, perhaps, by noting the tolerance shown by successive American administrations towards British disagreement with them. Considering the state of economic and, later, strategic dependence to which Britain was rapidly reduced after the war, there has been remarkably little cracking of the American whip.

The Suez 'veto' was one exception; the heavy economic pressure on the Callaghan government at the end of 1977 was possibly another. But there has been a long list of British 'aberrations', beginning with Palestine and the recognition of communist China, continuing with Eden's Indo-China initiatives and Macmillan's insistence on summitry, and ending with Denis Healey's establishment of the Eurogroup and Wilson's refusal to send even a token British contingent to Vietnam. All these discommoded the United States at the time – to put it no higher – but though the Americans naturally argued their case or circumvented British opposition in some other way, they did not often demand that Britain desist on pain of American sanctions, explicit or otherwise. It is true that there existed, in each of these instances, other practical restraints against American retaliation. Nevertheless, it is possible to detect in the correspondence of all American presidents and British Prime Ministers from Truman and Attlee to Nixon and Wilson a certain consideration, even deference, on the American side which was not so often displayed – at any rate until the 1970s – towards other allies. Macmillan's famous classical analogy (Greece = Britain: Rome = United States) was far-fetched as well as self-serving. But it did catch something of the sense on both sides that America was undertaking a global role that Britain was passing on. Never mind that this renunciation was not entirely voluntary; never mind that a number of British politicians and commentators regretted – and, as Lord Beloff's essay makes clear, still regret – the transition and believed that the Americans were making a poor fist of it. The fact remained that Britain had been there before. At the beginning – for instance, when the British inability to hold Greece and Turkey led to the Truman Doctrine – there was some grumbling about 'pulling British chestnuts out of the fire' (to quote a Congressman at that time). The fear of being sucked into Britain's nefarious imperial machinations was persistent. Later (in Henry Kissinger's opinion too late), this was replaced by a desire to profit from British experience and even to help sustain lingering British influence in the Third World for as long as possible. Later still, it has turned into profound exasperation with all Europeans, including the British, for not sharing with the United States the assumptions and burdens of a global struggle with the Soviet Union (a divergence whose growth can be traced in most of the essays in the non-European section of this book as well as in Professor Ullman's discussion of East–West relations). Nevertheless, for some years the notion of a torch being handed on cast something of a sunset glow over the relationship, as seen from Washington, and enhanced

**91**

the arguments against undermining the British by too many hard choices or bullying tactics.

That, of course, like most of the points I have discussed so far, represents matters from the American side. The perspective offered by the British contributors to this volume alters the picture considerably, though not perhaps as drastically as might be supposed. One is initially inclined to accept, as a working hypothesis, the common idea that the British have been much more sentimental about the relationship than the Americans; or, in other words, that they believed their own Churchillian propaganda and were frequently misled by it. It is a proposition which has received a lot of backing from the Europeanists in British public life, to whom it has become virtually axiomatic that our failure to 'catch the European bus' in the mid-1950s was almost entirely due to a national obsession with the 'special relationship'. Closer investigation shows that things were much more complicated.

For one thing the thesis does not take account of the strong currents of anti-Americanism that have flowed continuously on the left and right wings of British politics ever since 1945, often subterranean but apt to spring to the surface at moments of crisis. Since these are not discussed specifically elsewhere they are worth a brief mention here. The basic elements of the British left's hostility have not varied much over the years: a dislike of capitalism, a desire to think well of 'socialist' states if at all possible, and, above all, a belief (with a long lineage going back beyond George Lansbury and Ramsay MacDonald to the nineteenth-century origins of the Labour movement) that, since conflict in international relations is due to injustice and misunderstanding rather than clashes of legitimate interest, it is the mission of socialists to take a moral stand and to avoid power politics and blocs. These views informed the 'Keep Left' group, led by Michael Foot and Richard Crossman, which attacked Bevin's 'excessive subservience' to the United States in the late 1940s; they provide the instinctual basis for the Labour Party's defence policy published in August 1984. Experience had forced the non-communist Left to modify their opinion of the Soviet Union somewhat from the unclouded admiration of the war years; but the psychological difficulty of this shift has been eased by the gradual substitution of the United States for Britain in the villain's role of chief 'imperial' power. This last transformation, which corresponds, of course, to developments in the real world that have already been discussed, assumes special significance in Britain because it enables a whole segment of liberal opinion, spreading much wider than the left proper, to transfer feelings of guilt about the British imperial past to American shoulders – which are then cudgelled with redoubled vigour. More generally, however, it has produced a comfortable state of mind in which the two superpowers are lumped together in the same moral category and a new infusion of vitality is imparted to the old attack on power blocs and alliances.

The new American Right, which has joyfully discovered these quite antique phenomena in the last couple of years, appears to regard them as symptomatic of a new and general degradation of British will. They are wrong on both counts. Anti-Americanism of the type I have just described may have broadened its appeal since the Vietnam War, and again since the election of Ronald Reagan, but it as old as the cold war and has been very consistently held in check among the wider public, as countless opinion polls have demonstrated, by the commonsense perception that the United States is infinitely less of a potential menace to Britain than the Soviet Union and that the British need the Americans to help protect them from the Russians. The fact that the main opposition party in Britain became committed after 1979 to a position which, in effect if not quite in principle, contradicted this popular view was chiefly a result of the hermetic convolutions of its internal politics at that time; a party which had stuck to the bi-partisan policies of the 1945–79 era might have had a better chance of winning power in 1983. On the other hand it would be wrong to suggest that this left-wing critique of the American connection has been wholly without influence on policy – especially when Labour has been in office, but even, indirectly, when it has not. Attlee and Bevin were able to face it down by weight of prestige and personality, but it caused immense difficulties and divisions at the time of the Korean War. It suffused the nuclear disarmament movement in the late 1950s which in turn affected the Macmillan government's attitudes to East–West relations. It was the origin of the Wilson government's decision to stand aloof from Vietnam. And it has reappeared with renewed force in the 1980s.

Right-wing anti-Americanism has been less obviously influential. The Right has been generally resentful of the Americans' usurpation of British power, either out of pure national pride or on the more elevated ground that the United States helped to destroy a beneficent British world system without putting anything effective in its place. But these sentiments have been overtrumped by an even greater dislike of others. Resistance to communism, clearly at the top of the Right's priorities, has been difficult to sustain without at least some co-operation with the strongest anti-communist power in sight. Opposition to

British membership of the European Communities, another obsession, has also softened opposition to the United States whose alliance (along with the Commonwealth) has had to be presented as the only credible alternative. Nevertheless there have been periods when anti-American feelings within the Conservative Party have boiled over. Anyone who wants a strong taste of these sentiments, even in the immediate aftermath of allied victory in World War Two, should read the debate in the House of Commons on 13 December 1945 when the terms of the American loan were grudgingly approved, with 100 MPs opposed and 169, including Churchill himself, abstaining. Again, after the Suez débâcle, the 'Suez Group' of Tory MPs was a thorn in Macmillan's flesh throughout his Ministry, opposing not only every step in the dissolution of the Empire in Africa, but also every sign of 'weakness' in the face of American pressure as well. Had he not succeeded in pulling off the Nassau agreement with Kennedy he might have been in very grave difficulties with his own party. Subsequent manifestations have had less practical effect, but have still made a great deal of noise from time to time – the most recent being the Falklands War (so long as it looked as if the United States proposed to remain an impartial mediator in the dispute) and the Grenada affair.

It is obvious, then, that some quite important groups on the wings of British opinion have always been less than enchanted with the 'special relationship'. But it is also true that the pro-American centre has not been quite so intoxicated by mid-Atlantic rhetoric as is sometimes alleged. Innumerable quotations can be produced to show that British policy-makers have usually had a pretty hard-headed appreciation of what they were doing in relation to the United States. Stated crudely, their purpose has been to use the American connection to maintain British interests and security at a reasonable financial cost. They have from time to time miscalculated the degree to which the Americans would permit themselves to be manipulated or underestimated the price they would exact, but the fundamental British illusion has had much more to do with the old vision of Britain as a major independent actor on the world stage than with any very profound belief in the combined destiny of the English-speaking peoples. Ernest Bevin, for instance, who is rightly given the credit for dragging the United States back into the European arena in 1945 and 1946, never had any doubt that what he wished to do ultimately was to restore Britain's *ante bellum* position. The Americans were essential to Britain's economic recovery and also, while that recovery was taking place, to her security. He was determined that the United States should not lapse into isolation again and was therefore prepared to compromise a number of important issues, including Palestine, rather than sour Anglo-American relations. But his underlying attitude was summed up in a minute, written in January 1946, opposing a suggestion of Attlee's that we should withdraw from the Mediterranean: 'Let us wait till our strength is restored and let us meanwhile, *with US help as necessary* [my emphasis], hold on to essential positions and concentrate on building up UNO.' Those positions where the necessity of American help was accepted by Bevin were mainly limited to the realms of East–West strategy and economic recovery in Europe. Throughout the Attlee Cabinet's discussions of policy towards Africa, South-east Asia and the Indian subcontinent the American angle was rarely considered relevant at all; in the Middle East, it was regarded as an intrusive and usually very unhelpful factor. Bevin and Attlee would have relied on American help in the nuclear field if they could have got it, but neither had the slightest hesitation in going ahead with the British nuclear weapons programme when American co-operation fell through; it seemed the natural thing to do.

The slow death of this easy assumption about an independent status and freedom of manoeuvre has in my view been the crucial and traumatic British experience in the last thirty years. The growing disparity between British and American power was, of course, one important element of this but it is a mistake to think that it was, or always seemed, the most important one. British governments were aware that their strength and influence were shrinking in each of Churchill's three famous overlapping circles – the Commonwealth, the Atlantic, and Europe – but for the fact that the process advanced at different rates at different times and in different places muddled them and occasionally led them to believe that in one area or another it had stopped or even been reversed. The confusion was increased in the case of the Commonwealth by the sense of movement; the very act of negotiating, and then granting, independence in a succession of dependencies gave an illusion of power – that is, until the dependencies began to run out.

Psychologically speaking, the declension was marked by three phases. In the first, just described, the loss of power was mainly felt in the Atlantic and European 'circles'. The American loan and the abandonment of Palestine (essentially forced by the United States) signalled the one and the British withdrawal from Greece and Turkey the other. The decision to leave India, which looks objectively the most significant symptom of decline in this period, did not really seem so at the time, being generally regarded (in spite of the chaos of partition and the opposition of zealots like Churchill) as a statesmanlike gesture which had in any case been foreshadowed for the last twenty-five years.

In the second phase, roughly the 1950s, British attention turned primarily to weaknesses in the Empire circle. At the beginning of this period General Templer's remarkable victory in Malaya shored up the British position in the Far East for another decade, but the situation elsewhere showed that Bevin's dream of eventually re-establishing the world role on something like the old scale would have to be abandoned. The old Middle Eastern sphere of influence (Egypt and Iraq) began to crumble and following a deliberate decision of Macmillan's, the African empire was disposed of at breakneck speed. Meanwhile the British delusion of strength, or at least business as usual, was maintained in Europe and the Atlantic. Eden upstaged Dulles with the Geneva negotiations on Indo-China; Macmillan irritated Eisenhower by his independent summit manoeuvres with the Russians; almost all British politicians cold-shouldered the infant movement for European integration.

From the same psychological point of view, the third phase (the 1960s) was perhaps the most interesting, for it brought matters to a crucial decision point. The decision in question was not, as was then claimed by General de Gaulle and is still often claimed today, one between Europe and the United States. For the vast majority of British policy-makers, this was a false dichotomy. The United States was in Europe; Europe needed the United States. To maintain close security links with America and to try to retain some influence in Washington, whatever else one was doing, was only a matter of realism. De Gaulle's anti-American posturings seemed petty and dishonest since France ultimately relied on the United States as much as anyone else; they were also stupid, since to indulge in America-baiting without the strength to stand on one's own was to lose influence for no purpose. The debate in Britain was much more to do with a choice between unilateralism or multilateralism. The Left and the Right wanted various forms of independent national self-assertion – the Right tending to imperial nostalgia, the Left to little Englandism or, in the case of sublimated imperialists like Hugh Gaitskell, to visions of the new Commonwealth as a way of prolonging '1000 years of history'. As Macmillan and company perceived it, on the other hand, none of these options any longer offered a satisfactory degree of influence. Britain was running out of entry cards in Washington, and was 'losing out', as the phrase went, in Europe as well. A far more co-operative form of alliance diplomacy was therefore required in which a residual world position, easy relations with the United States and security and economic interests in Europe would, as it were, be pooled. This line of argument suited the United States as well, not so much because of a desire to have a 'Trojan Horse' in Europe (which is what the French alleged) as because the utility of the British as a major partner, under the old assumptions, was becoming hopelessly compromised by sheer weakness and the idea of using what was left of British power to build a more solid (and perhaps less expensive) European 'pillar' to the alliance was, in spite of possible drawbacks, extremely attractive on balance.

In one sense, de Gaulle actually proved Macmillan's case for him. By excluding Britain from Europe, and preventing the 'pool' being made for another decade, he forced a demonstration of the inadequacy of the 'independent' option. The Wilson years were a painful series of economic and political retreats made more humiliating by Wilson's own tendency to grandiose pretensions of power and statesmanship. Economic weakness brought on the withdrawal from east of Suez; and this in turn reduced British importance to the United States. Britain's influence in Europe was effectively nullified by the French. The Commonwealth was a broken reed, so far as offering Britain a serious global standing was concerned. Wilson's final desperate attempts to reopen the question of European entry, against all his own past views and the instincts of his party, were the most convincing proof of who had won the main argument.

Having said that, one has to admit that a subsidiary argument of a Europe-versus-the-United States kind has subsequently been forced on the British. Edward Heath recognized, as perhaps Macmillan did not, the emotional importance to the Europeans of a British 'commitment' to the Community. This appeared to mean, as in childish initiation ceremonies, proving the point by doing the thing you least like to do – in this case being nasty to the Americans. Heath duly obliged. As Henry Kissinger says in his memoirs: 'Heath dealt with us with an unsentimentality quite at variance with the special relationship. The intimate consultation by which American and British policies had been co-ordinated in the post-war period was reduced to formal diplomatic exchanges.' More substantially he snubbed Kissinger's Year of Europe in 1973 and later the same year joined other European countries in refusing to allow American planes to use British bases to reinforce the Israelis in the Arab-Israeli war. The last of these gestures was arguably an early example of a real conflict of interest between

Europe on the one hand and the United States on the other, but the rest do not seem, in retrospect, to have been either necessary or effective. They merely alienated the Americans without greatly improving Britain's relations with the Community. The same could probably be said in reverse of the opposite tactic, tried by James Callaghan, of trying to establish a particularly close and avuncular relationship à la Macmillan, with President Carter; it aroused European suspicions without paying any great dividends in Washington.

Margaret Thatcher's stance has been more equivocal – partly because it has actually been less consistent. Having started with a strongly anti-European instinct and an admiration for President Reagan's brand of conservatism (in many ways similar to her own), she was naturally disposed to assume that the 'special relationship' was alive and would remain efficacious if she built on her empathy with the President. On the other hand, not only has her government necessarily become more and more enmeshed in European Community affairs, but she has also had to swallow some humiliating demonstrations of the modern limits of British influence in Washington, notably the Grenada affair and the loss of an enormous telecommunications contract to French competitors in spite of her personal intercession with the President.

The truth of the matter is that since the 1970s Anglo-American relations, considered entirely by themselves, have ceased to be very important or very interesting. To be either, they have to be viewed in the context of American–European relations, a fact which strips them of some of their remaining sentimental trimmings. Leaving aside anachronistic red herrings like the Falklands and Grenada, the great question for the future has nothing to do with special relationships. It is how far European and American interests are going to diverge, and if so how to manage this divergence. Where there are serious disputes, the Anglo-American relationship forged in World War Two will not prevent Britain lining up with increasing regularity on the European side, for all sorts of hard-headed reasons to do with geography and economics. Where history and sentiment come in is in enabling Britain to avoid two psychological traps. One, into which the French are particularly prone to fall, is to lose sight of the fundamental interdependence of the United States and Europe and make empty anti-American gestures in order to satisfy national pride. The other, which is the peculiar tendency of the Germans, is to see the European–American relationship in the excessively blinkered focus of immediate domestic political and economic concerns and therefore to veer, sometimes quite wildly, between fear of being abandoned and fear of being a pawn in American hands. Britain's true value to the United States at present is not as a 'Trojan horse' in Europe, still less as an independent adjutant in world affairs; to the extent that she is successfully tempted by American blandishments or nationalistic nostalgia to be either, she loses her ability to play the modern role for which she is best suited by temperament and historical experience. That role is to act emphatically as the European power she has actually become, but to bring to European counsels the important elements of pragmatism, balance, and global perspective that are her distinguishing characteristics. In future this may often entail a multi-polar view of the world which the United States finds disconcerting and even hostile. But the British have developed since 1940 the important ability to understand the American mind better than any of their European partners. They are able to say, on the basis of long experience and in all sincerity, that trans-Atlantic conflicts of interest are manageable even among unequal partners provided there is a minimum of shared objective and provided both sides are prepared to devote real energy to cultivating the habits of close and civilized intercourse.

*Introduction: 'The Anglo-American Relationship' from **The Special Relationship**, edited by W. R. Louis and Hedley Bull, O U P, 1986, pp. 1–14.*

# How We See
# the Americans:

## Perceptions of the United States in Europe
## 1945–83 ▮▮▮▮▮▮▮▮▮▮▮▮▮▮▮▮▮▮▮▮▮▮▮▮▮▮▮▮▮▮▮▮

For the inhabitants of most West European countries, consciousness of the United States has been one of the dominant experiences of the post-1945 era. It is worth stating this clearly at the outset of any discussion of modern European attitudes to America, for it is a common revisionist fallacy, particularly on the European side, to suppose that in the years after World War Two America was no more than a powerful actor on the world stage with whom European states found it expedient individually or collectively to come to close terms. Such a picture does not convey the quite extraordinary degree to which non-communist Europe has been impressed, even defined, in the past thirty-eight years by its relationship with the other side of the Atlantic.

It is a cliché to say that that relationship has always been unequal, but the enormity of the inequality for most of the period often escapes comment and so fails to place present European feelings and prejudices in a realistic setting. The prodigious disparity of military power has naturally been etched on European minds from the start. Nor was there any question of economic parity or anything like it for at least the first twenty years. Europe literally depended on the United States. But it is not so much these particular contrasts in strength that matter as their all-embracing character. Scarcely any event of any significance anywhere in the international system since 1945 has not been affected in some way by the United States, and in the case of Europe the American factor has gone deeper than that. American power not only accomplished the defence of Europe against the Soviet Union and the re-establishment of the European economies; it provided the framework within which some kind of specifically European identity has dimly begun to emerge. What is more, the cultural air that Europeans have breathed all this time has been American air. The language, the images, the popular music and films, the technology and many of the values of the increasingly homogeneous international culture of the post-war world have all been dominated by America, and when we have most vehemently attempted to deny this or reverse the trend, we have demonstrated most clearly our awareness of its reality.

In these circumstances it is not surprising that European attitudes to America should have been varied and intense as well as being basically reactive. Any attempt to describe the whole range of these reactions or to trace them to their causes is out of the question in an essay of this kind. Nevertheless, at the risk of some over-simplification and over-generalization, a rough taxonomy can be produced, under two headings – 'The US as Friend' and 'The US as Adversary':

## The US as Friend
1 Military protector and standard-bearer of the free, democratic world.
2 Economic provider and 'locomotive' of the Western industrialized system.
3 Cultural and technological El Dorado.

## The US as Adversary
1 Political rival, ideological hypocrite, possible betrayer and potential source of World War Three.
2 Economic imperialist.
3 Land of decadence, immorality and irresponsible waste.

We shall see that these pictures of America are by no means mutually exclusive. They have been held in varying degrees and at various times by pretty well all political parties, perhaps all individuals, in every West European country. For that matter, they often all inhabit a single mind at the same time. But for the purpose of analysis they fall naturally into three pairs, representing the positive and negative aspects of, respectively, the political, the economic and the cultural approach. This is primarily a political paper. Economic 'perceptions' do not normally differ, at any rate for long, from hard economic facts and interests which are being dealt with elsewhere in this book; cultural 'perceptions', on the other hand, are so diffuse that only a very long study could capture them. I shall try to deal with both briefly at the end, but mainly as they seem to impinge on political attitudes.

## Political Perceptions

When World War Two ended, it was already clear that of the so-called Big Five the United States and the Soviet Union were in a class of their own. Britain was an independent force, but its resources were obviously overstretched and its underlying weakness exposed by Truman's abrupt termination of Lend-Lease; France and China had not much except pretensions and bluff to sustain their place at the top table. This fact did not, however, entail an immediate post-war acceptance of the notion that the United States and USSR would be rivals, each with its own sphere of influence, far less that Western Europe would automatically find itself in an American 'camp' while East Europe went to a Soviet one. The outlook in 1945 was much more complicated than that.

To begin with, whatever the underlying realities of power, Britain and France started from the assumption that their own pre-war spheres of influence would be maintained or restored to them. Britain still believed in its destiny in the Empire, in the Middle East, in the Eastern Mediterranean and initially in Germany itself. France, in the person of de Gaulle, had spent most of the war years attempting to demonstrate total independence, and had every intention of asserting an equal right to impose a repressive settlement on Germany as well as to repossess its patrimony in Africa, Indo-China and the Middle East. These ambitions did not fit in very easily to a framework of American tutelage or dominance. Meanwhile it was not at all clear exactly what were the intentions of the United States and the USSR. Both were, of course, the liberators of the continent, and it was generally assumed that they (with the British and to a lesser extent the French) would work together to appease and rebuild it in the spirit of the Grand Alliance. Churchill and a few others could foresee serious trouble with the Russians, particularly over Poland, but the real extent of Stalin's ambitions was wrapped in mystery. Similarly, though the general tenor of American policy was self-confident and interventionist, the American Congress was clamouring for a return to normality, and Roosevelt had told Churchill that American troops could not possibly be kept on the European continent for more than two years.

The attitude of West Europeans to the United States was thus ambiguous from the very beginning of the post-war settlement. They were grateful to the Americans for their part in the war. They admired American power and American generosity. They were highly conscious of needing American economic assistance, and this consciousness certainly applied to the defeated Germans as much as to the victorious British. They were also aware that they might need military assistance as well, and both Britain and France were determined to try at all costs to prevent a repetition of America's post-Versailles retreat into isolationism. At the same time, if American help was necessary they wanted it on their own terms, which meant the rejection of American anti-colonialist policies and resistance to America's tendency to feather its own commercial nest at the expense of its allies. (Anyone who wants a strong taste of the anti-American suspicion and resentment of this time is advised to read the debate in the British House of Commons on 13 December 1945, in which the terms of the American loan were grudgingly approved, with 100 M Ps opposed and 169, Winston Churchill among them, abstaining.) In British minds, moreover, there was another fear – the legacy of Yalta, Tehran and Potsdam – that the Americans might be tempted to do a deal with Stalin on many issues vital to Britain's European and imperial interests behind Britain's back. Even at this early stage the idea of American unreliability and/or American naivety in relation to the Russians makes its appearance.

The headlong descent of the United States as well as of Europe into the cold war naturally obscured these fears for a while. To put it crudely, the rush to huddle together away from the fate of Poland, Hungary and Czechoslovakia was bound to lead to the arms of the strongest non-communist state. The Truman Doctrine and Marshall Plan, both launched in 1947, seemed to provide the essential framework of a successful defence strategy – a framework, moreover, that did not interfere with traditional French and British preoccupations, freed resources for other purposes and (probably the most important plus from the French point of view) did not raise the German problem. Transatlantic troubles arose again only when the American determination to meet the communist challenge seemed likely (a) to encroach on British and French freedom of action, (b) to involve the risk of nuclear war and (c) to entail the rearmament of Germany.

The signature of the North Atlantic Treaty in 1949 might have been expected to raise just such issues, and indeed there was a certain amount of left-wing opposition, mainly in France and Italy. But less than a year after the Berlin airlift and the communist revolution in Czechoslovakia, the need to combine against the danger of Soviet aggression appeared very great. On the other hand, the danger of nuclear war seemed minimal because the American nuclear predominance was enormous. The rearmament of Germany did not at that stage arise.

It was with the Korean War that the acute difficulties began to appear. Quite apart from the strain it put on the Western economies just as they were beginning to feel the beneficial effects of the Marshall Plan, the war added for the first time two new thematic criticisms of the United States to those already mentioned. The North Korean aggression was flagrant; the implication of the Russians and Chinese in the plot seemed self-evident. And though the war itself seemed far off and unimportant to most Europeans, those who contributed to the UN force – the British, the French, the Belgians, the Dutch and the Turks – responded to the American call with a fair grace. The real damage to European–American relations was done by two other factors, by allegations that the United States had connived in the excesses of the Syngman Rhee regime and by the personality and behaviour of General MacArthur.

The accusations of torture, and even of germ warfare, that communist propaganda laid against the Americans were the first of a long post-war line and provoked European reactions that were later to become equally predictable – outrage on the left, anger on the right and incredulity softened by a *frisson* of uncertainty in the liberal centre. What caused the uncertainty, then as later, was the American association with a right-wing regime notorious for its brutality (though not, as a matter of fact, more notorious than the North Koreans subsequently became). The requirements of *Realpolitik* were not accepted as an excuse by moralists in the United States, who adhered to Wilsonian principles. In Europe, non-communist motives for criticism were more complicated. As in the later case of Vietnam, genuine distaste for the South Korean government and disappointment at America's declension from its characteristic ideals were mingled with censorious envy. The positive desire of many well-meaning, and otherwise sensible, Europeans to think ill of their chief ally, given the flimsiest chance to do so, and to apply standards of international behaviour that they would not dream of applying to their own governments, has been one of the most persistent and puzzling phenomena of the post-war world. Invited to explain their attitude, such people usually reply that, confronted with much evil in the world, it is rational for them to attack the greatest over which they have any influence, namely the actions of the American government. Perhaps there is some truth in this, but it is

**104**

none the less tempting to detect in these views a less conscious desire to demonstrate independence from, and moral superiority to, a power that is humiliatingly larger than one's own.

In the Korean case it is fair to say that American power was not wielded in a fashion likely to minimize such feelings. The superlative arrogance of MacArthur's suzerainty over the Far East was beginning to cause real alarm in America as well as in Europe long before the North Korean invasion. His conduct of the war itself was even more disturbing, for it implied irresponsibility not only in the sense that the wider consequences of carrying the war into North Korea appeared to be ignored, but also in that MacArthur no longer seemed to be under proper political control. His threat to drop atomic bombs in Manchuria caused an immediate, sharp revulsion of feeling in Europe and brought as phlegmatic a character as Attlee rushing to Washington in protest. This archetype – the 'gung-ho' general in dark glasses with missiles sticking out of his pockets – has haunted the Alliance ever since.

So as far as Europe was concerned, there was even more important fallout from Korea. The crisis brought to a head the central issue of the future of Germany. Acute American alarm at the supposed global implications of the communist incursion, together with the possibility of having to commit large ground forces in the Far East, caused the Americans to try to strengthen the European front by native levies. This meant German rearmament, a mere five years after the end of the European war. Such a violent change of course not only caused severe trauma particularly for the French; it also cut across the efforts of those like Schuman and Monnet who were trying to attack the German problem by economic rather than military means. The United States officially supported the Schuman Plan for a European Coal and Steel Community (ECSC), but the determination of the American administration to press on with the creation of a German army embarrassed those in France in favour of European integration as well as infuriating the nationalist right wing. Monnet adroitly shifted gear in order to bridge the European–American gap in a way favourable to European integration and came up with the Pleven Plan for a European Defence Community (EDC), but the long controversy had two important effects on Atlantic relations. First, it hardened the French Right in its belief that the US connection was imposing intolerable consequences on France, as well as enabling them to transmit this conviction to a wider French consciousness. Second, it demonstrated the tension that was liable to exist between plans and developments which were based ultimately on the presence of the United States in Europe and those that were independent European initiatives.

The ensuing period – roughly that of the Eisenhower presidency – was dominated for Britain and France by the problems of post-colonial adjustment, and it was unfortunate that during this painful process American foreign policy was in the hands of John Foster Dulles, a man who could scarcely have been less sensitive to the difficulties and dangers involved. The notion that the United States was determined to undermine its allies' interests in what was later to be called the Third World in order to further its own became deeply entrenched in Europe at that time – a result brought about partly by Dulles's aggressive Wilsonian rhetoric but partly by incidents in the real world. France complained that after initially supporting the French position in Indo-China and Algeria the US Administration had in effect betrayed them. The Vietnamese situation was particularly infuriating to French opinion because it seemed that a relatively friendly, if neutral, area had been divided by American policy into one communist state and one American puppet, both anti-French. The British likewise had the gravest suspicions of American intentions in the Middle East, especially in Iraq, where they felt that the United States had taken advantage of Mussadeq's nationalization of the oil industry in order to grab power for its own oil companies. For Britain the climactic event of the period was the Suez operation in 1956, torpedoed by the United States for reasons that even British opponents of the landing were unable to understand and with a degree of sanctimoniousness from Dulles that led so ardent an Atlanticist as Alastair Buchan to describe him as 'the most unattractive figure in modern history'.[1]

It may be said that the legacy of European resentment left by Dulles's rather self-serving form of anti-imperialism was relatively short-lived (though I would argue that it was an important element in the undercurrent of *Schadenfreude* discernible in European attitudes to the Vietnam War and subsequent American misfortunes). This is certainly not true of the difficulties created by his crusading anti-communism. This went far beyond Truman's policy of pragmatic containment and entailed not simply the deliberate resurrection of a re-militarized West Germany and the emplacement of pacts such as CENTO and SEATO in order to limit further communist encroachments, but ruthless resistance to anything that seemed to legitimize past communist gains or accept the status quo. This obviously ruled

[1] In a dispatch to the *Observer*.

out any advance towards a German settlement or the normalization of relations with communist China. But it also gave an extra, non-defensive significance to the doctrine of 'massive retaliation' which appeared (along with phrases such as 'brinkmanship' and 'agonizing reappraisal') at this time. The doctrine, primarily intended to reassure the West Germans by establishing an unbreakable link between their fate and the use of American nuclear power, succeeded in this purpose but at a cost. It promoted in Europe for the first time the idea that the United States was a *dangerous* power, capable of destroying the human race in defence of its own interests and preconceptions and without too much reference to anyone else's.

I have dealt with the first fifteen years after World War Two in some detail because almost every subsequent European attitude to the United States was moulded in this period, and the early casts have a clarity that have become blurred with repetition later on. A short survey of later developments in the three major European countries will serve to emphasize the point:

### (a) France

The long shadow of General de Gaulle has loomed over all Franco-American contacts since 1958. The essence of de Gaulle's achievement in foreign affairs, apart from the settlement of the Algerian question, was to substitute anti-Americanism for anti-Germanism as the mainspring of French national policy or, to put it another way, as the wall off which French nationalism has been bounced. The main basis for this reversal was the accomplished fact of German rearmament (which de Gaulle had denounced passionately at the time of the EDC debate but which had become irreversible by the time he returned to power). Having faced this fact he adopted it, as it were, and turned it with characteristic ingenuity against its inventors.

This possibility would not have been open to him had there not been a strong current of anti-Americanism in French public opinion created by the events recounted earlier, as well as a groundswell of belief that there was a need for a historical reconciliation between France and Germany. Nevertheless, it is an open question how far the French public ever shared the whole of de Gaulle's systematic anti-Americanism. Certainly he himself found it expedient to proceed slowly with his disengagement from NATO, and not simply from fear of what retaliation he might provoke from the United States. The whole process had to be prepared with the proposal in 1958 for a three power *directoire*, which seems to have been designed purely for the purpose of putting Eisenhower in the wrong; and the final completion of the design, with the French withdrawal from the unified command system of NATO, followed only eight years later. As a purely personal impression of those years, I seldom found a Frenchman who was not willing to concede – *in extremis* – that France's real position as a 'free rider' on the American system sat uncomfortably with Gaullism's more grandiose pretensions. This unease not unnaturally increased as the limitations of the grand design were exposed by Adenauer's persistent refusal to let go of the American apron-strings and by the increasing wildness of de Gaulle's attempts in the mid-1960s to compensate for this German infantilism. The *tous-azimuts* doctrine,[2] the scandal of the '*Vive le Quebec Libre!*' speech, the attempt to set up French axes with Moscow and Peking, had an air of desperation about them that made the more pragmatic nationalism of Pompidou and his successors a relief to French public opinion as well as to everyone else.

Nevertheless nationalism and cultural obduracy are permanent characteristics of France, and they have undoubtedly been given an anti-American bent throughout the post-war period in simple reaction to the pressures and encroachments of a predominantly Anglo-Saxon international environment. The Catholic and *marxisant* elements in the French intelligentsia have at least been able to agree on a common distaste for American values. French national pride has led to a fierce determination to maintain at least the illusion of freedom for French action. And yet two realities have constantly mocked these attitudes, and prudence has set limits even to the parade of the illusions. The first reality has been the Soviet threat and the second the possibility of a German 'sell-out' to the East. French logic cannot ultimately resist these pressures, and anti-Americanism is modified in words as well as deeds in fairly precise proportion to French perceptions of the Soviet and German dangers. When, as in the past five years, both have hung over Paris, Franco-American relations have shown marked improvement.

### (b) Germany

The post-war development of the Federal Republic of Germany and

[2] In the December 1967 issue of the *Revue de défense nationale*, General Charles Ailleret, the French Chief of Staff, recommended the 'all azimuths' targeting of French nuclear weapons. The implication that some French missiles would be permanently trained on Washington was so outrageous that it could only have been printed with the direct authority of de Gaulle.

the convolutions of German domestic politics have produced a wide variety of attitudes towards the United States, but they have never seriously shaken the perception of the German public that they have prospered by the American connection and by their membership of NATO. They are aware that the restoration of the shattered and defeated country of 1945 – so that it is now, in spite of division, the most powerful and prosperous in Europe – is owed in large part to the Pax Americana and to Marshall Aid. Gratitude does not always purchase a great deal in international affairs, but there is doubtless some significance in the evidence of the opinion polls which have shown a huge and consistent German majority not just in favour of NATO but also in favour of the Americans as such. This does not, of course, preclude disagreement with Washington, but an Allensbach poll taken in 1981,[3] after four years of intense argument and dissatisfaction with the Carter administration, showed that 30 per cent of West Germans still believed that the Federal Republic should always support American foreign policy.

This is a startling figure, but it is a fair guess that had such a question been asked in 1958 (and I have been unable to discover that it was), the answer would have shown 70 or 80 per cent, rather than 30 per cent, in favour of unquestioning acceptance of American leadership. A twenty-five-year declension has undoubtedly taken place, brought about by three factors.

The first of these is the comparative loss of American strategic power. On the level of conventional defence, the demonstration of fallibility involved in the loss of the Vietnam War gave a profound shock to all America's allies but particularly to one as exposed and neurotic as the FRG. On the nuclear level the same can be said of the moment, sometime in the 1960s (and certainly after the launching of the Sputnik in 1957), at which it became generally apparent that Soviet missiles could reach the mainland of the United States. This is not the place to discuss the intricacies of the subsequent strategic debate, but two points relating to German–American attitudes are worth drawing out:

1 There were other reasons for Willy Brandt's *Ostpolitik* than loss of American power, and these will be discussed in a moment. But it was certainly one factor. Henry Kissinger paraphrases the position of Egon Bahr, Brandt's closest adviser on these matters, as follows: 'If

**109**

[3] Quoted in the *Financial Times*, 4 November 1981.

Europe can no longer rely on American strategic pre-eminence and if Europe will not – or in view of domestic politics cannot – make the effort to defend itself, Europe, and above all the Federal Republic, has to seek safety in relaxation of tensions with the East.'[4]

2   The Germans have been remarkably logical and consistent ever since the 1950s about the kind of defence they would prefer – that is, conventional forces with a strong American contingent backed by the threat of first use of American ICBMs if conventional forces fail. All American attempts to vary this formula have led to trouble in the FRG for the very simple reason that all variations are less consonant with German interests. Mansfieldism would have reduced the American stake and therefore the likelihood of American retaliation. President Carter's notorious Presidential Memorandum 10, by partially abandoning forward defence, appeared to leave at least part of the FRG to its fate. American attempts to implicate the Germans more directly in nuclear defence, either by the multilateral force (early 1960s), neutron weapons (late 1970s) or modernization of theatre nuclear forces (early 1980s), have caused fearful misgivings, not so much because of German feelings of *pudeur* as because they imply a notion of nuclear war won on German soil rather than by a safe exchange of ICBMs overhead. (The fact that the TNF problem was raised in its present form by Helmut Schmidt himself was rapidly shown to have been an aberration.) The only really successful innovation in the sphere has been the establishment of the Nuclear Planning Group in 1966, a development which increased German influence without increasing German vulnerability.

The second factor in the development of German views of the United States has simply been the growth of German power. The economic aspects of this belong to another section, but a mixture of German self-satisfaction at the *Wirtschaftswunder* and exasperation at the 'inflationary mismanagement' of the US economy has obviously spilled over in the political and strategic spheres. Importunate American demands for a greater German financial contribution, whether to 'support costs' (the cry of the 1960s and 1970s) or to the protection of 'European' oil and other interests outside Europe (the cry of the 1980s), have aroused the instinctive question, 'Why us?' and the resentfully self-supplied answer, 'Because we have the money.' They have also served to underline the centrality of the importance of the FRG to the

[4] Henry Kissinger, *Years of Upheaval*, London, Weidenfeld & Nicolson, 1982, p. 147.

Americans and therefore led directly to German resentment over American failures to consult or over crude demonstrations of American power such as the attempt to prevent the sale of German nuclear technology to Latin America.

Finally, of course, there has been the question of East–West relations. A common German view is that *détente* – and therefore, in a sense, *Ostpolitik* – was invented by the Americans in the first place. This is not entirely true. Other factors, notably the building of the Berlin Wall in 1961, were pushing Brandt's predecessors, the Erhard and Grand Coalition governments, in the direction of a deal in central Europe which would at least enable some intercourse between the two halves of the country to take place. What is obviously the case is that nothing so radical as the German treaties could possibly have been accomplished in 1970 if the Nixon administration had not actively desired it for its own good reasons; and it is equally obvious to German opinion that once this regional framework has been set up it cannot be dismantled or even put at risk because it suits the United States for global reasons. What appears to the Reagan administration as German selfishness and parochialism seems to Germans to be resistance to another example of the Americans bullying their allies, ignoring their interests and conducting quarrels at somebody else's expense.

It is presumably this East–West area of policy that the 56 per cent who thought (in the opinion poll quoted earlier) that the F R G should be 'prepared to go its own way' chiefly had in mind, and it is possible to foresee this line of thought developing if superpower relations continue to be bad. There is little truth in the American suspicion of 'neutralism' in Germany. It is evident to any reasonably impartial observer – and is confirmed by the result of the last German general election – that if the Germans were really forced to choose between the American Alliance and their opening to the East, they would, however reluctantly, choose the Americans. However, the Russians can be said to have gained some control over German public opinion in the sense that its instinctive reaction to deliberate acts of Soviet provocation outside Europe may well be to move further from the United States and not closer. To that extent the Americans have a point.

### (c) Britain

Since 1960, Britain's view of the United States has been schizophrenic. The Suez crisis had demonstrated in a traumatic fashion that Britain's economic base was no longer strong enough to allow it to make major moves on the world stage in opposition to the American administration. Three possible alternative strategies were therefore available. It could simply withdraw into a Little England position; it could attempt to exercise influence mainly through the Americans; or it could retrace its steps and apply to join the European Community. The choice made by Harold Macmillan in the late 1950s was to try to combine the second (American) with the third (European) course. The picture painted to the country at the time of the first round of Common Market negotiations in 1961 was of a Britain leading Europe into its global heritage ('making Europe more outward-looking' was the phrase) and at the same time offering wise counsel and support, both on its own account and on Europe's, to the United States.

This prospectus did not work out. The part of Councillor-in-Chief to the American president appeared to have some validity at the outset, thanks to the rapport between Kennedy and Macmillan. It even appeared for a while to have paid off handsomely in the Nassau Agreement in December 1962 when American provision of Polaris missiles to the Royal Navy renewed Britain's membership of the nuclear club at a bargain price. But Harold Wilson's attempt to fill the same role was a dismal failure. Lyndon Johnson was not particularly susceptible to British influence, and as soon as it became clear that Britain was neither willing nor able to give serious assistance in Vietnam (and was, indeed, in such economic straits that a pull-out from East of Suez was on the cards) Britain's independent role in Washington became increasingly marginal. At the same time the European half of the plan was thwarted by de Gaulle who rightly saw that the British strategy was incompatible with his own.

It was ten years before the British could plausibly claim to be back on their original track – inside the European Community – and also able, by reasons of sentiment, language and personal friendship, to exert some influence on American policy. But by that time history had moved on. The withdrawal from the Middle and Far East had reduced British standing in Washington, and the lapse of time had ensured that the Community had hardened into a mould to which Britain could not now fit conveniently without breakages, hard feelings and niggling argument of an indeterminate duration.

Subsequent British governments have reacted to this situation in varying ways but without altogether solving the psychological problem. Heath attempted to make a clear-cut decision in favour of Europe. As Henry Kissinger says in his memoirs: 'Heath dealt with us with an unsentimentality quite at variance with the special relationship.

The intimate consultation by which British and American policies had been co-ordinated in the post-war period was reduced to formal diplomatic exchanges.'[5] He snubbed Kissinger's Year of Europe in 1973 and, on the outbreak of the Arab–Israeli war that autumn, joined other European countries in refusing to allow American planes to use British bases for the airlift to Israel. In the subsequent negotiations over a common energy policy for the Alliance, it was the Germans rather than Britain who averted a split with the United States. Where all this would have led in the long run, it is hard to say, but in the period of Heath's Prime Ministership it appears that the policy succeeded in alienating the Americans without vastly improving Britain's relations with its Community partners. Wilson and Callaghan put their weight on the other foot, Callaghan in particular aiming at an avuncular relationship, à la Macmillan, with Carter. Neither got a lot out of it. Mrs Thatcher's policy has been more ambiguous. An instinctive Atlanticist and much concerned with her dispute with the Community over money, she has turned with some enthusiasm to the Reagan regime, with which she is in ideological sympathy in any case. The purchase of the Trident submarines from the United States prolongs a close dependence in the defence field. On the other hand, her somewhat Gaullist desire for greatness and the paramountcy of British interests tempted her to back Lord Carrington's attempt to establish a distinctive European policy in the Middle East during Britain's 1982 Presidency of the Community even though this was heavily frowned on in Washington. Nothing much has come of it, but the possibility remains that Mrs Thatcher's confusion, being nationalistic, will prove as difficult for Washington in the long run as for Europe.

## Economic Perceptions

As is the case with Atlantic political relationships, the most important thing is the one most often forgotten in discussions of the future of the Alliance – the success of the post-war economic enterprise. The depression that has followed the oil shocks has clouded the splendid vision of unbroken progress and exaggerated the tensions that have always existed in the system, but if one takes the period as a whole, the increase in production and international trade has been staggering, both in America and in Europe. The interpenetration of the two economic systems has also been startling, with huge investment flows in

[5] Kissinger, op. cit., p. 141.

both directions. Both sides of the Atlantic are ultimately aware of this fact, and their awareness arguably constitutes a better guarantee of the American commitment to the defence of Europe than the North Atlantic Treaty. This vast system has not come into being without difficulty and argument, but once the process had been put on solid rails at Bretton Woods and set in motion by the Marshall Plan, nothing has been able to stop the juggernaut completely, and nobody, with the occasional exception of the French, has really wanted to try.

The points of friction have occurred in relatively few places:

1   European complaints of the abuse of American economic power. These have ranged from relatively minor questions to do with monopoly, arms procurement, oil concessions or the scope of American regulatory agencies, to issues connected with the overall monetary system. The only one of these to reach major crisis proportions was the appearance of huge dollar surpluses in the late 1960s. The European charge, led by the French and Germans but subscribed to also by Britain and the rest, was that Europe was being forced by the dollar-exchange system to allow the United States (a) to buy up European business at Europe's expense, (b) to pay for the Vietnam War on credit and (c) to export inflation. This argument had real political bite and led in the end to the devaluation of the dollar in 1971. Nevertheless, the sequel has proved the irrelevance of much of the dispute. It is doubtful whether the system of floating exchange rates that supervened is any less open to abuse by the strongest party or gives any non-American country any greater control over its economic fate than before. The fact is that the American economy is still stronger and more self-sufficient than the European and it affects Europe more than the European economy affects America. Europeans implicitly admit this in their constant demands that the United States should conduct its economic affairs differently in order to help cure European inflation (or alternatively European unemployment). There is no sign that this present reality will change in the foreseeable future.

2   American complaints that Europe is unfairly defensive. There is no doubt that the American open-market approach to the world economy contrasts strongly with European notions of managed trade and protection. The Europeans say, as others did of Britain in the nineteenth century, that free trade benefits the strongest party. Americans reply, 'It is the consumer world-wide who benefits.' The European Community is in part a defensive mechanism against the argument and American domination – a fact which Americans, blinded perhaps by analogies with American Federation, have always been reluctant

to acknowledge in theory. Having been forced to recognize it in practice, they are understandably hurt, and even vindictive, because their initial encouragement of the idea has not been rewarded. The question for the Europeans has always been, and remains, how high they dare build their defences without provoking political retaliation such as the withdrawal of American troops from Europe. The situation calls for nice judgement and has, on the whole, received it because the political stakes are higher than the economic ones.

3   Friction over economic relations with third countries. The appearance of Japan as a major actor on the international economic scene has given plenty of scope for triangular arguments and betrayals but has more often than not tended to force the Americans and Europeans to make common cause. More difficult have been questions of trade with developing countries, especially where Europe has had ex-colonial ties that discriminate against the United States. Trickiest of all have been arguments where what might be called strategic trade is involved – arms sales to L D C s, technology sales to the communist bloc. Americans have charged that irresponsible Europeans think only of their pockets; to which the European reply that the United States is equally careless of the way in which it unloads arms on highly unsuitable recipients and is hypocritical into the bargain, since it is quite willing to sell grain to the Russians when domestic politics demands it. Here, as in the case of normal trade, Europeans are being forced by political pressure to set limits on their own freedom of manoeuvre, but the affair of the Soviet gas pipeline in 1982 has demonstrated that nice judgement is required in these matters on the American as well as the European side. For just as there is an implicit political threat to the Europeans in the possibility of American withdrawal, so there is an implicit threat to the United States in German disaffection if the F R G's strategic interest in détente is put under excessive strain.

4   Oil. The difference between Europe's heavy dependence on imported oil, particularly from the Gulf, and the relatively light and diminishing dependence of the United States has been the source of much trouble and misunderstanding since 1973. North Sea oil has insulated Britain to some extent from the sharp end of the argument, but the F R G's vulnerability both to price increases and to interruption of supply is enormous. The technical arguments about price manipulation and crisis management do not concern us here, but the political issues raised merit brief examination. At the most primitive psychological level the question has been, 'Whose oil is it?' The Americans are firmly convinced that they are being asked to pull Europe's chestnuts

out of the Arabian fire, and that they are therefore entitled to demand that the beneficiaries of the operation buckle to and help. The European view is that if anyone is at risk in the Gulf it is the West as a whole, but that, in any case, threats to supply may well be greater if the West starts meddling there than if they let well alone and hope for the best. The picture of the US marines wading ashore in Saudi Arabia to hold the oil wells in the middle of a civil war, or parachuting into southern Iran to hold the Red Army at bay, looks less convincing in European capitals than in Washington. There is in this case, as in others affecting instability in the Third World, a belief in Europe that the United States is ham-fisted and obsessed with the communist menace, whereas the Europeans, being sophisticates with their knees browned in the Imperial sunset, are better aware of the subtleties required in dealing with the natives. There may indeed be something in this, but that does not, unfortunately, deal with the political problem.

## Cultural Perspectives

In the two or three years after World War Two, America was widely admired and envied in Western Europe as a civilization. This was not just a matter of gratitude or vague recollections of the Atlantic Charter and the Five Freedoms. At a mundane level America made people happy. Liberation went well with the tunes of 'Oklahoma!' and 'Annie Get Your Gun'. French intellectuals 'discovered' Faulkner and Scott Fitzgerald. Britain flocked to see 'Meet Me in St Louis' and 'The Best Years of our Lives'. Things American, like dollars themselves, had the additional attraction of being scarce and expensive. It was almost a decade before American nylons and ballpoint pens became a drug on the European market.

An important part of the history of American–European relations since 1945 has been the gradual fading of that dazzling vision of American riches and vitality. It is partly a tale of the restoration of Europe and European self-confidence; partly, perhaps, of a loss of American zest somewhere in the jungles of South-east Asia. It is also a story of assimilation. Europe has adopted American culture more or less wholesale, from Coke to blue jeans, has twisted and softened it in its own way and then re-exported it to its inventors as its own. Some of the best country rock is played today by European groups with Tennessee accents crafted in Frankfurt and Rotterdam.

This is particularly true of the most fundamental post-war criticisms of the United States, nearly all of which have originated in America and not in Europe. Of course many Europeans have rejected the United States and its values from the start. Some, like the French, felt that it threatened their language and civilization. Some, like the communist parties, disliked its ideology. The French Communist Party which invented the phrase 'coca-colonization', detested it on both counts. Others – the French and German Catholics, for example – felt it was immoral, with its emphasis on materialism and sex and its encouragement to youthful revolt. The British middle class hated it for its vulgarity. This was in-built prejudice, some of which has softened with time and some not. But for a radical critique of America's actions as they have occurred one has had to look elsewhere. Who invented the slogan 'Private affluence and public squalor'? Where did the ecology movement start? Who were the most passionate denouncers of McCarthyism and who led the revolt against the Vietnam War? Who first supplied the intellectual ammunition for the peace movement's assault on the idea of winning a nuclear war? All Americans. Europe has adopted and adapted these, like everything else – and sometimes with unexpected results. It is one of the crowning ironies of the post-war period that the greatest wave of unrest that swept Western Europe in the past thirty-five years, and the one that toppled General de Gaulle, should have been led by students 'radicalized' by the example of their rebellious brothers and sisters on the campuses of the United States.

*From **The Troubled Alliance**, edited by Lawrence Freedman, Heinemann, 1983, pp. 28–43.*

# Atlantic Cross-currents

President Johnson, whom I and a colleague consulted not so long ago on the subject of Anglo-American relations, replied with a characteristic metaphor and a wealth of expressive gesture, 'Britain,' he said, 'may dicker around in the night-clubs and dance with a few of the girls but in the end you'll always come home to bed with the same old girl.' Hmm! Always is a big word, Mr President. And what if the door is bolted or we find the old girl in bed with someone else?

If the conversation took place today (and if bandying sexual images with the president of the United States had suddenly become an easier exercise) these and perhaps still more graphic objections would immediately spring to the lips. The devaluation of the pound, the deepening of the Vietnam War, the British withdrawal from the Far East, the quarrel over troop costs in Germany, the growing protectionism of the US Congress and now the President's massive restrictions on American investment and travel all seem part of an escalating battle in which the US and Europe abuse each other with increasing violence and in which Britain finds herself caught in a lethal crossfire.

It needs no very great exercise in imagination to foresee a possible outcome in which the US retires to an aggressive isolationism, Europe turns in entirely upon itself, monetary restrictions mount, world trade declines and the under-developed world sinks still further into poverty and resentment. This result would clearly be a catastrophe on a global scale but it would also defer if it did not blast hopes for Britain's economic recovery. For how is an export-led boom to be engineered in the midst of a jungle of falling growth rates and trade restrictions?

**118**  Such horrific consequences are still only possibilities but they should be considered sufficiently alarming to make us extremely cautious about the conduct of British foreign policy during the coming months and particularly about our relations with the US whose own reactions are obviously the most potent factor in the situation.

Should we allow ourselves to remain the first line of defence for the dollar or should we join in the campaign for an increase in the gold price? Should we maintain some kind of presence in the Far East for the duration of the Vietnam War? Should we cancel the F-111? Should we denounce the bombing of North Vietnam? Should we cash the dollar portfolio? Should we reinstate export rebates? Should we expand sales to the communist bloc? These are only a small selection from a large number of questions which arise from our present economic situation and which are now being actively canvassed. In each our national interest, narrowly defined, obviously differs to some extent from that of the US, but in each it is possible to argue that our long-term interest depends upon deferring to the interests of the United States.

In those far off happy days of 1964 and 1965, it was relatively easy to maintain that there was a very close identity of interests between ourselves and the US. They and we were anxious for one reason or another to maintain the old sterling parity. They and we were anxious that Britain should continue to maintain a world role. We tried hard to achieve both and they were prepared to foot the bill when we could not. But this contact ended with devaluation and a whole new balance has now to be established in a situation in which most of the facts are intensely complicated. And the political atmosphere is highly charged with emotion.

On one side the perennial anti-Americanism of the Labour left wing has been given a vast new impetus and appeal by the Vietnam War. The ancient anti-American jealousy of the Right has joined forces with Gaullism and even the mildest Europeanism to create formidable political pressures on the government. Moreover the economic crisis allows these forces to clothe their instincts in perfectly respectable economic garments. Where defence cuts are concerned the argument is compelling, and even the demand for Britain to dissociate herself from the American enterprise in Vietnam can be justified on the grounds that it will make the left wing more willing to accept necessary but 'anti-socialist' cuts in public expenditure at home.

On the other side there are those who are anxious to push us to the opposite extreme of falling in closely with American wishes. The protagonists of the 'special relationship' have reappeared on the scene in alliance with the anti-Market group who are busy pursuing the shadowy image of a North Atlantic Free Trade Area.

This sense of confusion certainly extends to the government – and in its present mood of division and domestic turmoil there is no point in even guessing at the balance of the Cabinet on most of these issues. Mr Brown evidently wants us to pay a certain amount of attention to American susceptibilities – partly because he is a staunch Atlantic Alliance man and partly because he wishes to retain some vestigial influence on American policy in South-east Asia.

Mr Healey and the Defence staff would no doubt agree – though more perhaps because the Brown arguments tend to shore up their own position than for any particular love of the US. Mr Jenkins with his domestic preoccupations and his temperamental Europeanism tends to advise facing American wrath at a number of points.

Mr Crossman often seems in favour of a policy as near to socialist isolationism as it is possible for a self-styled internationalist to get. As for the Prime Minister, who can tell? He has been (with only occasional lapses) a pillar of the special relationship for three years; he likes hob-nobbing with the President, and he is looking for comfort after his European rebuff. On the other hand devaluation has taken him out of pawn, the left wing is breathing down his neck and the Vietnam question gives him a convenient hatchet to wield against Mr Brown if he ever wishes to do so.

These cross-currents make a very unsatisfactory environment for decision-making, and it may be helpful to return for a moment to first principles and consider how the balance of our national interest is arrived at in this area. The crude facts of the situation are very obvious. Europe (including the UK) badly needs access to the American market and to American capital and technology. They also, in spite of some East–West *détente*, continue to need the protection of American nuclear missiles, and the land forces which provide the trip-wire for them. On the other hand the US needs access to the European market and feels that her own security can best be defended at the ramparts of West Germany.

Since the US is the more powerful force her set of needs is ultimately less pressing than those of Europe, and there are definite, though extreme, circumstances in which her Congress and her government might decide that too high a price was being paid in order to fulfil them. There are also conceivable circumstances in which Europe might take the same decision – and in a number of fields General de Gaulle has already taken it. But in that case Europe and the French have to recognize that they will probably be hurt more than the US (as the latest balance-of-payments restrictions will doubtless prove).

Within this framework there are an infinite number of particular transatlantic arrangements in which the US and her partners balance advantage and disadvantage but they are always limited by two considerations – first if the Europeans flout American interests consistently they will eventually find their own highest interests curtailed, and secondly the fact that this threat is vast and clumsy means that it is unlikely to be used except in extreme circumstances. Therefore European countries can get away with a great deal where their own immediate national interests are clearly at stake.

The conclusion of this calculus for Britain is not at all certain. I should judge that if we were absolutely determined we could answer all the questions listed earlier in this article without calling down any more immediate sanctions than the withdrawal of some US bases in England and the increase of the cancellation costs of the F-111. All I would suggest, however, is that the cumulative effect of answering all these questions the same way, taken with the present American feelings about Gaullism and Europe in general, would be to drive the US appreciably nearer to actions and attitudes in which the interests of Europe and the UK would suffer more than her own.

*Financial Times*, 5 January 1968

# The Waning of Optimism

An ancient New Dealer to whom I once expressed admiration for American drive and energy retorted drily that the American formula for tackling any national problem is first to exaggerate it and then to forget it. This is a dictum which subsequent observation of the life-cycle of such 'American dilemmas' as car safety, the Negro family, chemical fertilizers, the death of the cities, rural poverty, the affluent society, and the militarization of the US has tended to confirm for me.

A topic makes a coy appearance for a year or two in esoteric books and learned journals. It is next 'identified' by some popularizing intellectual in an epoch-making best-seller. It is then discovered by the big news magazines and the television programmes and the cocktail conversationalists and the Congressional speechwriters, at whose hands it accumulates labels like 'tragedy', 'confrontation', and 'catastrophe'.

Finally two things happen more or less simultaneously. The Ford Foundation or a Congressional sub-committee or (in extreme cases) a presidential 'task force' recommends the expenditure of a billion dollars or so, and the American public becomes bored to death with the subject and turns to something else – secure in the belief that it is taken care of.

This system has disadvantages. It is haphazard and often lacks follow-through. But these have been handsomely outweighed, on the whole, by the fact that it results (as perhaps nothing else would) in the rapid concentration of vast resources of money and energy where it is needed. Progress in America is achieved in starts and jerks and crazy swerves but at least every American has been able to believe that it does occur – and in the past they have often been right.

This invincible optimism, this splendid assurance that there is no difficulty so great and no obstacle so high that it cannot be surmounted by the application of American technology and idealism have always produced in me (as in other world-weary Europeans) admiration and envy and scepticism in about equal proportions, but I have never had any reason before to doubt that Americans themselves would continue to display them.

These last six weeks have taught me otherwise. It now seems to me that the experience of the last four years has undermined and for the time being almost destroyed the old optimism. And perhaps it is not surprising. Billions of dollars, the whole physical weight of American military technology, and the moral weight of American democracy have been exerted to produce a victory in Vietnam; but the war continues to drag on. Vast resources of goodwill and money have been expended on the programmes of the Great Society, but so far as most Americans can see, all that happens as a result is that the Negro population goes berserk, the student population expresses its gratitude by occupying university buildings and shouting obscenities at the police, and the incidence of violent crime goes up by 15 per cent in a year.

These failures, unlike the other earlier failures, cannot simply be ignored. They lie at the root of American society. Their consequences are constantly being repeated in the most painful way, and the cumulative effect of these repetitions has been a crisis of self-confidence far deeper than the failures themselves really warrant. They are not only individual humiliations; they cast doubt on the most important element of the American Dream – that it is actually within reach. The moment at which large numbers of people begin to suspect that it might be unattainable is a crucial and dangerous turning point.

In theory a number of different attitudes to this crisis are possible. The first is to question the whole basis on which the system is founded – and this indeed is what many American commentators tell themselves (and their readers) that the country is doing. America, we are told constantly, is in the midst of a crisis of identity. 'What sort of a nation are we?' asked the late Robert Kennedy. Senator Eugene McCarthy has tried to ask radical questions about foreign policy, and was either misunderstood or slapped down by the Establishment. The yippies and hippies and college students are trying to ask fundamental questions about domestic policy, but their ideas have been too anarchic and most of them are not prepared to undertake the sheer hard work involved in political conversion.

These are perfectly good questions, but they do not in fact seem to be the questions most Americans are asking. There is as yet no really widespread scepticism in the US about the purposes of American society. Democracy, liberty, puritan morality, free enterprise – and the right and duty of the US to advance and defend them in the world – remain fixed and certain principles to the majority of Americans irrespective of failures, setbacks, and uncertainties.

Since these ideals are assumed to be essentially sound, some other explanation and some other remedy has to be found within the existing system for the failures which have occurred. And as it happens Nixon and Wallace offer one set and Humphrey the other. The fact that all three have rather stale old-fashioned styles has led a good many people to assume that they are all out of the same drawer. Nothing could be further from the truth. They express entirely different philosophies, and they appeal to an entirely different set of emotions.

The Nixon-Wallace reaction to failure and loss of confidence is defensive – to fall back on the bare minimum of certainty. Stop taking risks, stop stirring things up. Clamp down on troublemakers of all sorts, cut out welfare programmes that are wasteful, reorganize those that are successful, restore America to quiescence and hope that time and the Constitution will heal its problems.

The Humphrey reaction, on the contrary, is offensive. His absurd 'politics of joy' are simply a stubborn reaffirmation of the old optimism of the past. Success and happiness are just round the corner if we will only reach for it. There was nothing wrong with the Great Society except that there was not enough of it. So far as it went it was a howling success, except that the Congress would not give it enough money.

In logic, Humphrey has far the better case. Considering everything, the Great Society has indeed been a success. To take only two statistics relating to the anti-poverty programme – in 1961, 55 per cent of Negroes were below the poverty line, only 35 per cent are there today. In 1961 only 9 per cent of Negroes earned as much as the medium income of the US, today 35 per cent do so.

The argument that many of the programmes need reorganizing (particularly in order to give cities more control of funds) cannot be seriously disputed; but it does not vindicate the trend of Nixon's and Wallace's argument. Reorganization will help the programmes but without vast new infusions of funds they will not keep pace with the expectations which have been aroused. It is first and foremost a shortage of money which holds back the education programmes, and the

**124**

job programmes, and the cities programmes today, and since it is calculated by the administration that the end of the Vietnam War will only release $3–4 billion a year for new programmes, a fresh political impetus is clearly essential.

But where is it to come from? The trouble is that logic does not appeal to frightened and deeply dispirited people – middle-class suburbanites with homes to protect from 'them', blue-collar workers with record salaries to protect from welfare-state taxation, Southerners 'betrayed' by 'nigger-loving' Democrats, intellectuals disgusted with LBJ, truckers with sons in Vietnam and businessmen groaning under high interest rates.

Inspiration might succeed where logic fails. But the optimism which Humphrey preaches, though it is of the classic American brand, is threadbare from constant use and he is merely repeating endlessly what people have already ceased to believe. Perhaps the sheer repetition will itself revive their self-confidence, but the chances are that the majority will prefer to retreat for a while to a well-defended psychological fortress under the banner of 'law and order' and 'America first' – leaving a desolated countryside in the hands of the Negroes and the young.

*Financial Times*, 6 September 1968

# How Snobbish are the Americans?

*The Protestant Establishment* is already a famous book in the United States. It deserves to be. It tells the Top People of America that they are a bunch of snobs and racists who have betrayed their status, their money and their birth and richly deserve the oblivion to which history is consigning them. Of course, this has often been observed before but never in such impeccable academic terms and in tones of such poignant regret.

The author, E. Digby Baltzell, is a competent professional sociologist and is therefore able to document his case with formidable literary and historical zeal as well as adorning it with elegant logical models. But what gives his book its great force and distinction is the fact that he is also an upper-class Philadelphian of unimpeachable lineage and therefore wears with gloomy grace the toga of the Elder Cato recalling his fellow patricians to the stern duties of ruling the republic.

His central theme is well suited to this task. America, he assumes, needs an open aristocracy or representative upper class to give authoritative moral leadership and maintain a continuous cultural tradition. In the beginning it had one in the White Anglo-Saxon Protestant (WASP, for short) Establishment, which, until about the middle of the nineteenth century, maintained its virility and power by regular assimilation of self-made men of the middle class – including Catholics and Jews. A second period followed from the Civil War to the turn of the century when the Establishment, threatened by the immigrant hordes, became more and more exclusive but continued to hold a genuine authority because it still contained a large proportion of the national talent. In the present degenerate phase – presumably the last – the top WASPs have become a still more exclusive caste, less and less representative of the country at large and less and less willing or able to meet their responsibilities. They are now, on the whole, snobbish, anti-Jewish, colour-conscious and frivolous; and America is now at a stage where authority is in danger of degenerating into authoritarianism and an organic social order 'becomes an atomized horde of fearful, alienated and manipulated individuals'.

This romantic, conservative Jeremiad is confessedly based on de Tocqueville's classic diagnosis of the causes of the fall of the *ancien régime* and the analogy is worked out with sombre brilliance for the American environment over the last century.

But is it valid? Anyone who has had his antecedents sniffed over by an old-fashioned Ivy Leaguer, or been to a point-to-point in Virginia, or lunched with conformist young executives at a big corporation, or tried to take a Jewish girl to a private dance, or seen a swarthy-complexioned stranger being ignored in a country club, knows that the sheer ruthlessness of American upper-class snobbery can sometimes make the English variety look positively Franciscan in its charity. This may show the rottenness of individuals, perhaps even of a group, but it does not prove that the ideals Mr Baltzell admires are dead.

Mr Baltzell agrees that most of the old aristocratic *institutions* have moved enough with the times to remain representative. The Ivy League colleges are now crammed with clever parvenus of doubtful parentage. The clubs are full of intellectual Jewish 'riff-raff' such as Walter Lippmann and Arthur Schlesinger. Above all the Democratic Party had the effrontery to nominate and then get elected to the presidency an upstart Irish Catholic with the manners and money of an aristocrat. The big corporations have been slower to shake off the old conventions but even they are being forced to move by the tremendous competiton for talent. Mr Baltzell would no doubt argue that the new products of these old institutions are a rootless first-generation élite but it is hard for the outsider to see that they lack the essential virtues and ideals of a competent and responsible ruling class.

One suspects in the end that what Mr Baltzell is really complaining about is that the traditional leaders of the Republican Party are mostly a sorry, unaristocratic lot. Here, indeed, he's on solid ground. The tragedy of the Goldwater incident was precisely that the senator from Arizona (half-Jewish, by the way) was nominated as the result of a Western revolt against the cliquish upper-class Eastern Establishment. The radical Right might never have been so virulent if its leaders had been admitted as equals by the East at an earlier stage nor would it have been victorious if the Establishment hadn't been so lackadaisical.

Mr Baltzell makes the same interesting case about McCarthyism which in some of its manifestations represented a mid-Western Republican revolt against the smooth Eastern boys in the State Department.

Mr Baltzell is quite lyrical in his gloom about such examples of democracy unbridled by aristocratic authority; but even these seem to prove the corruption of the Republicans rather than of the republic. For Goldwaterism was trounced by the sheer common sense of the herd, and McCarthyism was allowed to flourish by the two copper-bottomed Republican 'aristocrats' who could really have stopped it – President Eisenhower and Senator Taft.

*Observer*, *26 September 1965*

# The Limits of the Presidency

The most intolerable of the many intolerable burdens of the president of the United States is that everyone thinks he is God, when he is not. Whenever, as at present, the papers are full of phrases about 'awe-inspiring power', 'the lonely pinnacle of responsibility' and so forth, it is as well to recall the words of Harry Truman musing, in the dying days of his own presidency, on the problems of his successor.

'Poor old Ike,' he said. 'He is used to the Army. He will say "I have decided on this or that" and he will give his orders – and then nothing will happen.'

Poor old Nixon. He, like every other presidential candidate, has claimed the power to call spirits from the vasty deep. But will they come when he calls to them?

In some ways, it is true, the power of the presidency has increased, is increasing, and in the opinion of a good many Americans, ought to be diminished. A president may move vast armies about the globe without so much as a by-your-leave from anyone, he can involve his country by degrees in a major war, he can even 'mash the button' without anyone being able to stop him.

The Federal government, of which he is the head, is now involved in the smallest details of the lives of the people and has even usurped many of the powers originally reserved under the US Constitution to the individual states. The president disposes of a gargantuan civil service with almost limitless powers of hiring and firing, and he can mobilize, through the prestige of his office, huge resources of brains and goodwill for the solution of any difficulty.

Confronted by this array of powers the ordinary citizen naturally falls back in stunned amazement. And yet, as if the powers themselves were not enough, everything else conspires to magnify them. The Press and television concentrates the whole force of its converage upon the presidency, dramatizing, personalizing and often, inevitably, distorting.

Equally, in the world outside, the president is not simply the head of the American administration. He has become the embodiment of the United States, Uncle Sam in the flesh, and the 'last, best hope of earth' in person. He is expected, almost single-handed, to feed the hungry, preserve the peace, defend the right and still keep his nose out of everyone else's affairs.

These are prodigious expectations – and the fact is that the real power of the presidency has not nearly kept up with them and in several ways has actually receded. In a sense this is fortunate for us all since only a Divine tyrant could fulfil them. But the sense of disappointment remains – and for perfectly well-defined reasons.

The original checks and balances of the American Constitution are still in existence. The Congress can frustrate the will of any president in the vast area of policy where he is obliged to consult it.

There are large and growing fields of industrial and field activity which the president is powerless to control except in the most superficial fashion. Above all, the sheer size of the problems which the president is expected by the public to solve has meant the creation of a bureaucracy of such prodigious inertial mass that it is virtually impossible for the president to move it.

These are the difficulties to which President Truman was referring. They almost entirely engulfed President Eisenhower, and though the phenomenal energies of Presidents Kennedy and Johnson have kept them at bay to some extent, they have certainly not receded with the years. To take only three examples – President Kennedy's ability to act in foreign affairs was curtailed by the fact that in spite of ruthless efforts he was never able to master the CIA, which drew him into the Bay of Pigs, or the State Department, which he complained was like 'a bowl of jelly'.

President Johnson's control over the economy was undermined by the Federal Reserve Board's quite frequent (and constitutionally guarded) refusal to follow the monetary dictates of the US Treasury, and more importantly by the refusal of the chairman of the House Ways and Means Committee during many months to sponsor the administration's tax increase.

The president can in theory surmount these obstacles. But he can almost never do so by main force. He must try to achieve his ends by horse trading, by threatening the withdrawal of patronage or Federal funds, by changing the personnel at the top and by appealing to public opinion – and in many cases he will try entirely in vain.

Furthermore, he only has a finite store of political credit with the public, only so much patronage and only so much personal time to devote to any single problem.

No one expects a great deal from Mr Nixon. He has had a bad Press and he is the standard-bearer of a party which has traditionally made a virtue out of the minimum of government activity. But even so we may still be expecting too much – not because Mr Nixon is a weak or reactionary man (though in some ways I believe he is), but simply because many of the things we hope for America or desire from her it is not within the power of any president, good or bad, to guarantee.

Broadly speaking the world expects and hopes three things from America in the next four years – that she should display an enlightened interest in the outside world, that her economy should continue to prosper and that what might be called the quality of American society should improve.

On the first two points President Nixon will have considerable room for manoeuvre – particularly at first. But he will be quite unable, for instance, to persuade the 91st Congress to increase aid to underdeveloped countries substantially and even if the Vietnam War ends, the chances of anyone successfully diverting large sums to social welfare, far less passing new social legislation, are remote in the extreme.

So far as the 'quality of life' issue is concerned, the most liberal president would find the situation beyond him as things stand at present. For example, only another catastrophe is likely to make the Congress pass a serious law for the control of guns and only another summer of riots will persuade the Congress and the city governments and the states that a superhuman effort still has to be made to eradicate the slums and ghettoes.

As for the more intangible flaws in American society – the crude commercialism, say, or the violence, or the obsession with sex – they are beyond the power of any single president, however elevated or idealistic, to eradicate.

Within these limitations there is, of course, much scope for success or failure in a relative sense. Relative success will depend upon Mr Nixon's ability to mobilize the system to achieve imaginative, if limited, results. Relative failure will result from his not knowing the right levers to pull or his refusal even to try. Triumph or tragedy will depend upon the mood of his countrymen – their willingness to take risks or their apathy.

*Financial Times, 1968*

# Looking Back on LBJ

President Johnson, in moods of depression, often used to paint a pathetic picture of himself in retirement, sitting in a rocking-chair on the porch of the LBJ ranch, 'just watching the Pedernales River roll past'. And quite right, too. It is part of the satisfying Victorian mythology which surrounds the American president that the lad who rises from log cabin to the pinnacle of power should be dashed once more into the depths of obscurity before he gets too big for his breeches.

Tradition also demands that as the world savours the gloomy moral of this tale, a few crumbs of sympathy should be thrown towards the hero of it – 'at any rate he was a decent man', 'he did his best and perhaps a little bit more', and all the rest of it. Later on, perhaps, as the new president gets into a mess, this sympathy will harden into reinstatement as intellectuals discover new virtues in his predecessor and make a good deal of money writing themselves into the history of the period – on his side.

The first stage of this process is already under way for LBJ, but it simply will not do. As a man and as a president he has shown tremendous virtues – guts, intelligence, energy, and, on many issues, great vision. He has been consistently underrated by the commentators and subjected to a contemptibly nasty campaign of vilification by the liberal Establishment, based as much on intellectual and social snobbery as anything else.

Yet I cannot believe that, when history draws the balance between his virtues and his failings and failures, the sun will come out on his side.

He has not, on balance, been a good president, still less a great one, for the simple reason that he has frustrated all his own best purposes by the one, single overwhelming error of the Vietnam War. It is all very well in the week of his retirement to count up his achievements, but wherever one looks at his record, even at its best, the baleful influence of the war overshadows everything.

Take foreign affairs. Johnson was very far from being the crude bungler here that his critics may quote. In particular, his attitude both to the Russians and to General de Gaulle was actually more subtle and restrained than Kennedy's busy interventionist leanings. He was more inclined to make approaches to Eastern Europe on a realistic basis and much more inclined to influence events in Western Europe with a light touch. Yet he could not escape the difficulty that Russia's position in the communist world was bound to make her show hostility to American policy in Vietnam or that the war was a godsend to de Gaulle in his arguments for a third-force Europe.

Again, the Great Society legislation – which is Johnson's ultimate justification – was desperately mauled by the war. Much of the programme – particularly medical care for the old, Federal aid for education and the anti-poverty programme – was a genuine breakthrough, and whatever the Kennedy lobby may say it was an achievement for which Johnson deserves most of the credit.

Some of it, certainly, was conceived under Kennedy, and Johnson was undoubtedly helped by the wave of emotional sympathy which supported him after Kennedy's murder. But in their final form the new measures were the product of Johnson's particular sense of social injustice, and the fact that they were passed was largely due to his brilliant exploitation of his own Congressional experience.

But it was still a hollow victory. Almost all legislation in the US has to be considered as 'enabling' law which only becomes a reality if the President has sufficient political leverage to see that it is properly financed and executed within the satrapies of powerful state politicians.

This is precisely what Johnson has lacked for the past two years. Expenditure on the war has given his Congressional critics the excuse to starve his programmes of funds, while his growing unpopularity in the country made it almost impossible to defeat the vested interests of machine politicians determined to keep the incursions of the Federal government into their territory under control.

This analysis could be extended almost indefinitely. The war has certainly affected the Foreign Aid programme and it has almost certainly influenced the racial situation indirectly by adding to the frustrations of the Negroes, the tensions of the white population and the administrative burdens of the President. In short the social progress of the US and its influence in the world have probably been set back by a decade and it is very hard to see how any foreign war, let alone an unsuccessful one, can be held to justify this result unless the integrity of the state concerned were actually threatened.

This, I believe, will be the judgement of historians on Johnson's presidency and it will be uninfluenced by arguments that he could not have known the consequences of involvement in Vietnam, that he inherited the commitment from Kennedy, that his advisers were all in favour of sending in the Marines in March 1965, and so forth. History has to judge by results, and though it may conclude that Johnson was a tragic failure it will still conclude that he failed.

Nor, I believe, will it entirely absolve him of a reasonable human responsibility for what has happened, for the causes of his error lie, to some extent, in his own character. It seemed to me as I watched him get further and further into the mire that he was the victim to quite a large extent of forces over which he could not have control. He was, for a start, under the shadow of Kennedy, and one can imagine what his opponents would have said if his reaction to the situation as he found it had been to countermand Kennedy's commitments to South Vietnam, to withdraw Kennedy's 16,000 'advisers' and to hand over the country to Ho Chi Minh.

Secondly, it is enormously difficult for a lay president, pressed for time and hemmed in by political considerations, to disregard the advice of his senior aides and of the military potentates, especially when these happen to coincide. Kennedy discovered this to his cost in the Bay of Pigs episode, and Johnson was another sufferer under the same system. The American Constitution is supposed to be a matter of checks and balances, but the sheer size of the Executive and the rapidity with which the pyramid of responsibility narrows means that where the Executive has to act by itself, as it must to all intents and purposes in matters of national security, there is a very little balance to be found.

Just the same, one can see in retrospect that these difficulties do not really offer an adequate excuse. The fact is that Johnson himself firmly believed that it was necessary for American interest to keep the communists out of South Vietnam. He had said as much in his memorandum to Kennedy after he had toured South-east Asia as Vice-President in May, 1961. The basic decision, he said, was whether to help Vietnam and Thailand or 'to throw in the towel in the area and pull back our defences to San Francisco and a fortress America concept

... we would say to the world in this case that we don't live up to treaties and don't stand by our friends. This is not my concept.'

One had only to talk to him for a short while to realize that he was out of his depth, for his conversation was loaded with superficial parallels between himself and Churchill and himself and Truman, though he had obviously never studied them properly. As a 'practical politician' he despised dogmatic theorizers and intellectuals, but it was precisely because he hardly ever read books that he was taken in by the theoreticians, and precisely because he was a fixer and not a dogmatic theorist that he could not recognize in Ho Chi Minh an opponent incapable of compromise.

The final charge against him, though, is that his vanity betrayed his political sense. His unwillingness to be shown wrong under any circumstances meant first that his position became unnecessarily inflexible and secondly that the 'credibility gap' between himself and the public widened so far that his effectiveness as president was weakened. The man who prided himself on knowing more about politics than anyone around him turned out to be incapable under pressure of sinking his own personality and recognizing when he was wrong.

Ultimately, of course, he did recognize it – and indeed it could be said that nothing became him in his office like the leaving of it – but that is poor consolation for a president who was determined to be one of the greatest in the history of the US.

It may be said that all this is really a demand for an impossibly high standard of character and competence in the American president. No man can do better than his best and this, assuredly, President Johnson performed in the face of a situation which was precisely that to which he was least well adapted by character and background. He did perform honourably, engagingly, often amusingly and sometimes even happily, but that is not what history will say – for history, alas, echoes Napoleon's criterion for a good general, that he should have luck.

*Financial Times, 17 January 1969*

# Vietnam and the American Mind

It is one of the clichés of political history that dictatorships are better at conducting a forceful foreign policy than democracies. Throughout the Cold War we have been used to commentators contrasting the feeble gyrations of the open societies of the West with the sometimes cumbersome but alarmingly effective operations of totalitarian regimes with no public opinion to worry about. Most of the discussion of the inter-Vietnam crisis has been cast firmly in this mould: on the one side the North Vietnamese, ruthless, devious and forcibly united; on the other the Americans, vacillating, fearful and restrained by domestic scruples and dissension.

Socialists find this general picture highly encouraging because it seems to show that 'the people' have more sense than their rulers. The Right is equally content because it seems to confirm the debilitating effects of excessive democracy, the permissive society and mass education. Just the same, the whole thesis is, in fact, dangerously over-simplified and, when applied to Vietnam, likely to be highly misleading about the way in which things will turn out in the future.

In the first place one of the things that strikes the outsider most forcibly about the whole history of the Vietnam War is how long it took for domestic political considerations to have much practical effect on it. At the outset American public opinion, if it had been consulted, would probably have supported President Kennedy's decision to put support troops into South Vietnam, but the fact is that Mr Kennedy did not bother much about this aspect of the affair. He simply acted on his own perception of American global interests.

President Johnson began to get worried – as well he might – when the war started to escalate in 1965, but he was able to take matters a very long way before opposition in the senate to the war and finally large-scale opposition in the country began to affect his policies. His initial decisions, like Kennedy's, were taken in accordance with the consensus in the foreign policy and defence establishments.

The second point that comes out very clearly is that American public opinion has never been really clear-cut about the war. The point here is not simply that there has always been at any given moment a sizeable minority of Americans who have felt either passionately for or passionately against the war – though that is certainly the case. The significant fact is that the majority had, and for that matter still have, a split mind on the subject. They are more or less weary of the war and want to get out of it, but they would also deeply resent it if the US were humiliated in the process.

The reality of the present situation depends upon this fact. The war was in effect 'lost' by 1969 and possibly earlier – by which I mean that there was probably nothing that the Americans could have done after that to prevent the eventual fall of South Vietnam to the communists, except by keeping a vast permanent army of occupation. President Nixon's 'Vietnamization' programme was really a confession of this defeat and certainly most Americans of my acquaintance have acknowledged in their hearts that it would probably entail the communization of the South at some future date, after the final withdrawal of the American presence.

What has happened in the last month is that the North Vietnamese have decided not to allow the US to lose gracefully in this fashion. They are not satisfied with success; they want victory. And Mr Nixon, rightly judging the mixed feelings of his electors, was bound to make some sharp reaction.

In other words, far from there having been a sustained struggle between the radical expansionist forces of the American Establishment, and the timid or restraining views of the American public, the development of the Vietnam War has been marked by confused interaction between a fairly clear-headed but not very efficient series of administrations and a distinctly confused but rather slow-moving body of public opinion.

The fact is that the average American, like the average man in most countries, is not by nature madly interested in foreign affairs. He is normally prepared to leave foreign policy to his leaders and to read foreign news in snippets on obscure inside pages of his local newspaper. Where foreign policy directly impinges upon him – in matters of war and peace or trade – he naturally becomes concerned more deeply, but even here he is prepared to take a good deal on trust until shooting actually starts or factories actually start closing down.

On the other hand he has strong nationalistic emotions. He wishes his country to be liked and respected and can be roused to short spasms of reaction to quite trivial slights, insults and ingratitude on the part of foreigners. Certainly, having been led into a war, he will be acutely unhappy unless he is able to claim some kind of victory, and the more expensive in blood, money and prestige the war has been, the greater this unhappiness will be.

All this is so obvious as to be scarcely worth setting down – except that so many people seem to have forgotten it. It seems, funnily enough, to have been overlooked by the Soviet government during the past few weeks – for how else can one explain the extraordinary risks the Russians have been taking except on the basis of a misappreciation of these factors?

The North Vietnamese behaviour in launching an offensive when they only had to sit back for a year or two and let South Vietnam fall into their lap is understandable on a number of hypotheses. The impetus in the North Vietnamese army may have been very great, or there may have been a deliberate calculation that by launching an offensive they could head off the dangerous possibility that the Russians and the Chinese might do a deal with the Americans at North Vietnam's expense.

What is really puzzling is the fact that important Russian officials should have been in Haiphong and Russian vessels in Haiphong harbour when the North Vietnamese offensive was launched. The first implies some Russian collusion at a time when the SALT talks and the Moscow visit of President Nixon (both of them, apparently, central to Russian policy) were hanging in the balance, and the second implies that the American reaction was unexpected. Did the Kremlin really believe that American public opinion was now so 'dovish' that the President could afford a humiliating débâcle in the South? It seems about the only plausible explanation.

The opposite mistake is made by those who assume that American public opinion is so violently united against the war that it will, over the long haul, cause the American administration to change entirely its traditional view of American national interests. The argument appears to be that isolationism, born of disillusionment, will now seize the American public and the Congress, and that they will promptly rush down the Gadarene slope to complete global irresponsibility –

dragging the administration with them. Europe will be denuded of American troops, and no American ally will be able henceforth to rely upon the support of any American administration when the going gets rough.

This argument seems to me to fly in the face of too many entrenched facts to be really plausible. It is certainly true that the old, world-wide crusade against communism is dead. The Nixon doctrine has already acknowledged this, and any president who got up next January and said the words of President Kennedy's inaugural – 'Let every nation know, whether it wish us well or ill, that we shall pay any price, bear any burden, meet any hardship, support any friend, oppose any foe, in order to assure the survival and success of liberty' – would be assumed to be at best a revolting cynic and at worst a raving lunatic.

The US will not bear *any* burden in defence of liberty. That is a blank cheque which will never be written again – for a number of reasons which have been discussed endlessly during the past two years. But that does not mean that the American Establishment intends to be stampeded by short-term emotion or even longer-term war-weariness into giving up geo-politics. Whoever is president – even the distinctly inward-looking Senator McGovern – and whatever resolutions may be passed by the Congress, American foreign policy for the foreseeable future will continue to be based on well-known foundations.

One of these is a viable great-power relationship with the Soviet Union. Such a relationship can only be conducted on the basis of variations on the status quo; and this seems to me to presuppose a limit, for instance, to the number of troops that the US will withdraw unilaterally from Europe. Massive withdrawals would risk upsetting the existing balance and have dangerous repercussions on other aspects of the Russian–American relationship. So long as this is so, I see no reason why the alliance should not survive. There will no doubt be strains and alarms and some troop reductions – but the essential elements seem to be secure.

The second foundation of American policy is bound to be the protection of a world-wide network of commerce and investment. An economically autarkic America engaged in a war of trade barriers and mounting capital restrictions might survive longer than most of the other combatants, but it would be an unpleasant experience for any American politician to try to sustain himself during the campaign against the fifth column of his own business community and labour force.

Of course foreign policy is not always conducted on a rational basis.

Mistakes are made and emotions aroused. But if one talks to American politicians and policy-makers at present – and I have had the opportunity to talk to a number recently – one does not get the impression that their mistakes are too likely to be of the dangerous kind. They will bend to the confused winds of public opinion, which are blowing around them at present, and some of their resulting actions may provoke anger and fear on this side of the Atlantic – particularly where trade and monetary policy are concerned.

It is a pity that with weak governments in Italy and Germany it may be hard for the Europeans to co-ordinate a cool, concerted reply. But the main thing is that the self-interest of the United States coincides on the great issues with that of Western Europe, and American public opinion is neither so coherent, so overpowering, or so foolish that it can undo this fact.

*Financial Times, 12 May 1972*

# When the Dominoes Begin to Fall

The astonishing crumbling of the bastions in Vietnam these last two weeks is the most poignant demonstration of the vanity of human wishes that fate and military incompetence have contrived since the destruction of the Athenian Expedition to Sicily. So it was for this that 50,000 Americans and God knows how many Vietnamese died; for this that $200 billion was poured out. To this end President Lyndon Johnson and his Great Society were ruined and the summit of American politics ceded to a bunch of political thugs. So much blood, so much treasure, so many words, so many consciences, expended for nothing and, indeed, less than nothing.

Much time and laborious sifting of evidence will have to go by before we shall be able to see this gigantic tragedy in perspective. As in the case of the Boer War (the nearest equivalent in modern times), the Left has the best tunes and the most persuasive singers, but it will be surprising if there are not many more or less convincing revisionist attacks, and some time about the year 2050 our grandchildren will conclude that it was all inevitable anyway.

Meanwhile, however, the American people – and the world at large – must face the situation as it is. It is now virtually certain that Saigon will fall – if not immediately, then within a couple of years at most. Even if it does not, Cambodia may be presumed to be lost and the chances of the Laotian coalition's surviving are remote. French Indochina having thus fallen after a thirty-year struggle, what will follow next? Anyone who lived in Washington during the 1960s, as I did, must be haunted at this moment by memories of the Domino Theory as expounded in endless briefings and interviews by Robert Macnamara and Dean Rusk, to say nothing of President Johnson himself.

The 'book' answer is that, for the time being at least, there is no reason to suppose that other dominoes will fall. Thailand and Malaysia both have economic and political resources to withstand a certain amount of pressure and insurgency. In the wider context of the balance of world power South-east Asia has already been discounted. Indeed, the disadvantages to the US of trying to hang on to it had been so vividly displayed for so long that it might almost be said to be a positive gain for American foreign policy to be rid of it at last. Neither China nor Russia can reasonably conclude from what had happened anything that they had not concluded three or four years ago.

This optimistic interpretation of recent events can even be extended so as to provide a magnificent vindication of President Nixon's foreign policy. An apologist might plausibly argue as follows: 'The Vietnam Peace Agreement two years ago was a two-way bet. Either the Thieu regime survived on its own account with only logistic support from the US (in which case all well and good) or if, very regrettably, it collapsed, then at least the American government would be distanced to some extent from the débâcle. In either case the policy of overall *détente* with the Soviet Union and communist China would ensure that global stability was maintained. We can now see the second of these bets paying off – the size of the dividend being easily computed by comparing the present calm state of the chancelleries with the frightful convulsions of paranoia that would have followed such a disaster twenty years ago at the height of the Cold War.'

Naturally we are not likely to hear this argument being put forward explicitly, either by Dr Henry Kissinger or President Gerald Ford. The administration's moral pressure on the American Congress will be kept up, and the charge is that had it not been for Congressional 'irresponsibility', none of the present disasters need have happened. If the US government had been allowed to spend the necessary amounts on support in armaments, President Thieu would not have felt obliged to evacuate the Highlands – the move from which, it is alleged, his military difficulties stem. Nevertheless, Mr Ford's insouciance is striking and significant. He, at any rate, is facing the inevitable with the air of a man who believes he has the important cards still in his hand.

But is he right? Can we really regard the collapse of Vietnam so coolly? The arguments on the other side need to be considered carefully before we relax. It is not only the question of what happens in South-east Asia now that American influence is drastically reduced that has to be debated. The whole state of America's relations with the rest of the world is in the balance.

In the first place, what light does the Vietnam affair throw upon the workings of the Nixon doctrine and Dr Kissinger's highly idiosyncratic style of diplomacy? The essence of the Nixon/Kissinger policy was that *détente* and military disengagement went hand in hand. The US could withdraw from the business of maintaining local stability by military means, thanks to the umbrella of super-power understanding. On the other hand, care had to be taken to compensate, by diplomatic means, for the loss of military muscle, otherwise local situations might get out of control and threaten the overall *détente*.

This policy has had some success, but its limitations are now coming to be more clearly seen. In Indochina, for instance, Russia and China have observed the rules of the game as laid down by Dr Kissinger. They held aloof (to at least the same extent as the US herself) from the military struggle and gave their blessing to the Geneva agreement. The trouble has been that one local participant, Hanoi, has not observed the regulations, and, having broken them, has put the US in the position of either having to accept an adverse result or else having to break the regulations herself with all that that might mean to relations with Russia and China.

The analogy with the Middle East is immediately obvious here, for, while it is true that Russia has been fishing rather more in those waters than in South-east Asia, her restraint has been fairly exemplary. The trouble has been that, from a 'disengaged' situation, the US has not had the diplomatic leverage to cope with the local situation to her own satisfaction. An American military guarantee to the State of Israel might have done the trick, but that would have broken the spirit of the Nixon doctrine, and possibly brought the US into direct confrontation with the Soviet Union.

The Vietnam collapse following so quickly upon Dr Kissinger's failure in the Middle East raises the spectre of other 'local' situations which might get out of control, and which the US has made herself virtually powerless to affect directly. Portugal is an obvious example. Iran, if anything should happen to the Shah, might be another. The whole concept of a stable world kept in equilibrium by a complex balance of relationships grouped around the central US–USSR understanding cannot take care of internal shifts of power, some of which may be of great international importance in an era of scarce energy resources and uncertain strategic perspectives. The capture of the Azores base and the Persian oilfield by forces favourable to Russia and hostile to America would, in themselves, be important changes to the balance of power. And coming after other reverses they might break up the game.

The situation is further complicated by the state of American opinion. At present Congress and public are reacting violently to the strains (financial, political and moral) of the last decade – and who shall blame them? Their perception of American interest, while not exactly isolationist, is more narrowly defined than at any time since 1947. Americans appear to be virtually unmoved by the prospect that Saigon will fall, and the spectacle of the American President of World Airways knocking South Vietnamese refugees off his aeroplane at Da Nang probably summarizes a widespread feeling of 'let's get the hell out of there'.

Even if Vietnam is followed by no more than the appearance of a communist government in Lisbon, some reaction seems to be highly likely to set in. The moralistic streak in American public life has not been removed simply by Dr Kissinger's say so, and there is no section of America more moralistic than the right wing. The proposition that it was reds in the State Department who sold out to the communists, which was Senator Joe McCarthy's cry in the early 1950s cannot be sustained this time since the State Department had almost no say in the matter since 1970. On the other hand an attack on the 'soft pinkos' in Congress may be a powerful Republican counter-attack.

These considerations leave out the whole question of the effect of apparent American losses on the balance in the Kremlin to say nothing of the effect on allies and waverers of all kinds. These effects may or may not be large. Just the same, if what the world is seeking is stability – and it surely is – then rapid shifts of fortune such as have occurred in Vietnam must be worrying. Not only do they alter the real balance of forces to some degree; they also, and far more importantly, undermine people's perception of what is stable. Gradual change is what diplomacy aims at and, if gradual change is impossible, then political skill must educate public opinion to be reconciled to something more rapid. The present directors of American foreign policy certainly cannot deliver public education and Vietnam must cast doubt on their ability to deliver gradual change itself.

# Watergate – the Damage to the Presidency

Conversations between a British visitor to Washington and his hosts, normally a little stilted at the outset, go with a swing these days.
– How are things in England?
– Not too good.
– Is that so? – Well it must be a relief to come to an even worse God-awful mess over here.
– Are you joking? You don't know when you're well off. Your inflation rate is still in single figures.
– So how would you like to swap your inflation rate for our president?

And so on. All good, clean, graveyard fun – and not much less painful because it is so obvious that the American situation is genuinely and fundamentally less serious than Britain's. The Watergate affair darkens the Washington horizon and the still rather insubstantial spectre of major recession haunts Wall Street, but elsewhere one is overwhelmed, as usual, by the vast underlying strength of the American economy, the openness and self-confidence of the society, and the supple durability of the political institutions.

I am writing this article, for example, in Tennessee, where a primary election for the governorship of the state is in full swing. There are no less than sixteen candidates for two party nominations, hardly any of whom will spend less than $100,000 on the race and several as much as $1 million – a lot of it their own cash. What makes them run? Greed? Probably not – there have been very few recent financial scandals attached to this office. Desire for power? Certainly – but power of a limited degree and duration. The Federal government has usurped much of the power of the states, and under the Tennessee Constitution the governor must bow out after his four-year term.

In the end, of course, the determining factor is sheer vitality expressing itself through a powerful political tradition. It is an exhilarating force to encounter – even a rather awe-inspiring one. But it is also deceptive; for it suggests to many conservatives that Watergate is irrelevant. 'Get out into the sticks,' one is told, 'and you will soon see all this squalid nonsense in perspective.' All this is true, up to a point, and yet it leaves two important things out of account.

The first is what one might call the psychological factor. The presidency is still, as it has always been, the visible symbol of the state and tone of American society, and its eclipse has all sorts of unsettling side-effects. In this respect people in Tennessee are scarcely less affected than those in Washington by the realization that the White House has been occupied during the past six years by a bunch of political thugs. Some are infected with cynicism, others are profoundly disturbed, but few are untouched. On this, more in another article. For the moment, however, let us concentrate on the second reason why the damage to the presidency really does matter – the practical factor.

Watergate has visibly harmed the policy-making functions of American government. This assertion is naturally denied strenuously by members of the administration; but the results are clearly discernible all over Washington. The wheels of government continue to turn. Papers pass across desks, meetings are held, day-to-day decisions are taken, laws are passed, departmental budgets are approved. But the mainspring of the whole system is broken.

The Congress, particularly a Democratic Congress facing a Republican administration in the last two years of its term, requires firm and patient handling. Appeals to the public must be made over its head, other forces brought to bear in aid of the government position, key senators and Congressmen must be persuaded, cajoled or threatened. The administration itself, being like every other administration a fearful tangle of warring agencies and interests, remains in a state of perilous deadlock unless the President intervenes to impel it in a particular direction.

President Nixon has neither the time nor the authority to exercise these functions. The ramifications of the Watergate affair, and the assault on the White House are so persistent and varied – new revelations and accusations appear every day – that it is inconceivable that Mr Nixon, beseiged in San Clemente or Washington, can devote more than half his normal attention to affairs of state. And even when he does exert his full pressure, what happens? As often as not bureaucratic opposition continues to fight a rearguard action, the Congress refuses to take the slightest political risk, and finally the public undermines presidential purposes by withholding its confidence.

Washington abounds with domestic examples of this paralysis, ranging from the question of land use and the energy crisis to the difficulty – even more acute than usual – of putting together an economic strategy acceptable to the Treasury, the Federal Reserve, the Budget Bureau, the various Congressional bodies and the business community. Even more interesting are the external examples – more interesting, but also, it must be said, more surprising, for as the apologists of the administration are quick to point out, it is in foreign affairs that President Nixon has had his main successes. Watergate has not prevented a Middle East settlement. It has not, apparently, had any serious effects on East–West *détente* nor has it been the slightest hindrance to a most remarkable improvement in US–European relations during the last three or four months. Henry Kissinger is in the State Department, and all's right with the world.

This interpretation of the situation is perfectly correct so far as it goes, but it does not do justice to the fundamental problems of attention and authority which apply in this field as in others. The whole argument over the Moscow summit meeting three weeks ago illustrates the difficulty. The State Department, in the person of Dr Kissinger, wishes to keep the dialogue with the Russians afloat and to stop what now threatens to become a ruinously expensive arms race in the 1980s. He therefore argues that the US should be prepared to exercise considerable restraint in the deployment of nuclear missiles in the near future.

The Pentagon, in the person of Dr James Schlesinger the Defence Secretary, possesses not only an institutional interest in maintaining and improving armaments but also a highly sophisticated and forcefully presented counter-argument about the de-stabilizing effect of nuclear parity between the superpowers at anything more than low levels of missile armaments. The water is muddied still further by the situation in Congress where the Conservative Democrat Senator Jackson is thundering about the betrayal. Outside, the liberal Jewish community is demanding pressure on behalf of the Russian Jews, and the great American public is preparing to resist, at the polling stations, tax increases to pay for armaments or anything else.

In normal times this battle would, with a bit of luck, be resolved by the simple expedient of the president first taking a rational decision, then playing off the Congressional forces against one another and going through to win. In this case the procedure has not been possible.

The president went to Moscow knowing (a) that large concessions to the Russians might lose him the support of the conservative senators whom he will need to prevent the success of the impeachment campaign; (b) that total failure in Moscow would be bad for his last remaining asset – his image as a creative international statesman; (c) that the next Congress may be so violently liberal as a response to Watergate that it is almost impossible to predict what money will be available for defence expenditure next year; (d) that Dr Kissinger is under heavy and increasing attack for his alleged part in the Watergate fringe activity of illegal telephone-tapping.

The administration argues, plausibly enough, that in practice none of these preoccupations alters the outcome of the Moscow talks in the slightest since the Russians were not prepared to do business on the subject of nuclear warheads except on absolutely prohibitive terms. But this apology misses the point. The president's freedom of manoeuvre was in reality severely curtailed, and the accident that the Russians, as it were, rescued him from the necessity of having to strain at his bonds cannot alter the fact or diminish its significance for the future. *Détente* from now on is likely to be at best at a standstill and possibly on the decline.

On the subject of relations with Europe much the same is true. It so happens that events have conspired to take most of the fury out of the mid-Atlantic storm that raged from the middle of last year until a month or two ago. The dollar overhang has disappeared, the Middle East war has ended, the energy crisis has partially receded, the governments of Britain, France and Germany have all changed and become more congenial to Washington and more realistic about the true balance of power within the Alliance.

All this is to the good. The trouble is that, thanks to Watergate, the US administration is neither ready to profit from the opportunity offered by this rearrangement of the pieces, nor in a position to act quickly and effectively if things go wrong in the future. Some observers in Washington argue, of course, that 'creative action' by the US is precisely what the Western Alliance has suffered from most in the past and needs least today, especially under a Secretary of State whose feelings towards Europe are as ambivalent as Dr Kissinger's. But even if this rather timid proposition is accepted, the existing stability is a precarious one. An economic crisis, a renewal of the energy problem, a quarrel within NATO, a haggle over trade (the Trade Bill is still hung up in Congress) – indeed, any unforeseen circumstances whose resolution requires action agreed by more than one American department for institutions would not infallibly be tackled with any great speed, resolution or tact while the President is tossed hither and thither on the waves of the Watergate scandal and while the old Eastern Establishment, which is the repository of much of the collective American wisdom about Europe, is either unwilling or unable to influence policy.

It does not seem likely that this situation will change much in the next two years. If Mr Nixon is acquitted, he will remain tarnished in exactly the same way until he leaves office. If he is successfully impeached, then Mr Gerald Ford can hardly be expected to fill the foreign policy vacuum. Old hands in Washington draw comparisons, ominously enough, between the scandals of the Harding regime followed by the isolationist incompetence and paralysis of Hoover. One does not need to go that far to see that we are entering a period in which the United States is likely to be unable to exercise her full strength. That strength remains and will be fitfully and unpredictably felt in the outside world – sometimes for good and sometimes not – but the culmination of the Vietnam War and Watergate has had an effect on the essential institutions of American government, which it would take a whole new generation of politicians to erase.

*Financial Times*, *19 July 1974*

# The Impeachment Begins

The long drawn out tragedy of President Nixon is clearly the highest of high drama, and with the start of the debate in the Judiciary Committee of the House of Representatives the curtain has now risen on the final act. Aristotle himself would have approved the classic arrangement of elements. The great man, benefactor of his country; the flawed character and unholy pride; the chastisement by the gods, worked with fiendish appropriateness through the victim's own weaknesses; the crashing reversal of fortune. All that is lacking is the final ruin and the final divine reconciliation, and while the second of these may be difficult to achieve there is no longer much doubt about the first. The Committee will almost certainly vote for impeachment and so will the House. The Senate may fail to convict, but Mr Nixon will be disgraced.

And yet for all these undeniably impressive ingredients the key to the spectacle remains, to the outsider, curiously elusive. As in revivals of Aeschylus or Sophocles, characters whose motives have seemed painfully clear suddenly act in inexplicable ways. Their values, which we assumed were the same as our own, turn out to be subtly different. Our critical faculties are aroused and our emotions turned off.

There are many examples of these oddities in the Watergate saga. Why, for instance, did the President make tapes of all his conversations in the first place? And why, when the going began to get rough, did he not make a bonfire of them on the White House lawn, confronting the courts and the Prosecutor with a *fait accompli* which he could have justified as a defence of executive privilege? These are questions to which even Americans offer divergent answers.

Some put down the original recording to the President's suspicious, hunted personality. Others explain that the new law making the sale of historical papers taxable says nothing about tapes. The President, prudent man, was trying to amass an archive which he could sell for several million dollars tax free. As for his astounding failure to destroy the evidence – was it some strange, residual sense of scruple, or a desire to retain ammunition with which to destroy John Dean and other friends-turned-enemy? Impossible to say, but in any case how can any European entirely comprehend any of these motives without having lived in a society which is (a) so dominated by money as America and (b) so deeply imbued with a consciousness of law?

Another obvious puzzle is why the President seems to have destroyed some damaging bits of evidence by erasing parts of the tapes, but left others, possibly equally damaging, untouched. He seems, even now, to be unaware of how deeply offensive his conduct has been, and can therefore hardly distinguish between what is political dynamite and what is not. The 'goddams' are deleted in deference to the susceptibilities of the Bible Belt, but conversations strongly suggestive of cover-up, victimization and illegality are left in.

The explanation for this almost certainly lies in the extreme isolation of the Nixon entourage in Washington. The White House is often portrayed these days as a beleaguered garrison, even a Hitlerite bunker about to be engulfed; but in reality it has been like that for most of the Nixon years. Perhaps the most revealing of all the endless quotations in the transcripts is the passage in the famous conversation between the President and John Mitchell on 22 March 1973, in which Mr Nixon compares his own actions with those of President Eisenhower, who dismissed his close aide Sherman Adams for accepting presents in payment for favours received.

'Now let me make this clear,' said Mr Nixon, 'I, I, I, thought it was, uh, very, uh, cruel thing as it turned out what happened to Adams. I don't want it to happen to Watergate ... That's what Eisenhower, that's all he cared about – Christ, "be sure he was clean" ... But I don't look at it that way. And I just – that's the thing I'm really concerned with. We're going to protect our people if we can.'

In other words, loyalty to one's subordinates represents a higher morality than 'cleanliness'. A stonewall solidarity is not only proved, it is a positive duty because it is only in this way that the implacably hostile forces of the Eastern Democratic Establishment and the liberal press can be kept at bay. As the President remarks elsewhere in the context of his 'enemies list', this was 'war' – and in a war, self-preservation becomes the supreme law.

This point of view is perfectly explicable in rational terms but is only emotionally understandable in the context of the whole social history of the Nixon presidency – its lower-middle-class rootless, Western and mid-Western basis; its self-righteousness and yet sense of inferiority; its strange mixture of defensive puritanism and compulsive materialism; its antipathy to Democratic liberalism – and Democratic liberalism's total contempt for and lack of sympathy with it. To Nixon's aides, like Haldeman and Ehrlichman, the capture of the White House in 1968 must have seemed only the beginning of a desperate struggle for survival in the midst of a completely uncongenial environment. The liberal Hosts of Midian could be seen prowling around the camp for six years ready to pick off any straggler, and what has happened in Watergate merely shows them massing predictably for the final assault.

All this, which the outsider can dimly see but finds hard to feel, is an important part of the Watergate drama. But the really central conundrum and the one which robs Watergate of much of its emotive power in non-American eyes is why in the world the Congress and the American public have been so hesitant about drawing the obvious conclusion from the evidence.

It is a truism, of course, that Americans revere the presidency, but when all is said and done the President is only an elected official whom the Founding Fathers of the Republic expressly provided should be capable of being removed by due process and without any vast taradiddle being made about it. No reasonably objective person reading the transcripts can really fail to be convinced that the President is guilty at the very least of attempting to pervert the course of justice and of attempting (probably successfully) to abuse his power for political and financial ends. So why not get rid of him and be done with it?

After hawking this tiresomely naive question around the US for the last three weeks, I have found a wide variety of responses. At the most practical end of the spectrum there are narrow political calculations. Republican Congressmen with safe majorities have to consider the outrage of their Conservative constituents as a betrayal of the party leader. There is a great deal of fussing and puffing on Capitol Hill about 'conscience' and 'history', but it would be naive to suppose that at least some Democrats have not worked out that they would prefer to go into the 1976 election with a discredited Nixon still sitting in the White House rather than with Mr Ford – a 'nice guy' doing his best in difficult circumstances.

Another equally practical, though less partisan, group is extremely dubious about the wisdom of creating a vacuum at the centre of American politics at this moment. To look forward in troubled times to at least two years of low-quality government – or to expect the Congress to fill the executive gap – are equally unattractive options even to many Democrats. Nixon, for all his faults, has experience and the ability to pick able subordinates. Mr Ford is at best an unknown quantity, at worst a fourth-rate disaster.

Again, there is a no-nonsense school of doubters. American politics, they argue, is inevitably a bit shady at the edges – just as American business is. It is reasonable enough to insist that the President does not commit illegal acts but to demand a complete abstention from cover-up for subordinates is to ask for the moon. Everyone does it, they say – and they point to Senator Kennedy who is said to have successfully covered up some aspects of the Chappaquidick affair.

These arguments shade naturally into more philosophical and fundamental fears about the longer-term consequences of impeachment. To many Conservatives, indeed many ordinary un-political Americans, it is simply a matter of instinct that the Head of State, like the flag, must be supported. To attack him is to attack law and order; to remove him is the equivalent of regicide. Such feelings come naturally, but they can be satisfactorily rationalized. If it is once shown that impeccable, even impossible, standards of conduct are required of the President on pain of instant removal, where is it all going to end?

Impeachment is the nuclear weapon of American politics. Drop it and you not only devastate friend and foe alike, you also have to start thinking about proliferation. Once one president is removed, may not the Congress acquire a taste for the process? The balance of the American system, struck at the outset round an equality in power, now depends for its stability and effectiveness upon a strong, even preponderant executive; to try to restore the pristine system by deliberately creating presidential weakness is a recipe for chaos and disaster.

Such arguments as these may not seem very convincing to the outsider but they are the deeply felt reaction to the crisis of many millions of Americans. It is easy to mock Mr Doar, the Democratic Counsel to the Judiciary Committee, for beginning his summing up the other day with a stammering apology: 'For me to speak like this – I can hardly believe I am speaking as I do or thinking as I do – the awesomeness of this is so – so tremendous . . .' But it is an authentic voice.

It is even easier to dismiss as sentimental rubbish the much-peddled **154** proposition that the whole Watergate process proved the strength of American institutions and the decency of the American public and politicians. The self-satisfaction of this belief is irritating, but there is no denying that given the strength of American feelings in the contrary sense, the true wonder is not that impeachment should have taken so long to get under way but that it should now be in train at all.

*Financial Times*, *26 July 1974*

# The Drawbacks of Gary Hart

## New York

The breakthrough of Senator Gary Hart in the Democratic primary elections is, frankly, a bit scary. I am not against Hart personally. In fact, whenever I have met or talked to him in the past there has been nothing whatever about him to belie the impression, which anyone would get from seeing him on television, of a 'pretty nice guy', reasonably intelligent, reasonably good-looking, reasonably liberal, reasonably (though not excessively) industrious.

He listens well, he seems open-minded and (unlike Governor Reagan when he campaigned for the Republic nomination) he has taken the trouble to travel quite widely over the years and acquire a nodding acquaintance with the main international issues. In short, though the press is digging away busily in the hope of discovering a guilty secret in his youthful past, he is a model citizen and a perfectly respectable senator for the state of Colorado.

The trouble is that there is no reason to suppose that on any objective criterion he is more likely to make a good president of the United States than anyone else of his age, class and background.

As far as his rivals in the primaries go, he has less experience of government than Mondale, less experience of command than Glenn and less gift of the gab than Jackson. He might, of course, like President Truman (to use a most obvious, post-war example) turn out to be a winner in spite of all previous appearances of mediocrity. But isn't there something badly wrong with a system which forces the US to put its all on an outside chance?

Two answers to this question are normally offered over here. The first is that Mr Hart has not yet won the nomination, far less the presidency. The spring primaries and caucuses that he has carried constitute a tiny base of the voters, and even if these victories create a momentum which gives him the candidacy of his party, he will be subjected to an examination of an altogether more searching and serious kind during the summer and autumn. If the voters believe he lacks the substance to pass this test, that will be the end of him. I find this argument all very well as far as it goes, but not particularly reassuring in the long run. If, at the beginning of November, the final choice is between a Hart discredited by the processes of US democracy and Reagan validated by them, the US Constitution hardly stands vindicated.

The second argument is more serious. The absolutely indispensable task of the US president, it is said, is to hold the country together; to sum up its own aspirations in his person; to be *accepted* as the president. This symbolic function is what, till now, President Reagan has successfully fulfilled, whatever his other faults; and it is this function that Jimmy Carter, with his curiously diffident manner and his born-again naivety, signally failed to perform.

The apologists for the US electoral process, which is about images and communication, say that it has at least this to be said for it – it tends to eliminate men who do not have the necessary charisma. If you cannot communicate with the majority of the population – and it is obvious that Glenn cannot and doubtful whether Mondale can – then you will not get elected.

This, again, does not seem to me a very comforting reflection, especially if you are not an American but are still, like many of the inhabitants of the planet, dependent to a greater or lesser extent on the wisdom of the American president for your survival. For one thing, a system which emphasizes the ability to persuade rather than the ability to make the right decisions is fatally one-sided. For another, as the Carter case showed, there is not even a guarantee that the system will in fact throw up a credible leader every time. Aberrations are quite possible, thanks to the American public's craving for novelty.

Novelty. Perhaps that is too harsh. The American people's real desire is for hope. The idea of progress, long since moribund in Europe, lives on in the US, combined with a ruthless belief that its victory lies in the hands of youth and the march of democracy.

Gary Hart, who talks and, better still looks rather like Kennedy, is the practitioner of this generation of politics. Mondale, who won the vice-presidency in 1976 on the basis of Jimmy Carter's appeal for fresh, new, country faces untainted by Washington, Watergate and so forth, now finds himself representing not only the past but the old 'machine' politics that every good democrat these days is supposed to abhor.

Where there is very high unemployment, as in Georgia and Alabama, Democratic voters are prepared to turn back to the 'machine' and vote for Mondale. Elsewhere, more emotional considerations reign supreme.

Nobody, except the most crusted reactionary, needs telling that there is a positive, even an inspiring, aspect to all this. The question is whether modern communications and particularly television have not made the effects so corrupt and unstable that democracy defeats itself. Hart is no more competent, no more attractive, not even any younger, than he was six weeks ago when he was no more than a small flip in the voting statistics and when the commentators were all writing him off, on entirely justifiable grounds, as a 'lightweight'.

One last consolation is sometimes proffered at this point. The system takes its revenge on people like Hart – as it did on Jimmy Carter. Those that live the image will perish by the image. People are either rapidly disillusioned by the failure of their heroes to cope with the problems of the real world or they simply get bored with their faces and demand new ones. In the presidential politics of the television era and the media 'hype', political capital has to be expended at a crippling rate – a fact that Mrs Thatcher is now having to learn the hard way.

There is a certain justice about this, perhaps, but does the resulting volatility make for good government? It is not easy to find satisfactory answers to these gloomy reflections. Constitutional shifts, like lengthening the presidential term, are not practical politics. And the only serious answer lies in a better-educated and more discriminating public opinion. The American press and the serious American television journalists will tell you that it is their responsibility and privilege to produce just this. But the experience of the last three weeks suggests that they have quite a lot to do.

*The Times, 16 March 1984*

# After Reagan's Landslide

The American people have just re-elected, in the biggest landslide since George Washington ran unopposed in 1792, a president whom history will surely show to be second-rate. This may seem an ungracious observation on the morrow of a great political victory, and possibly an irrelevant one in the circumstances. As Bernard Shaw remarked in a first-night curtain speech, when a solitary cry of 'rubbish' was heard amid the storms of applause: 'My dear sir, I quite agree with you. But who are we among so many?' Nevertheless, a certain amount of realism is obligatory if we are to deal with the problems of a second Reagan term.

Stated baldly, the situation is this: President Reagan, for reasons of temperament and capacity, is not on top of his job. He sees no reason to involve himself in the details of either foreign or domestic policy, and when forced by circumstances to turn his attention to them cannot usually absorb the information necessary to make a judgement on the merits of the case. There is no reason to suppose that as he goes into his mid-seventies this is going to change for the better.

This means that decisions are normally taken by reference to very different considerations: (a) the President's two simplistic and ultimately irreconcilable principles ('strength against the Soviet Union' and 'keep down taxes'); (b) domestic political tactics and 'image' and (c) the unfettered play of forces and personalities in the administration.

Mr Reagan won the election through a combination of luck and superlative marketing. He was lucky that the underlying strength of the American economy reasserted itself and produced a boom at exactly the right moment; even luckier that there has been no serious foreign crisis this year to expose the limitations of his leadership.

These strokes of good fortune cleared the way for him to identify himself as the legitimate custodian of the American Dream.

That vision of constant progress and endless abundance has burst forth in a blaze of conservative optimism. After Vietnam, Watergate, recession and the permissive society, the old values have proved their worth, the good old times have been restored and Old King Cole is on the throne again.

It goes almost without saying that this is an exceedingly precarious state of affairs. The chances of Mr Reagan's dream being exposed as a fantasy again within the next four years are rather high. The external deficit and the excesses of the administration's 'supply-side' philosophy are virtually bound to run the American economy into the buffers within a couple of years.

In foreign policy it is inconceivable to me that some major upset will not bring Americans face to face with the fact that all the tough rhetoric and military expenditure of the last four years has bought them very limited influence and very few new friends. If and when either of these eventualities occurs, the political reaction will be sharp and the administrative capacity in Washington for coping will still be minimal. When Mr Reagan shouts 'you ain't seen nothing yet', he is speaking truer than he knows.

There is a strong disposition among European governments to avert their gaze from these difficulties. In Mrs Thatcher's Whitehall, and among conservative commentators, rationalization is more or less mandatory. To put the matter at its most mundane level, we have to deal with the Reagan administration for the next four years and we may as well make the best of it; but why stick to such a grudging, practical defence when there are such splendid reasons of principle for accepting the inevitable with pleasure?

First and least pretentious of these is the man-of-the-world notion that no presidential election matters very much anyhow. Whoever is in the White House will be subject to the same large economic and political forces which he will tackle with the same illusion of power but the same reality of impotence. In Reagan's case this is compounded by the fact that the House of Representatives is still under Democratic control, and that the chairman of the Federal Reserve Board is a highly independent character.

A slightly more radical variation of this line is that Reagan's do-nothing attitude is either a sham, a good thing, or both. The internal inconsistencies of this theory are almost irreconcilable. It is perhaps just possible, however, to assert simultaneously that Reagan, like

Eisenhower, is a wily old bird who takes a far greater interest in the main decisions of his administration than he thinks it expedient to show, and that he deliberately keeps his activity to a minimum on the good Friedmanite principle that free market forces will do almost any job better than government.

Both these hypotheses seem to me to be fatuous pieces of evasion. It is certainly a truism that American presidents are carried to power on waves of popular feeling which they must ride or capsize. Ronald Reagan is on the crest of one such wave, and he cannot be expected to be anything but basically conservative in policy. It is also obvious that the separation of powers in the American constitution sets limits on any president. And here again, Reagan cannot hope to end the perennial Washington rivalries that weaken all American government.

And yet, within these limits, it still *matters* crucially who holds the presidency. For good or ill the system revolves around this sun. Without Truman there might have been no Marshall Plan; without Johnson no reconciliation of the blacks, and no Vietnam either; without Nixon no opening to China, certainly no Watergate.

Without Reagan, what? Well, to be positive about it one might say that the President, by helping Americans to think better of themselves, has added a little psychological fuel to the boom, and damped down protectionism. On the negative side it is possible that without Reagan there would be less anti-Americanism in the world, a better climate of East–West relations and a less hopeless situation in the Middle East.

It is not a very encouraging balance, and it has been struck almost by accident out of the over-simplification, muddle and indirection that I have described. That it is not a lot worse may be credited to Mr Reagan, if he is held responsible for his own luck and ours; but we had better prepare ourselves for some hard and dangerous times when the luck runs out.

*The Times*, 9 November 1984

# The American Raid on Libya

Three hard facts about the American raid on Tripoli emerge from the welter of speculation and argument.

– The US ignored the declared wishes and advice of its European allies, including Britain. Whatever ministers and officials may now say in public for the sake of alliance solidarity, there was an overwhelming consensus in the British government (not excluding the Prime Minister) – conveyed to the Americans in advance – that the attack was unwise. Quite apart from repercussions in the Arab world from which the whole West may suffer, it was thought most unlikely to deter terrorism, indeed might actually increase it, particularly in Europe.

– Washington acted almost entirely under the impulsion of domestic emotions and domestic political considerations. Warnings by European governments and Arab moderates weighed almost nothing in comparison with President Reagan's need to maintain credibility with American public opinion and vindicate his own mission of American national honour. The only sufficient external deterrent (because harmful to Reagan's domestic image) might have been a prior threat by Mikhail Gorbachov to cancel the summit entirely or to support Gadaffi with military force. But no such threat was made.

– The British government, and Mrs Thatcher in particular, were put in an intolerable position by the American desire to use their bases in Britain. Apart from the doubts about the wisdom of the enterprise, they knew there would be an enormous political row in which the anti-Americans would have a field day and Labour's cry about Britain being an American aircraft carrier would be raised in a particularly awkward form. On the other hand, as Mrs Thatcher told the Commons, an outright 'no' was out of the question since this would put the alliance under probably an even greater strain across the Atlantic.

It is all very well for Edward Heath and James Callaghan to say from the secure refuge of retirement that they would have refused permission, but things have changed drastically since their days in office. American public opinion is far jumpier and the prospects of American isolationism far greater. It is a measure of how far confidence has been sapped that British officials actually considered the possibility that the US might take advantage of the ambiguity of the old Churchill–Truman 'understanding' and go ahead and use British bases after 'consulting' Mrs Thatcher but without receiving her consent.

The strategy proposed by moderate critics such as David Owen might in theory have reduced the damage. This would have entailed insisting, as the price for consent, that the US should put itself 'on side' in international law by going to the UN Security Council and making a plea of self-defence under Article 51 of the Charter. Then, when this got nowhere, to consent only to the bombing of Libyan oil jetties in the hope of achieving by relatively bloodless military means the effect of an economic blockade. The fatal flaw in this rational compromise is that the Reagan administration was in no mood for it.

In the first place, the present American government loathes and despises the UN, which it regards as a kind of Soviet-dominated kangaroo court for the indictment of American policies. Secondly, it wished to humiliate Gadaffi, rather than simply put a squeeze on him. Thirdly, it was deeply suspicious of any advice or constraints urged by Europeans, whom it regards as whingeing appeasers.

The remark by General Vernon Walters, Reagan's special envoy, after his visits to European capitals sums up Washington's mingled mood of resentment, defiance and condescension: 'The so-called sophisticated Europeans only managed twenty-one years of peace between the world wars; under United States leadership we have had forty-one years.' In this atmosphere Mrs Thatcher probably achieved as much as was possible in getting the Americans to make a tiny concession to international public relations by talking more explicitly about 'self-defence' than they had intended. If she had said 'no', Washington would simply have launched a bloodier attack from the Sixth Fleet and acted with even more unilateral contempt for Europe in subsequent dealings across the whole field of international affairs.

The clear conclusion is that whatever the immediate fate of Colonel Gadaffi, the incident has widened the US–European gap within NATO. Washington's worst opinion of European 'wetness' will have been confirmed – not so much by the EEC's joint declaration on Libya but rather by the general atmosphere of doubt, irresolution and dissension in which it was promulgated. At the same time, the picture of Reagan as a dangerous cowboy will be even more indelibly printed on European public opinion, for what is his comment that he 'did what had to be done' but a paraphrase of the classic cliché of the doomed Western gunfighter that 'a man does what a man has to do'?

But the affair shows up far deeper troubles than that. The truth is that European interests in the Middle East really do differ in important respects from America's. In the past the assumption has been that such differences can be patched up by cultural understanding, joint decision-making and real compromise. The US, in its present mood, has increasingly tended to go its own way and follow its own emotional imperatives. The Europeans have become more and more disaffected and uneasy but are not yet strong or united enough to let go of American apron strings. The Soviet threat still keeps the alliance together – just. But the binding sense of shared destiny is being eroded very rapidly. It is a deeply worrying prospect.

*The Times, 18 April 1986*

# Reagan: the Truth at Last

The disaster which has engulfed the White House has been coming a long time. It has been inherent in the Reagan presidency from the very beginning in 1981, its nature perfectly obvious to any serious observer. It was spelt out in the memoirs of Alexander Haig, the former Secretary of State, and in David Stockman's account of his time as Budget Director. Every authentic anecdote to have emerged from the White House has confirmed it. The US has a president who does not have the intellectual energy or capacity required for the conduct of foreign policy, and the aides on whom he depends to do it for him are third rate. The results have been continuous squabbling within the administration, wild fluctuations of policy, and a long series of mistakes brought on by panicky attempts to impress domestic opinion with bogus ideological consistency and quick results.

These facts have been concealed from the American public for a number of reasons – partly Reagan's extraordinary skill and charm as a television performer but, more to the point, public self-deception. After Vietnam, Watergate, and the Tehran hostages nightmare they have desperately wanted Reagan to succeed, and since he has *acted* the part of the successful president to perfection nobody in the US (certainly not the media, still smarting from accusations of having brought down Nixon by foul means) has until recently dared or indeed wished to break the euphoric spell. Foreign opinion has been more perceptive, but there has been an understandable conspiracy among the European establishments to make the best of a bad job.

It is also fair to say, in defence of Reagan, that the underlying problem that has produced the present crisis is intractable and systemic.

**165**

In an era when foreign policy is the transcendent political issue of American government, the President cannot afford to relinquish control of it either to members of his cabinet or to the legislature. But if he tries to impose himself seriously on the subject (through some such instrument as the National Security Council or special advisers in the White House) he automatically sets up enormous tensions between his own machine and the powerful institutions – State Department, Pentagon and, above all, Congress – that have a vested interest in it.

And not only that. There is almost bound to be a tension between the man who seeks to ensure that the President's foreign strategy is carried out and the man whose job is to keep the President out of domestic trouble and sees foreign policy as a means or an obstacle to that end.

These are genuine difficulties, and it cannot be said that any president since Eisenhower has solved them wholly satisfactorily. The Nixon White House provided the classic demonstration of the problem, with the President's man, Kissinger, cheating Congress and bypassing the State Department and Pentagon, and Nixon's political 'minders', Haldeman and Ehrlichman, cracking dirty jokes with the President and quarrelling with and often bypassing everyone, including Kissinger, to keep the political lid on.

It was a sordid set-up, wasteful of talent and energy and frequently in violation of the Constitution, but it worked after a fashion because Nixon was a highly intelligent man with great international experience, Kissinger was a remarkable operator, and even Haldeman and company usually had enough sense to see when they were out of their depth on the international side.

The case against Reagan is that he has never managed to make the system work, even after a fashion. His national security advisers have been lack-lustre. His Californian political mafia, with the exception of James Baker, have been aggressively parochial and tactical in their approach to foreign affairs, and Reagan himself, too inexperienced and too unable or unwilling to grapple with detail, has never been able to control what has gone on at the centre of government. General Haig's picture of the Reagan White House as a kind of ghost ship whose sails move mysteriously and almost randomly with nobody on deck is a telling one.

Reagan rightly sensed that America was looking to him for confidence, security and peace (in that order). The first of these, being a psychological commodity, he has managed to restore by rhetoric and gestures. But he has never been able to provide more than the shadows

**166**

of the last two; consequently the effort to prevent even confidence slipping away again has had to become more and more frenetic; hence the disinformation campaign and Colonel North's laundering activities.

What has happened now is therefore far more significant than the subject matter of the Iranian row. The point is that the Reagan myth has been shattered, the illusion exposed. The conjuror's false pockets have been turned inside out and the emperor has been revealed in all his nakedness. Nothing will be the same again. Even if a little of the present scandal can be deflected from Reagan himself by the suitable sacrifice of scapegoats, the Democrats and the media will have no difficulty, over the coming months, in making the incompetence charge against him stick. Its validity flows from a fundamental and irremediable flaw in this administration, and people, having once seen it for what it is, cannot forget what they have seen.

The Times, 28 November 1986

# The Bicentennial

The lives of innumerable famous unfortunates from Socrates and Samson to Rudolph Valentino and Robert Kennedy testify to the fact that about the worst thing any fairy godmother can wish a man at his christening is that he should become a symbol in his lifetime. Too many hopes and fears should not be concentrated upon one head – or one nation.

The American Republic has been a symbol from the moment of its birth and now, 200 years later, it is still facing the two perennial fears that torment anybody in this situation. The first is that the realities of a violent world may make it impossible to live up to the vast expectations enshrined in the myth. The other is that fashion will change and the myth will then destroy rather than attract devotion.

America was born in liberty. This was true at the time in spite of the hindsight of history. The colonists may have been slave-owners or bourgeois proto-capitalists or male chauvinist pigs, but they did something which both they and the rest of the world then believed to be profoundly significant. As Edmund Burke remarked: 'A great revolution has happened – a revolution made not by chopping and changing of power in any of the existing states but by the appearance of a new state and a new species in a new part of the globe.' The literature of that revolution – from the Declaration of Independence to the Constitution itself – breathes the conviction that the old shackles were being hacked away and that a new age was about to begin. The quotation from Virgil's fourth eclogue which appears on the great seal of the United States, signals the belief that the new age was to be a golden one.

The achievements of defeating the colonial power and setting up a new political order based upon rational principles and the spirit of equality were separated in time, and may have seemed to some Americans of the 1780s as separated in principle. But to the Founding Fathers and to the world outside they appeared to be two necessary stages of the same historical act. Internal liberty and equality were not only made possible by independence, they were actually an extension of it.

Throughout the whole of the nineteenth century and a good deal of the twentieth the world witnessed an extraordinary effort on the part of the Republic to live up to this initial symbolism, and even to enhance it. In its foreign relations the US proceeded on anti-colonial principles and saw itself, and was seen, as being on the side of freedom and independence throughout the world – even within its own hemisphere. The war with Mexico in 1846 could be regarded as an aberration brought on by the slave-owning South. The war with Spain in 1898, for all the jingoism of the Progressives, could be portrayed with some justice as an anti-colonial war itself. There was nothing seriously selfish or aggressive in the spirit that prompted America's entrance into the First World War (or the Second); and Bryce could quite justly write in 1922: 'No great people in the world is equally pervaded by the wish to see peace maintained everywhere over the world.'

Then, quite apart from this general benevolence towards liberty for others, there was the enormous pull of the libertarian ideal for emigrants from Europe. Economic hardship and famine were usually, no doubt, the final cause of the great wave of impoverished people flooding across the Atlantic in the years from 1839 to 1939. But the image of Liberty waiting with open arms for the 'masses longing to be free' was immensely powerful long before her hideous statue was created in New York harbour.

Meanwhile, of course, within the US itself, the classic nineteenth-century recipe for a libertarian system was being applied. Liberty meant, to quote that arch-Liberal Bryce again, the expulsion of tyrants, the admission of the bulk of the nation to a share in power, the full control of the people of their representative assembly, the abolition of privilege and hereditary rank, and the opening on equal terms of every public career to every citizen. It also meant the curtailment of public expenditure, the public provision of education, and free trade. Once these things had been attained everybody could sit down and be happy in his own way, the free play of economic forces ensuring peaceful progress and the steady amelioration of the conditions of life.

Naturally there were flies in this *laissez-faire* ointment, but on the whole they were invisible to nineteenth-century intellectuals and publicists. What mattered to radicals and democrats (and what fascinated conservatives like de Tocqueville) was the fact that the Americans appeared to be putting into practice in the purest form available the precepts which the poets of liberty from Schiller and Shelley to Mazzini and Victor Hugo hymned.

This pristine admiration became gradually overcast in the twentieth century by other images – corruption, violence, and the power of the trusts. Attitudes were also complicated by envy and fear of American industrial power – feelings which were rationalized among the European ruling classes by contempt for the vulgarity of American riches and the intolerable provinciality of all but the most Bostonian manners. Later still, of course, there was the slump which produced the uneasy feeling that the whole American system was based on suspect foundations. But the symbolism of America as a land of the free still persisted. There was friction and a certain resentment inherent in the arrival of the Yanks on these shores in 1917 and 1942. But to the mass of Europeans the 'liberation' of 1945 was an American achievement which they cheered all the more loudly because it appeared to be so much what America had always been destined to achieve.

Two things strike me about this long saga. The first is that throughout it the external world's view of America was a mirror image of America's view of itself. The moralism and optimism of the culture never really flagged, except briefly in the 1930s. The second obvious fact, of course, is that in the thirty years since the war – a very short time in the whole sweep of American history – much of the historic symbolism of the US has been destroyed and with it an important element of the idealism that sustained and was sustained by it.

The trouble is that during this period much of the world has either redefined liberty or given it a lower priority than other virtues such as equality and stability. Western Europe was grateful in the 1950s for being saved from the threat of Soviet tyranny but deeply distrusted the crusading libertarianism of John Foster Dulles, when it seemed likely to lead to dangerous confrontation with the Russians. Again, the question has been raised whether the attempt to preserve the liberty of the people of South Vietnam at the cost of laying their country to waste was not a contradiction of terms. And is it libertarian to preserve other Third-World countries from totalitarian miseries by supporting their present repressive regime?

170 The Third World replies that the liberty that matters to it is not so much the old freedoms of speech and worship and property, but free-

dom from outside interference, freedom from exploitation by powerful external interests, and the freedom which comes from the removal of grinding poverty. Philosophically, no doubt, this last is a well-known confusion, but the reality is that America is now situated in a world, much of which assumes that its old virtues are at best irrelevant and at worst a cloak for naked self-interest.

Even Europe, which relies upon the old American conception of liberty to keep it out of the clutches of the Russians, tends to see its relations with America in terms of a balance of power rather than of shared ideals and libertarian political assumptions: We, like the Third World, want equality. We too have our interests to protect. We too have been shaken by the moral dilemma of Vietnam. We too are tending to downgrade liberty in pursuit of equality and to solve our problems by expedients which raise up the state at the expense of the individual.

In the face of this hostile environment the U S enters its third century on the defensive, and all the more so because the domestic prerequisites of nineteenth-century liberalism – unlimited land and space, geographical security, and a working population with limited economic expectations – are no longer available. In such a context the sudden emergence of Mr Jimmy Carter, a man who combines a fairly primitive idealism with the promise to solve domestic problems in a businesslike fashion and restore good relations with the outside world, is easily explained.

Whether he or anyone else can restore the American sense of destiny or the symbolism of 1776 in quite the old sense is doubtful. It is hard to be a hero in a world of such competitive diversity. But what the new President and his successors have it in their power to achieve is a demonstration in modern conditions of a truth that has never ceased to be effective in the past, whatever the mistakes or derelictions of the American government. This is that the American Constitution actually works – that a vast continent full of people can live together in one nation without resort to coercion and labour camps and secret police, and that it can do so without taking more from the outside world than it gives. This is a more modest claim to fame than those of the Founding Fathers, but if one looks round the rest of the globe and its miseries, it seems more than enough to be going on with.

*Financial Times, 3 July 1976*

# The British
# Scene

III

# Is Britain Really Ungovernable?

'Save me, Oh, save me, from the candid friend.' Canning's famous line should be applied to almost all members of the anglophile, liberal Establishment of the US – Dean Acheson, Stewart Alsop and now Mr Eric Sevareid – who try to tell us, doubtless from the best possible motives, what is wrong with the government of Britain. Their criticisms are founded, for the most part, on a view of these islands that was already anachronistic when it was formed during or just after the war, and now bears almost no relation to what we are or aspire to be.

Mr Sevareid's effusion on American televison this week was full of tell-tale solecisms. No one who had seriously thought about the real problems of this country in the 1970s would put Britain's 'ebbing military strength' at the top of his symptoms of decline, or would state that the argument about nationalization turns on a belief that workers in nationalized industries will 'joyously work the harder'. These and similar slips ('thousands of middle-class people move out of London every year, like New York') betray a lack of up-to-date understanding that ought to put us on guard against other generalizations contained in the critique.

But what are these generalizations? They are easily summed up. Britain is becoming 'ungovernable' because the political tune is being called by doctrinaire socialists and/or communists in the trade unions who believe that sharing wealth is more important than producing it and who wish to assist the long-range strategies of the Soviet Union. Some kind of 'backlash' (though not necessarily a military one) is building up in opposition to this process and heaven knows what will happen. I believe for reasons which I shall describe that much of this is beside the point. But the embarrassment is that the whole picture bears a startling resemblance to much of the gloom that is now circulating round the Conservative Party and in some quarters in industry.

As usual American comment merely repeats, in a form distorted by transatlantic nostalgia and over-simplification, the view purveyed by the British Establishment on its visits to the US. The demoralization of our own ruling class is mirrored in the contempt and concern of theirs.

What, then, is the reality? Is Britain really becoming ungovernable? Let us consider what this would mean. In the present context it would imply (a) that the present government and its advisers had a plausible strategy for dealing with Britain's economic problems, but were unable to implement their plans, thanks to the defiance of some section or sections of the community; or (b) that an alternative government and its advisers had a plausible strategy but could predict with fair certainty that they would be no more successful in implementing it than the government; or (c) that in the event of the present government failing, the attempt to introduce an alternative was frustrated by inadequate constitutional arrangements.

On the face of it all three of these conditions seem to have some relevance. It is true that the Labour government's attempt to control inflation by means of the social contract is being frustrated by the defiance of the trade unions, and it is quite arguable (though not yet certain) that the attempt to beat inflation by monetary restriction, as outlined in Mr Denis Healey's last Budget, will fail for the same reason. The Conservatives maintain, in some moods, that their own monetary policy would succeed where the Labour policy failed – presumably because it would be carried out with more ruthlessness – but it is a very commonplace view in Conservative circles at present that if fate wafted them into office next week, they would be even less able to cope than Labour. As for the third condition, it is frequently said in despairing tones around the Palace of Westminster that there is no certainty that Mr Harold Wilson and his colleagues will in fact be penalized for failure. The Constitution is not sufficiently flexible (even when there is only a government majority of three) to ensure that, when one set of politicians makes a mess of things, something else can be tried quickly.

It is these perspectives, and the prospect they imply of an almost endless drift and decline, which currently fill the vision of so many politicians, businessmen and commentators. It is likewise these perspectives which have produced in recent weeks a flurry of Conservative discussion about our constitutional arrangements. Sir Keith Joseph and others have been heard canvassing in private the virtues of electoral reform and a new Bill of Rights. The words 'legitimacy', 'authority' and 'consent' have been much bandied about, and even that constitutional last resort – the referendum procedure – has been referred to with indulgence in some surprising quarters.

The general argument is a familiar one. The problem, it may be said, is the Executive's subservience to the tyranny of a minority (in this case the trade unions) and its inability to mobilize the majority of the public to defeat it. Let us, therefore, take steps to re-enlist the majority on the side of the government, thereby restoring its authority and legitimizing any measures introduced to cut the tyrannous majority down to size. The introduction of some form of proportional representation would produce coalition governments and thus strengthen the centre. A Bill of Rights would reassert the claims of individuals against pressure groups (including trade unions). The referendum could be used as a device to protect entrenched clauses of the Constitution (and so prevent change) as well as to mobilize further support against 'over-mighty subjects'.

These devices, quite apart from their general attractions, have tactical advantages of various kinds appropriate to this moment. Electoral reform would naturally have the enthusiastic support of the Liberals and the nationalists. It would also greatly please the business community which (when it thinks about the matter at all) sees coalition government as the best hope of continuity in industrial and economic policy. (Mr Anthony Wedgwood Benn's much-publicized gibe at Mrs Shirley Williams during Wednesday's meeting of the NEDC touched a sensitive nerve precisely because everyone present was aware of all the coalition gossip, most of it built around Mrs Williams and her friends which has been going on at the interface of the business and political worlds for some time.)

The tactical point about the Bill of Rights is that it would offer undoubted advantages to the Left as well as to the Right. In return for the right to peaceful demonstration or protection from administrative abuse – all good radical stuff – the Left might be prepared to let through the right to free access to the Press or the right not to belong to a trade union. Certainly a plausible case can be made for the proposition that it is easier to curb the power of the trade unions by this kind of indirect device than by the frontal assault on them through an Industrial Relations Bill.

The difficulty about all this is not that these innovations are not valuable in themselves. On the contrary, they may be extremely valuable, particularly the Bill of Rights which is probably essential for the many reasons set out in Sir Leslie Scarman's brilliant Hamlyn Lecture, 'English Law – The New Dimension.'[1] The difficulty is simply that the remedies proposed do not *necessarily* cure the mischiefs complained of and even if they do so, it will only be after a long time-lag. Proportional representation has been known in some contexts to do no more than reflect the fissures of a divided policy and we cannot be sure that it would have the desired and opposite effect here. As for the Bill of Rights, its operation in producing a less frenetic and more unified society could hardly begin to show results for many years.

The truth is that mechanical constitutional devices cannot produce political stability if there is no fundamental agreement, any more than mechanical economic devices can produce stability in their own field. In each case the art of politics and political leadership is paramount, and there is no possible substitute for it. Authority and legitimacy have to be earned the hard way – by success, by persuasion, by cajolery, by bluff and by inspiration. Other things may assist, but they cannot substitute for these ancient crafts.

This brings us back to the outset of this discussion, for I assert (though I cannot prove) that the fault in British politics lies mainly with the politicians and not with the public, or the trade unions, or the business community. There is nothing inevitable about the tendency in British politics to give way to pressure groups, to tell the electors that they can have something for nothing or that their expectations, far from being excessive, are natural and just. There is nothing in the British Constitution which lays us open to these evils, indeed it always used to be asserted that our constitutional arrangements had precisely the opposite effect. What has happened is that British politicians, and perhaps the whole British middle class, has lost its nerve, and until it recovers it, the prospects are bleak. It is not that Britain is ungovernable; it is that the governors refuse to govern.

What, then, is the outlook? Not, perhaps, as bad as it looks. It seems to me that the present government, after a bad start, has at least the beginnings of a plausible strategy and in spite of its ludicrous divisions has given evidence that it contains some politicians of skill and character. I do not believe that its authority and that of Parliament has slipped beyond repair and I do not think that if, for instance, it chose to react vigorously to a further economic decline – whether by

**178**

[1] Published by Stevens and Sons.

fiscal means or even by the imposition of a wages freeze – that it would either fall or be disobeyed. The only proviso – admittedly a large one – is that it should show some guts and assurance in its handling of these affairs and that its opponents do not moan more than the circumstances strictly warrant.

Mr Sevareid does not seem to understand a great deal about the situation. But he can hardly be expected to understand more than those who confuse inability to govern with weak government.

*Financial Times*, *9 May 1975*

# The Power of the Prime Minister

How powerful is a modern British Prime Minister? Does he dominate the Constitution already, or, if not, are we at least on the move towards a presidential style of government? These questions have been asked at fairly regular intervals for the past 150 years – indeed, they recur at least once in every new administration. Each Prime Minister treats the office in his own distinctive style. He contracts or, more often, expands its potentialities to suit his own needs. After nearly two years of Mr Heath it is probably time for another look at this evergreen topic, and the arrival this week of a new book of lectures by Mr Richard Crossman, *Inside View*,[1] provides an admirable starting point.

Mr Crossman is almost incapable of being boring about anything (even pensions), but he has always been particularly good on this subject because he is acutely fascinated by power and, until 1964, was always excluded from it. His famous 1963 preface to the paperback edition of Bagehot's *English Constitution*[2] was the most eloquent case that has yet been made for the proposition that Prime Ministerial power has increased, is increasing and probably ought to be diminished; and what gave the whole thesis its edge was the element of obsession. It was like reading a hostile analysis of the politics of goldfish written by a cat.

Today, nine years later, the perspective is naturally rather different. It is all as brilliant and entertaining as ever, but much more balanced and relaxed about Prime Ministers than before, and the conclusion

[1] Published by Jonathan Cape.
[2] Published by Collins.

which will rightly be quoted in endless textbooks, is perfectly moderate.

> Prime Ministerial government does not mean that the Prime Minister is a dictator; it does not mean that he can tell his Ministers what to do in their departments. But it does mean that in the battle of Whitehall, this man in the centre, this Chairman, this man without a department, without apparent power, can exert, when he is successful, dominating personal control.

The trouble about this statement is that it is a generalization mainly from Mr Crossman's own experience of Mr Wilson, and it already looks a bit out of date. This is no fault of Mr Crossman's, since his lectures were delivered early in 1970 when he could not have guessed at Mr Heath's style of government. Nevertheless, the last two years do suggest that Mr Crossman may, for once in his life, have been wrong to put in qualifications.

I do not mean by this that Mr Heath is a 'dictator', any more than Mr Wilson was, but I doubt whether any member of the present administration would say that he 'cannot tell his Ministers what to do in their departments'. The fact is that the potentialities of the office have already been considerably extended by Mr Heath and they will almost certainly be expanded still further before he is done with it.

In order to pin down the changes which have taken place since 1970, let us take the six factors which Mr Crossman, in his lectures, identifies as the main sources of a Prime Minister's power and consider what has happened to them under the present regime. The two most effective and time-honoured of these, the right to appoint and sack Ministers and the right of patronage, remain neither greater nor less than they have always been.

We do not yet know whether Mr Heath is capable of being a good 'butcher', but he has certainly been as ruthless as any of his predecessors in using exclusion and inclusion in the ministerial team as a method of political control – 'buying off' potential trouble-makers like his Mr Peyton and Mr Amery with office but isolating and excommunicating the Powellite wing. He has reviewed political honours which his predecessor had (rather bogusly) suppressed, and though he is no more cynical in this than any other Prime Minister before him, it is certainly a valuable weapon in his armoury.

Control of the government's publicity has undoubtedly been tightened by Mr Heath to a greater degree than at almost any time since the war. This is partly a question of preventing ministerial leaks and divergences of view by sheer political dominance (to which we shall come later); but the Civil Service public relations machine has been brought more nearly under direct Prime Ministerial control than it has ever been before. The effort started by Mr Macmillan to co-ordinate publicity under a minister has, in effect, been eschewed, with the vital difference that the Prime Minister and an extremely effective senior civil servant do the job themselves.

Organizational control of the Civil Service has been moving the Prime Minister's way ever since Lloyd George forbade ministers to appoint their own Permanent Secretaries. But the setting up of the Civil Service Department and removing day-to-day control from the Treasury has probably speeded things up. This reorganization was Mr Wilson's doing, but it is Mr Heath who has really been the first to benefit from it.

There is a Minister for the Civil Service, Lord Jellicoe, but both he and his senior civil servants manifestly regard themselves as having been, above all, the instruments of the Prime Minister's drive to produce a more streamlined and responsive Whitehall machine. Under the old system a civil servant who was 'head of the Civil Service' worked to the Prime Minister as First Lord of the Treasury but until there was a separate department it was far more difficult for a Prime Minister to see what was happening or impose his will upon it.

Control of the organization in this fashion does not, of course, mean that control of policy in particular departments is any easier. That has to be achieved by other means, but as it happens these means are to hand. Mr Crossman identifies two main ways in which Mr Wilson used to get his own policies adopted – or at any rate prevented the adoption of policies to which he was opposed. The first of these is the power to decide the Cabinet agenda. (Mr Wilson seldom allowed his colleagues to discuss central economic issues.) This power still remains at Mr Heath's disposal.

More important, however, is the Prime Minister's associated power to organize Cabinet committees as he chooses and to select their chairmen. This is vitally important, because, as Mr Crossman remarks, the growth of the Cabinet committee system has made the doctrine of 'collective responsibility' very demanding:

collective decision-making is now fragmented, and many major decisions may be taken by two, three, four or five Ministers. But the moment they have been taken and minuted, they have the force of a decision taken by the whole Cabinet and are binding on a hundred-odd members of the Government.

Mr Heath has not only inherited but extended this system – apparently somewhat to the annoyance of his colleagues. He likes to set up small *ad hoc* ministerial 'task forces', occasionally even containing a senior civil servant, which are constituted to hammer out a policy for a particular purpose and then dissolve. The appointment of a small committee to prepare a new policy for Ulster was a case on the grand scale, and caused ministers not in that particular group to protest that by the time the 'initiative' emerged (which took a very long time) the government position was virtually fixed.

Such things have happened before in other regimes, especially where there has been a kind of 'inner Cabinet' – but Mr Heath seems to be systematizing the process and, of course, the more *ad hoc* groups that are created by the Prime Minister to override what might otherwise be a single departmental decision, the more real policy 'power' is concentrated in Prime Ministerial hands.

So far we have been only looking at Mr Crossman's strictly constitutional sources of power, and we have seen that Mr Heath is not only making the fullest possible use of them but, as I would argue, is also extending them in the process. Civil servants, who are acutely aware that the public is frightened of extensions of anyone's power – at any rate in theory – reply that what gives Mr Heath his pull is not really the exploitation of mechanical advantages but the overwhelming personal dominance he has over his colleagues.

This is certainly rather extraordinary, particularly at this period of the government's life. The normal cycle is for a Prime Minister to dominate his Cabinet immediately after an election (because he has won power) and immediately before an election (because he is indispensable to winning it again). In between, his departmental ministers become knowledgeable and cocky and have to be shifted round to remind them who is boss.

The fact that this has not happened is due to a number of things of which I would admit the most important has nothing to do with the Constitution. The key factor has been Mr Heath's decision to take an enormous risk while he was in Opposition and first of all work out a very detailed programme and second to entrust this work only to people who are more or less of his way of thinking. This might have had a disastrous result if the public had been scared off the policies or the party had split because too many important people had been excluded from its councils. But the gamble came off and the result is that a clear, long-term policy associated closely with the Prime Minister has been adopted, and is being carried out by people who are in no position to say they've changed their minds.

But this does not quite dispose of the constitutional argument, The point is that a strong Prime Minister leaves his office to his successor in a stronger position than he found it, and this I believe Mr Heath will do. The point can be seen very clearly in the case of the Central Policy Review Staff – Lord Rothschild's 'think-tank'. Here is an instrument designed to give greater coherence to government policy by briefing the Cabinet on the overall (that is, non-departmental) implications of its decisions.

Everyone is careful to say that this strengthens the collective power of the Cabinet, and indeed there is some evidence that it has encouraged individual Cabinet members to intervene more often in subjects outside their narrow departmental briefs. On the other hand, in the long run it is bound to strengthen the Prime Minister – and indeed many of the more 'managerial' ministers and civil servants intend that it should.

When Sir Burke Trend, the present Cabinet Secretary, leaves next year I should expect to see the Cabinet Secretariat losing some of its independent power and the CPRS moving, in practice, further into the orbit of the Prime Minister; but this will be a gentle and ambiguous process. Mr Heath's successor, however, will inherit a new instrument of great power and potential importance.

Whether or not this is a good thing depends on a view of the relative importance of efficiency and 'representation'. The checks and balances of the British system operate at present through the forces of inertia, and we are used to thinking that the best guarantee that nothing is done amiss is that nothing should be done at all. This is crazy in modern terms, but it has given birth to the opposite heresy that providing the thing gets done it doesn't much matter if some people think it is done amiss. I suppose Prime Ministerial government carries us nearer to the second danger as it carries us away from the first. What is urgently needed is to find new ways of 'controlling' the Executive which do not prevent the Executive becoming more effective.

*Financial Times, 5 May 1972*

# What the Monarchy Means Now

'**Y**es,' said the prominent Labour politician half-jokingly the other day, 'it's all been the most appalling success. We shall have them now for at least another fifty years.' This crack referred, of course, to the House of Windsor – and it may even be true. No one can possibly deny the remarkable double triumph of the Royal Family in the last three weeks. The monarchy has not been so popular for years as it is at this moment.

Nevertheless, if the British Crown is going to survive as a useful institution it is important to be clear what this success really consists of and what its limits are likely to be in the future. Both the Investiture of the Prince of Wales and the film on the Royal Family were gambles in state-craft but the fact that they both came off does not alter the boundaries within which the monarchy is forced to operate.

The Investiture, at its most important level, was a political act. It used all the symbolism of the state and the personal popularity of the Queen to assert the unity of the United Kingdom against the separatist pretensions of the Welsh nationalists just as, on a smaller scale, the first appearance of the reigning monarch at the General Assembly of the Church of Scotland earlier this year was a challenge to the pretensions of Scottish nationalists. This was an absolutely legitimate use of the Crown and one with many precedents (King Baudouin of the Belgians practically keeps his unhappy country together single-handed by these means).

It was also a use of the Crown which put the Crown itself mildly at risk. For if the force of nationalism had proved too great, or the popularity of the Queen and the Prince had been insufficient, the proceedings at Caernarvon would have made the political atmosphere worse if they had not actually broken up in death and confusion.

The reason this did not happen is partly that Welsh nationalism is still too weak but partly also because the Palace had taken pains to weight the balance on the other side – increasing the Royal stock of personal popularity by exposing Prince Charles and the rest of his family in a well-planned publicity campaign.

This campaign was itself a gamble. The public might simply have failed to take to the Prince, or they might have been bored by him. 'Royalty', according to Walter Bagehot 'is a Government in which the attention of the Nation is concentrated upon one person doing interesting things.' But, alas, most of the things which Royalty does today are uninteresting, and the spectacle on TV of a year of garden parties, official openings, and formal conversations might easily have been tedious.

The effort to lighten this picture by laying emphasis on the Royal Family's human qualities might have been even more disastrous. For, to quote Bagehot again, the life of monarchy is its mystery. 'Magic should not be exposed to the light of day.'

In the end, it seems, the balance was about right. There were enough glimpses of the bleak splendours of the monarchy's façade to satisfy the traditional or the snobbish, and enough peeps behind it to evoke human sympathy for the inmates. What we have seen, in short, over the last month or two has been the painstaking accumulation of popular capital by the Crown and its cautious expenditure in a relatively important constitutional cause. It has been a well-judged operation and its success has, of course, accumulated another fund of capital to be used on subsequent occasions.

Yet when all this has been said, the key difficulties about a modern constitutional monarchy still remain – the most glaring being the basic one of finding a role for the monarch which is not either trifling or self-defeating.

A good deal is written from time to time about the residual powers of the Crown under the English Constitution and these made their appearance once more in the film on the Royal Family. But they are nearly all, to be frank, mere moonshine. The Queen's theoretical right to dissolve Parliament has been in abeyance since William IV; and after the Conservative Party followed Labour's suit and instituted a regular leadership election, her freedom of manoeuvre in the choice of Prime Minister became virtually non-existent. In moments of excitement constitutional pedants dream of ingenious contingencies in which the Crown would regain initiative; but in fact Royal advisers have frequently made it clear that they will go to almost any length to keep the Crown out of party politics and to play safe.

As for Bagehot's classic description of the functions of the Victorian monarchy, it is now almost entirely outmoded. The Queen does *not* 'disguise the efficient parts of Government', far less 'make Government intelligible to the masses'. She can be said to give government 'the sanction of religion and morality' in the sense that her family leads a virtuous life. But these are rather pallid virtues by comparison with the claims which are normally made.

What we are left with, therefore, amounts to a dual-purpose monarchy. The first purpose is that of adding a little colour and vicarious glamour to drab lives, and carrying out the various cere-monial chores of the Head of State. But well though the British Royal Family performs this function, it is one which could be adapted to a republican constitution.

The other function is that of representing, through lineage, a continu-ous devotion to a particular form of government, particular constitu-tional conventions and particular liberties. It is rightly and reasonably believed that in case of dictatorship she would draw the country's attention to its peril by refusing to sanction constitutional im-proprieties. She would presumably be immediately exiled, but at least we should know where we were. The trouble with this justification is that, like the bee's sting, it is a one-shot affair which cannot be used in any but the direst circumstances and therefore cannot and does not protect us from minor constitutional encroachments. The Crown may be the defender of our liberties, but probably only when it is too late.

It is within these boundaries that Prince Charles will operate as Prince and eventually as King. He will open Parliament and hear the Prime Minister's gossip. He will be deferred to by ministers on minor points and ignored when the issue is important. He will be popular, and his popularity may, as at Caernarvon, help to preserve the unity of his realm. But the main reason why the system will survive is because it functions painlessly and because no one can think of a better one.

*Financial Times*, 4 July 1969

# Race and Mr Enoch Powell

At its most serious the crisis of race relations is a constitutional one. Mr Enoch Powell's speech was, of course, an explicit challenge on the race issue to Mr Edward Heath and the rest of the Shadow Cabinet (as well as to moderate opinion and to the immigrants themselves). But it was also an implicit challenge to traditional political practice and to the party system.

Mr Powell is the first major politician for many years to break with his friends in Parliament for the deliberate purpose of appealing over their heads to the mass of the electors in the country. The Conservative rebels on Suez and the Common Market were not figures of the first rank. Mr Aneurin Bevan's issues were fought out almost entirely within the Labour Party. And Winston Churchill in the 1930s addressed himself mainly to educated opinion, being realistic enough to know that he had little prospect of mass support for rearmament.

For even a rough parallel to Mr Powell's present situation one has to go back to Sir Oswald Mosley's during his quarrel with the Labour Party after the slump, or even further to Joseph Chamberlain's at the beginning of his Tariff Reform campaign more than sixty years ago. He has seized upon a genuine feeling of popular discontent with the policies of the two major parties; he has given it expression in the hectic language of the market place and he is in an excellent position to put himself permanently at its head.

We do not yet know what he will do now. Many of his former colleagues believe that he is feeling both Messianic and intensely ambitious. And though these estimates are possibly a trifle suspect just now, past experience suggests that Mr Powell is not the kind of man who sets his hand to the plough and then breaks off for lunch. It seems probable that we shall hear much more from him on the same lines and that his activities and utterances will be ultimately directed towards power.

The significance of this possibility can best be understood by looking at the obstacles which stand between this kind of enterprise and its fulfilment. A major inconvenience, naturally, is the difficulty of persuading large numbers of people to change their minds on any vaguely political subject. The opinion polls show that the majority of the public remain tolerant about coloured immigrants. This is not surprising or even, perhaps, particularly praiseworthy since a large proportion of the population scarcely sees a coloured face from one week's end to another; but it presents undoubted difficulties to the politician who wishes to alert his countrymen to the alleged dangers and deprivations that they are suffering at the hands of the immigrants.

However, the main barrier to a mass political movement is the working of the Constitution itself which has been evolved to produce the maximum stability compatible with a reasonable amount of freedom and to prevent the Executive being terrorized by sudden outbursts of popular feeling – whether organized or not.

The remoteness of MPs from the feeling in the constituencies has been a recurrent and reasonable theme of radical complaint for many years but there are moments when a certain amount of remoteness has its advantages. Classical doctrine maintains that constituents command no more than the individual 'judgement' of an MP; modern doctrine suggests more realistically that constituents pick a party and are entitled to expect no more and no less than that their MP should vote with it. But either way the Constitution interimposes a buffer zone between popular outcries and the decisions of political leaders. This is the strength of the system. Sir Edward Boyle is able with perfect propriety to defy the wishes of probably the majority of his Birmingham constituents by flaunting his support for the government's racial legislation; and Mr Ian Mikardo need have no hesitation in telling his dockers, when they arrive to lobby him, to belt up. The government and the Opposition leaders are still more protected.

To those who object that this is undemocratic the constitutionalist can reply that there is nothing to prevent an MP's constituency party disowning him and that the ultimate remedy for the man in the street lies in the ballot box at the next election. This system is a maddening brake on any kind of change but it does allow room for political leadership to work and it is a deterrent to demagoguery and extra-Parliamentary politics. In the first place, loyalty, combined with the power of the party establishment and the Whips for most of the time, impel the ordinary M P to pay more attention in the last resort to his leaders in Parliament than to his constituents. And provided that the leadership is united and flexible it is remarkably difficult to arouse outside forces strong enough to make the individual M P revolt.

Then again, the leadership itself is given plenty of time by the electoral calendar to deploy its own soothing arguments, side-track resentments, propose compromises and generally foster the kind of situation in which rebel-rousing political campaigns find it most difficult to exist.

This conventional machinery is all very comforting at such times as these – particularly when both government and Opposition are united in moving it into action in earnest. But in another sense the ponderous effectiveness of the whole arrangement is profoundly disturbing. For it is one of the main ingredients of our present troubles. The isolation of politicians, the in-groupiness of Westminster, the blandness of the Establishment, the tendency to sweep unpleasant facts under the carpet for the best of motives (as well as the worst), the irrelevance of many of the old party divisions to modern problems (and hence the tendency towards fictitious dispute or cosy agreement) – these are the main characteristics of the conventional system as the man in the street sees it today. The balance and stability of the constitutional machinery – which are his protection against revolution and tyranny – often seem less important than its increasing remoteness, irrelevance or incompetence.

By putting himself outside his party and appealing directly to the public, as it were against the 'system', Mr Powell has cashed in on these feelings. He sets up, in effect, as the champion not only of the oppressed white citizens of Wolverhampton but of everyone who feels serious alienation from politics. He is taking on the machine. That he has to some extent rung the bell is obvious from the chorus of praise for him for 'speaking out' and the chorus of abuse for Mr Heath and Mr Callaghan for 'hushing things up' – often from the most unlikely quarters.

I believe that the 'machine' is still likely to prove powerful enough for the time being to defeat intolerance on this issue. The Labour Party in Parliament is solid on it. The Tory leadership has (with one brief wobble over its amendment to the new Bill) been admirably firm on the basic principle during the last few months and now that it has been challenged by Mr Powell is compelled to be even firmer. Both sides are bound to take note of the racial grievances expressed in the last few days, but they have ample opportunity to tackle their causes without compromising with racialism.

But the danger still exists – both to racial harmony and in the long run to Parliamentary democracy itself. There is still time to tackle the problems of racial discrimination before Mr Powell's lurid images become a reality. And there is still time to give a new sense of purpose and reality to the activities of the political parties and of Parliament. But in either case the time is limited by the tolerance of the public – and the events of the last week suggest that it could run out on both simultaneously.

*Financial Times, 26 April 1968*

# If Gaitskell Had Lived

Hugh Gaitskell died on 18 January 1963. Ten years later he is still remembered and mourned not merely by the group within the Labour Party which is still, after all this time, known as Gaitskellite, but by almost anybody (with the possible exception of some of his old left-wing opponents) whose inclination or occupation obliges him to think about the state of British politics. This is a distinction given to very few politicians indeed. We watch the procession of public figures cross the stage and disappear into oblivion with varying degrees of detachment, regret, pity – and sometimes joy. But a deep and enduring sense of national loss? Almost never.

Everybody will have his own list of men in this most exclusive category. In my recollection Gaitskell and Iain Macleod certainly qualify. Possibly Aneurin Bevan and Archbishop Temple.

And on the wider world stage President Kennedy and Pope John. If one asks oneself what these men had in common which caused millions of their fellow beings to feel desolated by their deaths, it is obvious that pathos plays a part, and a sense of the malignity of the blind Fury which snaps the thread just at the moment of greatest potential. But, more important, was the instinct which we felt obscurely at the time of each catastrophe, that here was an individual who really had in his power and embodied in his person the ability to do something that desperately needed to be done and that no one else could do.

This feeling has not misled us about any of the men I have mentioned. We can never be sure exactly what any statesman would have achieved if he had lived longer, but we can certainly say whether his characteristic aims have in fact been realized – or even intelligently pursued – without him. The reality is that neither the United States nor the Roman Catholic Church nor the Church of England nor the Conservative Party nor the Labour Party is anywhere near the place to which Kennedy and John XXIII and Temple and Macleod and Bevan and Gaitskell were pointing. In fact, in every case, the institution is, in most important respects, facing in the opposite direction with no very real prospect of a turn-around.

This gap between past aspirations and present performance is poignant enough in the American and the religious cases; but at least something was achieved in them by the progenitors of the modern era. The Great Society programme of President Johnson flowed directly from the J F K impetus, and both the Roman and the English churches have made some progress towards a new dialogue with the laity.

Likewise the Conservative Party looked in worse shape a year ago than it does today. Iain Macleod's own unique ability to communicate with the electorate is still sorely needed; but there is not much doubt in my mind that he would have approved the slaughter of the lame ducks policy, the attempt to go for growth and the determination to call public opinion into the balance during Phase Two of the prices and incomes struggle.

The case of the Labour Party is far more doubtful. There are very few consolations to be found in its present plight – and it is the knowledge of what Bevan and Gaitskell – most particularly Gaitskell – might have achieved that makes this tenth anniversary perspective so melancholy.

It is hard to pin down exactly what this contribution was without lapsing into a series of negative comparisons with what in fact occurred. But, to put it as positively as possible, at the outset, I should say that by the end of their lives – and after the appalling doctrinal clashes of the mid-1950s – the two men had, in their different ways, come to represent the reconciliation of the opposing principles of reason and emotion within the Labour Party. Bevan was passion mellowed, finally, by wisdom. Gaitskell was logic humanized, finally, by emotion.

I am not saying that either man was ever as one-sided as his opponents portrayed him. Gaitskell was never a 'desiccated, calculated machine'. Nor was Bevan simply an irresponsible demagogue. But it was only at the very end that either fully integrated their political personalities and projected jointly to the country the vision of a coherent democratic party whose ends and means combined the force of the desirable and the conviction of the possible. Since that fairly brief moment of real credibility in the early 1960s, it has been downhill all the way. The Labour Party has won two general elections since then but mainly thanks to the impetus acquired at that time.

What has gone wrong? And what might Gaitskell, as leader of the Labour Party, have created or retained that has now been lost? There are many things one might suggest – sheer brains, for one thing. (Re-reading Gaitskell's speeches on almost any subject still gives a genuine intellectual pleasure which cannot be derived from those of anyone now sitting in the House of Commons.) But two things stand out. One is intellectual seriousness and the other is intellectual honesty. Gaitskell believed that political ideas really matter. And moreover he believed that other people thought they mattered too.

The result of these eccentric notions was that he was both far more radical and, funnily enough, more democratic than his successor. Having started off with certain fundamental ideals of social justice he then proceeded with rigorous care to think out the consequences of an egalitarian postition in a way which Harold Wilson has never been able, or perhaps wished, to do. And having reached his conclusion he aspired to convince by persuasive argument and exposition rather than by political manoeuvre.

If one reads his speech to the TUC in 1951 (when he was Chancellor of the Exchequer), where he was arguing for incomes restraint; or his exposition of the case for and against the Common Market at the Labour Party Conference in 1962, one can see his determination to treat the movement seriously. This was the reverse of the élitism with which he has sometimes been charged, for it was the product of a calm belief that people are quite capable of understanding sophisticated arguments and responding to them.

The corollary of this was, of course, that having made a serious case, he required a great deal of persuasion and equally serious argument to change it. His reputation for stubbornness was earned not so much because he could never be persuaded that he was wrong but because he required to be persuaded in a fashion which most politicians regard as inappropriate in political argument – namely by the force of logic rather than of expediency.

I have no idea how he would have finally decided on the Common Market issue. His contempt for some of the 'pro' arguments being put around in the early 1960s combined with his concern for the Commonwealth (particularly India) were obviously inclining him towards the 'anti' camp when he died. But the one thing that is absolutely certain is that if he had taken a firm decision as Prime Minister to enter the EEC he would have staked his own leadership of the party on maintaining consistency under another government.

The case against Gaitskell and in favour of the Wilson-style leadership lies, of course, in this area. Gaitskell's determination to have clarity and honesty led him to face issues head-on when Wilson (or for that matter Harold Macmillan) would have tried to fudge them. The famous Clause Four debate over the nationalization section of the party constitution provides the main ammunition today, as it did in 1959, for a defence of expediency and party unity as against doctrinal purity and tidiness.

Gaitskell was accused, with some justice of splitting the party unnecessarily over a form of words when he could have won the substance of the argument and kept the party united by a little judicious terminological inexactitude. And one can make the case against even harder by asking what he would have done in the long run about immigration. He committed himself passionately to an 'open door' policy for Commonwealth immigrants. But could he – or should he indeed – have sustained this admirable ideal against the wishes of an overwhelming majority of the party when the inevitable reaction set in from 1964 onwards?

This kind of question leads straight to the heart of the argument about the nature of political leadership in a democratic society – what it can achieve and what it cannot. The essence of the thing must surely be persuasion, either before the event or at most very soon after. A Prime Minister or party leader may either try to educate the country and his followers before he commits them to certain courses of action or, at a pinch, he can precipitate them into a new situation and hope to convince them that they like it afterwards. But whichever method he chooses, he has got to put his own words and his own reputation on the line. You cannot persuade unless you are prepared to make a case, and you cannot make a case unless you have some respect for your own arguments.

A leader cannot be expected to achieve the impossible and he is most unwise to embark on fights which are manifestly unnecessary – for which reasons Hugh Gaitskell was almost certainly wrong to go against Clause Four, and Harold Wilson can be forgiven for failing, in the short time at his disposal, to persuade the trade unions to accept Mrs Castle's legislation.

But the fact remains that there is no possibility of persuasion and none of progress unless a leader is prepared to commit himself on the great isues and, once committted, is prepared to follow his own logic and to fight his battles over and over again or die in the attempt. The point about Gaitskell is that he believed these things and acted on them. In the past ten years we have seen precious few others of whom that could be said.

*Financial Times*, *12 January 1973*

# Education and the Black Paper

It is a very long time since there has been a full-blooded political argument about education. Until recently, no subject emptied the House of Commons so quickly or caused fewer squalls to ruffle the placid surface of inter-party consensus. There were a few agreeable, ritual slanging-matches about the public schools and so forth, but by and large, since the 1944 Education Act, both sides have accepted a mildly progressive 'Butskellite' thesis that education is a 'good thing' and that the more people who have it the better.

One of the most significant political phenomena of the past couple of years has been to see this consensus breaking down under the strains imposed by massive expansion and limited finance. The Labour Party has remained in much the same position, for its supporters have nothing, or almost nothing, to lose in this field. But on the Conservative side we have seen a sense of unease among middle-class people in the country deepening to anxiety and affecting (as traditional democratic doctrine demands it should) the political arm of the middle class – the Conservative Party in Parliament.

Sir Edward Boyle who, as the last Conservative Education Minister, presided happily over the introduction of comprehensive schools and the implementation of the Robbins Report recommendations about university expansion, is now under almost intolerable pressure from his back benches to denounce the comprehensive system and to modify university expansion. And although he has the support of Mr Heath and the majority of the Shadow Cabinet at present, that is not necessarily immutable.

The latest move in this campaign – and one which sheds a lot of interesting light on its origins and objectives – was the publication last week of a so-called 'Black Paper' entitled 'Fight for Education' in which a number of educational traditionalists summarize their objections to the present situation and to future trends. The contributions to this symposium vary considerably in quality and in point of view, but a reasonably coherent train of thought emerges and reflects what an increasing number of middle-class Conservatives are feeling.

The central complaint is that quality in English education is being sacrificed to equality and to quantity. Egalitarian doctrines about 'equality of opportunity' are penalizing clever children who are being held back, and 'progressive' ideas about educational psychology are lowering the attainments even of the average. There is too much permissiveness and not enough formal teaching in primary and secondary schools. University education seems to be concerned with self-expression and not with truth and discipline. Far too many university students are wasting time and money. And in short, we are witnessing a 'progressive collapse' of our educational system.

This is a persuasive attack on present trends from a conservative point of view. It highlights a number of observable defects in things as they stand – inflexibility and overcrowding in schools, student revolution and chequered standards at universities – and connects them with a number of Conservative bogeys – 'progressive' nonsense about self-expression, lack of discipline and permissiveness. By linking the whole question to size and thereby pointing implicitly to a more élitist approach, the pamphlet draws upon deep springs of conservative thought about the hierarchical society and the imperfectability of human nature.

At a time when the emphasis is upon cutting public expenditure the attack on size has another kind of appeal as well. The preservation of the private system and a slowdown in the rate of university expansion have become economically as well as doctrinally attractive.

For the time being therefore we must expect to hear a lot more of this thesis, and it would not be entirely surprising if it sweeps away Sir Edward Boyle, when the new Labour Education Bill, now in preparation, is brought in. Even on the Labour side it will gain its adherents among the practical, no-nonsense school of education to which some socialist politicians and intellectuals belong. For while these will dispute the conclusions about comprehensive schools (which are approved because they provide adequate education for lower-middle-class children of average ability) they will agree that university students should be made to devote more of their time to practical, useful study and less to revolutionary hogwash.

Yet there are serious flaws in the whole argument both as a diagnosis and as a prescription. It recognizes that many of the difficulties of the education system arise from sheer numbers, but it does not acknowledge the political force behind these numbers or see where this force must inevitably carry us. It is an attempt to turn back the clock to a system of education which has already passed away rather than an attempt to come to terms with the future.

The basic change which has taken place over the past forty years is that we have moved from a two-tier system of education to a one-tier system of quite a different sort. The old system was devoted at the top level to the inculcation of middle-class values and virtues and a smattering of utilitarian knowledge and general culture. At the lower level it was entirely a question of producing a white-collared and working class with rudimentary skills enough to get a decent clerical job.

We now have a unified system in which the whole of the education system is geared to a society in which specific knowledge and qualifications matter more and more and class matters less and less. From the élitists point of view the damage has already been done and it cannot be reversed. Middle-class children already have to compete on terms of virtual equality with others for university places and subsequently for good jobs; the criteria on which they are judged are less and less accent and manners but more and more knowledge of specific skills and subjects.

Looking ahead, one can see that this tendency is now bound to accelerate with each generation. The competitive gap between public and grammar schools has already virtually disappeared, and in view of the rise in expectations it is impossible to believe that the gap between comprehensive and grammar schools will not eventually disappear as well. It is a difficult transition that we are making; and most of the confusion and reaction arises quite simply from this fact – not, as the authors of 'Fight for Education' would have it, from egalitarianism.

Students are rebelling against two main consequences of the new situation – first, the sheer crowding and impersonality produced by weight of numbers; and secondly the arid attempt to introduce pseudo-scientific disciplines into the arts and social sciences as a means of categorizing them in the rat race. The 'permissive' school of teaching is partly the result of genuine discoveries in psychology (particularly in the definition of 'intelligence') but quite largely an emotional reaction against the competitive pressures which teachers find themselves forced to apply to modern children. Even the revolt of the middle classes against the system is to some extent a simple reaction to the loss of prestige and security which a fully competitive educational system brings.

There is really nothing to be done about the ultimate cause of all these discontents – namely, the irreversible change in our social structure. Indeed, the political party which continued to ignore it would do so at its peril. To take comprehensive schools, for instance.

A recent NOP poll showed that 45 per cent of the country was in favour of comprehensives as against 43 per cent in favour of two- or three-tier systems; and of Conservatives 57 per cent were opposed. On the other hand, 62 per cent of the 21–24 age group, 50 per cent of the 25–34 age group and 54 per cent of the 35–44 age group were in favour of comprehensives. The breakdown by classes is also significant for while the AB class split 60-32 in favour of separate systems, the C, D and E classes split no better than half and half.

Whether we like it or not, therefore, any attempt to perpetuate a class-oriented, élitist view of education is likely to be doomed to failure. More may mean worse, in Kingsley Amis's famous phrase, at any rate for the time being, but 'more' is here to stay. The only question is, or should be, whether we can rescue the virtues of an élitist system – tradition, standards, and a wide view of civilization – from the utilitarian, competitive system which now applies.

This cannot be done by mere lamentations about the present numbers, for that is a waste of time; nor by cries for higher standards of scholarship, for this will only entail a more fearsome competition and more philistine pseudo-science. Both parties, and indeed industry, need to rethink from first principles the objectives of education; and I do not believe that this need necessarily lead either to the woolly excesses of extreme progressives or the élitist rigours of the right wing.

*Financial Times*, 21 March 1969

# The Fate of the Public Schools

Are the public schools due for the chop at last? It's not an unreasonable question at this moment. Generations of left-wing activists have been telling us that these institutions are the bastions of class-consciousness, snobbery, and inefficiency; and generations of public-school men (mostly, though not by any means all, Conservative) have informed us that they are the backbone of the country. In an election contest which is supposed to be about the modernization of Britain – and particularly of education – one might have expected that the issue would be the centre of violent party controversy. In a year, moreover, in which a leading Conservative Minister admitted publicly that he had refused to serve at least partly on the grounds that the Prime Minister had been chosen by 'a small circle of Etonians', the Opposition might have seized a chance. Nothing of the sort has happened. The Labour Party merely announce that they will 'integrate the schools with the state system' – which may mean in practice almost anything from a move towards some mild form of Direct Grant boarding-schools, to a complete and almost instant take-over following diversion to other kinds of education. The Conservatives present us with the pious thought that 'parents have the right to spend their money on the education of their children if they choose'; but they do not appear ready to lift a controversial finger in defence of this principle.

The reason for this rather coy political truce is not simply that about half of the likely Labour Cabinet went to public schools or sent their sons there; nor, for that matter, has a Conservative Cabinet containing nine Etonians and twelve other public-school men had a sudden rush of egalitarian conscience. The trouble is, most probably, that neither side wants to upset the floating voter. One of the Labour Party's major achievements under Mr Harold Wilson has been to win back at least the suspended disbelief of the professional middle classes, and this is not to be recklessly allowed to subside into distrust again. The Conservatives, for their part, are well aware that it would need only about two words in defence of the public schools from them to send their reluctant ex-member of 'Pop', ex-peer cricketer and poacher-catcher slithering over a precipice of farce, and the party after him.

This seems a sad commentary on the present initiative of the political parties, but it's also a pity for all of us, for the whole public-schools controversy badly needs revivifying. At this moment political pussy-footing has side-tracked it (as it has often been side-tracked before) into a question of 'value for money'.

The recent report of *Where?* has passed sentence:

> If a parent lives in a large town, there is a good chance that his local grammar school will be academically equal to the average public school and a good deal better than many . . . It is far better if in doubt to stick to the state system from the beginning than be faced with the choice of changing a child's school perhaps at a critical stage, or subjecting the family budget to intolerable strain . . .

This kind of judgement, logically impeccable as it is, is balm to the gradualist reformer. He can from now on relax in the belief that if the state system is academically as sound as the private and if we democratize the admissions system at Oxbridge and stop the tax loopholes through which doting grandparents are able to pour money for the education of the next generation but one, nobody can either need or afford to send his child to a public school. Unfortunately the headmaster of Bloxham (whose school came bottom of the *Where?* league table for A-level passes) gave the game away in his annoyance: 'There's more,' he said indignantly, 'to education than passing examinations.' Tom Brown's father made the same observation on the eve of his son's departure for Rugby. 'I don't care a straw for Greek particles or the digamma; no more does his mother . . . If he'll only turn out a brave, helpful, truth-telling Englishman and a Christian, that's all I want.' And one hundred and thirty years later Mr Peregrine Wors-thorne, writing in the *Sunday Telegraph*, remarked, 'I should like my son to go to a public school less because it would help him get into Oxford and Cambridge than because it would help him stay out of the Aldermaston march and suchlike follies.' Mr Worsthorne's idiom is a little different from the Squire's but I suspect he means much the same.

A *Daily Mail* survey carried out a few years ago showed that in a sample of ex-public-school products asked to say what they had got for their money, 37 per cent said 'social advantage', 29 per cent said 'more self-confidence', 14 per cent said 'career advantage', 6 per cent said 'leadership', 14 per cent picked other qualities (including, presumably, intellectual prowess). In short, so long as people think they can gain some or all of these advantages and 'the manners of an English gentleman' many of them will continue to scrape and save to send their sons to a boarding-school where the proper indoctrination can take place rather than a day grammar school where it might not be effective or a state school where the advantages simply do not exist. It would apparently matter little to them if the school taught but raffia work and tatting.

What is clearly needed for these people is another *Where?* league table showing the number of gentlemen turned out per 100 boys (with Bloxham triumphantly at the top, and Ampleforth at the bottom). This brings us to Mr Wilkinson's book, *The Prefects*,[1] for it is to this work that the compilers of such a table would undoubtedly have to refer. What Mr Wilkinson has done is to describe in immense detail the ethos of the Victorian public school in its heyday. He has isolated all the main virtues that were implanted and made to flower on what was often extremely stony soil. Self-control as shown in the character of the 'good loser' and the man who doesn't show off. Loyalty and co-operation demonstrated in the house and team spirit. 'Style', fostered by hallowed customs and rituals. Flexibility epitomized in the amateur ideal and a curriculum which avoided a single useful item of expertise. Responsibility inculcated by the prefect system.

I wish Mr Wilkinson had had more fun with all this. He could have made some hilarious and valid points with those glumly uplifting school songs and even with mottoes ('*vincit qui patitur*', '*clarior ex ignibus*', '*aut vincere aut mori*', and so on). And what about the school story? Dean Farrar and later Talbot Baines Reed and especially G A Henty were illuminating because they carried the spirit to the point of caricature. Take the hero of *With Roberts to Pretoria*, one Yorke Pemberton, aged sixteen – 'a typical public schoolboy, straight, and clean-limbed, free from all awkwardness, bright in expression and possessed of a large amount of self-possession or, as he himself would

**203**

[1] Published by Oxford University Press, 1963.

have called it, 'cheek', was a little particular about the set of his Eton jacket and trousers and the appearance of his boots; as hard as nails and almost tireless; a good specimen of the class by which Britain has been built up, her colonies formed and her battlefields won.' *The Prefects* describes his type with a good deal less brevity and vividness.

Nevertheless Mr Wilkinson is good and salutary, because the system he describes as it existed in the 1880s and 1890s is so little changed. Here, for instance, are two passages, from the recent book[2] on Marlborough, written by a group of the boys.

> On the whole it is the conscientious and efficient organizer, who is full of house spirit, has a strong character and personality as well as a good games record, who is normally made a prefect . . . Non-games playing prefects do exist . . . but they are very much in the minority . . . partly because the right sort of person with a forceful personality tends to project it into games, but it is also tied up with the fact that games are the basis of all house spirit, the force which is considered essential for the welfare of a house as a united co-operative body . . .

> The insignia of [prefectorial] office, white tie and coloured waistcoat or sweater, plus all the ceremonial of sidesmanship in Chapel and the prefect's table in hall help to emphasize this fact that they are the chosen apostles of the Master . . .

All Mr Wilkinson's ingredients are still there and all the utensils for mixing them – house spirit, games, ceremonial, tradition, authority. Yet Marlborough at present is known as one of the most 'modern' public schools with no fagging, little beating, a well-known progressive headmaster, and (to judge from the book) licence for a healthy dose of scepticism. There are, however, many more traditional schools, as anyone will appreciate who heard the unearthly howl of an Eton fag-call resounding round the ornate eaves of the St Martin's Theatre during the recent performances of Mr David Benedictus's play *The Fourth of June* and witnessed on the same stage the ritual brutalities of an Eton Library playing with its victims. In most essentials, at any rate in character-building, it seems that Eton, by reason of arrogance, and the smallest public schools, by reason of desperate traditionalism, have remained pretty well unchanged for eighty years.

And why should they change? one might ask. What is wrong with

[2] Kenneth Mason, *Marlborough*.

loyalty and responsibility and self-control and flexibility, that we should despise them or wish to alter the institutions which foster them? The reason for doubt lies not in the qualities themselves so much as the fact that experience, amply illustrated by Mr Wilkinson, shows that they can be too dearly bought. Even eighty years ago the public schools had distinct defects as 'leadership courses'. They did their job historically all right, tapping the middle classes for talent, making Victorian society more homogeneous than it would otherwise have been, and keeping alive some sense of values in the highly competitive and materialistic Victorian world. But they achieved this, in effect, by a series of brain-washing operations for which a high price had to be paid in terms of emotional growth and creative capacity. The famous report received by Peter Ustinov at Westminster – 'he shows great originality which must be curbed at all costs' – is a bit of a freak but not all that much. Originality at a public school is unsettling because it implies, if carried beyond a very limited distance, that the individual is prepared to put himself before society and to defy it – the unforgivable sin.

If, as is often said about them, the Victorian public schools had merely been producing empire-fodder – endless Indian Army sub-alterns and inhabitants of cantonment houses in a thousand parts of the globe – it might not have mattered so much (except for the wretched victims who must have been frequently bored to death). But they were also producing the central direction of the Empire, and it was here that the incapacity to imagine and foresee changes and to seize and use the imagination of others had disastrous effects in a world which changed as fast as ours has in eighty years. The mandarin class in China, with which Mr Wilkinson makes a long and elaborate comparison, was to this extent in a better situation in that its members could look back over the precedents of 1,000 years and be sure of finding something more or less relevant. The public-school leader has had to meet an appallingly bewildering world in which almost no precedents ever fully apply and in which Thucydides and Livy and Tacitus do not provide an adequate general guide. He has often failed disastrously. The products of the public schools in their heyday (i.e., from the late 1860s to 1900) were the generals who tried to fight the Boer War with the methods of the Crimean, and the First World War with the methods of the Boer War. They were the politicians who failed to prevent the slaughter in the trenches, and in the next generation failed to react to Hitler as a tragically new phenomenon. The period was illuminated by occasional flashes of genius which not even the public schools could extinguish – Churchill was at Harrow, Keynes at Eton, William Temple at Rugby – but the picture as a whole is one of appalling unimaginative failure at the top.

When one criticizes the present government and its predecessors on these lines one is, of course, criticizing the public schools, vintage 1920–30. But with the exception of Harold Macmillan (an earlier vintage), who did show considerable imagination in some fields, it is difficult to say that this generation has shown that things have changed. It is worth remarking in passing how entirely dominated the Tory Party still is by the public-school ethos. In the constituencies non-public-school men come in all the time from the Young Conservatives but the important offices still go mainly to public-school types with traditional public-school ideas. In Parliament, there is a generation of non-public-school Tories who came in via the wartime services but they are, as a class, rather regretted (especially at the moment). Of the twenty-two Tories who voted against the resale prices bill only five were from the big public schools while the persistent Tory rebels – the men who 'rock the boat' and to whom 'loyalty' is not the over-mastering virtue – are hardly at all from the traditional background. The Labour Party, which consists either of non-public-school men or rogue intellectuals like Mr Crossman, are even more difficult to whip in.

And what will the youngest generation from the public schools be like, assuming there is no reform? The book on Marlborough confirms such inquiries as I have made from present or recent public schoolboys and leads me to think that this batch will not be much different from the others. They may be better educated in the sense that they have a wider syllabus and better laboratory and library facilities; they may even be less brainwashed by discipline, herded less often on to the rugger field, and more at ease with the opposite sex. But boarding-school life among a group of boys who are there because their parents are rich is bound to be an inbred existence, cut off from the outside world and its real problems and guaranteed to build up the pressures to social conformity and caste prejudice.

Most of such people cannot be allowed to become 'leaders' in any real sense because the country cannot afford to staff its senior civil service, its Parliament, its industry, and its professions with characters who are by background and training so totally unaware of the feelings, reactions, and problems of the people they are supposed to be leading – the gap between the Executive and the subject is wide enough even without a class barrier.

**206**

It is frequently said that the public schools have lost their *raison d'être* now that the 'Imperial spirit' is dead. This is perfectly true – without the Empire the public schools have become, as someone remarked, a code without a creed. But that is only half the story. The fact is that up to the last war the Empire provided an infinite number of openings for the less-than-brilliant public schoolboy. The Home Civil and the I C S would be above him, but the Army, Colonial Police Forces and District Officerships lay ready and waiting for Yorke Pemberton. Now he and his friends are a drug on the home market. Ten thousand or so leave public school every year. Half (to be generous) reach a university. Another quarter are taken by Sandhurst or squeezed into the family firm or bought a place in the city. But the rest must try to impress industrial personnel managers and medical school registrars and heads of chartered accountant firms. Since it may be years before these boys lose their marginal snob-appeal it may be years before the best candidate has the best chance.

I have already argued that nothing will stop parents buying their children an education if it brings advantages like these. The choice before the reformer is therefore restricted. He can keep the boarding-school concept and therefore, almost inevitably, keep the idea of an élite (though he may enlarge the élite's catchment area and its humanity by making it open to a wider range of entrants). This would have the blessing of precedent since the original public schools achieved a very similar advance over previous systems; but it is doubtful whether the deep prejudice against boarding-schools among the working-class entrants that are wanted could be overcome. The alternative is to turn the schools into something entirely different, bearing in mind that their geographical position makes them virtually useless for day-student use.

The Conservative Party has naturally no intention of reforming the system. Why should it when its own values and even its existence are at stake? Nevertheless it would be pleasant to think that the Labour Party was really prepared to grasp the nettle.

*Encounter, May 1964*

# Mr Crosland and the Coffee Pot

**W**e live in stirring times. The Vietnam War still rages, President Nixon unveils a budget which may easily mean racial war in the US within the next decade, the British and French governments are faced with the possibility of £1,000 millions' worth of research money disappearing down the plughole, negotiations open in Vienna which could transform the post-war military situation in Europe – and Mr Anthony Crosland finds a £40 coffee pot in his cupboard. There is no doubt which of these momentous events is the most important. Mr Crosland's coffee pot has won by a mile.

Do I hear someone say there is something wrong with our values here? 'Frivolous', 'parochial', 'monstrously unfair to an innocent and respected politician' – the words spring readily to the lips. And they are all true. We *ought* to be able to appreciate the consequences of far-off happenings, and we ought, as journalists, to be able to sell newspapers by discussing '*The Future of Socialism*' rather than by splashing its author's name around in a totally fatuous fairy story suggesting petty graft.

And yet it is not as simple as that. For one thing this three-days' wonder is not just a whim of news editors in the popular Press. Of course, to anyone who has the faintest personal knowledge of Mr Crosland the whole thing was barmy from the start. But if one is to go on the reactions of one's non-political acquaintances, to say nothing of conversations overheard in bars, and the like, this was genuinely one of those stories which aroused echoes far outside the normal range of ordinary public events. And the interesting question is why?

The instinctive reaction of the most doom-laden school of politicians to this question will, I imagine, be to say that it all goes to show the depths to which parliamentary democracy has sunk in the public esteem. In a week in which the leader of the Opposition and the president of the CBI unite in scattering dark forebodings about the state of politics in Britain, it would be positively unfashionable to say anything else. The public, so the story goes, has become totally dis-illusioned with the catchpenny antics of politicians and is now not only prepared but positively anxious to believe anything, however sordid, about them and their activities.

There may be a bit of this muck-raking about it, of course – though if so, one can hardly say that things have changed very much in the past 3,000 years. Men have always been at least half delighted by scandal in high life, and for the simplest of reasons – namely that it puts the high and mighty in a position which normal people com-prehend and conversely enables the man in the street to see himself as no worse than the high and mighty. If the story includes sex it is better still. But the mere raising of the possibility that Mr Crosland was having his palm greased, even though it proved false, immediately made him seem a far more human figure, although a less admirable one. People do not like their politicians to be bent, but if they are, at least they can understand them.

On the whole, though, I should be inclined to draw a quite different moral from the incident. Far from betraying contempt and disillusion-ment on the part of the public it seems to me to show a touching faith and real concern about our central political institutions. It is an odd thing that we still adhere as a nation essentially to a middle-class late-Victorian morality in public life, even though every other vestige of that morality has been swept away or at least undermined; and this is all the more miraculous because so many of the social and administrative circumstances which produced this morality have changed as well.

And the oddest paradox about the whole situation is that at a time when materialism is probably more in the ascendant than at any time in the past two hundred years, the actual possibilities of 'getting at' our rulers have seldom been less. A cynic might say that this is because the wide boys can make more than enough without having to bribe anyone. But the fact is that any sensible person looking for a 'way in' to central government must conclude that it is scarcely possible to corrupt a Cabinet minister these days and scarcely worth corrupting anyone else.

Mr Crosland pointed out, quite rightly, that at the time he received his pot as Minister of Education, he was not responsible for awarding contracts. But even if a minister were in a position to push favours in any particular direction his chances of doing so would be very severely circumscribed by the machinery of his department and the corporate incorruptibility of the senior civil service.

A Secretary of the Environment might in theory be 'influenced' in taking some big planning decision, but at that level the fierce light that is focused on a minister by his colleagues, his secretaries and the Press would make it a very risky proceeding – even if his personal say-so produced the desired result. The complexity of modern society, which has increased the power of the bureaucracy and reduced the power of individual ministers, has also reduced the likelihood of corruption, at least at the very summit.

Lower down, among the rank and file on the back benches, the pointlessness of corruption is even more apparent. There is legitimate concern about the activities of public relations firms who retain MPs to advise them, but it is very doubtful whether these organizations get their money's worth. There is simply not enough power on the back benches to go round. It was not always so, of course. In the eighteenth century, the government found it necessary to bribe members on a massive scale out of secret service funds (in the early nineteenth century it was, though, more seemly to apply the money to the electors in the constituencies), but nowadays party discipline has made such expenditure otiose. Naturally PR men like to have an MP on their books because it impresses the clients and it may occasionally be advantageous to have a cocktail party at the House of Commons or a bit of gossip about how such and such a minister is tending to think about such and such a subject. But the amount of influence that can be brought to bear by even the most assiduous and committed backbench lobbyist is severely limited.

The reasons why this is so have something to do with the clubby atmosphere of the House of Commons (another survival from the nineteenth century), which enables members and ministers to assess the statements of their colleagues and to guess their origins pretty accurately – even if the outside world cannot. But the main reason is the more disturbing one that the pressures which MPs can now bring to bear on real decisions – either in debate, or in the back-bench committees or through the specialist committees of the House – is for the most part tenuous and even when it is stronger, that strength is a collective rather than an individual one.

The public does not realize this. Nor has it cottoned on to the fact that its concern would be much better directed to the possibilities of corruption in the place where one would really expect to find it – that is, in local government, where individual councillors have far more executive power, where the Press is less potent, where very large sums of money turn on the decisions of very few people, and where permanent officials are neither as numerous, as high-powered or as well paid.

Does all this mean that matters can be safely left as they are, or does the public's rather incoherent concern need to be met in some way? A battle about this is now being fought out within the Tory Party. One school of thought believes that there is genuine cause for worry about the whole question of outside pressures and recommends that there should be a register in which ministers and M Ps would be obliged to record at least the main sources of their income whether from shares or P R 'retainers'. This is passionately opposed by those who believe that individual members must be assumed to be behaving like gentlemen unless it is shown otherwise. They also argue that members must be allowed some privacy and that shareholdings in, say, South Africa would bring the House into unnecessary controversy.

My own feeling is in favour of the register. As Parliament and the Executive are at present constructed, corruption at Westminster is not a serious question. Moreover, if, as I hope, Parliament's power as a scrutineer is greatly increased in the coming years, it is important that as many 'interests' as possible are heard in it. Nevertheless, in the last resort, this power will be meaningless (and could probably never be recaptured) unless the public is absolutely certain that its own voice and no one else's is predominant.

*Financial Times*, 2 February 1973

# Ulster – the Foreboding

A true political earthquake is an awe-inspiring sight. Vast edifices topple, ancient façades crumble, cornices drop off and crash to the ground – and normally sane, level-headed citizens, feeling their world tremble, rush screaming mindlessly into the street. Such is the scene in Northern Ireland during the last week of the general election campaign.

The Ulster Unionist Party, for forty-eight years perhaps the most monolithic of any ruling political apparatus in the democratic world, is split from top to bottom. The Opposition is in splinters. And on the edge of the ruins prowl the religious extremists ready to pick off any of their shivering fellow-citizens who show any sign of straying far from their derelict houses.

To understand this extraordinary débâcle and assess the chances of building something worthwhile from the fragments one ought, as is usual in Ireland, to plod far back into history – to the seventeenth century and beyond. But to cut this long story short one may, perhaps, start with the partition of Ireland in 1921. At that time the Unionist Party was founded; and it was founded out of fear – fear that the constitutional stockade planted round the six counties of Northern Ireland would be breached and the Protestants within it submerged in the Roman Catholic hordes of Southern Ireland.

So long as the Protestants remained the overwhelming majority in Northern Ireland and so long as the external threat overrode any other political inclination, the Unionist Party relying on the support of the electorate could run the country pretty much as it chose. And for forty years it did so, not unnaturally, for the benefit of the Protestant majority and the comfort of its own members.

During the past five years, however, this fundamental balance has changed rapidly. In the first place, the external threat which provided both the justification and the cement of the Unionist Party has receded. The old animosities have faded from the South, and the Irish government no longer lays claim publicly to all of Ulster. The I R A gunmen have retired or been subdued by their own government.

Secondly, immigration from the South and the high Catholic birth-rate have reduced the Protestant majority in the North to something near critical proportions. There are now just over 750,000 Protestants to about half a million Catholics. This influx might have increased the embattled nature of Unionism, but it has not. For the Catholics have increasingly come to recognize the economic advantages of living in Northern Ireland with British National Security benefits and the National Health Service, and though they are demanding equality with Protestants as citizens, their republicanism has been softened.

The results of these shifts are shown by an opinion poll carried out by the University of Strathclyde recently, which shows that for both Protestants and Catholics, Northern Ireland's economic problems take precedence by a huge margin over religious issues or the constitutional question. Only 40 per cent of Catholics now appear in favour of a united Ireland and 35 per cent of Protestants are in favour of at least greater co-operation with the Republic. In spite of the much vaunted 'link with the U K' only 38 per cent of Protestants thought of themselves as 'British' and 68 per cent of Protestants and 81 per cent of Catholics thought that people of the opposite religion are 'about the same'.

These findings cannot be taken to mean that the old bitterness is entirely dead. Ulster is predominantly rural and the whole mystique of Protestant freemasonry, the Orange lodges, the walls of Derry, the Battle of the Boyne, King Billy and all the rest of the anti-Catholic paraphernalia, is carried on with fervour; and in a situation in which the pace of change became too fast or Catholicism became militant or violent it would take very little to fan the flames of extremism once more.

The Reverend Ian Paisley is the most flamboyant exponent of this last-ditch Protestantism. He is a spell-binder, a Bible-punching demagogue, and not without his own grim sense of humour. To hear him tell his congregation of Free Presbyterians to pray that, 'the gallows which the tyrant O'Neill has prepared for God's chosen people should become the instrument of his own destruction,' and then break off with the words, 'I wouldn't want you to take that literally or I might be accused of telling you to put a rope round his neck' – is to realize the extreme possibility of innuendo and irony. His appeal at present is severely restricted, but under some circumstances he could become almost infinitely dangerous.

It is this situation, with its new possibilities and dangers, which Captain Terence O'Neill, the Unionist leader and Prime Minister since 1963, is trying desperately to control. He evidently recognizes that the increase in the Catholic population must force the Unionist Party to try to come to terms with its sectarian opponents, and he has been feeling his way with infinite caution in this direction since he came to office. However, events have moved too fast for him since last summer. The Civil Rights Movement, which suddenly caught on with its march on Londonderry and its cry 'One man, one vote', is really an attempt by the Catholic minority to claim political power, particularly in local government, commensurate with its size.

As soon as its ability to put mass support on to the streets was shown last autumn, it became clear that the pace of change would have to be speeded up. The riots in Derry and Armagh not only threatened to provoke a dangerous Protestant backlash, but also involved the Westminster government, upon whose goodwill and economic support Northern Ireland, as an entity, must depend.

The quarrel between Captain O'Neill and his dissident followers ultimately arises because they do not recognize the urgency of this situation. The Prime Minister managed to push through a five-point programme of reform in November including, in effect, the abolition of religious discrimination in local housing, the appointment of an Ombudsman, and a review of the local government franchise; but in the process he had to dismiss his hard-line Minister of Home Affairs, Mr William Craig, and face the resignation of two other important Cabinet ministers. Later there was the call by twelve back-bench Unionist MPs (out of the thirty-seven in the Party) that he should resign himself – and finally, this week, Lord Brookeborough, the Grand Old Man of Unionism, denounced him.

It is probable that if he had asked for a vote of confidence from his party the Prime Minister would have got it by about twenty-two votes to fifteen but he has preferred to appeal to the electors over the heads of his party in the hopes that he will gain a clear mandate from moderate opinion to build still further bridges to the Catholic community.

The difficulties inherent in this operation are enormous. Captain O'Neill has a vast personal following. His appeal on television in December for individual support produced 120,000 signatures and the

214

opinion polls show that he is preferred by 91 per cent of Catholics and 58 per cent of Protestants. However, these preferences can only be given practical expression where 'O'Neill men' can be substituted for the dissidents, and since the dissidents in all cases control their local party machines this has meant that 'O'Neill' candidates have had to be put up to run against official Unionist candidates.

The troubles of the fourteen O'Neillists, pitchforked suddenly into constituencies where they may have few links, with no organization and facing the well-oiled official machine are indescribable. Their opponents have been astute enough to stand blandly on the party's rather vague manifesto, and, being mainly friends of the aristocratic Prime Minister they are exposed to jibes about upper-class carpet-baggers.

The trouble is that the O'Neill Unionists can only get in if they win the support of a large number of Catholics, and unfortunately, though Catholics may prefer O'Neill to his colleagues, the opinion polls show that where there is another Opposition candidate available more than half the Catholics will prefer such a man to either sort of Unionist.

Captain O'Neill could in theory have increased his appeal to Catholics if he had forthrightly endorsed the principle of 'one man, one vote' instead of merely saying he will set up a Commission to consider it; if he had appealed for Catholics to join the Unionist Party instead of merely supporting it; or if he had formally endorsed the O'Neill men instead of simply attacking their opponents. But this, so far, he has refused to do.

The fact has to be faced, in any case, that the gamble he has taken may not come off. His friends believe he can emerge from the election with a new balance in the Parliamentary party of twenty-seven to ten. This is a very optimistic assessment, yet much less success would make it very difficult for him to continue.

To make matters worse he is undoubtedly an arrogant, sensitive and difficult man who takes very little pain to make his policies palatable to Parliament either by dressing them up for what they are not, or by bonhomous gestures to his colleagues and his back-benchers.

There are thus the most daunting hurdles both of personality and policy to be cleared before the vision of a non-sectarian, moderate and united Unionist Party is turned to reality. And until it does the chances of it being confronted by a non-sectarian, moderate and united opposition are at least as remote.

At present the main opposition is provided by the Nationalist Party with nine seats. Being traditionally Catholic and in favour of union with the South its days are theoretically numbered for the same reasons that confront old-style Unionism. As its leader, Mr Eddy McAteer, a once fiery but now almost extinct volcano, admits sadly, the bread-and-butter issues are taking over and blurring his vision of a united Ireland. But although he can now be heard talking of housing and unemployment he does so without much conviction or the necessary economic expertise.

This failure has often led to the charge that the Nationalists are simply Green Tories whereas the logic of the situation calls for a Social Democratic or left-wing opposition – and there is truth in this. The trouble is that the Northern Ireland Labour Party, which has two seats at present, has failed to provide this alternative, partly because it has become identified with Protestantism and partly because its industrial preoccupations have been a severe handicap in a country nearly half of whose inhabitants live on the land.

The People's Democracy Party, formed last October from the Civil Rights movement, might in time bridge this gap. It is fielding eight candidates and a great deal of amateur enthusiasm. But it is torn by the same doubts as the Student Movement – whether to remain a pressure group, with anarchist overtones, or try to work through conventional political machinery. The Republican Labour Party is swimming against the partitionist tide.

The Northern Irish electors are faced, then, with a situation of tremendous uncertainty. The old landmarks have disappeared quite suddenly and there can be no question of rebuilding them on the same sites. There is neither time nor materials to build the modern 'quake-proof political structures which will eventually be necessary. For the moment all the people can do is to choose between Captain O'Neill's temporary and undoubtedly leaky structure and the prospect of camping in quarrelsome discomfort among the ruins.

*Financial Times*, 20 February 1969

# ... and the Descent to Civil War

It cannot go on like this. Northern Ireland cannot stand very much more. The situation has deteriorated steadily now for two years. But the speed and steepness of the descent to civil war is now increasing at such an alarming rate that we must now be quite close to the point where it is literally uncontrollable.

It is important to recognize where this 'point of no return' lies – the moment when the Protestant population loses all confidence in the system and starts to take the law into its own hands.

If the IRA continues to blow up innocent civilians and gets away with it, it will not be enough that Mr Faulkner and the British Army are doing their best. We shall see the long-heralded 'Protestant back-lash' start to take effect, not simply in the growth of political extremism but in the appearance on the streets of the Ulster Volunteer Force – the Protestant mirror-image of the IRA. Once a subterranean war of vengeance starts to be waged, then the two communities will rapidly be drawn into violent confrontation.

The fear that this last horseman of the Ulster Apocalypse might gallop on to the scene at any moment has been the dominating motive of Whitehall policy for many months. The introduction of internment two weeks ago was only the latest of a long series of decisions based on the proposition that whatever else was done, London was bound to back, and indeed try to strengthen, the only institutions which are capable of keeping the Protestants within moderate bounds – the Unionist Party and the Stormont system.

Efforts to placate the Catholic minority were important and possibly even essential, but they could never be carried to a point at which the Stormont government of the day felt itself seriously endangered by the reaction of its own supporters.

This order of priorities has resulted in a good deal of progress – as the recent Stormont government White Paper on reforms of local government and so on has shown – but it has always meant that progress has been at least one step behind the demands of the Catholics. At each stopping point along the road there has been an area of manoeuvre between what the Catholics wanted and what the Protestants would put up with. And because of fear of the Protestant backlash the measures actually produced have always fallen just short of this target area.

With each crisis that has occurred the Catholics have put up their price and the Protestants have reduced their tolerance, and the question which now confronts Mr Heath and Mr Maudling is whether the Catholics' minimum demands have not now become greater than anything that the Protestants can stand. Has the window closed, and if so, what can be done to open it?

This rather abstract way of putting the central question is best brought to life, perhaps, by looking at some of the proposals for a 'new political initiative' which are currently going the rounds in London and Belfast and measuring them against what each side now regards as its own political realities. In ascending order of 'radicalness' these are:

**Proportional representation.** The introduction of this system for elections to the Stormont Parliament has been advocated by moderate Catholics for years and would certainly produce a body of Catholic representatives more commensurate with the size of the Catholic population. It has certain drawbacks, notably a tendency to produce political stagnation and possibly a larger number of Protestant extremists, but if it had been introduced three or four years ago it would have undoubtedly helped meet Catholic aspirations in a moderate fashion.

It will be recommended, in all probability, by the Crowther Commission on the Constitution, whenever that reports; but Mr Faulkner may well introduce it himself, with Westminster approval, within the next six months. The Protestants could now 'wear' it, but it would be totally inadequate, in the present atmosphere, to calm Catholic feelings.

**The enlargement of the Stormont House of Commons.** Even if future constituency boundaries in Ulster are less blatantly gerrymandered than they have been in the past, the present fifty-two members of Stormont would not, even on a proportional representational basis, contain a large enough number of Catholics to form an effective opposition. As with proportional representation this suggestion has now become liberal orthodoxy and is likely to be implemented without making any difference to the political situation on either side.

**Local government reforms.** These are already being put into effect as a result of a number of inquiries, including the Cameron Commission and the Macrory Committee; as a result of these, new district councils are to be elected in October of next year on the basis of new boundaries and one man, one vote. This programme might be slightly speeded up – and in view of the fact that the last local elections were in 1967 they could well afford to be.

However, apart from genuine technical difficulties and delays, there is an overwhelming flaw in these reforms from the Catholic point of view, namely that they leave the new councils without direct control over the most sensitive areas of policy – housing, education and health – so that even if Catholics gain nominal power in particular areas of the country they may still be thwarted on control over policy.

**More Catholics in government.** Here we reach the point at which the lines of Catholic expectation and Protestant refusal begin to approach each other. Catholics are now interested in nothing less than a genuine shift of power in their direction at the centre of the administration of the province. It is a moot point, however, whether any of the present Catholic 'leaders' could afford to join a Faulkner government without losing all credibility with their followers.

For instance, Mr John Hume, the Londonderry M P, has said that he and his colleagues will not co-operate with the present structure any more and that it must be swept away. On the other side it is equally doubtful whether Mr Faulkner could survive if he took into government men who had openly, within the last months, identified themselves with a movement which is devoted to the destruction of an independent Ulster.

**More drastic changes in the constitution of Northern Ireland.** The least extreme of these would, presumably, be the formal retrieval of some functions now vested in the Stormont Parliament by Westminster, but leaving the framework of the present arrangements intact. The most obvious candidate here would be to put the entire control of security, including the police, under the Home Office in London.

But there is a wide range of possibilities involving the complete restructuring of the Stormont system, with various combinations of British military responsibility and local elected or appointed control. Mr Hume and his friends have never, unfortunately, spelt out exactly what they have in mind, but it seems to be something in the nature of a Northern Ireland regional council, backed by Westminster guarantees that the reforms already instituted would not be reversed.

At what point, in theory, the present Unionist leadership would feel obliged to throw in its hand is scarcely relevant since any of the proposals would be regarded by the Protestant population as being on the high road to a sell-out to the South and would be resisted violently for that reason.

To sum up these options: the first three would be acceptable to the Protestants but would simply leave the Catholics in much the same frame of mind as they now are – that is, alienated from the system and perfectly willing to provide the cover for a long IRA campaign of bombing. The fourth would be resisted by both sides equally at present. And the fifth would result in an almost immediate confrontation between the two communities with the British Army desperately trying to control both sides.

When politicians are faced with a series of such intolerable choices there is, not surprisingly, a high premium on arguments which offer a respectable excuse for sticking to the status quo and this is, in effect, what the Stormont government is arguing today – as it has in previous situations.

The official line coming from Mr Faulkner's direction is that the activities of the gunmen are being curtailed, that Messrs Paisley, Craig and the Protestant right wing are, on the one hand discredited but on the other hand dangerously menacing; that the Catholics can be detached from the IRA by resolute military means; and that the process of detaching them may possibly be helped along at a later stage by some minor reforms short of a genuine shift in power.

As I said at the outset, to go on like this seems to me to be a recipe for absolutely certain disaster. There is no reason to suppose that the IRA cannot sustain its present level of activity for a very considerable time or that the Catholics will not continue to support them indefinitely if political reforms do not reach a level considerably higher than anything Mr Faulkner envisages.

Furthermore, although the Protestant right wing may not be particularly menacing to Mr Faulkner for some while, it could be extremely menacing to the Catholics. There is, of course, an ironic possibility that if the Protestants start to take their Sten guns out of the lofts the Catholics may feel rather differently about the British Army – but by that time it will be too late.

The British government at Westminster is faced, therefore, with an intolerable dilemma. If it backs the Faulkner government's 'stand-pat' line, it could have a communal war on its hands. If, on the contrary, it tries to impose a more radical programme on Stormont, it may produce political complications which could end at the same destination by a slightly different route – for it might well enrage the Protestant Right without actually placating the Catholics.

In this choice of evils I believe Mr Heath has very little to lose and might have much to gain by taking the bolder course and by trying to devise a package which would offer the Catholics the prospect of a real increase in power at the centre. It would, of course, be a gamble – but then, so was internment. That was a gamble which did not come off, but with a little luck and skill this one might.

The possible ingredients of such a package are, I believe, being examined in Whitehall at present and though I have no means of telling what bits of it are now to the fore, it is clear that to have any chance of success they would have to include the following minimum elements:

**1**  An instrument (perhaps a re-formed Upper House at Stormont) which would guarantee the Catholic community at least the ability to *block* legislation which affected them.

**2**  Machinery which would rapidly produce an effective Opposition in the Lower House with a membership proportionate to the strength of the Catholic community.

**3**  Machinery which would increase Catholic participation in the administration of services such as health, education, and welfare.

**4**  Some machinery which would bring eminent non-political Catholics nearer to the centre of affairs.

**5**  A fresh guarantee that the border is not at issue.

**6**  An understanding that all these changes should be within the framework of the existing constitutional set-up.

Such a programme would undoubtedly put Mr Faulkner at some political risk and it would fall short of the position now taken by the Catholic members of Stormont. On the other hand there is some reason to think it would have the support of Mr Lynch in the South and, I suspect, of the Northern Ireland business community. Certainly it is better than sitting still and waiting for the final deluge of events.

*Financial Times, 27 August 1971*

# The Twilight of the Old Tradition

Mrs Margaret Thatcher's victory is a major portent and, as with most other events of significance, it is hard to say whether skilful management, great good fortune, or some deep historical current was the most powerful agent in the affair. Certainly there is a real ring of truth about the picture of the whole enterprise as a brilliant stroke of political opportunism – a daringly successful commando raid on the heights of the Tory Party.

We now recognize, as one usually can with hindsight, that the defences were astonishingly demoralized and incompetent. If we assume, as I think we may, that Mr Heath regarded Mrs Thatcher as the least desirable of all the candidates, with the exceptions of Mr Hugh Fraser and Mr John Peyton, then it was absolute insanity to provide her with an ideal jumping-off point in the leadership of the Conservative assault on the Finance Bill. It was also fatal, though more understandable, for Mr Heath's minions to try to attract votes during the first round by decrying Mr William Whitelaw, whose position in the second round was undoubtedly weakened by these manoeuvres.

Then again, the timing and procedure of the election itself were uncovenanted pieces of luck for Mrs Thatcher. If Mr Heath had gone immediately after the October defeat (as Mr James Prior earnestly advised him to do) Mr Whitelaw would have been a certainty. He would have been equally safe under the old 'magic circle' processes of consultation – though it would have been more difficult to dislodge Mr Heath. Under a relatively straightforward procedure, like the Labour Party's, Mrs Thatcher might still have won, but she would have had a harder fight because there would have been a full field of candidates in the first round, and her 'bandwagon' would have been much more difficult to get under way.

But still, Mrs Thatcher seized her chances with great skill and certainty. Many people have remarked on the astonishing sleight of hand by which she managed to detach herself from the collective responsibility of the Heath government and Shadow Cabinet. But one might also cite the enormous self-control of her campaign, her very professional handling of the Press and her faultless use of the dangerous feminine card – different, but demure, gallant without being managing. She said remarkably little and simply allowed her opponents to trip themselves up.

Mrs Thatcher is, in short, a very lucky woman but her luck has been of the kind that seems almost inevitable, being drawn, as it were, by magnetic attraction to someone who will know how to seize it because the moment has come. This feeling of inevitability is hard to pin down and has very little to do with whether or not one predicted the result. It is more that when the result has been produced it suddenly fits into a wider pattern that one had only dimly seen before and which, now it is seen, endows the new fact with fresh meaning.

If one asks what is the larger significance of Mrs Thatcher's elevation, the answer is that it seems to mark the end of an historic process lasting about a century. To put it crudely, the history of the Tory Party in this period has been its movement from being the party of landowners with some bourgeois additions to being a bourgeois party with some working-class additions at one end and some land-owning relics at the other. But this rough characterization does not do justice to the evolution of the party's sympathies which has not been nearly as rapid or as clear-cut as that implies. The indoctrination of the rising industrial middle classes of Victorian England with some of the values of the aristrocracy, the admixture of ideas appropriate to the government of the Empire through the public-school system, the influence of nineteenth-century idealism and religion – all this produced a British middle class very different from its counterparts on the Continent – blander, less aggressive, more tolerant, more high-minded, more complacent. And the Tory Party naturally followed suit.

Of course, Conservatism also became the party of industry and 'big business' – partly because land-owning property diversified into industry, partly because the rise of Labour and the collapse of the Liberal Party left industry with nowhere else to go. But the dominant ethos of Conservatism for the whole of this century has been that of Oxbridge, the Armed Services and the professions – the inheritors of late nineteenth-century imperial tradition, with all its paternalism, its assumption of superiority, its relative honesty of purpose and perhaps its indolence. Every leader of the Conservative Party from Balfour to Lord Home was more or less in this tradition (Baldwin and Chamberlain imported some of the industrial strain, though in a slightly attenuated form; Bonar Law brought in a weird Scottish element). And the men who have surrounded them in Conservative Cabinets have been of the same mould. But, the trouble has arisen because, while the personnel at the top has remained very much the same, the middle class, which still forms the backbone of the party, has been changing.

Some of these changes have been economic, the result of inflation or rationalization or aggressive trade unionism which has vastly reduced differentials and has actually put many workers in a higher income bracket than their supposed superiors in the hierarchy of the middle-middle and lower-middle classes. Other changes are cultural and psychological. The collapse of empire has removed an outlet for energy and an easy road to status. The post-war revolution in education has produced a generation which no longer sees the values of the upper-middle class as relevant, thereby not only sowing doubts about these values themselves but creating a sense of unease and uncertainty about the future even among those who still subscribe to them.

At the same time there is the fact that the management of the country has been manifestly unsatisfactory. If industry and the civil service and the government has been in the hands of the old tradition these last twenty years – and it largely has – who wants to aspire to it? If Britain is living in an alien world as a small and unprotected island, what is the point of behaving as if one could still afford the grand gestures and easy-going ways of sixty years ago? And if the middle class is an undefended minority surrounded by a sea of workers on the make, what is the point of adopting attitudes of tolerance and effortless superiority such as the rulers of the Conservative Party still embrace? If life is going to be tough, then let us be tough as well and to hell with immigrants, layabouts and the poor in general. We want security and stability and the assurance of status for ourselves and our children and we are prepared to fight for it.

This is the cry that has been coming from the suburbs for at least a decade and the fact that it has some force in reality has not, of course, made it any less powerful. Indeed, the perception of some of the same things has demoralized the upper-middle class as much as any of the political difficulties that have followed from these pressures. The institutions of British government, which have been in the hands of this class for so long, are all in disarray and the reason is that it is so hard to reconcile high-minded responsibility with the hard facts of the modern world. The main instrument in recent times of this high-mindedness has been Keynesian economics, combined with a belief in the patriotism of the inhabitants of these islands and their amenability to old-fashioned 'leadership' either in politics or industry. The failure of all these has left the old tradition without any answers to socialism on one side and *laissez-faire* on the other. They have in many cases simply given up.

What has happened in the Tory Party this week does not show the final débâcle on the political front. There is still, oddly enough, an enclave of the old tradition in the Labour Party. But it may signal its eclipse in Conservative politics. In a way, this should have happened ten years ago when Mr Heath became leader. It was thought then by many who voted for him and by many in the country, that he represented precisely the repudiation of the old ways that they desired – he was self-made, he was classless, he talked the language of managerial efficiency and to some extent even the language of the free market. But it turned out that he was no repudiation at all. He had acquired all the preconceptions that he was supposed to be rejecting. He was a liberal in social matters, he felt great responsibility for the unemployed, the low-paid and the immigrant. Moreover he turned out to believe in 'leadership', a dialogue with the workers and economic intervention on a large scale.

This is not what he had been elected to represent, which was the main reason his party never felt happy with him. If Mr Heath had brought off an economic success, no doubt he would have been forgiven and the old tradition would have received a new lease of life. But the tools broke in his hands as they had in others, and the result has been a violent rejection in favour of something that seems much more like the new look. Needless to say Mr Whitelaw, who is the living epitome of the old style, could only have survived if there had been an effective conspiracy of the old guard to have him.

Whether Mrs Thatcher is quite so clear-cut a representative of tough middle-middle-class-based values as is generally supposed, is not yet certain. To judge by her writings and speeches she has far more of its characteristics than Mr Heath. Unlike the traditionalists, she knows nothing of foreign affairs, for one thing; and she lacks both the manners and the temperament, of the upper-middle-class tradition.

Strangely enough, Sir Keith Joseph has almost all the characteristics involved – high-mindedness, social concern and the required touch of intellectual arrogance. The fact that he happens not to believe in the ability of his own class to order the economy better than the sum of individual choices seems almost an accident. Where, in all this, a new synthesis lies is the main question of Mrs Thatcher's reign. Perhaps there will not be one. But whatever happens, a new era seems to have begun.

*Financial Times, 14 February 1975*

# Mrs Thatcher and the Tides of History

**M**rs Margaret Thatcher's appearance on 'Panorama' last Monday night was something of a landmark. It not only disclosed her increasing command of herself and of the medium; it allowed the general public (as opposed to privileged audiences) to see, for the first time, some of the genuine passion that lies beneath her elaborately groomed and normally cautious exterior.

One senses a deliberate gamble here. Her instinctive sympathy with middle-middle-class values has been overlaid in the past by the necessity of keeping the Conservative Party together and not alienating large groups of voters. And even now, as we saw on Monday, she plays really contentious issues, like picketing and immigration, with what can be described as a 'forward defensive prod'.

Yet the 'Panorama' performance bears out reports that her colleagues and advisers are having increasing difficulty in restraining her from throwing at least some of this caution to the winds. She is increasingly enthused by the righteousness of her cause and she seems to believe, with increasing certainty, that she has caught the spirit of the times. A full-blooded 'Campaign For Freedom' is not by any means to the taste of all the Shadow Cabinet, and they must have shuddered no little at her jaunty referencee to 'Winston's speeches' (echoes of his disastrous attempt in 1945 to equate the Labour Party with the Gestapo still reverberate with terrifying effect around Conservative Central Office). But it is beginning to look as if the Leader is going to go ahead in the belief that her own instincts and the tides of history and public opinion are all flowing in the same direction.

In allowing herself to appear in her true emotional colours like this, Mrs Thatcher is risking a great deal. She is staking a lot on people actually being 'fed up with collectivism' in the sense she requires, and she is throwing away the element of surprise in the belief that the momentum of her campaign can be sustained and increased right up to polling day – whether that is this autumn or next spring or the spring after.

It is impossible to tell whether she is right. If she is, she will scoop the pool, if not, she will put people off – perhaps to a disastrous extent. Certainly the British voter is always capable of being carried away by a crusade if the timing and subject matter are right, but there is nothing more pathetic in politics than a crusade which has not caught on or which has lost its momentum. But a crusade requires, of its nature, a certain element of exaggeration; it is an invitation to suspend rational doubts for a higher end. And life in this rarefied atmosphere cannot be sustained indefinitely.

Let me illustrate what I mean by taking four of the notions contained, either explicitly or implicitly, in Mrs Thatcher's television broadcast. The viewer may sympathize from the outset with the thought behind them or he may be swept along by the force of the rhetoric against his will. But can he be expected to go on accepting the beautiful certainty and simplicity of the flowing propositions indefinitely?

The Labour Party is on the high road to communism. The argument proceeds as follows: Mr Callaghan has to rely on the eighty votes of the Tribune Group in the House of Commons; all eighty are 'extreme left-wingers'; therefore, Mr Callaghan is under the control of the extreme Left. Again, there are Trotskyists in the Labour Party; Mr Callaghan cannot turn them out; therefore he has compromised with them. Once you start to compromise with the Left you will be swallowed up; therefore Jim Callaghan will be swallowed up, as East European Social Democrats once were.

The emotional cladding of this thesis is all very impressive. The flesh creeps as Mrs Thatcher, her eyes darting from side to side, declaims: 'If you don't fight when the knock comes at your neighbours' door, what right have you to expect them to fight when it comes at your door?' But reduced to its essential elements as a statement about the real position of the Labour Party under Mr Callaghan, it is really absurd.

The Tribune Group is a motley collection which wields far less power as well as being far less radical than the Bevanites whom Mrs Thatcher mentions with tolerance. The Trotskyites in the constituency parties and the trade unions are a genuine problem, but they are less of a problem than they were three years ago, and they have about as much chance of 'taking over' the Labour Party in the foreseeable future as they have of taking over the Conservative Party. It may well be excessively purist to object as a matter of political morality to Mrs Thatcher putting out this over-simplified stuff if she thinks she can make a good cry out of it. The question is whether she is wise to do so, given that the voters, if they have time, tend to dislike this sort of exaggeration.

The key to economic expansion is lower taxation. There is a strong emotional charge to this thesis deriving not merely from everyone's natural desire to be taxed less but from Mrs Thatcher's own idealized view of what makes people tick. The idea is that private industry in general and small businesses in particular can lead the recovery of investment if they are given the proper incentives. Similarly, managers in industry, and small business managers, will work harder if their personal taxation is cut. A lot of other themes are woven in here, including a strong element of Puritan moral uplift. Thrift and self-reliance will come with the restoration of market forces, as well as prosperity. But the basic picture is a romantic and nostalgic one, and it is no accident that Mrs Thatcher has taken recently to talking a good deal about the Victorians.

Can such a picture stand the wear and tear of political life and economic reality for another twelve months, if necessary? It has the advantage of being evocative, particularly among a section of Conservative voters whose immediate economic interests appear in it under a very favourable guise. It also, clearly, has a particular reality in Mrs Thatcher's imagination which means that she is very good at putting it across. The trouble is that the simplification of the argument necessary to fit into this framework does violence to too much of the real economic argument.

Even within the 'Panorama' framework, this became apparent, for, in order to answer the natural charge that her policy would be just the Tories helping the rich again, Mrs Thatcher was obliged to answer that the reduction of taxation all the way down the scale would be necessary. The point was not pursued, but it does not require great ingenuity, once one has got this far, to impale the Conservatives on the horns of the old dilemma – either the tax cuts at the middle and bottom end of the scale are chickenfeed, or they are widely inflationary, or they entail cuts in social expenditure so draconian that not even the most resolute Conservative government could contemplate them. I am not saying that skilful politics in office might not finesse this problem.

What is questionable is whether the emotional certainties of the That-cher approach can be sustained between now and the election.

Trade unions do not confront governments but each other. This is what one might call the 'naive monetarist' theory – the belief being that government, having set its monetary target, can simply stand aside and let the unions scrabble for their share of wages and employ-ment. It is an attractive dream, especially if one subscribes to the Thatcherian moral precept that people ought to be made to realize that where they sow, there will they also reap. One might also argue that, in a modified kind of way, Mr Healey has successfully injected some of this philosophy into his own approach to the unions.

Nevertheless, in the form in which it appeared in the 'Panorama' interview and in other recent pronouncements, it is moonshine. How-ever much Mrs Thatcher may say that it is not her business to de-termine miners' wages or nurses' wages or dustmen's wages, the public will hold her responsible at the ballot box for the consequences of industrial action or unemployment, and if the electoral quinquennium is thought to be the wrong time-scale, others are no better. At the short end, foreign investors and sterling holders are unlikely to de-monstrate practical support for Mrs Thatcher's philosophy in a major industrial crisis; and at the long end, no responsible government can simply watch the country's industrial base being undermined by a prolonged deflation made necessary by union activities. This is so obvious that the exercise of trying to maintain the opposite merely causes doubts about Mrs Thatcher's judgement in precisely the places she most wishes to promote her own reputation for hard-headedness – namely, the City and industry.

Freedom is indivisible. The whole idea of freedom as an overriding priority of Conservative doctrine, at this time, is enormously muddled. It is partly the traditional cry of the Conservative Party against socialist government. But there is a new dimension added as a result of the capture of some influential Conservative minds by the Hayekian re-statement of the *laissez-faire* philosophy. Also involved is the question of the Rule of Law which has been given a new authoritarian twist by some Conservatives which Hayekians and the libertarians would by no means find congenial.

There is nothing particularly fresh about this stew of ideas – which, in fact, contains most of the usual brands of Conservative thought. What is perhaps new is the intensity with which Mrs Thatcher now puts forward these not altogether compatible ideas. On the one hand, she evidently feels close to the National Association for Freedom from whose ranks she has drawn advice and speechwriting. On the other, she is appealing to the spirit of freedom and compromise.

The link is that the internal contradictions of Conservatism are most manageable if Conservatism remains pragmatic. As soon as doctrine rears its head the difficulties become very great – and normal voters take fright.

Until recently Mrs Thatcher has shown herself well aware of this fact and acted upon it. It will be an interesting departure if she now turns it over.

*Financial Times*, *15 July 1977*

# What Has Become of Our National Pride?

It is a great relief for all of us to be allowed, on the highest government authority, to dismiss at least one and possibly two of the possible causes of this week's riots. Unemployment is no more than a mild contributory factor. After all, there has been high unemployment elsewhere without riots (has there not?), and some of the culprits were too young to be employed anyway. Even race, it seems, cannot have been the primary cause, at any rate in Toxteth, since so many of the rioters were white.

The trouble with this yarn, apart from the fact that it defies common sense, is that it leaves us with no plausible scapegoats – except the parents of the rioters and, for those of a leftward bent, the police. I hope therefore to be forgiven for putting forward another set of culprits altogether – namely this government and, to an only slightly lesser extent, its two predecessors.

This accusation is based on the proposition that the horrible events of the past week are only the latest symptoms of a deeper malaise – the fact that the government itself and the subsidiary organs of state, the police, the civil service, and the armed forces, are suffering from a loss of authority. The reason is not simply that it is hard to respect a government that is divided and apparently unable to deliver economic success or a bureaucracy that is on strike; it is also that the forces of law and order do not have an entirely credible entity to represent. They should, and in one sense do, represent 'the community' or to put it more grandly, the British nation.

But those whom they are trying to control, whether black or white, no longer seem to share a positive vision of what this country is and what it might be to be British. In other words, we have lost, or at least mislaid, some of our collective sense of assured national identity. Lacking this overriding sense of shared purpose and loyalty, is it surprising that the British policy has a tendency to disintegrate into a collection of pressure groups, social classes, regional groupings, economic vested interests – and races?

The main assumption underlying this question is, of course, open to challenge. I shall be told that British nationalism, even jingoism, is alive and well and living in the Labour Party, on the football terraces, in the correspondence columns of *The Times*, and at No. 10 Downing Street. And are we not about to celebrate with vast popular acclaim an event which testifies to the enduring power of the greatest national symbol of all – the Crown?

To these objections I reply that there is a large element of strain about most of these manifestations. They lack the easy assumption, certainly of the superiority, but even of the validity of things British that we were able to show thirty or even fifteen years ago. When Mrs Thatcher is complaining about being 'swamped' by immigrants, or the National Executive of the Labour Party is denouncing the EEC, or English football fans are bashing every Swiss head in sight, they are all reacting defensively, seeking to define Britishness by reference to others rather than by knowledge of ourselves. Only the Royal wedding has some of the old panache, but even then we seem to be embracing it with a kind of desperate fervour that is itself revealing.

But assuming that I am right about the underlying uncertainty, the question is whether politicians can be expected to provide the missing psychological ingredients. Some will certainly say they cannot. Minimalism, after all, is a concept of government which can be applied beyond the immediate bailiwick of Mr John Biffen. And yet if one examines three main areas where national unity has been an immediate issue in recent British politics, the charges against our political leaders stick.

(1) Unlike the French, who have never had any difficulty with the concept of black Frenchmen, or the Americans, who brought themselves, mainly by moral exhortation, to accept full equality of rights, the British have lacked the self-confidence and the political leadership to adopt a mental definition of 'Britishness' which for practical purposes includes blacks or which persuades blacks to adopt it themselves. Successive governments since the mid-1960s have taken an entirely defensive attitude to the race issue. It has been bottom of the list of priorities, a vote-loser.

In spite of endless Cassandra warnings from those working in the field, nothing serious has been done to spread equal employment opportunities for blacks throughout Britain's economy, to reform police complaints procedure, or to make the coloured community feel that they had a stake in being British – that authority, in other words, was their authority.

(2) Politicians have been altogether too apologetic in the face of 'small is beautiful' arguments and have failed to produce a persuasive defence of 'diversity in unity'.

The alternatives open to us are not necessarily 'big' or 'small'; they may be 'small, frantically and unsuccessfully trying to struggle on its own' and 'small, with its own independent functions, bound productively into a wider union'.

This confusion had a baleful influence on the Devolution debate. The political battle was basically fought between hard-line centralists and hard-line devolvers, the Devolution Bills being uneasy compromises between the two camps rather than being offered as a genuinely constructive way of making Britain work better.

At the other end of the scale the EEC debate has also been a victim. The Common Market has been presented to the British public either as the dawn of a brave new supra-national era or as a diabolical conspiracy to suppress British sovereignty, rather than as a framework in which Britain worked more constructively and harmoniously with its neighbours.

(3) The economic policies of the present and the immediately preceding governments have been not only unsuccessful (thereby smothering any stirrings of national self-confidence) but have positively reduced national unity. There is nothing intrinsically incompatible between a left-of-centre government and a purposeful national consensus; but the last Labour Government caved in to a sectional interest – the trade unions. Similarly, there is nothing which shows that individualism and liberty cannot be reconciled with a strong state – indeed it has been the stock-in-trade of Conservatism for 200 years that it is best qualified to reconcile the two. But under the Thatcher government the Conservative slogan of 'one nation' is mocked by the vast chasm which stands between employed and unemployed.

Nobody supposes that politicians can produce a genuine national self-confidence and patriotic consensus overnight. (It is easy enough to whip up jingoism in a hurry but that, as I said earlier, is a different matter.) Nor can anything be achieved by mere exhortation. (If it could, Mrs Thatcher's attempt to instil some British pride into her listeners by a frankly nationalistic approach would have produced the

**234**

desired effect long ago.) What we need, and what we have not had for twenty years, is a settled spell of good government and moderate, persuasive political leadership.

All the same, government, by its actions and by its presentation of issues, has a choice between staking out the claims of a valid British state which deserves the loyalty of its citizens and their faith in its future; or it can allow all this to go by default. One does not get the impression that Mrs Thatcher and her colleagues are thinking in these terms; and they are suffering for it. Patriotism, as Nurse Cavell wrote, is not enough; but unless there is enough of it around government becomes very difficult.

*The Times*, *8 July 1981*

# The Gains and Losses
# of the Falklands Victory

The Duke of Wellington's dictum that a victory is the greatest tragedy in the world apart from a defeat does not obviously apply to the Falklands. Our casualties have been miraculously light and we have achieved some solid objectives for them.

First we have kept our promises to the Falkland Islanders and prevented their coming under a particularly unpleasant regime. The moral satisfaction of this is tempered by the knowledge that the promises ought to have been constructively modified long since and that in keeping them we have shattered the islanders' way of life for ever; but still, it is nice to be virtuous.

Moreover, in this case virtue is accompanied by profit. We have restored our own international credibility and that, from the beginning, was by far the most powerful reason for going to war. To have allowed a third-rate power like Argentina to humiliate us would have damaged our interests over the whole range of foreign policy because it would have demoted us in the eyes of governments who, however sophisticated, are used to categorizing other nations in remarkably simplistic ways.

The speed, efficiency and courage with which the military operation was carried out, the remarkable degree of national unity behind the campaign, and the determination of the Prime Minister have all made a deep impression. Mrs Thatcher may well discover, as President Nixon, General de Gaulle and Mr Begin have done, the genuine international advantages of being regarded as a dangerous customer and possibly slightly mad.

So far, so good. Tragedy will, however, arise if we are unable to put the sacrifices of lives and limbs that have been made to the construction of a co-operative peace with Argentina and, even more, if we draw absurd triumphalist conclusions from what has occurred. Some extraordinarily delusive ideas have been spawned in the excitement of the last two weeks and they may do us serious and quite unnecessary damage if we allow them to harden into axiom.

**We have shown that aggression does not pay.** We have done nothing so far-reaching. Would that we had. We have shown no more than that aggression by a state against a stronger one normally does not pay – which may have to be demonstrated from time to time but does not carry many Brownie points. If we had wanted to show the unwisdom of aggression in general we should have had to put together a far more formidable international coalition than we were able in the event to construct.

The fact that neither the United States, the United Nations nor the European Community was in a position to make the Argentines withdraw by political, military or economic measures still leaves the field wide open for strong aggressors. The Chinese, for instance, could march into Hong Kong tomorrow at minimal international cost and without our being able subsequently to do anything to oust them.

The moral is that we should try to strengthen all kinds of international instruments for keeping the peace. But that, apparently, is an option that does not now appeal to the predominant nationalism of the British Cabinet.

**We have transformed our national temper.** A lot of people, perhaps most people who have not borne responsibility or had relatives at risk, had, to put it bluntly, a lot of fun out of this war. It has been fought a long way away and yet it has had a spice of genuine danger about it. It has been, morally speaking, pretty straightforward, with the British in white hats and the bad guys playing (by and large) by accepted old-fashioned rules. Above all, of course, we have been winning for most of it.

This excitement is neither surprising nor sinful. The question is whether it has changed anything. The war, like every major military operation this country has engaged in since the Crimean War, has naturally uncovered the good things and bad things in the British national character: on the one hand, for instance, the vein of patriotism and hardiness, on the other, the smaller but unmistakable vein of ranting, xenophobia and jingoism.

It has also shown, very inconveniently for the right wing, that despite permissiveness, pornography and pot, the young of England is at least no more degenerate now than in the days of Byron or Rupert Brooke. Port Stanley was won on the playgrounds of Neasden Comprehensive.

The snag is that there is no particular reason to suppose that it will now be any easier to 'cash in' these characteristics for, say, less disruption or more managerial enterprise in British industry than it would be if we won the World Cup. Those results can be achieved only by quite different and much more subtle and arduous means.

**We have proved that we alone are the best defenders, as we are the sole judges, of British interests.** Up to a point this is a truism. No man is likely to put so much effort into any task as he does into that of protecting his own security. But nothing that has happened since the beginning of April shows that we are anything less than deeply dependent on other actors on the international stage. The military operation itself relied heavily on American intelligence; and without the support of our European partners in the United Nations and in the matter of arms embargoes and economic sanctions the position would in all sorts of ways have been much weaker.

If one looks at the wider scene and the longer term, it is even clearer that our freedom of action over the Falklands is severely circumscribed. We cannot defend them indefinitely without either over-straining a still very sick economy (the figures leaked to the press on this point by the Ministry of Defence are at least three times more than they should be) or running down our commitments in NATO.

In the first case the electors may have something to say, in the second our allies will have every justification in pointing out that we are weakening the most important element of our security. We shall also be under the heaviest possible pressure from the United States administration to reach a compromise solution with Argentina because of the effect of the dispute on the whole United States position in Latin America.

The probable Thatcher reply, that we cannot compromise over sovereignty after the sacrifices we have made, meets the unanswerable reply that the wider interests of Great Britain as well as of the West as a whole are crucially involved in preventing South America slipping into the sphere of influence of the Soviet Union.

**Mrs Thatcher is the greatest British ruler since Queen Elizabeth I.** She is not. Her real gifts – industry, and great tenacity – are no less counterbalanced by her equally real weaknesses – impetuosity, inflexibility and narrowness of vision – than they were ten weeks ago. She deserves every bit of her triumph after a remarkable performance, but she is still a very lucky woman – not simply because she took some hair-raising military risks but because the crisis itself was one in which her strong points were displayed to the best advantage and her demerits consistently cast far into shadow by the pigheadedness and stupidity of the Junta.

Her worshippers, of course, believe that the problems of the British economy and the other more complicated problems of British foreign policy are susceptible to her virtues and indeed that the new force and authority that may have been given to them by the Falklands will make them irresistible in other fields. Perhaps they are right. Perhaps her luck will hold here too. But, to put it mildly, there is grave danger that in these fields she will in the following months come up against issues in British society and industry or in the international scene, in which it is her vices that will be in the ascendancy and her virtues in eclipse. In such a case, unlike the Falklands, the gains could be non-existent and the casualties immense.

*The Times, 18 June 1982*

# Is This Really What Is Wrong With Britain?

Everyone thinks that the politics of his own country is ultimately impermeable to the intelligence of any foreigner, however learned and friendly. It belongs, together with regional accents and national cuisine, to the list of arcane mysteries whose subtleties we guard most jealously and which nobody from outside ever 'gets quite right'.

This is all nonsense, in fact nobody really understands the politics of his own country, if it comes to that, and the acute foreign observer may well manage to see the wood when the native is grubbing around at the roots of the trees.

There are few better general introductions to American politics, even after a century, than Lord Bryce's *American Commonwealth*,[1] and there are very few better short accounts of our own policy than Samuel Beer's *Modern British Politics*.[2]

This elegant feat of American scholarship which came out in 1965 at the height of Wilsonian (Harold Wilsonian that is) optimism is a classic and will remain one because it presents an ideal picture of how the post-war British system is supposed to function.

The fact that the ideal has apparently fallen into precipitous decline since then, cannot blur the achievement and, in a way, only enhances its value. Nevertheless the question of how Professor Beer, himself, would account for our fall from grace is one that arises naturally from the work and has often been asked.

**240**

[1] Published by Putnam.
[2] Published by Faber, 1969.

The answer has been a long time coming, but two weeks ago it finally arrived in another short, majesterial book, *Britain Against Itself*,[1] a distillation of detached judgements which clarifies and fortifies all the articles and books you can ever have read on the 'What's Wrong With Britain' theme.

To summarize a book of this density is inevitably to abuse it, but, briefly, the Beer thesis is as follows. The 'Butskellite' political consensus of the 1950s and early 1960s (which was the basis of the professor's earlier admiration) contained the seeds of its own destruction. Once the Conservatives joined the Labour Party (as they did in the late 1940s) in conceding that government had responsibility for the economic and social order, a malign process, which Beer calls, rather repulsively, 'pluralistic stagnation' set in.

Because the strategic alternatives offered by the two parties began to look much the same, the choice became concentrated on narrower interests. The parties competed to corral votes of pressure groups which themselves became more and more fragmented, numerous, and individually powerful (though collectively powerless) in the process. In the 1970s the Conservative and Labour parties each attempted an ideological break out from this trap but were forced back by political pressures to a 'collectivist conception', in which all forces cancelled each other out and immobility reigned supreme.

These developments might not have been so destructive, in Beer's view, if they had not been closely linked to another fundamental change that has come over the British political system during the past two decades. This change amounts to the virtual disintegration of the old British political culture, with its hierarchical values, its strong party system, its belief in parliamentary sovereignty and Cabinet responsibility and, above all, its foundation of trust based, to a considerable extent, on the class system.

Such a culture, had it still been in position, might have prevented the group interest proliferating or might at least have ensured that they were brought together and dealt with in a manageable way. But without strong parties, without the habit of deference to authority, without a belief if say, one's own trade union exercises self-restraint, others will do likewise, there has been nothing to prevent the creation of a vicious circle of fragmentation, political impotence and loss of belief in the system as a whole.

[1] Published by Faber, 1982.

Another of Beer's interrelated themes is the growth of a romantic populism, also undermining the old values. Beginning in the 1960s, he has seen in Britain as elsewhere in the developed industrial world, an emotional reaction to collectivism. 'Small is beautiful', 'do your own thing', the students' revolt of 1968, the Beatles, the revival of Scottish and Welsh nationalism, the pressure for electoral reform, Tony Benn's appeal to extra-parliamentary forces, Enoch Powell's popular nationalism, the SDP's insistence on one man, one vote – all these are, in Beer's thesis, collective manifestations of a revival of popular consciousness which, in its political aspects, might make the foundation of a genuine revival of the British radical tradition.

This account of what has occurred is not necessarily definitive. In fact, it seems to me to have the important defect, among others, that in its emphasis on cultural and structural factors, it skates too easily over economic decline as a cause, rather than simply an effect, of political changes.

The problem, from the point of view of Beer's thesis, is quite fundamental, for it is not at all clear what the cultural origins of our economic woes actually are, or how they are connected with the decay of the political culture that he is talking about.

His pointers to the future do not look quite satisfactory either. He believes on the whole that non-collectivism is here to stay, but of the three non-collectivist futures he identifies for us – Mrs Thatcher's, Mr Benn's and Mr Jenkins's – he is a bit ungenerous to the first and too uncritical of the last two.

In the case of the New Left and the Alliance, I think that for once Professor Beer is blinded by American idealism in being so sure that either of them really finds its mainspring in the kind of radicalism he approves. Mr Benn's rhetoric may well be no more than a well-tried demagogic means to a collectivist end, and Mr Jenkins, an élitist to the core, does not even feel it necessary to bother with the rhetoric.

And yet, oddly enough, I believe this gloomy prospect is lightened in the least likely way – namely the existence of Mrs Thatcher. I agree with Beer in doubting the efficacy of her policies, deploring the crudity of her methods but on the basis of his own arguments ought he not – ought we not – to take comfort from her example?

She may, for all I know, wreck the country in the short term, but
**242** she has at least shown in the last twelve months that political determination can defy the pressures and inertia that Beer has described so well.

If anyone has broken the Butskellite mould, it is she; and what she has broken, others may put together again in a different and more creative pattern.

*The Times*, *22 October 1982*

# Dr Owen's Roaming Political Fancy

In politics, as in racing, a special aura hangs about the man in form. For the moment, however brief, he seems to have some kind of unique insight into the secrets of the universe, which causes other superstitious mortals to crowd in behind him in the hope of picking up the odd grain of fortune, but at a slightly respectful distance, for fear of breaking the spell.

The man in political form at present is Dr David Owen, and his political opponents, as well as his followers, have been listening with rapt attention to what he has been saying at the SDP conference at Salford.

It is easy enough to account for this on a rather mundane level. Dr Owen is the first party leader to put his wares on display since the election. He is, moreover, young and is therefore thought to hold one of the main keys to 'post-Thatcher' politics. Indeed one can legitimately speculate that Mrs Thatcher is beginning to feel the first cold breath of political autumn on her cheek. Boredom and disillusionment with the Conservative government have not yet set in in earnest; but since the election the public and the media have already got as far as asking themselves what comes next.

Socialism certainly does not fill the bill – or at least Mr Kinnock is not yet in a position to restate it in a plausible form. Even Liberalism has a weight of historic associations to contend with. New ideas, or at least a new synthesis of old ones, seem needed, and Dr Owen has them on offer.

All this has given freshness and importance to the Salford debate. Nevertheless, it is clear that Dr Owen's claim to attention goes beyond mere novelty. The point is that he claims authority. To say, as he did in a radio interview the other day, that he is 'leading from the front' is putting it mildly. His speeches were so far in front of his followers as to be virtually out of sight.

Indeed, as I listened to his interventions as well as his leader's speech, I was reminded, absurdly, of that Napoleon of crime, Carl Peterson, whose titanic struggles with Bulldog Drummond enlivened my childhood. Devotees may remember that, in one of the adventures, we are offered a delightful glimpse of the arch-villain, who is naturally a master of disguise, seated before his mirror at the crucial instant of creating 'a new character'.

Later would come the dreary micrometer readings of nose width, the meticulous notation of eye and hair colour, and the laborious assembly of minor characteristics in the famous black booklet. At this moment, his artistic soul was free to range far and wide; and, being in a good mood thanks to the satisfactory progress of the crime of the century, he created a jolly, elderly gentleman with twinkling eyes and mutton-chop whiskers.

Dr Owen is not, perhaps, at such complete liberty to follow his whims as Peterson, and next year he will certainly have to pay close attention with his micrometers to consistency. But, given the present incompleteness of the SDP's programme and the newness of his own mandate, he took a unique opportunity to let his political fancy roam.

This is all very well – and so far as his immediate audience was concerned, he got away with it. On the whole, they seemed to like what they heard, and in any case would not have given him the bird on his first appearance, whether he had read extracts from the thoughts of Chairman Mao or the collected works of Friedrich von Hayek.

The crucial questions, still unanswered after Salford, are (a) whether the wide public, to whom Dr Owen was directly appealing, approve of his idiosyncratic mixture; (b) whether a political party, let alone an alliance, can actually coalesce around the Owen philosophy.

On the first point, it is evident that Dr Owen himself has been convinced for some time, and certainly since the Falklands, that he actually understands what the British people want at this time. It is the completeness of his conviction on this score that gives him his compelling quality at this moment, and it is on the probability of his being right that his claim to authority stands.

But *is* he right? It is clear from the thoughtfully nervous reactions to the speech that a lot of the professionals in other parties believe he is on to something of permanent significance – and I agree with them. For the amalgamation of three simple and successful elements from the opposite poles of the old political debate – on the one hand, patriotism and a competitive market, and on the other the continuation and improvement of the welfare state – does indeed, so far as it goes, offer a plausible popular framework for a post-Thatcher political prospectus.

It cuts away so much of the accumulated cant of the last thirty years. The Owen style – quite deliberately earnest and uncompromising – is another point on which he is probably more in tune with the public than are his critics.

The difficulty is to turn these assets into tangible political and institutional power. For one thing, the philosophical framework is paper-thin and, as Dr Owen knows, full of gaping holes, particularly on the economic side. For another, it is still not clear from Dr Owen's disquisition what *interest* the SDP is appealing to, apart from 'all sensible, serious, enlightened people within earshot' – a category apt to be smaller than expected when it is actually required to put its hands deeper into its pockets on behalf of the poor.

Finally, there is the old, nagging question of the SDP as a party. Is it to be defined primarily as 'people who passionately agree with Dr Owen's diagnosis and prescription'; or 'people who are fed up with one or other of the main parties and don't fancy the Liberals', or 'people who have paid their subscription and want a bit of power and interest in life'?

The SDP has come a long way in the last two years, but looking round the hall at Salford University, while I could see plenty of the last two categories, I was not sure how many were yet in the first.

*The Times, 16 September 1983*

# Keith Joseph's Idea of a University

My first reaction to Sir Keith Joseph's green paper, with its bleak accountant's view of higher education as a kind of service industry which needs to pull its socks up and pay its way, was to dive for the bookshelf and re-read the classic case for the liberal education: John Henry Newman's lectures in Dublin in 1852 on the 'the idea of a university'.

Newman regarded a liberal university education as 'the process of training by which the intellect, instead of being formed or sacrificed to some particular or accidental purpose, some specific trade or profession or study or science, is disciplined for its own sake, for the perception of its own proper object and for its own highest culture'. The object should be to cultivate 'the force, steadiness, the comprehensiveness and versatility of the intellect, the command over our own powers, the instinctive just estimate of things as they pass before us . . . the idea of scientific method, order, principle and system, of rule and exception, of richness and harmony'.

This passage is worth reproducing because it reflects ideals that were commonly accepted by very practical people at the height of Britain's industrial success, because it sums up the underlying assumptions of more than a hundred subsequent years of British education and because it indicates precisely what is lacking in the Thatcher government's approach to this subject.

It is unfair, no doubt, to expect Sir Keith Joseph to write like Newman. It also is true that the green paper covers its flank by disclaiming, in a couple of grudging sentences, any desire to set a low value on the general cultural benefits of education and research. But it provides no vision of what the value of higher education actually is.

The tone of the green paper is uniformly grey, narrow, niggling, and bureaucratic. If we take it together with other pronouncements we are confronted with the picture of a government which is not just downgrading the intangible benefits envisaged by Newman, but is turning its back on them in a fit of anti-intellectual revulsion.

The underlying assumptions of the green paper seem to be that British universities are unacceptably 'non-cost-effective' because their research has not been as 'profitable' as it should be. Furthermore they actually bear a serious responsibility for the bad performance of the British economy since the war because they have been too snobbish about business and money and have not turned out enough useful, dynamic graduates. This, in turn, is mainly because they have been too 'academic' – that is, they have thought too much about training minds and not enough about fostering entrepreneurial or encashable skills such as engineering and computer science.

The conclusion is that the weight of limited government money will in future be thrown behind research shown to be 'productive' and departments shown to be 'useful'. This will enable us to cut back expenditure with some semblance of respectability, as well as rooting out the ivory tower élitism that has brought Britain to its knees.

The charge of anti-business snobbery in the universities, as elsewhere in our society, has had a large grain of truth in the past, although (through the simple working of the labour market) much less today. But where is the government's justification for burning down the house in order to cure a little rising damp?

Almost nothing is right about the argument, either in theory or practice. The government assumes that there would have been better economic performance if we had produced a higher proportion of scientists. It produces no comparisons, however, to disprove the argument of many experts that the proportions in this country have been very little different from, say, Germany or America. How does it know that in the 1990s the kind of skills required will not be the 'generalist's' ability to think quickly and independently (which already causes industry to favour Oxbridge graduates) rather than specific scientific knowledge?

Again, how can British universities hope to attract first-class teachers, far less prevent an appalling long-term brain drain, if no money is provided for research that cannot prove its worth within three years? If all the best graduates take to entrepreneurial occupations, who is going to teach in the secondary schools, particularly if the teachers are to be held down in the hierarchy of society by the government's public sector pay policy?

There are two common-sense answers to all these questions. One is that any government – particularly one trying to think in utilitarian terms – ought to try to cover as many bets about the future as possible. Instead of rationalizing its failures by ideologically motivated guess-work and even more dubious statistics, it should spend far more on every level and type of education. Some waste is a price worth paying to secure and improve our most important national resource.

The other answer is that nothing in this field can be done without the co-operation of intellectuals; the government may dislike or despise them but it cannot hope to educate if it makes no effort to understand and compromise with them. The fact that their priorities include a love of truth for its own sake and a belief that it is, in Enoch Powell's word, 'barbarism' to attempt to evaluate higher education in terms of economic performance, has not been faced by the government.

Mrs Thatcher has been heard to remark that she finds scientists who do research 'so boring'; that is her privilege. But her political instincts ought to warn her that an important part of her middle-class conservative constituency still has the sense to agree, in its heart, with Newman's tremendous peroration: 'A university training aims at raising the intellectual tone of society, at cultivating the public mind, at purifying national taste, at supplying true principles to popular enthusiasm and fixed aims to popular aspirations, at giving enlargement and sobriety to the ideas of the age, at facilitating the exercise of political power and refining the intercourse of private life.'

*The Times, 31 May 1985*

# Crumblings of
# Discontent

I have thought, and written, for six months that this government was at last in real political difficulties, not primarily as a result of any complicated psychological or even ideological failings but from the cumulative operation of the simple factors that normally bring down governments – economic failure beyond the limits of plausible excuse or explanation; lack of new ideas and/or middle-aged self-reproach and panic about the lack of new ideas; and inevitable boredom, on the part of the voters, with old ideas and old faces. This process of deterioration is pretty remorseless once it starts and defies cosmetic repairs such as Cabinet reshuffles; the question is how long it will take to reach the critical stage.

I had thought until recently that it would take a good while yet; but now I am not so sure. The vultures and coyotes are beginning to circle. When the *Economist* thinks it is safe to make a tentative swoop, as it did last week, you can be sure things look pretty bad. And I notice that other politicians and commentators, scenting decay, are now trying occasional rushes at the government's flanks that they would not have risked a few months ago.

The instincts of these predators are usually pretty reliable. But what is particularly ominous for Mrs Thatcher is that there is now a certain pattern in the attacks. To change the metaphor, we are moving into the phase of the government's life in which the political myths and images that will determine the next election are being manufactured. Once one of these 'stories' becomes established in the public mind it will be almost impossible to get out – and indeed every subsequent event will be slotted into the pattern.

Opponents are still experimenting to see what 'fits', and there are doubtless further modifications to come. But the main elements are already there and their arrangement is beginning to take on some uniformity and coherence.

The latest variant goes something like this: Britain under Mrs Thatcher is like a splendid Victorian mansion that has been allowed to become a slum lodging-house. The spacious rooms have been divided into sordid tenements and let for exorbitant rents; there are no amenities because they don't pay; nothing works properly, nothing is repaired; the brass and mahogany fittings have been flogged off to speculators; worst of all, the occupants, brutalized by desperation and misery, have turned nasty and not only carve up each other and anyone else who comes around but have actually taken to marauding expeditions into the neighbourhood.

As it happens, a lot of this yarn seems nonsense to me – and I say that as someone always out of sympathy with this government's approach. Britain and the British are not noticeably shabbier or more vicious than they were ten years ago or than most other denizens of the civilized world now are. I could take you tomorrow to a dozen cities in the US where, after four years of fantastic boom, there is as much deprivation – and far more filth and litter – than in Liverpool or Glasgow. On the whole, the Germans remain more neurotic, the French more selfish and the Italians more feckless than we are.

For really aggressive drunkenness go to Helsinki or Tokyo. If you want to see broken-down infrastructure try travelling on a commuter train between, say, New Brunswick and Newark, New Jersey, or driving along a small town street in Fluvanna County, Virginia; if you want to get mugged, carry a shoulder bag in Rome or travel on the New York subway at night. Drug abuse is on the increase in Britain, as elsewhere in Europe, but it is still infinitesimal in the whole country compared with any one of the five largest cities in America.

One could go on indefinitely. The truth is that all the industrial societies have perennial problems in adjusting to social and economic change. The Thatcher government can fairly be attacked for making this predicament worse by adopting the wrong strategy for growth and doing too little to cope with the adverse consequences of its own doctrines or, to put it another way, for failing either to arrest Britain's economic decline or to reconcile the British people to it. But there is actually very little visible evidence *so far* – as opposed to suspicion and prediction – to show that Thatcherism has inflicted more permanent damage on our society than Reaganism has on America or socialism, under President Mitterrand, has on France.

**251**

Certainly violence on the picket lines or on the football terraces cannot be laid at the charge of any government, still less of the rest of society. We are not, thank God, a tribe, and the Chief Rabbi's attempt (in a letter to *The Times* last Saturday) to turn us into one is horribly misguided. We should stop hooliganism because it is harmful and ugly, but the last thing that is appropriate is to dignify an act of collective violence, committed by a few idiots in the name of perverted national pride, by inverting their offence and matching it with an orgy of national contrition.

Yet, from a political standpoint, the kind of cautious, rational objection that I have just been putting forward is completely beside the mark. The fact is that public opinion evidently *feels* humiliated and that a national orgy of penitence, or something very like it, was what actually took place. That is what spells trouble for Mrs Thatcher. People, particularly middle-class people, are finally getting frightened by an endless vista of deterioration which they sense will eventually affect the quality of life. They feel depressed and guilty about it and they are looking round for someone to blame.

If I am not mistaken, something like the 'story' of the beautiful residence being brought to ruin is now quite close to becoming the authorized version. Everything fits in – unemployment, privatization, the refusal to spend money on the national infrastructure, the philistinism of the green paper on higher education, the specious parsimony of the new social security proposals, picket violence, the Bradford fire and the Brussels riot.

There is some ironic justice in all this, of course. It is Thatcherite patriotism that is now being turned against its inventor. But I doubt whether that thought will be much consolation to the Prime Minister.

*The Times*, 7 July 1985

# Why Our Politicians Don't Persuade Us

Consensus is a rare plant in British politics to-day – which is not perhaps surprising, since so many people expend so much energy in trying to extirpate it. At the risk of being denounced by the entire fraternity of commentators and politicians, however, I should like to try this week to reinstate one modest proposition on which reasonable observers of our present political situation could agree. This proposition is that our most urgent need is for more persuasive political leadership.

During the last ten years this has not been a fashionable view. Indeed it has been assailed from all sides. One branch of the left wing has attacked it on anti-élitist grounds. Political leaders tend to be anti-egalitarian officer-types, or if they were not, they were very soon seduced into that way of thinking. What we needed, therefore was not more leadership but more workers' control, more participation all round and more decentralization to break up the units of power on which the old leadership battened.

Another critique, even more powerful in the last five years, has come from the opposite direction. This has been the neo-liberal suggestion that Britain has been 'over-governed' by Oxbridge know-alls who have attempted to impose their own values and prescriptions on the country, and particularly on the economy. This Keynesian hubris has been followed by the appropriate nemesis, and everyone has been forced to recognize that interference with market mechanisms, even (perhaps one should say 'particularly') with the best of motives, ends in disaster. What was required, therefore, was a period of benign neglect all round or at least a retiral of the politicians to the touch-line.

In order to avoid the charge of being grossly unfair to either the

Benn or the Joseph school of thought, I should say that neither they nor their allies would regard the attack on political leadership, as such, as being the main thrust of their case. But it has undoubtedly worked out that way from an 'objective' point of view (as the Marxists would say). The animus against the Gaitskellites in the Labour Party, and the old paternalist/interventionist wing of the Tories – to say nothing of the obloquy heaped upon the Treasury mandarins from all sides – has tended to carry the argument further than was intended, at any rate by the politicians involved. But still if the role of a politician was to be simply a foghorn through which the voice of the people could be broadcast through the land, or alternatively a rather passive referee in a free-for-all game, it became rather difficult to attach any useful meaning to the concept of political leadership at all.

It seems to me that some of the dust kicked up by this rumpus is now beginning to settle, and in fact the much-maligned politicians can once more be discerned in a worthwhile, independent role. Most sensible monetarists, for instance, now admit that one cannot divorce economics from politics. The idea that pressure on the political system can be removed by setting monetary targets and allowing the market to settle distributional problems has had to be abandoned, for nobody will believe monetary targets are an act of God. To put it at its very lowest, people have to be persuaded to accept the 'inevitable' if they are not going to pull the place apart: and there is nobody but the politician to do the persuading.

On the other side, one can also sense a reaction, though it is perhaps more difficult to be sure about. As usual men's minds are swayed by the crises of the moment. These happen to be the next phase of the social contract (with the particular problem of British Leyland very much to the fore) and the question of devolution. Nobody in the centre of the Labour Party supposes that another round of incomes policy will be imposed on the unions simply because they take a deferential view of Mr Healey's Balliol accents; but neither do they suppose that a free ballot of all the trade unionists in the land or the application of the full principles of worker participation to British Leyland would solve the problem either. Somebody has got to go out and persuade the unions collectively and singly that it is in their long-term interests to accept another round of wage restraint or another period in which traditional differentials, like those of the Leyland toolmakers, are squeezed. Once again it can only be the political leaders, whether parliamentary or trade unionist, who can do it.

In the case of devolution, the point is even clearer. The reason that the government is in its present mess is that it failed to prepare the ground properly for its own proposals. There was never any real attempt to explain to the English electorate in simple and powerful terms what was going on in Scotland; there was not even more than a half-hearted attempt to rally support in Scotland behind the particular proposals that were chosen. The difficulty was not that the politicians failed to listen to the voice of the people. There were endless discussions, soundings and constitutional confabulations. The difficulty was that these revealed, not surprisingly, a clash of interests for the politicians to resolve – preferably by devising some reconciliation and then 'selling' it all round. Until this is done, it is pointless to try to short-circuit the process by means of a referendum, for that will only reflect the clash of interests once again.

Of course there are other lines of approach to our problems than the two mentioned here – some of them raising fundamental and perhaps even insoluble problems. Is it true, as many political scientists have been saying for some time, that socio-economic factors have produced a crisis of expectation which threatens liberal democracy with extinction? Is it true, as Mr Fred Hirsch argues in his absorbing new book, *Social Limits to Growth*,[1] that the increasing scarcity of some social goods like privacy or prestige adds a new twist to the screw? Very likely it is, and some fairly drastic changes in social ethics and even individual psychology are going to be necessary if we are to avoid the worst consequences. But whatever the dangers, they cannot be averted (if we exclude dictatorship or brainwashing or the revival of some powerful anti-materialist religion) except by persuasion and example. And in our western society, politicians, whatever their weaknesses, are the only individuals who are universally recognized as having a legitimate right and duty to try to persuade us.

What we should be looking for, therefore, is not some method of dispensing with politicians or bypassing them by the application of direct plebiscitory methods to decision-making in politics and industry. The problem is to impart as much legitimacy as possible to what politicians do and say.

It seems to me that we have not thought clearly or hard enough about this and that some of the solutions to our present problems which are proposed are either irrelevant or positively harmful to this end. Contrary to some constitutionalists, for example, I cannot see that a Bill of Rights or a written constitution would be at all profit-

[1] Published by Routledge.

able, for it would hand over to the courts a mediating function which ought to belong to the political process. It is arguable, again, that a politician elected by proportional representation of some kind will carry more conviction than a politician or group of politicians elected by the present method – but I rather doubt it.

What matters is that the political system should be as open and flexible as possible and that it should appear to be responsive, without being subservient to the wishes of the electors and the needs of the time. Very little of that can be said to apply today – for which three main defects can be blamed.

First there is the extremely closed and arthritic nature of the party system – which binds a politician to a narrow-minded group of supporters and gives him, in most cases, virtual security of tenure thereafter. The normal way proposed for breaking this carapace open is to try to destroy the existing parties – or at any rate the Labour Party – by some means or other. But this course faces the well-known objection that the parties usefully canalize interests which might be driven to extra-parliamentary pressure and action if the party route was closed. An alternative approach therefore suggests itself – that is, to open up wider possibilities for the individual politician at constituency level.

If, for instance, an MP knew that he had to resubmit himself every five years for selection by all registered Labour votes in his constituency or by all members of his local party; and if it were taken, as a matter of course, that it was as natural to challenge him in this 'primary' election as to challenge an American Congressman, a number of things might follow. First, he would be obliged to try to widen his party support as much as possible, bringing in new members, in order to be sure of not being displaced by a small clique. Second, he would tend to be less set in his ways and more likely to be a one- or two-term man. Third, having got to Westminster, he would be in a stronger position *vis-à-vis* his party leaders – not in the sense that he would be less easy to remove, but in the psychological sense that he would have a broader base within the party.

Another beneficent fall-out from this kind of innovation might be its effect upon the constituency representation at party conferences – particularly the Labour Party conference. If the conference was more representative there would be far less objection to its nominal influence on the party programme, indeed it might even be an asset. Equally, I hold the heretical view that a genuinely representative conference would have some claim to a partial role in the election of the party leader.

The other two major defects of the present system are old stories. One is the question of parliamentary control of the Executive. In spite of all the difficulties and objections it is becoming obvious to all but the most entrenched traditionalists that we must move to a more effective committee system at Westminster and give individual M Ps the resources to make it function properly. The other problem is the matter of open government. Our senior politicians and bureaucrats are still deeply imbued with the spirit of secrecy – partly for secrecy's sake and partly because business is easier to push through. Until we have some further progress on this front, legitimacy and credibility will inevitably be clouded.

In conclusion, I must admit that this outburst has been prompted by a weekend discussing the problems of electoral politics with some visiting American politicians. It is a well-known trap, of course, to suppose that one can transport political systems across the oceans or that experiences which appear comparable are so in reality. All the same, after making every allowance for the deep differences in our traditions, I came away depressed by the limited possibilities and in-flexible assumptions of our own system at present compared with the openness, vitality, and representatives of theirs.

*Financial Times*, 4 March 1977

# IV

# Great Contemporaries and Others

# Robert Kennedy

There was never the slightest doubt. Senator Robert Kennedy was an outstanding man – a passionate idealist, a ferocious worker, and an intensely compelling personality. He stood for all, or nearly all, the causes which I approve. He was utterly charming and helpful to me on the two or three occasions when we had any serious conversation. Yet why was it that I never totally trusted or liked him?

This may seem a tasteless approach to his memory on the day after the appalling tragedy of his death but I know of no other by which to confront the contradictions of his character. He baffled and worried almost as many Americans as he captivated. He was a man who aroused ardent admiration and ardent distrust in about equal proportions and there is unlikely to be either honesty or ultimate truth in any judgement of him which does not acknowledge its personal starting point.

For many of his critics this starting point was a specific grievance. Liberals remembered that he had once worked on the staff of the infamous Senator Joe McCarthy; trade unionists remembered his relentless pursuit of James Hoffa, the Teamsters Union leader; Democratic officials recalled the ruthlessness and even brutality of his relations with them while he was managing his brother's campaign for the Presidency; businessmen knew that he was their bitterest opponent in President Kennedy's entourage during the fight over steel prices. All these groups to some extent disliked and feared him for no other reason than he had bruised them. A good few detested him blindly.

For others, the starting point was an equally blind adoration. What he did or failed to do scarcely mattered. He talked the language of idealism and youth. He was immensely attractive. And above all he was the standard bearer of the Kennedy name – the man who would avenge his brother and restore to Washington the departed glories of the New Frontier.

My own starting point was probably just as irrational, being based largely on disillusionment. I deeply distrusted the enormous gap between the Robert Kennedy image and the man as I could observe him. The image which he deliberately projected and to which he obviously aspired was that of a younger version of the President himself – philosophical, sardonic, stylish, relaxed, radical, and decisive. The Bobby Kennedy I could see was a quite different person – unreflective, tense, insecure, conventional, indecisive, and extremely emotional. I did not see how such a man, living between myth and reality in this fashion, could possibly be trusted to run the affairs of a great democracy or indeed the free world.

Looking back on it, I do not think that this conclusion was wrong. But I can now see that the premises on which it was based were far too harsh. They did not do justice to Kennedy's appalling difficulties – both psychological and political. And they did not take account of America's deep need for a personified ideal – which he had become.

He was, as a matter of fact, most of the things I have listed. He was immensely, even recklessly, brave in physical terms but disappointingly timid politically. The agonies of indecision through which he went before invading New York State and running for the Senate from it, or challenging President Johnson on Vietnam, or recently running for President against Senator McCarthy, are only the most publicized of his doubts. He seldom took a public stand on anything unless he had gone to immense pains to inspect the damage it might do him and even then he was constantly worrying whether he ought not to tone it down after all.

It was this caution which accounted for the extraordinary ambiguity of his political attitudes during recent months. He was against the war in Vietnam but frequently warned against prolonged negotiations. He denounced the Negro ghettos yet hesitated to recommend a radical and expensive attack by the Federal government upon them. He cared deeply about Latin America and yet never moved far beyond the most cautious and orthodox expressions of dissatisfaction with the present Alliance for Progress.

What he might have done in practice if he had ever come to power we shall now never know. In private, however, his attitude to issues was more straightforward. One had only to talk to him for a few moments to be aware that he saw many issues in very simple terms. Unlike his brother he had not (to quote a friend of his) 'travelled in the speculative area where doubt lies'. It was not (contrary to what is often said) that he was intensively and exclusively pragmatic. He was genuinely humane in large things as well as small. His imagination latched on to a number of abstract ideas – youth, death, poverty and equality.

He had, moreover, an introspective and melancholy streak which made him touchingly worried about his own ability to put policies into effect. But he did see many issues and personalities in black and white. He was desperately anxious about 'doing what is right', and once he had seen an issue in this light, as he did the questions of racial equality or labour rackets or poverty or mental retardation, his mind and abilities seized upon it avidly.

At these moments he was at his most impressive and effective but even then one could never be quite sure that political considerations would not cause the crusade to be abruptly halted in its course or that the means by which he had chosen to pursue it would not turn out to be chillingly ruthless. His two greatest practical achievements – the management of his brother's campaigns and his handling of racial questions during his term as Attorney General – were brought off when his vast energies and his imagination marched hand in hand and there were others about to see that his competitiveness was kept within bounds. At other times his initiatives were apt either to fizzle out (as happened with mental retardation), or assumed the character of a vendetta (as happened over Jimmy Hoffa).

Many people have theorized about the origins of these strengths and weaknesses and it has been pointed out that the seventh child (and third son) in a vast, brilliant and closely knit family was likely to feel a desperate urge to excel. What is probably more significant, however, is the overpowering sense of responsibility which Kennedy felt for the image and reputation of his brother – and the obvious doubts he had about his ability to discharge it. He knew that for all his own abilities he did not have John Kennedy's intellect or his grace or his power of decision. Yet he knew that he had to follow the destiny of the family.

Much of his caution over the last few years may have been due to his understandable desire not to drag this image in the dust through failure or to throw away the splendid inheritance with which he had been entrusted through rashness. Yet ironically it was his caution and his refusal to risk it all until it was too late which was already threatening to tarnish the gold by the time his assassin struck. The young had already gone over to Senator McCarthy and in spite of his success with the Mexicans in California some observers were convinced that the poor and the Negroes were beginning to desert him.

Looking back, one can sympathize with his hesitations. The dilemma was really insoluble. The trouble has been that time has given John F. Kennedy's presidency a glow that never was on land or sea. To live up to the recollections which exist of it among the young, the liberals and the down-trodden sections of American society would have forced Robert Kennedy to take up positions which, in the present mood of America, would probably have led to electoral disaster. President Kennedy found it possible to be both progressive-looking and politically successful. His brother was forced to choose between the two and fell between them.

Yet, at the end of the day, it would be wrong to say that his long efforts to avoid this fearful choice were entirely wasted. For four and a half years there was a man in high office in the US in whom the hopes for a younger, juster, more equitable America were personified. Simply by his name, his dignity and his image, he helped to keep alive – and, more important still, keep rational – the aspirations of millions of Americans who might otherwise have taken to the streets or to despair. Now that he is gone it is hard to see where else these hopes can be enshrined.

*Financial Times*, 7 June 1968

# Iain Macleod

With the death of Iain Macleod the Conservative Party has lost its most formidable politician. He had flair, toughness, a devastating wit and, when required, a healthy streak of cynicism.

During the Tory leadership crisis of 1963 Harold Wilson told me that he regarded Macleod as by far the most dangerous contender from the Labour point of view, and I am sure he was right. Macleod had what no other member of the Conservative front bench then possessed or now possesses – an instinct for the political jugular vein and a real taste for blood.

But he had something still rarer in the modern Conservative Party – the power to transmit political excitement. Year after year at Tory Conference after Tory Conference, amid a desert of technocratic minutiae, his was the only oasis where vision and principle were allowed to come into their own. His big, harsh voice would worry away at some alleged iniquity of socialism, tear it apart, scatter brilliant derision over it, and then, leaving it for dead, would soar up to some splendid Tory Empyrean, where Crown and Commons walk hand-in-hand and Order, Honour and Loyalty preside benignly over all.

In Parliament, from the moment in 1952 when he took on Nye Bevan ('a health debate without him would be like *Hamlet* without the First Gravedigger') he was always good value. At his best he was a star of the first order. Hunched over the dispatch box he would adopt a lucid, pleasant, conversational tone for five or ten minutes at a time, then he would trail his coat a little, mocking his opponents with the lightest touch of mockery. There would be an interjection from somewhere below the gangway and slowly the whole of his body would swing round like some great gun being brought to bear, a smile of satanic anticipation would spread across his face, and the broadside would blow the opposition out of the water amid a gale of laughter.

This unique talent for making the ideas of Disraeli live in the minds and laughter of a big audience could hardly have been so effective if Macleod himself had not been deeply romantic and had not tried to practise what he preached in his own public and private life. From the moment he arrived in 1946 to join Lord Butler's team at the Conservative Research Department, he was deeply committed to changing the pre-war image of the Conservative Party as an alliance of business and the upper classes in which the working man had no part.

He insisted to his dying day that he was not a Conservative, but a Tory in the sense that Disraeli and Lord Randolph Churchill had used the term – that is to say, a man who believes fiercely in the responsibility of the state to protect the whole body politic, including the poor, and if necessary at the expense of the rich.

In Macleod's subsequent career these preoccupations could be seen clearly at four different periods. First there was the foundation of the 'one nation' group in 1950 with Angus Maude and others devoted to a more positive and analytic approach to social problems than the Churchill opposition had shown during the years of Attlee's government. Again, as Colonial Secretary during the 'wind of change' period he saw himself first and foremost as the constitutional protector of an oppressed African majority in central Africa.

As Leader of the House of Commons, characteristically he regarded the House primarily as a forum for the discussion of great issues and the redress of grievances and not (in the modern fashion) as an instrument designed to help the Executive govern more efficiently. Finally as Shadow Chancellor, and briefly as Chancellor, he concentrated heavily on trying to produce a 'property-owning democracy' by means of tax reform, and on such problems as child poverty and unemployment.

There was, of course, something old-fashioned, paternalist and hierarchical about this. In the same way he believed instinctively in an aristocracy of merit, if not of blood, with its duties, responsibilities and its privileges – all the more so, perhaps, because he was not born into it.

He was the son of a Yorkshire doctor. He went to Fettes and not to Eton, his Cambridge college was not a smart one and nor was his regiment. But he was still fascinated and attracted by the 'ruling-class' world of Whites Club and racing and country houses, and his vitriolic attack on the 'magic circle' which chose Lord Home as successor to Mr Macmillan owed, one suspects, as much to his hurt at being excluded from it as to any sense of outrage that the constitutional proprieties had been breached or the 'informal' voting rigged.

This is not a criticism of him, for it would have required a saint to stand the treatment that was meted out to him on that occasion. He was joint Chairman of the Conservative Party, he had been conspicuously loyal to Harold Macmillan, and he was a leading contender for the succession. He was emphatically entitled to some consultation; and he did not get it.

His decision to retire to his tent at the *Spectator* instead of serving under Sir Alec was courageous or foolhardy according to one's point of view, but it was an act of quixotry quite in line with his character and with the ideal of Tory *noblesse oblige* which he carried around with him.

The paradoxical truth is that in general, though he was quite capable of fighting dirty when he had to, he behaved much better than many of the existing 'ruling class' who constantly criticized him for being tricky, devious or 'too clever by half'. A good example of this was his strong support for Mr Nigel Fisher in the row with his Surbiton right-wingers; and an even more meritorious example was his immediate statement of sympathy and friendship for Mr John Profumo, after the latter's resignation and after most had run for cover. He voted against the Kenya Asians Bill and submitted Mr Duncan Sandys to a withering blast of scorn for taking the opposite line. 'Your Kenya constitution is devastatingly clear,' he wrote. 'So is Hansard. So are all the statutes. And so therefore is my position. I gave my word. I meant to give it. I wish to keep it.'

Why, then, with such splendid polemical gifts, so much drive and ambition and so much real idealism and decency did Macleod never really enjoy the success that ought to have been his? Why did a man who wrote so well and spoke so well fail to 'get across' in a bigger way with his party and the public. He was never really very close to the premiership and although he was one of the best known of modern politicians he never climbed very high in the popularity charts. The answer, as always, is a complex mixture of chance and temperament and timing – all the more interesting and tragic in this case because success meant so much to him.

Certainly bad luck had a good deal to do with it. The frightful arthritis which crippled his spine progressively in the last few years was perhaps the worst cross he had to bear, for he had been an active, athletic man and the pain was intermittently very great. He bore it with enormous courage, but it did sometimes make him irritable and preoccupied. Another mischance was to have been put, by Harold Macmillan, into a political position at the Colonial Office in which it was virtually impossible to succeed.

He could not, like Mr Wilson, take refuge in the fact that Britain had no power to enforce her will in southern Africa, for in his day it was universally accepted that the Colonial Secretary was at least an equal partner in the debate with the African Nationalists and the white Rhodesians, and yet his real ability to influence events was not much greater. He had to bluff desperately and in the process earned the vindictive mistrust of the right wing of the Tory Party. The crowning misfortune is that he should have died at this moment, when, after a decade of opposition and minor offices, he was at last in a position to make a major contribution again.

But though chance played its part it must be said that his own temperament and talents had something to do with it. I worked closely with him for a year when he was editor of the *Spectator* and I was its political columnist. He taught me a lot about politics and he was fantastically generous in allowing me to express views which he regarded as dangerously heterodox. I regarded him as a friend. But he had a kind of detachment, deepening sometimes into profound melancholy and suspicion which could be extraordinarily chilling. In the gregarious, gossipy life of politics this quality jarred many people and gave him a reputation for coldness and calculation which was really undeserved but which did him a good deal of damage.

Then again, one has to admit that he lacked a spark of creative, practical imagination. He was not a great innovator. He left the Health Service pretty much as he found it; and the *Spectator* and the House of Commons were the same. At the Colonial Office he followed lines which were laid down by Macmillan and by history. As Minister of Labour he was tough and successful where his predecessor had been weak and expensive; but he operated strictly with the instruments and machinery as he found them.

On this record it cannot be automatically assumed that he would have been a great reforming Chancellor on the lines of his mentor, Lord Butler. Nevertheless, he still had a fighting chance. He was slowed down by the economic situation he discovered when he came in. He lacked the feel which Mr Maudling has for macro-economics, or the passionate interest in micro-economics which Sir Keith Joseph would no doubt bring to bear if he were chosen as Macleod's successor.

Yet Macleod did have three priceless attributes in dealing with the central problems of the economy.

First, he had a genuine concern about what ordinary people want and a genuine feeling for what makes them tick. This instinct was what made it possible for him to seize political issues with such dexterity. Any tax system which he devised would have been very well based on individual psychology rather than on intellectual neatness or industrial convenience. Secondly, he would have been certain to protect the interests of the poor. Macleod's form of Tory romanticism was revolted by poverty, exploitation and human waste. He favoured lower income-tax and selectivity in the social services, but he would have spent as much as the Labour government, if not more, on the relief of hardship at the bottom end of the scale.

Lastly, whatever had been devised would have been launched with enough panache and style to ensure that it got a fair run. He used to say of himself that he and Enoch Powell were the only two people in the Tory Party who had any real passion for words and that this was why they were the only Conservative politicians who were really able to move their fellow countrymen.

He was quite right. Perhaps there are others on the government benches who could fill the Chancellorship with as much political insight and as much genuine compassion – though I doubt it. But there is no one with the same ability to give his policies perspective, to set them in the framework of a coherent attitude to life or, in short, to give them that independent life which only great politicians can impart to the dry stuff which passes for politics today.

*Financial Times, 22 July 1970*

# David Lloyd George

In September 1916, when the Liberal–Conservative coalition led by Asquith was tottering to its doom, Bonar Law confided to Sir Edward Carson (presumably by way of excusing himself for failing to plunge in the fatal dagger) that he distrusted Lloyd George, the most likely successor, more than he distrusted Asquith. Carson replied: 'No, that one [Lloyd George] is a plain man of the people and though you mayn't trust him, his crookednesses are all plain to see. But the other [Asquith] is clever and knows how to conceal his crookedness.'

The exchange, which is rather surprisingly thrown away in a footnote in this latest volume of John Grigg's massive but admirably vivid life of Lloyd George,[1] really sums up the whole argument, then and since. Either one believes that Lloyd George's crookednesses were so glaring that they cast real doubts over his whole career or one believes that his defects were in a sense a necessary part of his genius, that only 'a man of the people', as careless of the rules of conventional morality as of every other contemporary convention, could have smashed the complacent shell of Edwardian society, inaugurated the welfare state and carried his country through the First World War.

To my mind the greatest among the many virtues of Mr Grigg's biography is that he invariably tackles this central question head-on. At every dubious turning point in his hero's career, which is to say on practically every page, he is at hand to weigh not just the practical arguments for each possible course of action but the moral arguments as they would have appeared to Lloyd George and his contemporaries and as they seem to us today.

**270**

[1] *Lloyd George: From Peace to War 1912–1916*, Methuen, 1985.

On this basis Lloyd George does not come too well out of the new volume. The Marconi scandal of 1912, for instance, with which this instalment opens, is subjected to the Grigg method with pretty devastating results. Lloyd George's purchase of shares in American Marconi while Chancellor of the Exchequer was, in Mr Grigg's conclusion, 'an impropriety only a little short of corruption'.

The brazen hypocrisy and evasiveness of Lloyd George's subsequent defence is pitilessly compared with his vicious attack on Joe Chamberlain during the Boer War for a far lighter offence; and his appeal for sympathy on the ground that he could have made ten times more in business than in politics is dismissed in short order: 'it is not self-evident that he would have emerged any richer than he did from his career in politics. Had he emerged ten times as rich he would have been a plutocrat indeed.'

Mr Grigg is much less censorious towards Lloyd George's sexual adventures and handles the early stages of his long relationship with Frances Stevenson, which started at about the time of Marconi, with great sympathy. Having fallen deeply in love with a girl twenty-five years younger than himself, Lloyd George did indeed treat her with real tenderness and unusual honesty – though of course on his terms, not hers. But alas, even this picture of chivalry is clouded by the extraordinary story of the chevalier's attempt to marry her off in 1916 to the former stationmaster at Holyhead who was to be a complaisant 'cover' for the safe and indefinite continuation of the affair.

As for more public questions of policy, on which Lloyd George's record stands or falls, Mr Grigg has to put on his black cap on a number of occasions. Some of these have been recounted before as when the wretched King George V is instructed by Lloyd George, as Minister of Munitions, that it is his patriotic duty to take the temperance pledge for the duration of the war in order to give an example of sobriety to his subjects working in the shell factories, and, having done so, finds that neither L G nor any of the rest of the Cabinet follow suit.

Less well known, and more damning, is the background to Lloyd George's famous patriotic speech in the Queen's Hall in September 1914. Those who listened with tears in their eyes as he lamented being too old to fight and exhorted his compatriots, with superb eloquence, to make supreme sacrifices could not know that he had written to his wife a month earlier instructing her to tell their son Gwilym that he must on no account be bullied into volunteering abroad.

Scrupulous frankness about these episodes makes championship of the countervailing qualities all the more convincing. Lloyd George's phenomenal energy, his strategic flair and his rampant rhetorical imagination all come across with great vividness in this volume – partly because of Mr Grigg's seductive combination of nicety and gusto but partly because his subject was at the height of his powers in these years. (Who else, with the possible exception of Aneurin Bevan, could have coined the phrase 'hands dripping with the fat of sacrilege' to describe the Duke of Devonshire and his rapacious forebears?)

A more unexpected but definite flavour that also emerges in this 1912–16 *mélange* is loyalty. Lloyd George was never an easy colleague, being an inveterate 'leaker' from Cabinet and, like Churchill, a restless interferer in all sorts of business that was not strictly his own. Nevertheless Mr Grigg makes a good case that, although Lloyd George was frequently frustrated by Asquith's failure to establish a firm wartime grasp and was obviously going to be the main beneficiary of a change at the top, he refrained from intrigue until the very end – and even then was a genuinely reluctant conspirator who was more concerned with the proper machinery for directing the war than with politics and personalities, including his own.

At the end of the book one is left with a proper sense of Lloyd George's transcendent gifts and the inevitability that in a crisis they would eventually elbow aside all doubts as well as doubters. Thus Mr Grigg remarks at the conclusion of the Marconi affair: 'perhaps the public reaction, or lack of it, reflected a true sense of the national interest as well as a shrewd understanding of the frailty of politicians'.

And yet, the frailties linger in the mind. It is all very well to say, as Dr David Owen did the other day, that Lloyd George is likeable because he was 'a bit of a rogue'. But the whole trouble is that he was both better and worse than that. He mobilized and saved the nation but his 'crookednesses' eventually did a lot to debase the language and standards of British politics.

Were we bound to pay for the one with the other? Received opinion, including I suspect Mr Grigg's, is that we were. For myself, I am still not convinced.

*Observer, February 1985*

# Alec Douglas-Home

The seventieth birthday of Sir Alec Douglas-Home is an anniversary pregnant with the two commodities that PR men find most useful – nostalgia and personal sentiment. As in architecture, so in politicians: ripeness is all. The last great amateur; a man of honour; a fine innings. The phrases spring easily to the mind and will provoke, in about equal proportions, assent and mockery among the world at large.

And yet it would be wrong to be too cynical about the official phrases that will undoubtedly be showered upon the Foreign Secretary within the next few days. As the thoughts of any objective person range backwards over his long career, it is impossible not to feel a very genuine (and alas, rather unusual) glow of admiration and affection for so durable and likeable a politician. He has been consistent, he has been modest, and (most attractive and rare of all in political life) he has managed to retain a sense of proportion – about the political process, about foreign affairs, and about himself. Dean Acheson's remark about Harry Truman applies to Sir Alec: 'He has never let his personality come between himself and the job.'

This is all entirely admirable, and particularly so at a time when politicians are generally supposed to be ambitious, self-seeking and unprincipled. What is more difficult is to see through these agreeable personal characteristics to a fair and balanced view of Sir Alec as the man who has personified, even if he has not conducted, so much of British foreign policy in the last twenty years.

There are two problems here. The first is the unpleasant difficulty that the activities of any British statesman of the last forty years have to be placed in a long-term historical context of a decline in national power. Sir Alec has had to work with extremely unpromising materials. His record from Munich onwards (though it is really unfair to implicate him in that episode merely on the basis that he was Neville Chamberlain's Parliamentary Private Secretary) has not contained a high proportion of spectacular diplomatic 'success' up to the present, and it seems unlikely that it ever will. Unlike Arthur Balfour, another Conservative ex-Prime Minister who remained Foreign Secretary into his seventies, Sir Alec is unlikely to crown his career with anything like the Versailles Treaty or the Statute of Westminster. But how much of that is Sir Alec's failure?

One may argue that he has been hampered by his lack of Balfour's intellectual brilliance, though for my own part I should say that in the practical business of diplomacy his dogged honesty probably made up for the Hegelian subtlety of Balfour's mind. The real difference between them was surely the difference in their freedom of manoeuvre. Balfour disposed of forces, diplomatic and military, which enabled him, in conjunction with a Prime Minister of genius – Lloyd George – to call the tune. And he was probably the last British Foreign Secretary who was really able to do so. Sir Alec, by contrast, has been engaged from the outset, both at the Commonwealth Relations Office and subsequently in two spells at the Foreign Office in conducting a rearguard action.

This being so, the Douglas-Home record has to be judged on rather limited criteria. The real question is whether, during the long recession which has more or less coincided with his public career, he has made the most of his opportunities, limited though they have been, of influencing events to the benefit of this country.

On this basis, it seems to me that posterity is likely to deal fairly kindly with what the Foreign Secretary has done. The retreat from Empire has been conducted with some skill and remarkable lack of friction. We retain the ability to inflict unacceptable losses upon an invader, and we have managed to keep or acquire some influence over the policies of our two most important neighbours today, the US and the continent of western Europe. To throw off the accumulated psychological preoccupations of 150 years within so short a time has been a process requiring remarkable flexibility and Sir Alec, as one of those who might have been expected, by heredity and temperament, to be least flexible, has served an invaluable purpose in showing the most crusty backward-lookers how to come to terms with reality.

**274** The flaw in this achievement has been that he himself has never quite dared to carry his own perceptions to their logical conclusions or to follow them fast enough. In the two years between 1940 and 1942 when he was immobilized in a plaster cast he had plenty of time to exercise his remarkable ability to boil down a complex mass of data, with the aid of a laborious common sense, to a few strong, simple ideas. The central one of these seems to have been a thoroughly conservative (in the philosophical sense) view about the nature of power. Another, allied to it, was a deeply sceptical, if not actively hostile view about the nature of Soviet communism.

These views led him, as they did Harold Macmillan and others during the post-war years on a natural progression of thought and of policy. The Empire was all very well as a British power base at first, but after a certain point its weakness was bound to feed on itself, and Britain could only maintain her freedom of action and her security in Europe (where the communist menace was acute) by a close alliance with the United States. When this new power base appeared to be becoming unreliable he turned reluctantly to the expedient of a United Europe.

The unfortunate thing has been that at no time has he ever quite come to terms with the consequences of these shifts. As Commonwealth Secretary he was always apt to overestimate British influence, particularly in Africa. Even now, there is a certain self-deception in his attitude towards Rhodesia. Similarly, in the mid-1950s and early 1960s he did not perceive just what being an American client involved. He was in favour of the Suez operation, for instance, and I can still recall the contempt and disgust in the voice of Lyndon Johnson as he described to me Sir Alec's behaviour over the sale of buses to Cuba.

He was late in being converted to the idea of entry to the EEC. He was brought round, I fancy, mainly because he still believes that Russia has not changed her spots. Like many of his officials he is convinced that the Soviet Union can be expected to behave with ruthlessness and great power, and, in addition, he believes that as communists they mean exactly what they say when they threaten to bury the capitalist system. The American nuclear umbrella is becoming increasingly unreliable and therefore we must consolidate our power and security in between Russia and the US.

It is no surprise at all to hear that he is extremely sceptical about the declarations of Mr Brezhnev in Washington and inclined to believe that Mr Nixon's domestic difficulties – both economic and political – have led the Americans down a potentially dangerous path. But to judge by his speech in the House of Commons on Wednesday (as well as from other indications) he has still not drawn the full implications for British foreign policy.

'In all the summitry going on,' he said, 'it is membership of the EEC which gives Britain the right to have some notice taken of Britain. Alone, Britain would have been in danger of being bypassed, but within she can now talk on equal terms.' This is, frankly, rubbish. Britain as the possessor of nuclear weapons has been consulted about future security arrangements in Europe. As an old and fairly vociferous ally of the US she has some residual claim to be informed about the overall direction of American policy. As a power with large forces in Germany she has a place in the negotiations for mutual force reductions. And so on. But there is no reason as yet to suppose that any information has been given us as an individual nation on the strength of our EEC membership.

What the Foreign Secretary has apparently failed to recognize here is that it is only by pooling resources with Europe that we can hope to get additional mileage in terms of power politics out of our membership of the Common Market, and then not as an individual nation but as a constituent part of a new, emerging power. The political case for joining the EEC certainly rests on the search for a new locus of power, but that power will never be greater than the sum of the power of individual members until each contributes to the whole in a way which Sir Alec instinctively shies from.

This account of the Foreign Secretary's diplomatic progress is, of course, ludicrously simplified. But I have made it thus on purpose to bring out the single most striking fact about it. Sir Alec, unlike some of his colleagues and opponents – more perceptive or more obtuse – has almost exactly paralleled the emotional pilgrimage of the country during the period, its confusions, its self-deceptions and its reluctant realism. We have as a nation seen fairly clearly what was happening in the world. We have done what we must with some resentment, with many a lingering backward glance, and occasionally with dragging feet. We have done it, by and large, sensibly and honourably – and by and large too late. Sharing this record with Sir Alec, we should spare him a fraternal salute.

*Financial Times*, *29 June 1973*

# Oswald Mosley

Oswald Mosley is mildly in fashion these days – not, one imagines, a situation which he finds particularly encouraging. Better to be madly admired, as he was in the 1920s or wildly detested, as he was from 1936 until his virtual retirement from active politics ten years ago. After a life so full of violent colours, deliberately daubed, the modest degree of tolerance which now crowns his old age must seem like the monochrome seal of history.

So in a way it is. The story is done. And yet in a sense I doubt whether we have yet got Mosley in historical perspective. We are still oscillating uneasily between acceptance of powerful myths created in the 1920s and 1930s and a revisionist determination to challenge and destroy them. Mosley's career is a test case in the two crucial controversies of the period – the question of responsibility for the slump and the question of responsibility for the Second World War; and since these debates are still being conducted (particularly the first) with one eye on the contemporary scene, Mosley continues to play a vicarious part in modern politics even after he has left the stage.

Mosley himself, in his brilliant apologia *My Life*,[1] naturally aligned himself in order to suit his own case, taking the conventional left-of-centre view of the economic question but an ultra-revisionist view on appeasement. Robert Skidelsky, who now produces the first major academic study,[2] follows much the same line. Mosley, in this portrait, is a man of impetuous, unconventional genius thwarted by the mediocrity of a bourgeois Establishment. He was one of the first to embrace

[1] Sir Oswald Mosley, *My Life*, Sanctuary Press.
[2] Robert Skidelsky, *Oswald Mosley*, Macmillan, 1975.

Keynesian economics and one of the very few members of the 1929 Labour government to put forward a coherent strategy for dealing with the crisis. So far as the foreign policy of the 1930s is concerned, Mosley, by then in his fascist phase, was no doubt guilty of all sorts of excesses, but was it not, in fact, true that Britain could have had peace if she had (as Mosley recommended) left Hitler a free hand in eastern Europe and hedged against his double-crossing us by a massive programme of British rearmament?

It is all very attractive and up to a point, convincing. It looks even more plausible, indeed, than it did seven years ago, when Mosley's autobiography came out, because we are living through an economic and political crisis so dangerous that the comparisons with 1929 can scarcely be avoided. A world which faces the prospect of calamitous unemployment, communist advance and social collapse is prepared, once more, to look with a certain amount of indulgence upon 'men of action' who offer incisive solutions in return for sacrifices of liberty.

And yet the contrary case also cries out to be made from the analogy between our present discontents and those of the inter-war years. Mosley had very remarkable qualities, and Mr Skidelsky is very good on them. Tremendous courage, great energy, a high and original intelligence and above all a superb gift of the gab. He also had serious failings – the self-taught man's tendency to over-simplify, the egotist's capacity for self-deception, the vain man's need for mob-adulation and the autocrat's intolerance of opposition. Mr Skidelsky does not gloss over these traits either.

But the point is that this combination of merits and demerits was not altogether accidentally united and from the midst of our present discontents we may ask ourselves: (a) Was there not something very half-baked about the economic autarky which Mosley envisaged as an integral part of the economic strategy he was propounding in the late 1930s? (b) Did not the mandarins and the City have a point when they claimed that the Mosley proposals would lead to inflation and a loss of competitiveness in British exports? (c) Were not Mosley's ideas about state interventionism in industry and nationalization of the banks open to the same objections of freedom, of confidence and of efficiency which have been advanced against Mr Wedgewood Benn? (d) Quite apart from any considerations of taste or morality involved in Mosley's admiration for Hitler and Mussolini, was it not dangerous to suppose that we could cut ourselves off from a major war on the European continent between Germany and Russia or even, if you like, cheer on Germany from the sidelines?

More generally there is the problem of the man who does not have what R. A. Butler used to call 'the patience of politics'. Anybody who has ever brought creative passion to the political process knows how infuriating established institutions can be but there is a high price to be paid for trying to appeal to 'the People' over their heads. Not only, as Enoch Powell will bear witness, are they apt to defeat you in the long run, but it is almost impossible for the demagogue to avoid following the audience rather than leading them.

Mr Skidelsky shows that Mosley's British Union of Fascists had a greater following throughout the 1930s than has often been supposed. But the striking things about the whole movement were first, the ease with which an allegedly incompetent government managed to outflank it, and secondly, how corrupted Mosley himself became by the constant need to whip up his followers and prop up his own position. I have always found excuses (including Mr Skidelsky's) for the anti-semitic slant of Mosley's activities pretty unconvincing. What is the point of being a Fuhrer if you are obliged to pander to the worst prejudices of your adherents?

Mosley was, and is, an intensely interesting figure in many ways and Mr Skidelsky's book, painstakingly researched and perfectly fair, is genuinely absorbing. Mosley himself deserves credit for this, for the reason is that he charged head on at the central issues of his day. But the tale of how and why he came to grief does not yet lend itself to apologetics. If Britain should finally 'degenerate into the position of a Spain', as Mosley predicted in 1932, or alternatively if the present political system collapses and some future dictator is in a position to dictate the history of the inter-war period, perhaps he may be vindicated. In 1975 his ideas still seem at best highly debatable and at worst infinitely destructive not only of the lax, easy-going liberal democracy he despised but of civilized society itself.

*Financial Times*, 3 April 1975

# Dwight Eisenhower

**P**erhaps only Pope John and President Kennedy among the great figures of our time have brought out more affection and goodwill in great masses of people than General Dwight Eisenhower. When he was elected President in 1952 he was a popular hero, the liberator of Europe, to a vast multitude of people far outside the confines of the US. Far more remarkable, he was still a popular hero when he left the White House eight years later.

The intervening period had not been notable for the growing popularity of the US and its government; and some of the major causes of irritation were directly associated with Eisenhower's presidency; yet, astonishingly, no muddle, no disaster, no brute assertion of American power from Guatemala to the U-2 incident seemed to make any difference. Nothing could disarm the magic of the famous Ike grin, the bright blue eyes and the arms stretched wide to embrace the whole world. The subsequent years have changed little. He has had many detractors but hardly a single enemy.

Current fashion is tearing his record as President to shreds; his influence in his retirement has been negligible and even his reputation as a soldier and as Allied Commander-in-Chief in the later stages of World War Two has been effectively assailed. Yet beneath the most violent assaults on his quietism, his naivety or his conservatism lies a bedrock of admiration for his honesty of purpose, his decent humanity and his extraordinary talent for bridging the gaps between men. History is unlikely to rate him as one of the best American presidents but it may easily conclude that the popular instinct about him has been right and that his human virtues enabled him – at any rate in his first term – to make a significant contribution in America and in the world at a moment in time when other more sophisticated attributes might have been less valuable.

It is hard to remember how gloomy the outlook was both at home and abroad when Eisenhower entered office at the beginning of 1953. The Korean War was dragging on, Stalin was in the final awesome throes of his dictatorship, Senator Joseph McCarthy was on the rampage, and the whole fabric of American life was shot through with bitterness and fear.

The achievement of the Eisenhower administration was to face the dangers and to a great extent defeat them. The Korean War was ended without the American economy slithering into slump. By the manufacture of the H-bomb, the more immediate challenges of communism were halted but without new American lapses into militarism or isolationism. Senator McCarthy was admittedly crushed without any effective assistance from Eisenhower, but it was he who bound up the wounds afterwards; and above all it was he who restored calmness and dignity and a little charity to the political scene.

All this was impressive. What, then, went wrong? And why, after a relatively short honeymoon period, did an air of purposelessness and drift begin to overwhelm even the efforts of a James Hagerty (without a mention of whose shamelessly brilliant activities as White House Press Secretary no account of the Eisenhower years would be complete)?

An explanation which has often been given is the effect of Eisenhower's three serious attacks of illness during his term of office. He had a slight stroke in 1958 and even before his re-election to a second term he had a serious coronary thrombosis in September 1955, and an attack of ileitis necessitating major surgery in 1956.

His popularity survived these traumas (as his 10 million majority in the 1956 election showed) but his activity did not. His doctors ordered much relaxation and his absences on the golf course became more prolonged and apparently more absorbing.

But the real trouble went far deeper. It arose from Eisenhower's stubbornly traditional conception of the American presidency. He was far from being a weak man. Rather he practised inaction with almost incredible strength. He was used to command and his outbursts of temper were legendary. When he saw a need to exercise his authority he did so with decision – as he demonstrated, for instance, in his celebrated showdown with Governor Faubus of Arkansas in 1957.

Nevertheless, his whole conduct was coloured by fixed ideas about his role, which came as much from the experience of a soldier-diplomat and the moralism of a Kansan Protestant as from orthodox Republicanism. Much of the air of muddle and slackness arose, for example, from his refusal to press his case on Capitol Hill or appeal to the country with it. The reasons, estimable in an individual and fatal in a practical politician, were that he violently distrusted demagoguery and believed in what he called the 'slow, gradual power of persuasion'.

He had a strong sense of the dignity of the presidency. There were many admirable results of this. It reinforced his temperamental aversion to 'personalities' and ensured, for instance, that although he despised Adlai Stevenson as a 'faker', he never attacked him personally in either of their election campaigns. On the other hand, the drawbacks to this approach were fearfully apparent when Eisenhower consistently refused to take the lead in stopping McCarthy (and there is not much doubt that he could have done so) because, as he said: 'I will not get down into the gutter with that man.'

Most serious of all, perhaps, his character as well as his military experience led him to a peculiar view of the proper relation of a president to his Cabinet. In Washington, as in the European War, he believed in delegation; he picked his generals and then let them get on with their campaigns. If they did anything outrageous, or started fighting each other instead of the enemy, he would intervene with charm and compromise but only rarely with firm authority. Even this was not exactly weakness, for he always took the responsibility. But it often looked remarkably like it, since the President's preferences, in so far as they were known, so often seemed to be disregarded.

These preferences were not by any means all orthodox at the time. His wartime experiences had made him an internationalist, with an internationalism which was quite prepared eventually to embrace Russia. He had a most humane detestation of war and a strong urge to disarm. He aimed at freer trade and lower tariffs. He talked sensitively about the aspirations of developing countries and the need for increased foreign aid. He believed in all the republican virtues of thrift and self-reliance but when confronted with real social needs his instinct was generally to throw doctrine out of the window. He even liked the British – and said so.

Roosevelt, Truman, Kennedy, Johnson, all succeeded in imposing their views on their Cabinet, if not upon the Congress. But Eisenhower hardly ever persuaded John Foster Dulles, his Secretary of State, to relax his moral crusade against the Russians (scarcely more often his suspicion of the British), or George Humphrey, his Secretary of

Defence, to spend two cents where one would do half the job. They and their colleagues, once picked, were nearly always allowed their heads. And the sad thing is that the President's instincts were often shown subsequently to be righter than theirs.

The personal code which produced these strange, tentative results during Eisenhower's presidency led him in retirement to one of the greatest blunders of his career – the failure to use his influence to stop the nomination of Goldwater. But it had no such catastrophic side-effects during World War Two. He had come late to combat command and he was not a profound strategist. But he never needed to be; for both in North Africa and in Europe there were competent generals under him to fight the battles in detail and politicians and higher strategists galore above him to prevent global miscalculations. Thus Eisenhower was able to concentrate upon what he could do super-latively well – the imparting of unity to a vast mass of men – all within the framework of the things he believed in – loyalty, morality, harmony – and for an end that was clearly and safely determined for him.

Yet presidents, unlike generals, must find their own ends and fight every battle themselves. Their enemies are multiplying all the time and to use old weapons in the old way is to invite certain defeat. Eisenhower the President, fighting the complexities of modern society with the armaments of George Washington, lost, but he lost honourably. And who shall say for certain that a nation which chooses as its leader a good man rather than a clever one is wrong?

*Financial Times, 1969*

# Aneurin Bevan

It is odd that when Roy Jenkins was discussing the near-misses of British politics last week he did not mention Aneurin Bevan. Among those who might have made it to the very top, Bevan is a particularly interesting example, because such an extreme one. Here was probably the greatest orator in English of the century with a natural flow and sense of timing as great as Lloyd George's, with an even richer vocabulary and a far better-stocked mind. He had the rank and file of his party in the hollow of his hand, a complete mastery over the House of Commons, a famous record as Minister of Health, and a devoted group of close admirers to spread his gospel abroad. He was a genuinely big man who brought excitement and glamour and moral depth to the politics of his time. Why was it that he failed to reach the summit?

We have waited a long time for Michael Foot's reply[1] to this central question about his hero. The marvellously vivid first volume of his biography[2] left us stranded more than ten years ago at 1945 with the *enfant terrible* of the wartime parliament poised on the verge of office as the youngest member of Attlee's Cabinet. Now, with all the rest of the story in his grasp, it doesn't seem to me that Mr Foot quite faces the issue. In fact he makes the conundrum still more puzzling by the sheer persuasiveness of his advocacy. Bevan, he demonstrates with absolute justice, was not the rabble-rousing revolutionary that his right-wing opponents and the Press continually painted him. He turned

[1] *Aneurin Bevan 1945–1960*, Davis-Poynter.
[2] *Aneurin Bevan 1897–1945*, Granada.

out to be an impressive administrator and in his struggle with the BMA over the National Health Service (one of the most absorbing parts of Mr Foot's book) he hardly put a foot wrong. He was also a deeply serious and reflective politician to whom ideas were meat and drink and whose devotion to parliamentary democracy was as passionate and absolute as his opposition to totalitarianism in Russia or anywhere else.

In the controversies around which all the troubles of the 1950s centred, Bevan's propositions, closely examined, were nearly always sustainable and have sometimes proved right where his fiercest orthodox critics were wrong. An exception was his initial line on the H-bomb which he genuinely seems to have believed Russia and the United States would give up if Britain showed the way. But on German rearmament his line of approach – temporary neutralization pending wider disarmament – might have been worth giving a real try. And although he acquiesced in the vast British armament programme at the time of the Korean War when he was inside the Cabinet, his criticisms of its utter unreality at the time of his resignation a few months later were actually perfectly correct.

In view of Bevan's relatively blameless record in all these arguments, we are forced to look towards two other explanations of his difficulties. One possibility is that he was thwarted by villainous opponents who wilfully misunderstood his position or stabbed him for their own ends. The other is that there were important destructive elements in his character that escaped the protection of his intellect.

Not surprisingly, Mr Foot plumps for the first of these alternatives. Men in black hats are much in evidence and have to be shot down one by one. Herbert Morrison is a great plotter whose 'substitute for a guiding hand or a real grip was a finger in every pie'. Hugh Gaitskell appears on the horizon as 'the pedantic spokesman of the Treasury's most arid doctrines'. Even Attlee, though granted grudging tolerance, is still the 'arch-mediocrity'. The real killer is Arthur Deakin of the Transport Workers who personifies the iron hand of trade union bureaucracy which dictated, as to some extent it still dictates, the course of events within the party and was determined, according to Mr Foot, to destroy Bevan simply because he showed signs of dangerous originality.

This interpretation is all very well so far as it goes. A lot of people were gunning for Bevan. But why? Some of Gaitskell's and Morrison's animosity might be plausibly put down to jealousy. But Attlee was secure enough and as for the union bosses, they had no fundamental quarrel with him until his resignation in 1951.

The real answer is that Bevan had temperamental characteristics which made it extremely probable that the British political system would reject him. With his warmth and talent went an enormous egotism and a very excitable Celtic sensibility. This combination was the key to his genius as a speaker but it made him an almost impossible colleague. When his personality was allowed to blossom without restriction, as it could in the Ministry of Health, he was all right. But as soon as the practical difficulties of the government required him to make sacrifices either of status or of substance he immediately started to pull the place apart.

Mr Foot constantly tells us that Bevan despised 'personalities' and thought exclusively in terms of principle. But to everyone except the immediate coterie of Bevanites the tantrums with which his stands of principle were often accompanied looked remarkably like the sulks of frustrated ambition; and the violent *ad hominem* style in which he launched them made 'personalities' inevitable. The charitable gloss on Bevan's predicament is that genius in politics is a form of passion and that if the British were less frightened of passion they would be better at harnessing it. But still, other political giants have bowed their passions to the yoke – and indeed Bevan himself did so at the end of his life. In the meantime his colleagues had a point.

Two things prevent Mr Foot from acknowledging this. The baser motive is his determination to rub the noses of his contemporary opponents – Jenkinsites, pro-Marketeers and other undesirables – in the contrast between the 'magnanimity' of the Left today and the 'viciousness' of the Right in the days of their pride. The more admirable reason is his overflowing love and admiration for his friend.

He is much too honest in completing this portrait to suppress the warts altogether, but he has softened them and arranged them artfully so as to set off the rest of the features to the best advantage. The appalling outbursts of personal vituperation, for example, are mentioned but are treated with a sparing and, if possible, humorous touch. The blurted indiscretions are reinterpreted or contrasted with the chilly sobriety of others. The end result is not exactly hagiography. Mr Foot's own intelligence and experience keep it in the real world. It is perhaps more like one of those splendid Renaissance profiles, glowing with life and colour and sincere admiration, but somehow leaving one with the certainty that the other side of the face, if one could only see it, must carry lines or even disfigurements more revealing than anything in view.

*Observer*, 7 October 1973

# Ramsay MacDonald

It was an interesting and ingenious gesture of Anthony Wedgwood Benn's to circulate to his Cabinet colleagues last November the Cabinet minutes of the 1931 crisis. The long, child's history of the Labour movement contains many touching illustrations but none so inspiring as the picture of Arthur Henderson and his gallant band of true socialists shaking their fists in defiance of the international bankers while the arch-traitor Ramsay MacDonald and his lantern-jawed henchman, Snowden, slink off to Buckingham Palace (where else?) to complete the sale of the working-class to the Tory bosses.

This edifying scene, in which, incidentally, a rather shamefaced Benn senior can be dimly discerned in the back row, was presumably intended to strike such terror into the hearts of the Callaghan Cabinet that they would immediately reform their ways and adopt the *Tribune* Group's 'alternative strategy' of a siege economy. But oddly enough it seems to have had, if anything, the opposite effect. A number of ministers, notably Anthony Crosland, were reminded, not simply that the cuts proposed by the I M F last year were chicken-feed compared with what was being imposed on the unemployed in 1931 but, more important, that if they actually succeeded in defeating the Prime Minister and the Chancellor in Cabinet they would simply bring down the Labour government without preventing the cuts from being made.

The failure of Arthur Henderson and the others to face the same reality in August 1931 is naturally the foundation stone on which David Marquand rests his defence of MacDonald in the first major biography[1] anyone has dared to write of the great apostate. Broadly

[1] *Ramsay MacDonald*, Cape, 1977.

288

speaking, his thesis is that MacDonald did not understand the new Keynesian economics, nor did he seriously challenge the conventional wisdom that anything was better than that Britain should come off the gold standard. But then neither did any of his opponents in the Labour Cabinet at the time. Even Ernest Bevin and the TUC did not at that stage deny that some sorts of measure had to be taken to hold the parity. Once this was admitted, then the argument for balancing the budget was unassailable because nothing else would restore foreign confidence in sterling. MacDonald accepted this logic and, moreover, being a patriot, threw his own reputation into the scales by becoming Prime Minister of a national coalition with the 'class enemy'. The 'loyalist' ministers ran away and put the preservaton of Labour unity above the national interest.

This line of argument, which is pretty much what MacDonald himself adopted in a series of astonishingly savage letters and speeches after the split, seems touching and plausible in the light of recent events. The reason why it was overwhelmed in 1931 (and, for that matter, may not satisfy the Left or the trade unions even now) is partly that MacDonald committed the fatal error of running a subsequent general election campaign against his own party – and winning. But there was a more fundamental problem in the fact that MacDonald's 'treason' was obviously no aberration and could therefore be portrayed by a brilliant propagandist like Laski as the long-contemplated product of an 'unsound' character:

> Timid, indecisive, vain of applause, he shrank from the price of un-popularity among a society [i.e. the Conservative upper classes] he had growingly come to esteem . . . Its own faith in its standards gave him standards he could not otherwise attain.

Marquand's book attempts to demolish this attack – not by denying that MacDonald acted in character, but on the contrary by showing that the actions that destroyed his career sprang logically from an able and honourable mind and from the experience of the forty years of Labour politics that had preceded them. In other words, he was more than most, a consistent politician and it is not really possible to blackguard him for 1931 without having to cast aspersions on his extraordinary achievements earlier on.

What were these? The first, which emerges more clearly than ever before from Marquand's intricate researches, was his success as a conciliator. MacDonald was elected leader of the Labour Party in

1911 mainly because he had shown during the previous decade as its secretary that he was the one man who could reconcile the Independent Labour Party and its militant socialism with the rather erratic pragmatism of the trade unions and other Liberal converts. He was able to straddle this gap by force of personality but also because his particular theory of socialism was suitable to the exercise. Marquand makes us understand that, to MacDonald, socialism was an ideal state of society, or rather, perhaps, a state of mind, in which everyone recognized his overriding duty to his neighbour. We were gradually evolving in Darwinian style towards this high condition, and while the pace of the evolution could be hastened a little by pressure on behalf of the needy it could never be forced. Socialism would be built on the success of capitalism, not its failure. It was not a weapon in a class war; it was not even the exclusive prerogative of a party, though Labour was the most promising base for socialist activities.

These views fortified MacDonald in a highly effective stance, once described as 'vehement moderation', during the protracted struggle to establish Labour as the legitimate rival of liberalism within the Constitution. But they were bound to lead to tension as soon as economic circumstances revived Marxist notions and the sectional interest of the unions. This happened in the stormy period of industrial unrest between 1911 and 1914 when he adopted an ungrateful 'honest broker's' role, supporting strikers' demands but berating their methods and telling the House of Commons in February 1912:

> We are too fond of imagining there are only two sides to a dispute . . .
> There is the side of Capital, there is the side of Labour and there is the
> side of the general community; and the general community has no
> business to allow Capital and Labour, fighting their battles themselves,
> to elbow them out of consideration.

After the war the class question rapidly came to the front again. MacDonald quickly became disillusioned with Lenin and embarked on a bruising struggle to prevent Labour joining the Third International. He remained aloof from the General Strike, which he described in his diary as 'one of the most lamentable adventures in crowd self-leadership of our labour history'. After this, 1931 does not seem so surprising. Indeed the question arises why the bust-up between MacDonald's national conception of Labour and the class conception did not occur sooner.

**290**

The answer which emerges from Marquand really has to do with MacDonald's Scottishness. In the first place there was a moral dimension to MacDonald that transcended the theoretical argument and it was a morality of a peculiarly Scottish kind. He was a spellbinder with the voice and language and appearance of an Old Testament prophet. He appealed to the ordinary worker by foretelling the coming of a new Heaven and a new Earth and the day when the tears would be wiped away from all eyes. His principled opposition to the First World War – for which he gave up the leadership – made him the hero of the ILP idealists.

His other asset, still more distinctively Scottish, was his ability to skip across the class boundaries at a time when they were particularly high. Marquand is extremely good on all this. MacDonald was a genuine working-class lad from Lossiemouth, but he was at the same time quite obviously a man of hard-headed practical ability, a man of great natural dignity, and a man who had imbibed a liberal education at one of the purest founts of nineteenth-century learning – a small-town Scottish high school. Upper-middle-class Fabians like the Webbs were always uncomfortable with him, perhaps because he was difficult to patronize, but the Establishment accepted him because they could not place him in the normal categories and the workers were proud of him because he was accepted by the Establishment.

As in the case of his theoretical position, a certain price had to be paid for these advantages. Like other contemporary Scotsmen on the make – Lord Reith or John Buchan for instance – he displayed a certain naive snobbery and vanity. He had a Celtic streak of mawkishness and another of rather self-pitying pessimism which was deepened still further by perennial loneliness (his wife died in 1911). A typical diary entry on New Year's Eve 1917 begins:

> I cannot go to bed till the New Year comes in, and the Old is at the point of death. It demands an account of my stewardship to take with it – where? Who knows? Maybe into nothingness. What can I say? Work, work! Effort, effort! That is all.

Another, in 1919, ends, 'I read for consolation Gibbon's *Decline and Fall* and the Minor prophets.'

Such a man was indeed susceptible to the psychological comforts of flattery, particularly from women: hence his vulnerability to the Laski line of attack. But the achievements remain – and so does the fundamental dilemma of every Labour leader from MacDonald to Callaghan. The choice lies between a national mandate soured by trade-union disenchantment or a class programme leading to electoral disaster.

When this beautifully intelligent book was begun more than a decade ago it looked as if Harold Wilson, like MacDonald, might still take his chance on the first option; when it was finished last year he had abandoned his party to the second and fled the scene. David Marquand is too subtle and perhaps too political an historian to say that Mac-Donald took the wiser part. But the case is made, nevertheless, that he took the braver.

*New Statesman, 4 March 1977*

# Neville Chamberlain

Neville Chamberlain was born on 18 March 1869, and his centenary will be celebrated next week with the usual discreet festivities and the usual pious attempts at rehabilitation.

The Conservative Research Department, which he founded, has already produced a highly complimentary sheet of notes on his career for the use of anyone who wishes to defend him. But who will wish to try? Perhaps Lord Butler, his Foreign Under-Secretary, or Sir Alec Douglas-Home, his Parliamentary Private Secretary, or Mr Malcolm McDonald, his Dominions Secretary, or Mr Geoffrey Lloyd, the inheritor of his political bailiwick in Birmingham, will make a stab at it for old times' sake. Perhaps Mr Iain Macleod, who produced an unfashionably laudatory (and, in my opinion, much underrated) biography a few years ago will return to the charge.

It is a hopeless task. Chamberlain still stands for the twin disasters of the 1930s – appeasement and unemployment. The words carry an intolerable weight of emotion which neither party can afford to unload. The Conservative Party is still not ready to face the fact that the appeasement of Hitler was the first result of a secular decline in British power which continues to this day and which Sir Anthony Eden's Suez disaster was a desperate attempt to prove non-existent.

Similarly, the Labour Party derives much of its emotional uplift from the myth that unemployment is the great enemy as it was before the war and that the National Government, with Neville Chamberlain in the van, was its diabolical exponent. To examine Neville Chamberlain's life is to attack these beliefs at their root, as well as shedding an unwelcome light on some of the less creditable episodes in the history of each party. Political prudence, if not justice, suggests that Chamberlain should be left in peace.

293

Yet there is something in the man, a certain nagging honesty, a dogged ability, which demands to be heard. And if that were not all there is something so massively Conservative about him.

He once said he wanted to 'get rid of that odious title of Conservative', indeed he started off as a Liberal, like his father the great Joseph Chamberlain, and then as a Liberal Unionist. But he was in fact the archetype of the Conservative Party of the 1960s. He really was everything that Mr Edward Heath and his young followers would like to be – hard-headed, efficient and mildly progressive – and he shared their characteristic defects, being inflexible, arrogant and humourless. If anyone wants to know what the chairman of Great Britain Ltd would probably be like they have only got to go back to Chamberlain.

It is against this kind of conservatism – the conservatism of the Birmingham businessman with the precise mind, the conservatism with a passion for constructing institutions, and if necessary intervening decisively with all the force of central government – that the Powellites and the Tory romantics are rebelling. Whether they are defending Biafra (like Czechoslovakia – a small country that we know nothing of) or attacking regional policy, they are in search of principle instead of pragmatism; of an ideal model instead of the best working model that can be put together in the circumstances. Chamberlain's career is enormously relevant to this argument, for it shows with exemplary clarity the virtues and limitations of the busy, pragmatic approach.

The virtues are not to be underestimated. Chamberlain's achievements in the field of domestic reform were, in their day, almost prodigious. Lloyd George remarked sneeringly of him that he had made 'a good mayor of Birmingham in an off year'. But having devoted twenty years of his life to local government (he only entered Parliament at the age of fifty in 1918), he was in fact a far better administrator than Lloyd George and at least as close to understanding the practical problems of the man in the street.

His work as Minister of Health (which then covered Housing) between 1923 and 1931 was genuinely valuable and explicitly directed to 'the improvement of social conditions'. His Housing Act of 1923 was the basis of a highly successful housing drive. His Contributory Pensions Act of 1935 produced the first comprehensive scheme for insurance against illness, old age and widowhood.

A series of measures, of which the main ones were the Rating Act of 1935 and the Local Government Act of 1929, completely overhauled and revivified local government. Later it was he who was responsible for taking away unemployment relief from local authorities altogether and setting up the National Assistance Board.

As Chancellor of the Exchequer, loyalty to his father, or perhaps the brainwashing of a liberal imperialist upbringing, led him into one of his few dogmatic flights of fancy – the tariff protection measures of 1932 and the futile attempt to set up Empire Free Trade at the Ottawa Conference. But within the orthodoxy of the day his general approach was remarkably enlightened, including, as it did, a cheap money policy and a Special (that is, depressed) Areas policy of which Cobden and Mr Enoch Powell would have heartily disapproved.

All this does not make Chamberlain exactly the 'social reformer' and 'Tory Democrat' which Mr Macleod would like to make him out. For most of his measures were devoted primarily to tidying up a mess. 'I cannot,' he wrote, 'contemplate any problem without trying to find a solution for it.' But it was the practical challenge of setting a muddle to rights by rational means which attracted him; there is little evidence of any grand social designs in the Gladstonian or even Disraelian sense. He was, as A. J. P. Taylor remarks, a 'meticulous housemaid'; he was no Frank Lloyd Wright.

At the same time he was nothing like the ogre that the Labour Party has painted him and nor were his or Baldwin's governments. The cuts in unemployment benefit which were supposed to, but did not, avert the fall of the gold standard in 1931 were supported by Chamberlain; but it was Snowden and the international financial community who imposed them and not he. As Chancellor subsequently, however, he received all the odium of not increasing them and for the baleful workings of the means test. He got none of the credit when the rates were raised and the means test was softened by the arrival of his Assistance Board.

His real trouble here, as in foreign affairs, was that he was a cold fish – as pragmatists so often are. It may be that a sensitive nature and an early sense of failure caused by the collapse of the sisal-growing venture, with which his father entrusted him as a young man, made him withdrawn and difficult.

But the Labour Party spotted, quite rightly, that he was conducting policy largely as a logical exercise. He lacked warmth, he lacked a higher vision and he lacked a sympathetic imagination.

And this, of course, is precisely where his foreign policy came unstuck as well. He was confronted with a dangerous mess in Europe and believed that by the application of pure practical reason he could sort it out. The Versailles Treaty had produced some anomalous results and had left large numbers of Germans under foreign sovereignty. Very well. By the 'orderly operation of treaty revision' he would set it to rights.

He failed to take into account the possibility that he was not dealing with a rational situation. Hitler was an opportunist and a dreamer. The British public could be swayed by emotions of fear, shame, honour, and morality and it was by no means certain that they could be made to accept any 'reasonable' arrangement in which their Prime Minister might acquiesce.

The arguments which have been advanced in defence of appeasement and the Munich agreement are perfectly sound – up to a point. At the outset the British public did not, to quote Chamberlain's own words, 'care a hoot' whether Sudeten Germans were in Germany or Czechoslovakia, and there was indeed no guarantee that the French or the Dominions would support us in a war over Czechoslovakia. We did gain time. Perhaps war was always inevitable. But the fact remains that Chamberlain had entirely lost control of events. He misread the dictators and in consequence showed weakness when strength was required. He ignored British public opinion at the outset but then allowed it to stampede him into giving guarantees to Poland and Czechoslovakia which could not be fulfilled short of total war. He went to war in the end at a time and on an issue he had not chosen, and without any chance of leading to victory.

These were all, ultimately, failures of imagination and they were compounded by an absolute intellectual certainty. Those who disagreed with him were brushed aside as idealists or mischief-makers. The chairman and his three closest associates decided what was best for the company. The Board and the shareholders were given little say.

It was all done quite coolly and with the best of intentions – mainly to prevent the company's progress being delayed, its profits reduced or the reasonable expectations of its workpeople (as interpreted by the chairman) being disappointed. It was, at the outset at any rate, a sound business strategy but it was not political leadership – and indeed it never will be.

*Financial Times, 14 March 1969*

# The Many Faces of Harold Macmillan

Actors are notoriously hopeless subjects for portraiture. The Garrick Club is lined from floor to ceiling with scenes of wild animation and fantastic costume. But the faces, Kean and Siddons and Irving, are as dead as putty and the eyes as blind as beer-tops because when it came to the crux, the artist simply had to give up. It is the same with Macmillan. The Carlton, if I remember right, is already adorned with a particularly blank-looking portrait of him in the full regalia of a Chancellor of Oxford University, and one could decorate a new bar very cosily with pictures of his other favourite roles – the crofter's grandson, the survivor of the Somme, the poor man's friend, the scourge of the socialists, the Duke of Omnium, the man in the white fur hat, and the philosopher-king.

Even in North Africa during the war when he was at his most independent and effective he could not resist the temptation to pose. Harold Nicolson recorded in his diary, after seeing him in Algiers, that his dispatches were really brilliant 'in the style of Macaulay'. Vicky used to hit off all these characters marvellously (as well as inventing one of his own, Supermac); Mr Sampson draws them very well, too.[1] But neither Vicky nor Sampson manages to make them seem expressions of a single, real personality lurking somewhere behind those drooping eyelids and toothbrush moustache.

Mr Sampson actually identifies no less than four proto-Macmillans: the Scottish publisher, the radical intellectual, the Guards officer, and the duke's son-in-law. I myself would eliminate the fourth as being

---

[1] Anthony Sampson, *Macmillan, A Study in Ambiguity*, Allen Lane, The Penguin Press, 1967.

simply an extension of the first. Aristocracy has a well-known fascination for the middle-class combination of romanticism and self-interest (cf. John Buchan). But even supposing we accept Mr Sampson's four Macmillans as the irreducible minimum, there remains the problem of accounting for all the other parts he played.

As one watched Macmillan in action, it seemed that his public attitudes were of two kinds. The first were poses adopted quite deliberately for tactical reasons. Welensky's description of Macmillan's tearful assurances over the Central African Federation is a fair sample of this type of dissimulation. Again, the plummy right-wing persona he took on in the final Churchill government was not always frightfully convincing, but it served its purpose of winning over the Knights of the Shires. The retreat from Africa and the advance to Europe were both conducted by Macmillan under the most outrageous histrionic camouflage.

One's attitude to these performances rather depends on whether one thinks the particular ends justify the means. Personally, since I believe a certain amount of deception is inevitable in politicians who want to get to the top and stay there, and I strongly agreed with Macmillan's imperial and European policies, I found I could swallow a good deal of his methods. I am much less ready to do so in retrospect.

The trouble was that Macmillan most often used his pragmatic wiles in the service of a second and different series of attitudes, equally theatrical and far more disastrous. These sprang from some real experience, such as the Flanders trenches or the Depression, or the Anglo-American operations in North Africa, but they had been romanticized and rehearsed so often in his mind that they had become stereotyped travesties. It was the regimental officer who automatically assumed that loyalty was more important than ability and accordingly kept Selwyn Lloyd and Lord Dilhorne in office for five long years and eventually bequeathed Sir Alec Douglas-Home to his party. It was the Member for Stockton-on-Tees who believed that unemployment was the greatest enemy and gave us a series of fitful consumer booms when we needed one steady investment one. It was the Minister Resident in Algiers who actually believed his own facile doctrine that Britain is the Greece to America's Rome and that it was our chief destiny to influence the United States.

Mr Sampson argues that both kinds of deception were a national necessity, papering over the cracks in British self-esteem and edging the Conservative Party towards the contemporary world. If so, the advantages were bought at a very high price. Britain managed to maintain a special relationship but thereby lost the European enterprise. Socialism in England was finally destroyed but the economy was set back ten years. Loyalty and 'unflappability' rescued the Tory Party after Suez but at the cost, eventually, of disillusioning a whole generation with politics and politicians.

The fact is, as Mr Sampson regretfully admits, Macmillan had no consistent aims. He took the parts that came to him and played them for all they were worth. He enjoyed them for all they were worth. He enjoyed himself thoroughly and, for a while, so did everyone else. Eventually, of course, reality intruded and he was hooted off the stage.

*Financial Times, 2 July 1967*

The pieces that follow are reviews of the volumes of Harold Macmillan's autobiography:

# His Finest Hour ▬▬▬▬▬▬

*Winds of Change*, the first volume of Mr Macmillan's memoirs, abandoned its hero in 1939, a rather obscure, donnish Conservative back-bencher with a reputation for glum rebelliousness and an unfashionably statistical social conscience. At the end of this new instalment[1] Macmillan is the virtually undisputed master of the Mediterranean basin, the maker and unmaker of governments, the overlord of armies, the daring but subtle author of fantastic diplomatic coups and the servant of nobody except Churchill and Roosevelt.

This remarkable transformation was due in part to luck. Macmillan as an anti-Munich rebel certainly earned a place in Churchill's government, even though he arguably deserved a better fate than that of becoming Herbert Morrison's (and later Lord Beaverbrook's) Parliamentary Secretary at the Ministry of Supply. But he would probably never have emerged from a worthy obscurity if he had not been dissuaded by Brendan Bracken, at a crucial moment, from resigning from the Ministry of Supply or if two other possibles had not turned down the job of British Minister in Algiers which Macmillan took on in December 1942.

[1] *The Blast of War, 1939–45*, Macmillan, 1967.

**299** ▬

On such frail foundations the careers of many Prime Ministers have been erected. The peculiar fascination of the *The Blast of War* derives from the highly idiosyncratic skill with which Macmillan seized his chance when it came. Fulsome tributes have already been paid by a number of participants to this skill – not least by General de Gaulle who was a major beneficiary of it. But recorded in Macmillan's own dry way the story gains plausibility because the reader, in a sense, becomes the victim of the same wiles which drew rings round enemies and allies alike.

One never quite sees how the trick is done, but the easy flow of words carries one along and suddenly the results are there. General Giraud, the right-wing puppet of the Americans in North Africa, is first reconciled with de Gaulle and then eased out in his favour; the French Fleet in Alexandria is brought over to the Allies; the Italian government is induced to surrender; the Italian king is forced to abdicate but the monarchy is saved from the wrath of the Americans; the Greek communists are brought to the conference table and Churchill is forced to accept that 'scheming medieval prelate' Archbishop Damaskinos as Regent of Greece.

Macmillan was not, of course, the sole author of these successes. In some cases the military situation was the deciding factor, in others the Americans took the bit between their teeth. But in each episode Macmillan's hand moulded events – all the more powerfully because his interventions were concealed behind the same studied mannerisms and the Edwardian understatement which permeates the memoirs. Who else would have written 'Rene Mayer became Secretary for Communications. This appointment was novel in two respects. In the first place he was a Jew; and secondly he was an expert on the matters with which he was to be entrusted'?

Macmillan's success was based on three foundations. First he used far more imaginative sympathy than anyone else in the field. For example, to the Americans and even to Churchill, the internal squabbles of the French were an irresponsible descent into petty personalities. Macmillan had the insight to treat them as a struggle over high principles and over the legitimacy of the French state. This enabled him to gain the respect of both sides in the quarrel and to avert a total breach at a number of ominous turning points. The necessary ruthlessness was there, of course, and in the final struggles of Giraud, Macmillan cabled his office, 'Giraud has been an unconscionable time dying. Let him die.' But at least Macmillan understood what he was doing.

His second asset was that he worked as far as possible with and through the Americans. Eisenhower, who was in command in Algiers, was understandably annoyed at the arrival of a British politician and Macmillan gives an hilarious account of the first frosty interview. But by dint of frankness and tact he rapidly gained the friendship of his American opposite number, Robert Murphy. In the end the relationship became to some extent an alliance of the two 'men on the spot' against London and Washington whose frantic cables were often put on one side and sometimes entirely disregarded.

This was Macmillan's third great virtue. He had the courage to stand up to Churchill when he knew he was right. As he himself admits, this lack of awe was partly due to distance, but he stuck to his guns even when the great man descended on North Africa in person roaring furiously that Macmillan was too pro-French and was disobeying his orders.

It is impossible not to feel that this was Macmillan's finest hour. He may perhaps feel this himself, for buoyancy and power and imagination and intense enjoyment come through every line of this volume. It is an exciting book for this reason and also a sad one because one knows the immediate sequel: the let-down of victory, the frustrating years of opposition, and the return of cynicism. Still further ahead one can feel the irony of the fact that Macmillan's foreign policy as Prime Minister was wrecked by the misapplication of his wartime experience. After Algiers he believed he could maintain Britain's position by manipulating the Americans. He also thought he could handle de Gaulle. Both beliefs turned out to be disastrously mistaken. But after reading this book one feels they were understandable.

*Financial Times*, 7 September 1967

# The Post-War Years

If ever there was a politican whose rise was due to phenomenal luck, brilliantly seized, it was Harold Macmillan. He and chance between them turned what looked like a very unpromising assignment to Algiers into the key political post in the Mediterranean. The centrepiece of the present volume [1] is the tale of how, having been palmed off with the Ministry of Housing in Churchill's 1951 government, he made his

[1] *Tides of Fortune*, Macmillan, 1969.

reputation with the party and the wider public as the magician who conjured 300,000 houses a year virtually out of thin air.

The narrative skids to a halt on the precipice of the Suez fiasco and in its last pages he mourns Eden's decision to take him away from the Foreign Office at the end of 1955 and put him in the Treasury. But here again the tide was flowing in his favour. For if Macmillan had remained Foreign Secretary it is doubtful whether Suez would have occurred, and if Suez had not occurred, Butler would not have lost favour with the party, and if Butler had not lost favour he would almost certainly have succeeded Eden in the premiership.

Churchill once told Macmillan that 'politics is not a flat race; it is a steeplechase'. And the virtue of Mr Macmillan's autobiography is that it takes us round the course at a spanking pace without losing sight of the surrounding countryside, the niceties of the race or the abilities of the opposing jockeys.

During the first third of this book the Attlee government naturally makes most of the running. And their performance is observed with the usual dry wit and delicate touches of the claw. Yet considering the reputation that Macmillan acquired between 1945 and 1950 as an almost childishly heavy-handed partisan, it is remarkable how detached his judgements now are. The old Adam occasionally appears in extracts of contemporary diaries. Thus (5 October 1950): 'Cripps was away in his clinic. He is said by some to be ill, by others to be mad. Since he has always been both I expect him to return and resume his post as Chancellor of the Exchequer.' But by now, charity has prevailed. We hear of Cripps's 'penetrating clarity', his 'deep Christian faith' and his 'ability amounting almost to genius'. Aneurin Bevan receives lavish praise and even Morrison, who obviously irritated Macmillan intensely, gets his meed.

But the main character of the book, perhaps even more central than the author, is Churchill. The great man has been painted from almost every conceivable angle by this time and one had thought that there was not much more to be said. Yet Mr Macmillan succeeds not only in producing some splendid new Churchillian *mots* ('it is never necessary to commit suicide, especially when you may live to regret it'), but also in convincing one that the old man's last administration has been seriously underrated, particularly on the domestic side. The shades closed in during the last eighteen months and Macmillan, though he does not go to the lengths of Lord Moran, certainly indicates how dark they were; but during the first two years the promise of 'work, food and homes' was abundantly fulfilled – and largely because the Prime Minister insisted on these priorities.

In foreign affairs, where Churchill and Eden might have been expected to shine, the record is not so good. In particular the mistake of perpetuating the Labour government's failure to respond to the European movement was a calamitous error for which we have paid a terrible price. Macmillan himself, having been one of the chief moving spirits in the establishment of the Council of Europe, watched appalled as first Labour and then his own leaders failed to meet the challenge. He confesses that he nearly resigned from the Cabinet on this issue in 1952 but refrained, partly because he was deeply immersed in housing, and partly out of loyalty to Churchill whom he is inclined to blame less than Eden. It is hard to blame Macmillan in these circumstances, particularly given the mood of the times. Yet it was not simply Eden who wanted to go on playing the old game of balance-of-power politics; but Churchill himself, when it came to the crucial questions of status and sovereignty, was not prepared to face reality.

Macmillan, with his far deeper understanding of the French, his streak of cynicism and his flexibility, saw it all much more clearly, and it is possible that if he had been left at the Foreign Office longer he would not only have had the sense to stay out of Suez but might also have been able to save two or three precious years on the European front. But then, if he had, he might never have caught the tide to Number Ten.

*Financial Times, April 1969*

# Top of the Bill

The old Entertainer finally makes it to the top of the Bill. After a brief, light-hearted turn as Chancellor of the Exchequer (Premium Bonds and all that), and a rather ambiguous supporting role in the Suez drama, the great Macmillan Bandwagon starts to roll. A quick, soft-shoe shuffle over to the Turf Club to celebrate with Ted Heath on game pie and champagne, a brisk disposal of 'local difficulties' in the casting of bit players like Lord Salisbury and Mr Peter Thorneycroft – and the show is on the road. Washington, Moscow, Paris, New Delhi, Canberra . . .

The histrionic parallel is irresistible in spite of being so hackneyed. Vicky the cartoonist and satirists like Mr Peter Cook did not 'invent' that inimitable tilt of the gibus and the twinkle of patent leather shoes. They merely spotted what they were meant to spot.

There was a sense, of course, in which Mr Macmillan's flamboyance was not assumed at all. The mere arrival of a 63-year-old Balliol Exhibitioner of the pre-First-World-War vintage at the summit of British politics was bound to produce some bizarre effects. He himself remarks for instance in a characteristic passage of this new volume [1] on the intense preparation he had to make before answering questions in Parliament about nuclear tests, for, as he says, 'unfortunately my knowledge of these high matters stopped at Lucretius'.

Yet, as this quotation proves, he delighted – and for that matter still delights – to heighten these oddities. *Riding the Storm* abounds in memories of these touches of artifice.

Sometimes it is a physical detail like the white fur hat which he took on his visit to Moscow that brings it all back. More often it is a turn of phrase or a tone of voice. 'One of the main reasons why people get out of gilt-edged,' he notes in his diary in 1957 'is the fall in the value of money and the attraction of gambling in equities. This has affected even Archbishops; buying equities to the ecclesiastical mind has all the fascination of gambling without its moral guilt.'

Again, when reproved by Butler for failing to contribute to a Cabinet discussion on social questions he notes his reply: 'No, no. I quite understand what it is you want to do. You want to popularize abortion, legalize homosexuality and start a betting shop on every street. All I can say is if you can't win the liberal non-conformist vote on these cries you never will.' All highly artificial, virtually pointless and quite amusing.

This elaborately mannered irony produces, I find, exactly the same progression of emotions in me as a reader as it did in me as a political observer and voter. First amazement, then admiration, and finally surfeit. The whole Macmillan style was only really effective when it was obviously allied with serious achievement. The contrast between his mock insouciance as Chancellor in 1956 and his really serious purpose as revealed by the Treasury minute he quotes, is a particularly impressive example of this.

His style also sets off to great advantage the deadly serious arguments with the Americans about nuclear weapons and the grim farce of his bouts with Mr Krushchev.

Where the unflappable manner really breaks down in the book as in real life is when it deteriorates into cynicism or a failure to look unpleasant facts in the face.

**304**

---

[1] *Riding the Storm*, Macmillan, 1971.

Of the cynicism there is perhaps less in this volume than one might have expected, perhaps because it only takes us to 1959. At Suez, where Macmillan is often accused of playing a pretty devious game, he has no difficulty in making out a case for his own consistency. It is only when the 1959 election starts to loom that a certain deviousness creeps in.

The charge of lack of realism is much harder to rebut, for in a sense the Macmillan style reflected the situation of the whole country at the time. The assumption of effortless, amateur superiority is really an attempt to keep up appearances – which was exactly what the British government's besetting sin in the late 1950s consisted in. Macmillan flitted to and fro masterminding international initiatives – and indeed his book is nine-tenths about foreign affairs – but the whole structure rested on extremely flimsy foundations – a special relationship with the United States which could not last, a position at the head of the Commonwealth which was plainly transitional, an all-or-nothing nuclear strategy (the Sandys Doctrine) of wilful naivety.

A good deal of statesmanship consists in bluff and hocus-pocus and Harold Macmillan was a great artist in both – as well as being an extremely intelligent and sensitive man. His Prime Ministership was successful when he used these gifts deliberately in the service of limited ends; but one senses all through this book a widening gap between art and real life.

*Financial Times*, *April 1971*

# Muddling Along ▬▬▬▬▬▬▬▬

The thirty-year shadow which passes over the reputation of almost any public figure some time after his retirement has now engulfed Mr Macmillan – and there is indeed an extraordinarily dated air about this volume.[1] The two years which it covers – from the 1959 election to the autumn of 1961 – were dominated, for Macmillan, by preoccupations which seem light-years away.

Berlin, Cyprus, the Gulf, Laos, the Congo and the endless round of conferences, telegrams, personal messages, hot-line telephone calls, summit conferences and all the rest which accompanied them seem, after a decade, either trivial or insoluble by a British Prime Minister. It

[1] *Pointing the Way (1959–62)*, Macmillan, 1972.

is easy to say now, that instead of master-minding futilely all over the international landscape under the delusion that Britain was still a great power, Mr Macmillan should have concentrated on the far more urgent task of putting the domestic economy to rights.

This seems to me to be an unduly harsh view both of the book and its author. It is true that Mr Macmillan does not really do himself justice in this part of his tale. The organization of the book is faulty both tactically and strategically. There are some confusing chronological jumps and the writing in the passages which cobble together the crucial quotations from his contemporary diary have lost some of their verve. More seriously, the pace is terribly slow and the painstaking record of diplomatic courtesies actually gives an exaggerated impression of the uselessness of the whole exercise. If Mr Macmillan could have telescoped this and the next volume together we should have got a better perspective as well as being relieved of some pretty excruciating *longueurs*.

And yet even in the midst of the most arid patches the ability and energy of the man come through. The shrewd political sense and the histrionics are there in good measure, of course, and are neatly illustrated by two quotations within a few pages of each other. In the first, he remarks in a note to Selwyn Lloyd at the Foreign Office: 'It may be that Khrushchev is working for a summit conference without the Chinese. In that case it would certainly not be bad politics for me to take the lead in suggesting it.' In the second he is insisting at the Western summit in December 1959, that he would only agree to Paris as the place for the first in a series of meetings on Berlin if future meetings were envisaged in other cities: 'Chancellor Adenauer then somewhat cynically observed that such a plan was helpful in winning elections. I replied rather angrily that I was not thinking of elections but of our duty to God and to mankind.' But throughout the book one is being constantly reminded that in addition to this kind of superficial dualism in his character, there was application and seriousness and a thoroughly civilized view of the potentialities and limits of political action.

The case for saying that these qualities were misapplied during the 1959–61 period rests heavily on historical hindsight. The fact is that in 1959 the world was faced with a number of urgent problems over which Britain did indubitably still have some residual influence. After a few years of John Foster Dulles and Nikita Khrushchev the possibility of a real explosion over Berlin seemed overwhelming; and if, indeed, the big confrontation had taken place there instead of over

Cuba three years later Britain would, willy-nilly, have been right in the middle of it. It is very hard, therefore, to say that the elaborate quadrille which Mr Macmillan danced in order to influence Presidents Eisenhower and Kennedy on this subject was a waste of time.

The problems of Africa, which took up an enormous amount of energy during these years, were equally hard to avoid. Britain still had direct responsibility in the Rhodesias and, through the still powerfully emotional Commonwealth link, some marginal influence in South and West Africa. Moreover, for historical reasons Africa was still at the centre of Conservative Party politics. If one casts one's mind back to these realities, Macmillan must be said to have given the subject no less attention than it demanded. He knew very well what he had to do – to withdraw under a smokescreen. And he did it. He gives himself away very creditably when he remarks, coolly, in his diary after the Congo crisis: 'The Conservative Party in Parliament has been much shaken. The real reason is that Members (who have up to now shut their eyes to the realities of the modern world) have been rudely awakened. Britain (or France or Germany or any European power) can no longer exert a decisive influence on these world events.'

The basic failure of Macmillan during this period was not really strategic at all. He knew that the Empire was finished and he came to realize that Britain alone could not influence the US as much as a united Europe – hence, partly, his historic and perfectly correct decision to apply to join the EEC. On the economic front at home he grasped, as many of his minutes and diary entries show, that 'stop-go' policy was having a disastrous effect – hence his courageous and interesting attempt, with Selwyn Lloyd, to institute an incomes policy and a more flexible exchange-rate policy. The trouble was that he relied too much on wishful thinking and generalization in trying to achieve his long-term aims.

He thought he could 'fix' General de Gaulle on the basis of his wartime contact with the great man in Algiers; he believed that the 'special relationship' with the US would last in a meaningful sense. Until he had taken us into Europe, he believed that the Commonwealth would tide us over the awkward transitional period until the EEC could be made to take the underdeveloped world seriously; he thought we could muddle along with the British economy until it sorted itself out of its own accord. None of these things turned out to be quite true. Whether a younger man would have changed his policies more quickly after 1959 or, having changed them, prosecuted them with more vigour and more attention to detail is a moot point. But by 'moot point' I mean one which is genuinely debatable. It is a cliché that Macmillan became Prime Minister ten years too late and though this book tends to confirm the judgement it would be a brave historian, even now, who would say on the available evidence that he was certain of it.

*Financial Times*, 8 June 1972

# Ringing Down the Curtain ■■■■■■■■■■■■■

It is exactly ten years, all but a couple of weeks, since Lord Home stunned the Conservative Party Conference at Blackpool with Harold Macmillan's message announcing his resignation. Macmillan's political reputation was already in steep decline at that moment and during the subsequent decade it has fallen still lower into the abyss of fashion that swallows every public figure some time after his official demise. Now, I fancy, there are signs of a revival.

This is partly a matter of luck. Happy is the Prime Minister who is followed at Number Ten by Harold Wilson and Edward Heath. Beside the inconsistency of the one and the impermeability of the other Mr Macmillan's characteristic vices take on a rather softer aspect. Then, of course, historical perspective helps. The achievements of the Macmillan era – in particular the successful retreat from Empire – seem more valuable with time; and the failures – especially the fumbling attempts to escape from economic 'stop-go' – appear more pardonable because they were no more unsuccessful than subsequent tries.

Yet one should not overlook the influence of the great man's own conscious efforts. Behind the mask of decrepit detachment which Mr Macmillan has worn with his customary panache during the ten years of his retirement, there has burned a consuming desire to justify himself and beat back the shadows which darkened the last years of his Prime Ministership. Five volumes of lengthy reminiscence have taken us from the mud of Flanders to the moment, in about the middle of 1961, when things began to go badly wrong for him; and the steady drip of ink from his pen has sketched a most convincing and appealing picture.

The earnest, humanitarian survivor of the trenches; the stylish wartime proconsul in North Africa; the wizard of the Housing Ministry; and finally Super-Mac, the unflappable restorer of the fortunes of the Conservative Party – as this procession has lengthened, the chorus of criticism has gradually fallen silent and the strains of praise have been heard in the land.

With the possible exception of the volume covering the Second World War which rippled with recollected excitement, the series has not been particularly electrifying or even outstandingly well written; but it has been a major achievement none the less. The sense of seriousness behind the elaborate amateur façade of a political personality evolving and deepening, of an acute intelligence and a romantic nature harnessing itself to political realities has been movingly sustained and it has had the desired effect of forcing us to look at its author with new admiration and understanding.

But now comes the crucial test. The sixth, and final, volume [1] of the saga is the story of the years which destroyed Macmillan as Prime Minister and, after a short delay, the Conservative government with him. Can the old Entertainer pull his final rabbit from the hat and show that this débâcle was the result of malign forces or blind mischance and not, as many people thought at the time, caused mainly by the weariness and cynicism of the Prime Minister?

The answer is ironic. Mr Macmillan has produced one of the most vivid and absorbing instalments of his serial. By the use of copious quotation from diaries and minutes of the period he tries to show the authenticity of his own version of events. And yet it is his own contemporary words which constantly betray him. A persistent whiff of political decay wafts back over the years.

'We had only five abstentions in the division,' notes Macmillan at the end of a big debate on the Common Market in 1961. 'But there are very many *anxious* Conservatives. It is getting terribly like 1846. Anyway none of these . . . can be Disraeli to my Peel.' Or again, after the Stockton by-election in 1962 he diagnoses the strong Liberal vote with his usual acumen: '[The Tory discontented] really are tired of us – of our faces, our caricatured faces, our appearance; above all they want a whipping boy. They are also bored.' And yet he cannot help adding: 'However, within a few months the great European issue will have to be fought out. This will bring a sense of reality and excitement.' These quotations do not exactly dispose of Hugh Gaitskell's conviction that the whole European enterprise was tainted by the Prime Minister's short-term, selfish view of the operation.

Or take another incident of this period – the Cuban missile crisis. The impression which Mr Macmillan now attempts to convey is that of the older statesman standing at the elbow of young President

[1] *At the End of the Day,* Macmillan, 1973.

Kennedy with wise and staunch advice. But this is not the impression which was given in Washington at the time. Many of the Americans involved believed that the Prime Minister panicked. Macmillan accuses Gaitskell of not being very 'robust' on the subject. But reading between the lines of Macmillan's contemporary minutes it is clear that at the outset, at least, he himself bristled with objections to the American course of action.

All through the great events of this volume – the dismissal of Selwyn Lloyd and six other members of the Cabinet, the economic difficulties of '61, the Common Market negotiations and the Profumo scandal there runs the common thread of a lack of touch, a loss of nerve. Survival has ceased to be regarded as the just reward of real success and has become an end in itself. Honours become mere playthings ('I got an Earldom for David [Kilmuir], a Viscounty for Mills and CHs for Watkinson and Maclay. I told Tim Bligh to ring up Selwyn and say that in the emotion of our talk I had forgotten to offer him a CH, would he like it?'). It is all very well for the retired Olympian in the final words of his book to exhort the British nation to 'restore and strengthen the moral and spiritual as well as the material base on which they have rested for so many generations' but it was he, after all, who coined the slogan 'you never had it so good' and he who once remarked contemptuously that if people want a sense of moral purpose they should go to their Archbishops for it.

Of course the final collapse was not entirely the Prime Minister's fault. He is abundantly entitled to feel bitter with the newspapers over Profumo and with some of his colleagues and supporters for their back-stabbing activities when the going got rough. Chance and boredom also played their parts. But in the last resort there was some rough justice in the fate of the Macmillan administration, and somehow this is conveyed through Mr Macmillan's final pages. It does not destroy the value of his earlier years as Prime Minister – but it gives the vast work a dying fall. For those who like happy endings this will be a disappointment but for those who like politics the way it is it will seem an appropriate and even satisfying finale.

*Financial Times*, 27 September 1973

# His Last Bow

There can't have been many sadder sights in the history of British politics than the Prime Minister's exit from the House of Commons on Monday night. Head more bowed, shuffle even more pronounced than usual, white as a ghost, he seemed to totter with complete finality out of the Chamber amid the howls of the Opposition and the faint counter-cheers of his own side. As he turned at the Speaker's Chair to face the House again some of his supporters rose and Mr Macmillan's last glimpse of the battlefield must have been of Lieut.-Col. Sir Walter Bromley-Davenport desperately wiggling his massive fingers in farewell with the expression of an inexperienced father trying to comfort a crying baby. Was this to be the end of the road for the man who rebuilt his party after Suez, the author of the 'wind of change' speech, the great Common Marketeer, the tireless correspondent of Mr Khrushchev and one of the most adroit politicians there has ever been? The cruelty of politics is no respecter of persons.

*Spectator*, *21 June 1963*

# V

# The Commentator at Large

# The Uncommitted Voice

When I wrote here last week about the political detachment produced by a stay in hospital, a friend commented: 'But you're always detached.'

The undercurrent of reproach in this remark carried my mind back nearly twenty-five years to a conversation with Anthony Crosland. I had just started in political journalism after a period as a theatre critic, and Crosland was extremely friendly and encouraging. It wasn't long, however, before we were engaged in a fierce altercation about an article of mine in which it appeared that I, who had accepted the Crosland version on two or three recent issues, was now rejecting it on this latest question, in favour of a line that was not only un-Crosland-like but positively Conservative. I can still see Tony towering over me and shouting: 'You'll never influence anyone unless you join up.'

My immediate reaction was to take refuge from this formidable onslaught in a young man's fever of moral indigation. How dare this political hack dictate his seedy partisan compromises to me? Was it not my vocation to seek truth without fear or favour?

At the time these questions seemed to me unanswerable, and yet the more I saw of political life and the way that political opinion in this country is formed, the more I found that Crosland was stating an important truth and one which has been a challenge to my political aloofness ever since.

Its force is that it is based on two simple facts of human nature: people are more willing to listen to their friends than to anyone else and people distrust unlabelled products.

All politics – and indeed every process of persuasion – is deeply influenced by these axioms and in the British political tradition they have been elevated to the level of high principle.

Our institutions are mainly eighteenth- and nineteenth-century constructions, founded on the existence of a political class (drawn from a small range of families and professions, schools and universities) which could be relied upon for predictability. If you knew who a man was, you could make a very fair preliminary guess as to what his political opinions would be; and once you had confirmed these by personal contact, you would be pretty sure that if they changed subsequently it would be by slow and well-signalled degrees.

Those who acted otherwise were liable to be tagged with a damaging label of flightiness and irresponsibility. The Chief Whip in one of the Palliser novels, arguing against giving the politically fastidious Phineas Finn a government post, summed it up in a characteristic hunting metaphor when he said, 'These Irishmen won't run straight.' Only the transcendent force and genius of Gladstone enabled him to overcome the bitter charges of unreliability which flowed from the many tergiversations of his long career.

Of course, the atmosphere of British politics has been transformed, but far more of it remains here than in, say, France, Germany or the United States. Not only do practical British politicians continue to cry: 'Damn your principles, stick to your party', the British voter apparently still tends to dislike politicians and parties without a settled, easily identifiable position. The maverick MP who attempts to turn independent may last one election on his personality, but rarely more. I suspect that at least half of the difficulty experienced by the SDP comes from an obscure feeling, even among people who profess to admire independence of mind, that a group of politicians who put their principles above party and have no obvious 'interest' cannot be wholly serious.

If this is still the prevailing political culture of the country, how can a political journalist make any real impact? Is he not bound, as Crosland implied, to tie a label round his own neck? If he does so, and is identified, say, as a 'Conservative' commentator, he may be largely ignored by anyone except Conservatives, but he will be able to influence an important half of the political spectrum, he will be admitted to the genuine confidence of Conservative politicians, and he will be allowed a good deal of judicious heterodoxy and independence within the Conservative camp.

**316**

On the other hand, if he opts for a wider independence and the luxury of choosing without an easily recognizable rationale between the politics and opinions of the various parties, and of praising and criticizing politicians without any detectable bias, he will probably be distrusted and, if possible, brushed aside by all parties alike.

My own temperament, in spite of Crosland's warning, has taken me over many years along this latter track; and I am sure that I have, in the Crosland sense, been less 'influential' upon the politicians than if I had backed a party or even an intellectual tendency, such as monetarism, which would have given me an affiliated identity.

I am also sure, as I was not at the time of my argument with Crosland, that there is no real comfort for me in any priggish consciousness of journalistic virtue. A reporter should try to report the facts, but beyond that, if his opinions are invited and if they fall into a clear pattern, and if that pattern happens to be socialist or Conservative, why should one be expected, as an honest man, to put them on the rack of a phoney impartiality? It will rapidly become apparent to the readers where the writer stands, and they can take it or leave it.

There is no good reply in principle to this argument and most of the practical weight is also on its side. On behalf of my own position I can only offer three arguments. First of all, in spite of the fashion for 'commitment', the uncommitted voice has its own right to be heard.

Secondly, detachment is not necessarily the same as either indifference or intellectual opportunism. The permanent concern and internal consistencies of any but the most trivial cross-bench mind will become apparent in time.

Thirdly, detachment is the state of mind of the majority of the British public towards politics. Politicians want loyalty but the ordinary reader may occasionally want to hear from someone more like himself.

These defences, now that I see them on paper, do not look impregnable, but they are the best that I can honestly offer. And in any case, it is too late to change.

*The Times*, 25 May 1984

# An Old-fashioned Sort of Chap

Early in 1985, when I wrote a column attacking the government's policy in a controversial field, a friend mentioned the piece, and his agreement with it, to the Permanent Secretary of the department concerned. The mandarin replied, with an air of regret that managed to be both charitable and dismissive: 'Ah, yes. But David is an old-fashioned sort of chap.'

Well, I suppose it happens to all of us in the end. I have not, at fifty-three, quite reached the age when all Permanent Secretaries begin to look young, but looking old-fashioned to Permanent Secretaries is no doubt the stage before it. I have been sufficiently shaken to ask myself, as a New Year exercise, whether the charge is true and, if so, if there is anything I should do about it.

A literal-minded defence is not too hard to construct. For am I not the very model of a modern communicator? I watch television; I keep up with the political gossip of dozens of countries; I am instructed by my children in 'teenspeak' and the finer points of the charts.

Am I not the possessor of a computer which I have learnt how to manipulate for all sorts of professional purposes? Can I not summon up a vast library of facts on my desk at the touch of a button?

'Yes,' replies the disembodied voice from Whitehall, 'but your mind is irredeemably stuck in the 1960s and a lot of your attitudes in the nineteenth century. You are an élitist with a typically useless Oxbridge classical education. You belong to a class and a generation that cannot understand the ruthless, competitive modern world.

'You are hung up on all sorts of outdated, *bien-pensant* notions like the welfare state and consensus politics and the Robbins Report and the Atlantic community and the European ideal and economic aid to the Third World. You sometimes sound like Ted Heath, for God's sake! Your sort made up the old Establishment and a right mess you made of it. Thank heavens Mrs Thatcher and her lot came and swept you all away.'

There are a lot of possible replies to this list of crimes, ranging from, 'Well, there were actually some aspects of the welfare state I never approved of' to 'You're from the same background as me, Mr Permanent Secretary, and you used to say and stand for most of the things that I do until self-interest caused you to adopt the Prime Minister's coloration.'

But these do not really take the argument much further. We have all, in fact, had to change our tunes drastically in the last twenty years – partly because of Britain's continued economic weakness, partly because of changes in the international environment, and partly (to be fair) because the Thatcher 'revolution' has carried conviction in some respects, the initial shake-up in British industry and the reform of trade union law being the most obvious.

The important question is not so much which 'old-fashioned' (i.e. unfashionable) opinions and attitudes should be thrown out as which ones still deserve to be rescued from the Thatcherite holocaust.

A full answer to this question could only emerge over many articles, but my New Year reply comes under three summary headings, corresponding to three guiding principles of my youth.

**Pragmatism.** One of the objects of the traditional British middle-class 'generalist' education was to instil the kind of self-confident scepticism that would enable a man to make reliable practical judgements.

The concept of 'reliability' was limited in some ways by cultural conformity and imperial necessity; and of course it was not thought, until very late in the day, that women might need the same qualities. But still, the system at its best taught people to stand on broad general principles, to clear their minds of cant, to be suspicious of ideology and ready-made solutions, and to look first for the answer that would work even if consistency had to be invented afterwards.

In spite of all the contemptuous labels that have been hung round its neck in the past few years – 'opportunism', 'cynicism', 'superficiality', 'lack of conviction', 'wetness' and so forth – this commonsensical frame of mind, which naturally tends to centrism, has preserved us from extremism and folly in the past, and the lack of it has been the most dangerous deficiency of the present government.

**Responsibility.** Our class system is dying, but only a very large, rich country can maintain stability and efficiency without some kind of élite, preferably as open as possible to talent, but still confident of its abilities and legitimacy. One of our problems is that our élite has lost that confidence, and many of those who have pulled and are pulling it down have neither the real self-confidence nor the instinctive 'feel' to take its place.

A meritocracy should try to preserve at least some of the virtues of the old paternalism, including the preservation of 'high culture' and the operation of such ancient rules of thumb as 'wealth is a trust', 'power means responsibility', 'see the men are fed first' and 'leadership is one part decision, one part persuasion and one part example.'

**Internationalism.** British pragmatism has prevented us ever becoming quite so hooked on international rules as the Americans at their most moralistic, but there was a rough consensus during the twenty post-war years in which my opinions on these matters were formed, around a self-interested large-mindedness in British foreign policy.

We recognized, by and large, that for a country as economically vulnerable as our own, an orderly retreat from Empire, participation in an open and generous international economic regime, a maximization of intangible cultural and historic assets, and a judicious trading of notional independence for real influence, first with America and later with Europe, were in order.

Nobody need pretend either that we have always lived up to these principles, or that the present government has entirely abandoned them. But we often seem to me to be even crazier in our weakness than the Americans are in their strength to exchange 'old-fashioned' outward-lookingness for self-deceiving nationalism and catchpenny isolation.

I can foresee that all three of these principles will come under fierce attack in 1986 – from pre-election populism, from protectionism, from sheer shortage of cash. But I am equally sure that anyone who unrepentantly proclaims their validity in January 1987 will still have the present and the future, as well as the past, on his side.

*The Times, 3 January 1986*

# Lingering Echoes of the Raj

## Madras

Remembrance Sunday in Madras. A nice conjuncture. There is a lot for the British to remember in the city of Clive and Cornwallis. In fact 'all our pomp of yesterday' is on ruinous display here. The spacious imperial boulevards, now renamed after obscure Tamil politicians, are potholed, their lofty façades covered with a riot of small shop signs. The big administrative bungalows are partitioned into mouldering tenements. The monuments of Victorian Madras – the colossal headquarters of the southern railway (a kind of Indian St Pancras) and the High Court building (a glorious confection of domes and turrets) are falling to pieces.

The less essential amenities of Empire have been swept away with a deliberate hand. The racecourse has been closed for the moral good of the masses, the governor's mansion is a crumbling hostel for impoverished state legislators. The East India Company's magnificent banqueting hall, though still in use by the state establishment, shares its facilities with the Tamil Nadu raffle.

It is a melancholy prospect – but not quite in the way you might suppose. There are worse fates for any civilization than to have its artefacts recycled by its successor. The Indian jungle and the apes reclaimed the imperial relics of the Moguls. It seems better that a jungle tide of humanity should engulf the remains of the British Raj. But what is really saddening is that in Madras the intangible benefits of British India are now being submerged as well.

In Delhi a Westernized élite calls the administrative tunes. In the booming economic centres – Bombay and Bangalore (India's silicon valley) – a cosmopolitan, modernizing business class is in control. Here in the sleepy south east, as in many other parts of the provinces, the British and American-educated middle class is being shut out from power.

Populist politicians have captured the mass vote by a mixture of charisma, linguistic nationalism and ruthless machine politics. Priorities have changed. Free food comes before buildings and roads and adequate power supply. Educational opportunity comes before standards. The peasant takes precedence over the urban poor. This can be seen to be an inevitable and even a desirable stage in Indian development. Certainly it is politically effective.

In the state of Tamil Nadu it does not matter that the chief minister, an ex-film-star called M. G. Ramachandran, has had a stroke and can barely communicate, that a lot of his ministers are stupid and some corrupt, that the Madras business community is in despair. The present state government will win the next election with a landslide.

The trouble is that under this kind of regime the economic future is mortgaged to the political needs of the present. The fact that the past is also sold up would not matter so much, except that in India the recent past – Western modernization – is also the key to the economic future. The intellectual remnants of the Raj are the foundation on which their future will be built – if the foundation and its custodians survive.

And are they surviving? Does life still stir in these ruins? Come with me to the Armistice Day Service at St Mary's, the seventeenth-century garrison church of Fort St George, the old seat of British government in Madras. It is a wonderfully odd occasion – part still very British. A harassed English clergyman, clearly an ardent member of the peace movement, leads us reluctantly through a heavily bowdlerized service from which all reference to the possibility of a just war has been firmly removed and a hymn of his own devising about 'the mud-splashed slums of Madras and the rubble of Vietnam' inserted (to the tune of 'Cwm Rhondda'). The British deputy high commissioner and the German consul general read the lessons.

A great cloud of British-Indian witnesses looks down on the proceedings from the memorials on the walls – Colonel Neill who died in 1832 'from the effects of a *coup de soleil*', Josiah Webbe (1770–1804) 'whose extensive knowledge of the Eastern languages forwarded his rise to stations of high trust where his ambition was fired to exalt the honour and interests of his country', Major Langley R E, 'who died from injuries received in an encounter with a tiger', the Rev. Christian Gericke, 'destined to labour in a peculiar vineyard (that of the conversion of the natives of India)'.

But the church is full to overflowing. The path is lined by Indian girl guides in full rig. Two Indian civilians wearing Second World War medals lay vast wreaths. The Indian garrison commander leads a prayer. An Indian professor gives the sermon and quotes from Wilfred Owen. And we all, both British and Indian, listen in silence to the 'Last Post' and sing 'Abide With Me'.

Follow now to a big party at an Indian house the same night. With only half a dozen exceptions the guests are middle-class Indians. Much whisky and gin and tonic. Much talk of recent trips abroad and of children in Britain and the United States. Many shrugs and curses at the state of Tamil Nadu politics.

The room is called to order. It is to be a musical evening, a sing-song. Sheets are handed round. A charming Indian musician (whose first name is Handel because his father had heard *Messiah* the night before he was born) seats himself at the electric organ and for the next hour plays a string of English and American tunes. Everyone bursts into song – 'The Lincolnshire Poacher', 'Swannee River', 'Get Me to the Church on Time'.

Suddenly we turn a page and swing into 'Pack Up Your Troubles in Your Old Kit Bag' and 'It's A Long Way to Tipperary'. I have a feeling that Wilfred Owen and Major Langley R E, and even the Rev. Gericke, would be pleased.

*The Times*, 14 November 1986

# Wonderful Chess:
# Spassky versus Fischer

'Spassky ees *kaput*.' The old Argentinian grandmaster Miguel Najdorf looks like a late Roman emperor and sounds like a bassoon, so this comment, pronounced with explosive force in a Reykjavik restaurant the other day, naturally caused a great hush to fall over the assembled diners. Having secured our attention the great man lowered his voice: 'I will tell you why.' Another dramatic pause. We all leant forward. 'Spassky is finished because he won the second game.' He sank back in his chair as if stunned by the beauty of his paradox and the entire room nodded in admiration and agreement.

Heaven knows if Najdorf is right; perhaps he is. Bobby Fischer forfeited that second game of the World Chess Championship three weeks ago when he sulked in bed instead of turning up at the board; but ever since, his ascendency over Boris Spassky has been clear. Did Spassky feel somehow unmanned by this free gift of a point? Did the dawning possibility that it was perfectly possible to lose the match even with this advantage sap his morale? I doubt if Spassky will ever tell us the answer.

His permanent expression of placid good humour is as inscrutable as it is unvarying. But whether Najdorf's guess was good or bad, his little performance in the restaurant was revealing. It showed the extraordinary capacity this match has had to arouse passionate interest among people who scarcely knew the moves of chess, and it also pinpointed the source of the fascination. The fact is that the match is not a cool intellectual struggle so much as an absorbing psychological drama.

This drama is being played out on several different levels. There must surely be some element of gamesmanship in Fischer's antics. The endless tantrums, the escalating demands, the nerve-wrenching 'will-he-won't-he' delay before his appearance at the beginning of each game – all must take their toll of an opponent, and Fischer, who has always had a very shrewd eye for his own self-interest, must be very well aware of the fact.

But that is not the whole story. His behaviour is entirely of a piece with his strange, obsessive character and his past record stretching back to long before his days of pre-eminence. The psychologists can have a field day with Fischer – the broken-home background, the overpowering Jewish momma, the escape into a non-human world, the emotional immaturity, constitute a classic case. At the chess-board or away from it he has always been as unstable as gelignite.

To watch him in action is to sense the torture and the tension at work in him. He shuffles like a bear on to the stage, blinking at the lights and the public. He fingers the chess-men on the table as if to establish some mystic connection with them. He twines himself torturously around the limbs of his special swing chair. His hands knead his temples feverishly and his body alternates between galvanic tension and sullen lassitude.

The fact that the fans still continue to flock to him is not simply a tribute to the transcendent beauty of his play but stems from a realization that in human terms Fischer is a sad, vulnerable figure who needs the love and acclamation of his fans. The odd thing is that if one talks to some of the grandmasters who have had to deal with him and suffer his whims, most do not take violent exception to his goings-on. Gligoric, the great Jugoslav master, is devoted to him and Spassky himself would have walked out long ago if he had not actually liked him.

It is this picture of a man at the mercy of a total obsession which is so irresistible; the fact that his adversary is so different both as a man and a chess-player adds to the piquancy. On the one hand Spassky is a highly disciplined product of the Soviet school of chess with its emphasis on thoroughness, detailed analysis and strict training; on the human level, although he is a man of great self-control (he sits like a heron at the chess-board, motionless for hours together) he is basically an easy-going extrovert who enjoys a glass or the company of a pretty girl. In both respects he is the complete opposite of Fischer whose chess style is a unique combination of limpid strategy and romantic tactical improvisation, and whose life-style excludes women, drink and indeed almost everything except chess itself.

This is the kind of stuff of which great fights are made. In games, as in the great military confrontations in history – Hannibal and Fabius, Pizarro and Atahualpa, Wellington and Napoleon, Montgomery and Rommel – it is the combination of personal and cultural rivalry that makes the contest memorable. And what is so satisfactory to the chess-player is that in the Fischer–Spassky bout, this obvious temperamental clash is matched by a contrast in purely chess terms that lives up to the same dramatic standards.

In view of some of the things that have been said about Spassky during the past week, it is important to emphasize that the games (with the possible exception of the eighth) have been wonderful chess. Fischer's wins in the third game and the sixth are among the finest that have ever been seen in a world championship match.

The originality and yet inevitability of the process invites the kind of metaphorical excesses that land the writer in 'Pseuds' Corner'. But it needs play of a superlative order from the opponent to bring out this kind of masterpiece. Spassky, even off form – and he is playing well below the form at which he won the title from Petrosian – is not only a superb chess-player but, what is more important for a match like this, a sporting and enterprising one as well.

As incumbent champion he could easily have tried to put up the shutters and played dull, drawish chess, leaving Fischer to batter himself against an iron technique. But in fact he has chosen to risk his title in a series of imaginative pawn sacrifices. In the first game he tempted Fischer to his doom by these means and in the fourth and seventh games he nearly broke through.

The reason he failed to do so is of course to do with nerves and the incalculable psychological tension which a match like this sets up, but it is also to do with age and talent. Chess-players, like other creative artists, tend to conform to a predetermined cycle. Under the age of thirty they rely on the quickness of their brain to ensnare their opponents in tactical complexities. After thirty, as their own thought processes slow down and their experience deepens, they tend to rely more and more heavily on strategic wisdom and pure technique to carry them through. Spassky has followed this course, Fischer has defied it.

Fischer has been thought of since his teens as a strategic master of the first order but one who has been vulnerable on the tactical side. Spassky had obviously decided to take advantage of this supposed chink in Fischer's armour by going all out for wild situations where Fischer will feel out of his depth. Alas, it has turned out that Fischer's tactical perception is now at its peak, and apart from one or two lapses, particularly in the first and seventh games, he has made virtually no mistakes in situations of hair-raising complication.

Spassky himself, on the other hand, who is thirty-five, is finding tactics at this level of competition burdensome and time-consuming and has been unable to find the strategic touch to compensate. In a few years, no doubt, Fischer will be finding the same, but at the moment there is no doubt that he is the best chess-player in the world.

*Financial Times*, *1 August 1972*

# Wonderful Chess: Kasparov versus Karpov

When Mrs Thatcher remarked at the opening of the World Chess Championship in London that politics was like chess, she committed an error that could only have been made by somebody who played one of the two games but not the other. They are utterly and essentially dissimilar. But I am grateful to her for the mistake, none the less, since she gave me an excuse to demand a ticket for the Karpov–Kasparov match and smuggle into this column one of the great pleasures of my life.

The last time I watched top-class chess was fourteen years ago in Iceland, where the dotty but glorious Bobby Fischer was defeating Boris Spassky and breaking, all too briefly, the long Russian hold on the world championship. I don't suppose anyone who witnessed that encounter will ever expect to see anything like it again. Quite apart from the East–West symbolism with which the whole affair was tinged, Fischer had the capacity, like Muhammad Ali or Ian Botham, to create atmospheric electricity in almost limitless quantities.

The chess itself was superlative, some of the best ever played in a match. But the quality of the drama also had something to do with its staging. Reykjavik, poised remotely between two continents and bathed for twenty-two hours a day in pale, unearthly summer light, provided the ideal setting for a struggle on a cosmic scale.

After this exalting experience the elaborate Edwardian gloom of the Park Lane Hotel, where the present world championship is being contested is bound to seem depressingly mundane. And yet the magic still works. The familiar whiff of brimstone still surrounds the two figures hunched on the stage. The same mesmerized silence enshrouds the 200 watchers in the semi-darkness of the auditorium. The corridors are filled with the same knowing commentary in a dozen languages: 'They're following Smyslov's line' . . . 'His black squares are very weak' . . . 'Of course the game was lost six moves ago.'

But how is one to explain all this to the Prime Minister or indeed any other newcomer to this arcane world? Easiest to understand, perhaps, is the element of mortal combat in a match like this. Television has made us all conscious of it in the highest reaches of tennis and other one-against-one sports. And yet chess is more personal and more punishing than the rest. Chess is about power and the domination, not just of a medium, but of another mind. Losing a serious game is a devastating blow to the ego, because there is no shred of chance involved in the loss. This adds another dimension to the ruthlessness of sport in its highest reaches.

A lot has been written about the politics of the Kasparov–Karpov match and the fact that Karpov is the goody-goody darling of the Soviet chess establishment while Kasparov is the embarrassing Jewish *enfant terrible*. No doubt this is a factor but the truth is, on the one hand, that Kasparov's unorthodoxy, even at the fiery age of twenty-three, is strictly limited; and on the other, that there is quite enough in the psychology of master chess matchplay to account for the mutual hostility of the combatants without having to look for political explanations.

Another source of fascination is the question of style. All chess matches display the interaction of differing temperaments, but Karpov and Kasparov provide a particularly classic contrast – the first slow, cautious and remorseless; the second imaginative, adventurous and mercurial.

The sixth game of this match, which I happened to watch, offered a wonderful illustration. Karpov chose an extremely safe but boring opening with which to defend the black pieces. Kasparov managed to conjure up a brilliant new line involving a pawn sacrifice in return for a dangerous attack, but finally overreached himself – as Karpov presumably intended – and had to scramble unceremoniously for a draw.

But in the end the mystery remains, for chess is not basically a spectator sport. Half the people who watch tennis and boxing have never raised a racket or a glove in their lives. Not so chess enthusiasts, 90 per cent of whom are addicted to playing the game and who, when they come to a show like the Karpov–Kasparov match, are in a sense actually playing. I doubt if there is anyone there who doesn't believe some time during the evening that he or she has spotted the brilliant move that the champion has missed.

What is the source of this addiction? What drew me as a boy to spend whole days in the old Gambit chess rooms in Cannon Street, pushing pieces around in an atmosphere thick with herbal tobacco smoke and Yiddish badinage? Why did I waste whole weeks at Oxford vainly analysing openings I would never use? And why, even now, do I have to ration myself, like a reformed drunk, to half a dozen games a year?

To those who really want to know the answers I would recommend David Spanier's delightful book *Total Chess*.[1] But as an interim reply, I should say that the appeal of chess lies in its finiteness. It forces logic and judgement and imagination and determination into a limited arena. It is a microcosm of life, but life that is perfectible, life with the uncertainties drained out of it, life that can be moulded. You lose by your own mistakes, and if you do not make a mistake you cannot lose.

Here lies the flaw in Mrs Thatcher's comparison. Politics is life with all its chances and imperfections intact. Human begins are not obedient, unlike chess-men; and even if you succeed in pushing them around with perfect precision you may still lose the game. Politics is part of the fluid, haphazard, approximate stream of existence. A game of chess is an escape, a vision and, if you can play it as Kasparov and Karpov can, a work of art.

*The Times, 15 August 1986*

[1] Published by Sphere, 1986.

# Theatrical Sketches

## Look Back in Anger ▰▰▰▰▰▰▰▰▰▰

The operation slip is signed, sealed and delivered, the lights are on and the instruments laid out, the heavy breathing of the surgeon mingles with the hiss of the sterilizer; and who should be wheeled in but John Osborne's problem-child stripped of its Royal Court clothes, anaesthetized into inactivity by print, and its agonized belly bared to the knife. The great question can at last be answered: what on earth is wrong with the patient?

After several hours of nerve-wracking exploration it is evident that there is nothing organically wrong at all. Construction? A trifle distended here and there but nothing dangerous. Language? A little hypertrophy perhaps, but this may be all to the good. Characterizations? A few nervous spasms and one superfluous organ, still nothing fatal about that. We can only take it that the whole trouble is psychosomatic and sew up the sufferer as fast as anyone will hand us the gut.

Exchanging the operating table for the psychiatrist's couch has its drawbacks. For instance, remarks that one might in the ordinary way dismiss as childish *jeux d'esprit* assume a horrid significance. Take the following striking fancy: 'She will pass away, my friends, leaving a trail of worms gasping for laxatives behind her – from purgatives to Purgatory.' What is sinister about this is not that it is morbid and unpleasant – we get plenty of that in the consulting room – but that it is a clumsy and passionate attempt to shock the bourgeois, surely a case of development retarded about thirty years. And in case it is said that I am foisting on to Mr Osborne the opinions of one of his characters – a crazy kid if ever there was one – here is a piece from a stage direction for which Mr Osborne alone can claim credit (he is describing the hard, genteel woman who, in spite of herself, throws her body to the non-U hero): 'Her sense of matriarchal authority makes most men who meet her anxious not only to please but impress, as if she were the gracious representative of visiting royalty. In this case the royalty of that middle-class womanhood, which is so secure in its divine rights that it can tolerate the parliament and reasonably free assembly of its menfolk.' One has only to read this to see at once, what one had suspected from watching the play, that the social opinions and pre-judices of Jimmy Porter bear quite a lot of resemblance to those of Mr Osborne himself. One can, therefore, without many qualms, measure the claim (not, to be fair, made by himself) that Mr Osborne speaks for his generation by looking directly at his hero, and conclude, again without qualms, that it is a ludicrous one.

For Jimmy Porter is, in fact, a dodo. He is an Angry Young Man, sure; he is an Outsider, sure. But it is not our own society that he is excluded from and furious with, but that of the 1930s. He gatecrashes weekends and house parties (as if anyone had the money to give them these days); he talks bitterly of the afterglow of the long Edwardian sunset (as if it had not long since faded from the sky); he goes to what he sneeringly calls a White Tile University and hasn't the gumption to do more than keep a provincial sweet-stall (as if intellectuals were still hit by the slump).

'Aha,' says the more subtle surveyor of the contemporary scene, 'you have missed the point. What he (and we) are *really* angry about is not having anything to *be* angry about. He is an Outsider by tempera-ment with nothing to be outside – fearfully frustrating.' The interpreta-tion derives from a single passage where Jimmy says 'There aren't any good, brave causes left. If the big bang does come and we all get killed off, it won't be in aid of the old-fashioned grand design. It'll be just for the Brave New Nothing-thank-you-very-much,' thereby, according to the pundits, speaking for us all. I suppose some people believe this, and I suppose, too, that even when we are all adjusted to present circumstances many people will be angry because they are not angry that there is nothing to be angry about. But do we, therefore, as a generation, spend our time tilting against thin air, so frustrated because the last real windmill has been pulled down that we must manufacture them again in our mind's eye, like that middle-class *Waste Land* which Jimmy wants to sweep away and over whose inmates his sexual victory is so lovingly celebrated? I doubt it. We are all far too busy trying to humanize the spacious, but still rather drab, blocks of flats which have sprung up in their place, a less glamorous, but far more rewarding, oc-cupation.

If I am right, then *Look Back in Anger* is either the expression of an unrepresentative and pernicious nostalgia of bitterness or a play with an anachronistic hero. If, as I prefer to think, it is the latter, no great harm is done, for it is also a brilliant picture of a neurotic tossing on an emotional bed of his own making and talking, as no hero has talked for years, in authentic and sometimes magnificent modern English. The difference between a hero talking modern English and a Modern English Hero talking is obvious and vital – or so it seems to one protesting, if not precisely angry, young man.

*Spectator*, 1 February 1956

# The Balcony ▐███████████████

It would be tempting Providence rather too far to taunt the Lord Chamberlain at this moment with being, like Baal, asleep or on a long journey; in any case I hope he has been neither but has been to see this week's plays, which include a brothel scene, a brace of homosexuals, several adulterers and an old-fashioned feast of rapine and wholesale murder. He may, for all I know, have been one of those carried fainting from the first night of *Titus Andronicus*, but if he stayed the course one or two truths may, with luck, have struck home. First, that this Shakespearian orgy, which is open to all, is far more likely to debauch the mind of youth, or for that matter age, than the carefully diluted discussion of pederasty at the Comedy or the 'What the egg-head saw' peepshow at the Arts, to which one can only gain admittance by the elaborate pantomime of becoming a member of the appropriate Theatre Club, or the desperate expedient of becoming a critic. Second, that pimps and homosexuals need not in themselves be particularly corrupting. Third, that since whores lie considerably thicker on the ground than, say, Dowager Duchesses, they are, on balance, likely to make better subjects for plays. Fourth (perhaps I am allowing my enthusiasm to run away with me), that he had better do something about it.

Take the case of that pillar of French disrespectability, M. Jean Genet. He has had the brilliant notion of setting a play about the papier mâché illusions which go to make up a man's façade in the most potent of all Freudian forcing-grounds – a fetishist's brothel. Here you may meet the gas-man who dons a bishop's regalia and

**333**

absolves the whore whose wares he is purchasing, and the other small-time tradesmen who dress up as generals or judges or desecrators of the Immaculate Conception before proceeding to work. Queen of this establishment is a business-like harridan by the name of Madame Irma, with a vocation for a job which she insists must be performed in rigorous earnest. The rites are punctuated throughout by the clatter of machine-gun fire, for at the time of the play there is a fierce revolution in full swing in the streets outside; things are going badly for the old regime and the queen and most of the rest of the government have been murdered. It is a brainwave of the Chief of Police, a friend of Madame Irma's, to produce her and the other inmates on the balcony of the establishment as the real queen, bishop, judge and general, thus cowing the mob into obedient adoration and introducing a regime of which the Chief of Police is the dictator and they are the permanent figure-heads.

This account is a gross simplification of a plot which seethes with symbolism and cracks with characters, but one can't help feeling that a little simplification would not have done the play any harm. M. Genet's violent quarrel with his producer shows that he has not realized how much of his play is practically unproducible – in the second half of it a fog of symbolic rhetoric descends with appalling suddenness; one peers through the pea-super-egos and catches glimpses of strange distorted figures, Power (sexless), Justice (dumb), Religion (bound), which, as one clutches them, fade exasperatingly into the mist. Peter Zarek does his best with the production but the acting might have been better – only Selma vaz Diaz as Madame and Hazel Penwarden as the rebel whore perform with much gusto, the rest move with the wooden control of those who are not amused. This is, though, a serious play and an interesting one; as for its corrupting influence – only the addition of a Lord Chamberlain as part of the mythology of the brothel could make it more harmless.

*Spectator*, 3 May 1957

# Flowering Cherry ▌

I forget who said that the test of a good play is its ability to stand up to a really bad performance. In any case he was wrong – the acid test is the ability to stand up to a really good one, and a harder trial for **334** *Flowering Cherry* on this count it would be very difficult to imagine. The point is that Robert Bolt, having written a play stuffed with every instrument of depressant realism (not barring the kitchen sink), has found himself presented with two stars who have specialized for years in the most intoxicating kind of magic – transformation by distillation. Sir Ralph Richardson's appearances are now pure fire-water. That great round face, those deep eyes as big as millstones, that slurred, lilting voice contrive to pour out all that is mundane and miserable about day-to-day existence and yet send one home lit up with the warmth of everything that is poetic and magnificent about it. Celia Johnson is almost as potent. The mere sight of her back bent over the washing-up is the quintessence of humdrum heroism. I know of no one else who could make the line 'These soup-spoons are dirty' sound like a commentary on the human condition.

This is all very magnificent but one cannot help feeling that it is not quite what Mr Bolt had in mind. Jim Cherry is a middle-aged insurance agent whose inability to cope with life is compensated by grotesque braggadocio and pitiful dishonesty. He loses his job and dare not tell his wife, he bullies his son but lets him take the blame for a petty theft which he has committed himself; he says he can bend an iron bar but gets a heart attack as soon as he tries – not surprisingly since he is almost permanently under the spell of gin and cider. One by one his deceptions are breached until only his last line of defence is left – the dream that what he would really do if he had the chance is to farm fifteen acres of apple orchard in Somerset, a land of waving blossom where men are men and the work is hard but clean. Alas, this bluff is called as well and his wife, whose struggle to believe in him has lasted as long as there is hope, gives up in despair. All this is sad and bitter. Imagine it played, perhaps, by Paul Scofield and Megs Jenkins, with all the snivelling self-pity, the ludicrous deception, the squalid bickering left in its harsh, original colours. Imagine in yourself, as I suspect Mr Bolt imagined it, the shock of recognition, the disgust and the anger. As it is I doubt whether you will feel it, for Sir Ralph and Miss Johnson are not true realists, they transcend realism, they peddle dreams. It amounts to this, that if you came for the tragedy of which they are capable you will not find it – it is not in the play; if you came for the sequel to *The Critic and the Hearth* by the earliest of the Angry Young Men you will not get that either – for it is not in the actors.

# Last Gasp

**B**y the time I was in hospital there was no doubt what had happened, and it was already hard for me to move my hands; yet I lay for a while in that queer limbo which one sometimes inhabits at the beginning of an illness, somewhere between physical discomfort and mental ease: life flickers past as comfortably and remotely as an Ealing comedy, but the seats are hard and a man is smoking a herbal mixture in the row behind.

I was even surprised when a pretty, coloured nurse threaded her way through the maze of screens and began to count my breaths with a stop-watch in her hand. Although I told her peevishly that it was impossible to behave normally while she stood over me like someone sucking a lemon at a flautist, she only went on counting. She was right; unease crept in by degrees, the seats became more cramped, the screen more and more blurred.

It was so blurred that I cannot remember what the iron lung looked like when I first saw it, though I have gone over it since with the kind of threadbare affection one reserves for worn-out loves. It is, in fact, a long box, monstrous and coffin-like, with a bellows attached. One end slides out like the drawer of a filing cabinet, and on this drawer the patient is laid, his head sticking out where the handle would be. The file is closed on him, the bellows make a vacuum inside, and he breathes out as if someone had sat on his chest. Of course, there are minor subtleties and refinements attached: a dial like the ones on the old kind of pressure cooker, a number of glass portholes, and a Heath Robinson type of electric bell covered with batteries and connected by numberless bare wires to thin air. Not surprisingly, there is always a new model just coming out. I stayed in the old model for six weeks, and it saved my life.

It is not an easy machine for the beginner. He breathes whether he likes it or not, and it is some time before he likes it at all. If he works against the rhythm of the thing, he splutters and gasps, and the bellows creak on without paying him the slightest attention. He cannot return the compliment because it is as if an asthmatic dormitory were tossing on its rusty springs all round him; there is an ominous click and deep grunt, followed by a noise like the pulverizing of many sardine tins, a pause, and then the whole machine gathers itself together for a final, long-drawn wheeze. Sometimes a porthole is left unlatched, the pressure drops, and the alarm bell peals out, filling the corridor with running feet that are hardly audible above the din.

Yet after a time all this sank from the surface like invisible ink, and I slept. Even the waking world was peopled by dream figures as insubstantial and shimmering as heat haze. Some were known by their sounds even when they could not be seen: the click of the nurses' heels and the almost metallic rustle of starched aprons. Some materialized on silent feet from nowhere at all: the matron in steel-rimmed spectacles and a blue dress, an orderly with white overalls and a blue chin. Some battered all the senses at once: the bustle of the doctor's round, the babble of hushed voices, the ring of faces grouped deferentially about the great man, the halo of ether.

There was the hospital carpenter who tried to make a contraption to let me read. He was a thin man with a white, lugubrious face and a voice that sighed like a swing-door. He said he disapproved of new-fangled nonsense, taking all his measurements ostentatiously with a piece of mouldy string; but he was apparently not surprised (nor was I), when he came back with a large and complicated bookrest made of orange crates, to find that it wouldn't fit. He was only a little more ruffled when he returned for the fourth time to find that some friends of mine had forestalled him with a functional model in perspex and aluminium. 'That stuff'll look silly in five years' time,' he said.

The room itself came alive – a curious, topsy-turvy, fish's-eye world, over whose banks these creatures peered. The ceiling – a great, white expanse of it – dominated everything, like an East Anglian sky, its blues in the gashes of missing plaster, its clouds the cracks by the cornice, and like a child I could see anything in it: a map of the Mediterranean, the Taj Mahal, the profile of a Greek girl with incongruous mutton-chop whiskers. Another piece of plaster hung above my head by a cobweb, a puppet as dead as an autumn leaf until a draught set it dancing Petrushka-like, spinning, swinging, jumping ecstatically, sinking mournfully, while the lung kept up its accompaniment, comfortable and cacophonous.

Yet the comfort depended on the cacophony, for while the patient can lie inside the lung like an oyster in its shell, he is safe, and can let worry wash round him like the outgoing tide; once the bellows are turned off and the din hushed, all the discomfort comes rushing in on him again, with the fears that had left him weeks ago behind it, and they find him defenceless. He longs for his lung as much as a tramp might long to get into the police cell out of the rain, and for the same reason: ease and security are worth paying for in self-respect. For it is a battle against his own fears and laziness that he is fighting as much as against his physical weakness. Breath comes to him only in small, hard lumps that have to be shaken down like pills; but he cannot help feeling that he would take them without a murmur if they were sugar, if he were not demoralized, if he were the kind of person he had always wanted to be. Pride demands that he should spend a little longer each day breathing his own air; everything else demands that he think of plausible reasons why he should not. Which would have won on my own battlefield I do not know. Luckily the implacable efficiency of the hospital solved the problem, because protests were useless. In six weeks the din had ceased for good.

*Spectator, 14 October 1955 (his first contribution)*

# The State of
# Our Democracy

Ten years is not, *pace* Sir Harold Wilson, a very long time in politics, but it is quite a large chunk of the working life of one political reporter. My first article in this series appeared in September 1967, and since the present one will be my last, I hope that I shall be forgiven if this Politics Today contains more than the usual amount of Politics Yesterday – and even the day before.

It has been a strange, disturbing decade in the political life of this country, and more than usually difficult to analyse, I fancy, because on the surface so little seems to have happened since 1967. The institutions have survived, the political personnel is identical and even the political situation is uncannily similar – the same left-wing government is engaged in a race against time to restore its popularity by right-wing measures. The ebb and flow of events in the world – the extraordinary surge of revolutionary sentiment in 1968, the climactic denouement of the Vietnam tragedy, the enlargement of the Common Market, the convulsions following two Middle East wars, the body blow of the oil price increase – all this has rushed past and there stand Westminster and Whitehall and Fleet Street, a little shabbier, a little more neurotic, but otherwise to outward appearances unchanged.

In the face of this obstinate immutability, a collection of weekly articles on yellowing pink paper is bound to look restless and panicky. It is not simply that one can now see, as one could not at the time, that (say) Mr Wilson's problems with George Brown were less significant than anyone, including either gentleman concerned, supposed; for it is the normal way with historical perspective that these kinds of mountains should be reduced to their proper molehill proportions. What is more alarming, at any rate for our self-esteem is the possibility that all the long-term trends that political commentators like me have been hunting so diligently throughout this time are insubstantial fragments of our own fears.

The conventional wisdom, to which I have frequently subscribed and which I have occasionally helped to create, has played about with a wide variety of ideas. But the central core of the diagnosis of 'what's wrong with British politics' has been a cluster of notions about the state of representative democracy. The symptoms have been variously identified as the decline of Parliament, the gulf between government and governed, the dictatorship (and at the same time the impotence) of the Executive, the growth of extra-parliamentary centres of power and the attempt of governments to come to terms with them in a corporate state. And the cure equally has been variously prescribed as proportional representation, the more frequent use of referendums, primary elections, a committee structure in the House of Commons, a bill of rights and a written constitution to mention only the most popular patent medicines.

Having used so many words discussing all these in the past, I do not propose to take any more now. All that needs to be said is that both the diagnosis and the prescriptions are challenged – at any rate in their radical forms – by the present state of affairs. An extreme apologist of the existing system (which I am not) is entitled to argue that the evidence is not yet complete. Of course, he might say, we have had troubles – who hasn't, after absorbing the squeeze on real living standards which OPEC imposed on us? It's hardly surprising under these circumstances, he would add, that the unions and the Labour Party should come under fearful left-wing pressure to take actions which are not really in the long-term interest of the country or even their own members. But what has happened subsequently, according to this argument, is that the British Constitution has once again demonstrated its innate flexibility and balance.

Even at the height of the panic after 1973 it enabled the British people to impose a curb on an unrestrained tyranny by producing a hung Parliament. Now, as another general election approaches, the Labour Party has been impelled to put in a highly conservative Prime Minister and to allow him to edge the whole movement, including the unions, back to the high central ground of British politics. The Conservatives, who also went on an ideological binge, and for much the same reason, are also being forced gradually to conform to the normal laws of the system.

What may emerge, then, if this line of reasoning is correct, is a vindication of a good many things that had been under fierce attack for some time – notably the party system itself. Nobody denies that this has been weakened in the sense that there is no longer a large permanent membership of dependable loyalists. The electorate has become more volatile, more 'American', as it has become better educated. But if it should emerge at the next election (as it is beginning to emerge from the opinion polls) that a high proportion of the electors are willing to run out and vote for the existing parties, then it might well seem that there has been nothing much wrong that a little economic prosperity could not put right. The reason the familiar landmarks still stand is that they have never been as badly undermined as everyone thought.

This would be a comforting conclusion, to my mind, if it were true – not because there is any special magic about British institutions; or even (though this is certainly an important point) because really radical constitutional changes are extremely unsettling until they have gained the patina of time, and usage; but because the successful operation of something like our present system would be a sign that our politicians had at last recovered their own balance and adapted themselves to new circumstances. If they can do so they can make almost any system work, including, with minor adaptations, the present one; and if they cannot there is no system yet devised by man which would enable them to govern the country satisfactorily.

Turning over the pages of my cuttings book, it seems to me that the most significant thing I have been reporting, though I have not always realized it, is the decay of a political culture and the demoralization of a political class. The British political world and its occupants have not yet discovered a convincing reaction to the very rapid movement of British society in the last ten years along the path towards a mass culture already travelled by the Americans – a world of high expectations and high demands which brushes aside slogans like 'More Means Worse' with the answer: 'Well, we'll have more anyway.'

The fact is that the assumptions of the whole of the Conservative and Liberal Parties and at least half the Labour members of Parliament are in a contrary sense. They instinctively subscribe to the fears of unbridled democracy of the Victorian middle class – outlined, in a famous passage, by John Stuart Mill:

> Is it reasonable to think that even much more cultivated minds than those of the numerical majority can be expected to be will have so delicate a conscience and so just an appreciation of what is against their

own apparent interest that they will reject the innumerable fallacies which will press in upon them from all quarters as soon as they come into power, to induce them to follow their own selfish inclinations and short-sighted notions of their own good, in opposition to justice at the expense of all other classes and of posterity?

In accordance with these precepts, it is not simply institutions or the Constitution which isolate the average British politician from the pressures of the mass electorate, it is education and the long paternalist tradition of British politics.

That this is not a frame of mind in which it is easy to cope with today's political problems, the experiences of most of the leading politicians of the past ten years show. Sir Harold Wilson himself believed that the way to meet the new demands was by manipulation. Sometimes he gave in to pressure, but for the most part he paid the electors in false coin of gestures and rhetoric which he tried, with some success, to get the media to put into circulation for him. The most casual acquaintance with his Cabinet – to say nothing of a reading of the Crossman Diaries – shows that almost all of them were frightened paternalists who were well aware of 'the people', but never trusted them enough to take them into their real confidence.

Mr Heath was a more purposeful paternalist in that he knew what he wanted to do; but he hadn't a clue about how to mobilize the necessary consensus in favour of his measures. His administration was even more secretive than its predecessor and even more inclined to rely upon the simple authority of Parliament – as if the country at large had not changed. When he finally, and in desperate straits, did appeal to the voters, it was too late.

This being the prevailing mood, it is not surprising that the most interesting politicians of this period (apart from the Prime Ministers) have been the four who have given most attention to the problem of coming to terms with a mass electorate; nor is it surprising that all four have betrayed deep schizophrenia on the subject. Iain Macleod tried to revive a kind of Tory democracy of the variety advocated by Lord Randolph Churchill, but he never had time to work out its implications in practice and one may guess that he was both too cautious and too autocratic to have made much of it. Roy Jenkins likewise did his best to take his Home Office measures to the country, but was temperamentally too fastidious to relinquish the pleasures and security of an Asquithian élitism.

342

Enoch Powell and Anthony Wedgwood Benn have come nearer

than others to starting a genuine dialogue with the mass electorate. But both have spoilt their case by excessive self-interest, and Mr Benn's credentials have been vitiated from the start by his failure to resolve the tension between the kind of participatory democracy he is talking about, and his penchant for extreme forms of socialist planning.

More widely, the main problem is that most British politicians don't realize that there is a problem. The long delay in countenancing television in Parliament, the fanatical jealousy of parliamentary committees to the arcane integrity of their proceedings and the still determinedly amateur, clubbish atmosphere of the House of Commons have shown how far there is to go.

I have picked this aspect of our difficulties to discuss rather than others in my farewell to this page, because it has haunted me personally for the whole period I have been writing. By background and temperament I share all the values and fears of Mill. But journalism imposes other values of its own – a belief in public discussion, a distrust of closed societies and a belief that ordinary people can be persuaded (contrary to Mill's expectations) to act rationally and far-sightedly if things are adequately explained. That is why the political event which has given me most pleasure in ten years was the referendum on the EEC. We shall not solve the problems of modern society by government diktat. The distribution of power and wealth and amenity is too complex and too sensitive to be encompassed either by paternalism or by a return to *laissez-faire*. The only alternatives are education, persuasion, debate, trust.

*Financial Times*, *11 November 1977* (*his last contribution as Political Editor*)

## FOR THE BEST IN PAPERBACKS, LOOK FOR THE

In every corner of the world, on every subject under the sun, Penguin represents quality and variety – the very best in publishing today.

For complete information about books available from Penguin – including Pelicans, Puffins, Peregrines and Penguin Classics – and how to order them, write to us at the appropriate address below. Please note that for copyright reasons the selection of books varies from country to country.

---

**In the United Kingdom:** For a complete list of books available from Penguin in the U.K., please write to *Dept E.P., Penguin Books Ltd, Harmondsworth, Middlesex, UB7 0DA*

**In the United States:** For a complete list of books available from Penguin in the U.S., please write to *Dept BA, Penguin, 299 Murray Hill Parkway, East Rutherford, New Jersey 07073*

**In Canada:** For a complete list of books available from Penguin in Canada, please write to *Penguin Books Canada Ltd, 2801 John Street, Markham, Ontario L3R 1B4*

**In Australia:** For a complete list of books available from Penguin in Australia, please write to the *Marketing Department, Penguin Books Australia Ltd, P.O. Box 257, Ringwood, Victoria 3134*

**In New Zealand:** For a complete list of books available from Penguin in New Zealand, please write to the *Marketing Department, Penguin Books (NZ) Ltd, Private Bag, Takapuna, Auckland 9*

**In India:** For a complete list of books available from Penguin, please write to *Penguin Overseas Ltd, 706 Eros Apartments, 56 Nehru Place, New Delhi, 110019*

**In Holland:** For a complete list of books available from Penguin in Holland, please write to *Penguin Books Nederland B. V., Postbus 195, NL–1380AD Weesp, Netherlands*

**In Germany:** For a complete list of books available from Penguin, please write to *Penguin Books Ltd, Friedrichstrasse 10 – 12, D–6000 Frankfurt Main 1, Federal Republic of Germany*

**In Spain:** For a complete list of books available from Penguin in Spain, please write to *Longman Penguin España, Calle San Nicolas 15, E–28013 Madrid, Spain*

## A SELECTION OF FICTION AND NON-FICTION

### A Confederacy of Dunces   John Kennedy Toole

In this Pulitzer-Prize-winning novel, in the bulky figure of Ignatius J. Reilly, an immortal comic character is born. 'I succumbed, stunned and seduced . . . it is a masterwork of comedy' – *The New York Times*

### The Labyrinth of Solitude   Octavio Paz

Nine remarkable essays by Mexico's finest living poet: 'A profound and original book . . . with Lowry's *Under the Volcano* and Eisenstein's *Que Viva Mexico!*, *The Labyrinth of Solitude* completes the trinity of masterworks about the spirit of modern Mexico' – *Sunday Times*

### Falconer   John Cheever

Ezekiel Farragut, fratricide with a heroin habit, comes to Falconer Correctional Facility. His freedom is enclosed, his view curtailed by iron bars. But he is a man, none the less, and the vice, misery and degradation of prison change a man . . .

### The Memory of War and Children in Exile: (Poems 1968–83)   James Fenton

'James Fenton is a poet I find myself again and again wanting to praise' – *Listener*. 'His assemblages bring with them tragedy, comedy, love of the world's variety, and the sadness of its moral blight' – *Observer*

### The Bloody Chamber   Angela Carter

In tales that glitter and haunt – strange nuggets from a writer whose wayward pen spills forth stylish, erotic, nightmarish jewels of prose – the old fairy stories live and breathe again, subtly altered, subtly changed.

### Cannibalism and the Common Law   A. W. Brian Simpson

In 1884 Tod Dudley and Edwin Stephens were sentenced to death for killing their shipmate in order to eat him. A. W. Brian Simpson unfolds the story of this macabre case in 'a marvellous rangy, atmospheric, complicated book . . . an irresistible blend of sensation and scholarship' – Jonathan Raban in the *Sunday Times*

**Bedbugs**   Clive Sinclair

'Wildly erotic and weirdly plotted, the subconscious erupting violently into everyday life . . . It is not for the squeamish or the lazy. His stories work you hard; tease and torment and shock you' – *Financial Times*

**The Awakening of George Darroch**   Robin Jenkins

An eloquent and powerful story of personal and political upheaval, the one inextricably linked with the other, written by one of Scotland's finest novelists.

**In Custody**   Anita Desai

Deven, a lecturer in a small town in Northern India, is resigned to a life of mediocrity and empty dreams. When asked to interview the greatest poet of Delhi, Deven discovers a new kind of dignity, both for himself and his dreams.

**Collected Poems**   Geoffrey Hill

'Among our finest poets, Geoffrey Hill is at present the most European – in his Latinity, in his dramatization of the Christian condition, in his political intensity . . . The commanding note is unmistakable' – George Steiner in the *Sunday Times*

**Parallel Lives**   Phyllis Rose

In this study of five famous Victorian marriages, including that of John Ruskin and Effie Gray, Phyllis Rose probes our inherited myths and assumptions to make us look again at what we expect from our marriages.

**Lamb**   Bernard MacLaverty

In the Borstal run by Brother Benedict, boys are taught a little of God and a lot of fear. Michael Lamb, one of the brothers, runs away and takes a small boy with him. As the outside world closes in around them, Michael is forced to an uncompromising solution.

# FOR THE BEST IN PAPERBACKS, LOOK FOR THE 🐧

## A SELECTION OF FICTION AND NON-FICTION

### The Beans of Egypt, Maine  Carolyn Chute

Out of the hidden heart of America comes *The Beans* – the uncompromising novel about poverty and of what life is like for people who have nothing left to them except their own pain, humiliation and rage. 'Disturbingly convincing' – *Observer*

### Book of Laughter and Forgetting  Milan Kundera

'A whirling dance of a book . . . a masterpiece full of angels, terror, ostriches and love . . . No question about it. The most important novel published in Britain this year' – Salman Rushdie in the *Sunday Times*

### Something I've Been Meaning to Tell You  Alice Munro

Thirteen brilliant and moving stories about women, men and love in its many disguises – pleasure, overwhelming gratitude, pain, jealousy and betrayal. The comedy is deft, agonizing and utterly delightful.

### A Voice Through a Cloud  Denton Welch

After sustaining a severe injury in an accident, Denton Welch wrote this moving account of his passage through a nightmare world. He vividly recreates the pain and desolation of illness and tells of his growing desire to live. 'It is, without doubt, a work of genius' – John Betjeman

### In the Heart of the Country  J. M. Coetzee

In a web of reciprocal oppression in colonial South Africa, a white sheep farmer makes a bid for salvation in the arms of a black concubine, while his embittered daughter dreams of and executes a bloody revenge. Or does she?

### Hugging the Shore  John Updike

A collection of criticism, taken from eight years of reviewing, where John Updike also indulges his imagination in imaginary interviews, short fiction, humorous pieces and essays.

**The Book Quiz Book**   Joseph Connolly

Who was literature's performing flea . . .? Who wrote 'Live Now, Pay Later . . .'? Keats and Cartland, Balzac and Braine, Coleridge conundrums, Eliot enigmas, Tolstoy teasers . . . all in this brilliant quiz book. You will be on the shelf without it . . .

**Voyage through the Antarctic**   Richard Adams and Ronald Lockley

Here is the true, authentic Antarctic of today, brought vividly to life by Richard Adams, author of *Watership Down*, and Ronald Lockley, the world-famous naturalist. 'A good adventure story, with a lot of information and a deal of enthusiasm for Antarctica and its animals' – *Nature*

**Getting to Know the General**   Graham Greene

'In August 1981 my bag was packed for my fifth visit to Panama when the news came to me over the telephone of the death of General Omar Torrijos Herrera, my friend and host . . .' 'Vigorous, deeply felt, at times funny, and for Greene surprisingly frank' – *Sunday Times*

**Television Today and Tomorrow: Wall to Wall Dallas?**
Christopher Dunkley

Virtually every British home has a television, nearly half now have two sets or more, and we are promised that before the end of the century there will be a vast expansion of television delivered via cable and satellite. How did television come to be so central to our lives? Is British television really the best in the world, as politicians like to assert?

**Arabian Sands**   Wilfred Thesiger

'In the tradition of Burton, Doughty, Lawrence, Philby and Thomas, it is, very likely, the book about Arabia to end all books about Arabia' – *Daily Telegraph*

**When the Wind Blows**   Raymond Briggs

'A visual parable against nuclear war: all the more chilling for being in the form of a strip cartoon' – *Sunday Times*. 'The most eloquent anti-Bomb statement you are likely to read' – *Daily Mail*

# FOR THE BEST IN PAPERBACKS, LOOK FOR THE 🐧

## A CHOICE OF PENGUINS

### Adieux: A Farewell to Sartre   Simone de Beauvoir

A devastatingly frank account of the last years of Sartre's life, and his death, by the woman who for more than half a century shared that life. 'A true labour of love, there is about it a touching sadness, a mingling of the personal with the impersonal and timeless which Sartre himself would surely have liked and understood' – *Listener*

### Business Wargames   James Barrie

How did BMW overtake Mercedes? Why did Laker crash? How did McDonalds grab the hamburger market? Drawing on the tragic mistakes and brilliant victories of military history, this remarkable book draws countless fascinating parallels with case histories from industry world-wide.

### Metamagical Themas   Douglas R. Hofstadter

This astonishing sequel to the best-selling, Pulitzer Prize-winning *Gödel, Escher, Bach* swarms with 'extraordinary ideas, brilliant fables, deep philosophical questions and Carrollian word play' – Martin Gardner

### Into the Heart of Borneo   Redmond O'Hanlon

'Perceptive, hilarious and at the same time a serious natural-history journey into one of the last remaining unspoilt paradises' – *New Statesman*. 'Consistently exciting, often funny and erudite without ever being overwhelming' – *Punch*

### A Better Class of Person   John Osborne

The playwright's autobiography, 1929–56. 'Splendidly enjoyable' – John Mortimer. 'One of the best, richest and most bitterly truthful autobiographies that I have ever read' – Melvyn Bragg

### The Secrets of a Woman's Heart   Hilary Spurling

The later life of Ivy Compton-Burnett, 1920–69. 'A biographical triumph . . . elegant, stylish, witty, tender, immensely acute – dazzles and exhilarates . . . a great achievement' – Kay Dick in the *Literary Review*. 'One of the most important literary biographies of the century' – *New Statesman*